The Nephilem

Published by Pershing

Printed in Great Britain
Although every precaution has been taken in the preparation of this book, the publisher and author assume no responsibility for errors or omissions. Neither is any liability assumed for damages resulting from the use of information contained herein.

ISBN 978-1-7397050-2-2

Foreword / Dedication

For Poogie and the day our music died

Epigraph

"...We got many moons that are deep at play
So I keep an eye on the shadow's smile
To see what it has to say
You and I both know
Everything must go away
Ah, what do you say?"

-Red Hot Chilli Peppers "Dark Necessities"

Acknowledgements

My book has been twenty years in the making and there are many people close to me with whom I've shared my dream of writing this book. First, I'd like to thank those of you who contributed to the physical creation of my book. I am immensely grateful for the skill, guile, craft and advice of Charles N. and Peter C. It has been an absolute pleasure working with such wonderful collaborative people, where I learned many new skills and took so much narrative advice. Thank you to my editor, Velma Christie, for being so prompt with my manuscript over her Christmas holiday time, and so patient with my query. You've all been a pleasure to work with and I've learned so much from you.

I have special thanks to my main contributor Maham Aziz for the front cover illustration and the many chapter illustration openings. I almost feel this book is partly hers as she has contributed so much visually and inspired me to create increasing complex visions. To Carma Naudé, an amazing tattoo artist who lives a quite hectic lifestyle that finds her off the grid for months at a time. Her sacred geometry drawings are amazing and though at times I doubted she could give me the detail I wanted; I should have never doubted her. I really do hope you enjoy both their contributions as much my own. my I have listed their contribution below with the chapter names:
• Maham Aziz (front cover, Paramour, Solomon's Party, Sarah's Smiling, The Riding In of Autumn, The Riding In of Winter, The Riding In of Spring, The Riding In of Summer, Going To Barça, Swim To Shore, Swim To Me, Say Goodnight To Tomorrow)
• Carma Naudé (The Eternal Game Constellation endpaper, Sun Is Shining, Extended Absences, Lunch With Nathaniel, Skuld, Twice Remembered, Once Lived, What Is, Is Coming Into Being, Psalm of Lament: Yasmina, You Can't See Where Your Eyes Can't Follow, Zaragoza, Seth, S'Palmador, Moirae: Of Owls and

Crows, The Mending of Catherine)

• Lauryn Wilson (ying-yang fish endpaper)

I'd like to thank and acknowledge the important contributions of my beta reader community. Your feedback has been invaluable. I learned so much about my story because of your contribution and it gave me confidence that the vision that I set out for the book was the right one. I was especially pleased with the added advice many have offered outside of the formal feedback. Many thanks to Danny Kaye, Glory Olowosoyo, Karly Marlow, Ionut George Mereuta, Nina M. Miller and Ana Corral Vuille.

I'd like to thank a long-time friend Jay Astill, who in the very early days helped me to develop my thought on the subject matter. Jay, with his incredible imagination and talent for character building undoubtably helped to bring The Nephilem story to life over twenty years ago, it is to him I owe the eclectic cast of characters such as Nathaniel, Solomon Vaughn and Seth – I thank him for giving them to me. Though he might raise an eyebrow about how I changed them, I really did try to write a story that he would proud of.

To my family, my two children, my daughter, Lauryn who is studying English Literature, I hope you find inspiration in my work and work ethic. I hope this book is a lesson in never talking yourself out of chasing your big dream. To my son Ashley; at the start of this book when The Nephilem was little more than short fairy tale and folktale style stories in my head. When my son was still a little boy, I'd read him short bedtime stories based on The Nephilem. Sometimes I had written them, but most of the time I made them up on the bedside spot. My bedtime storytelling is something I am sure he has no adult recollection of. There is something to be said in having the non-judging ears of an innocent child taking in the woeful ramblings of a storytelling parent. His bedtimes gave me the imagination to develop the world of The Nephilem aloud night after night – and he could not possibly know how thankful I am to him for this.

Of course, for the past ten years it has been my wife, Debbie, which has had to put up with my woeful ramblings of out loud storytelling. Debbie has been a fantastic life partner for me on this journey; she has been a great sounding board for the many female voices in this book and because of her wonderfully creative artful eye, she has been quick to give me feedback on my illustrative concepts. For her to take in the most minute details involved in this book whilst managing her own creative projects is impressive stuff indeed. Her support has been unwavering, honest and a yardstick.

For this project my literary heroes and roles models are those of old classics, though I did draw from a couple contemporary works as well. I also pull inspiration from musical heroes, art and cinema as well. I learned so many lessons about connecting to the audience from them. I like to thank the works of classic fairy tales, E.T.A Hoffman, F. Scott Fitzgerald, Neil Gaiman, Quentin Tarantino, Grant Nieporte, Julio Medem, and Guillermo Del Toro. The music, the sounds, the emotions from the catalogues of Bob Marley, Surface, Astrud Gilberto, Corrine Bailey Rae especially "I'd do it all again" and Janet Jackson's 'The body that loves you' haunted me throughout the books process.

Lastly, I'd like to thank God. I know it is customary for everyone from award show winners to top level athletes to people who battled against the odds to achieve a lifelong ambition to all give praise and thank God. But this time, my thanks is literal. Without God's existence, our belief system in him as a deity or a ritual, this book would simply not exist at all because ultimately this book is about God. And so, to God, I give thanks.

Contents

PROLOGUE
Chapter 1

"You *shall* go to the ball, Cinderella!" Catherine grinned and clapped as her big sister twirled a swishing circle in her new evening dress. "Perhaps your Majesty would care to address the huddled masses." She dropped an extravagant curtsy and threw open the elegant French windows leading to the balcony.

The smells of roasting garlic, charcoal grills and moped fumes quickly filled the marble-floored apartment as Carmelita ignored the balcony and clicked across to a heavy scrolled mirror. She turned first one way, then the other as the diamonds cascading down her neck glistened and winked against her dark, flawless skin.

For a moment, both sisters fell silent as Catherine joined her, also resplendent in her own gown and matching ruby accessories. "Did you really think we'd climb this high?"

Carmelita turned to her little sister and smiled fondly. "With you two beautiful belles by my side, I never doubted it for a moment!" She turned back to the mirror and traced a sculptured fingernail along the string of brilliant gems resting comfortably on her ample bust. "Just think, some poor kid with an empty stomach and bare feet probably dug these up. Most likely got paid in cigarettes and booze. There's always agony behind the beauty."

Catherine's expression changed to something between determined and thoughtful. "No need to dwell on that stuff. We didn't make the world this way. There must be thousands of poor bastards born into that darkness every day, but how many end up *wearing* the diamonds rather than digging for them?" She gently squeezed her sister's shoulder. "Come on, we'll be late, and I don't want to keep the mayor waiting on our first date."

Carmelita rolled her eyes. "This again? Just wait till I tell your sister."

Catherine feigned a hurt expression. "Hey, this is the closest *I've* ever got to a genuine bigshot. Makes me kinda hot to tell the truth."

The older sister took the younger by the arm as they walked to the tall double doors leading out of the apartment. "Now, don't you get tunnel vision over one provincial mayor- This is a big deal and we've no idea *what* kind of whales we could land if we're smart. There could be bankers, arms dealers, playboy gamblers and mysterious Middle Eastern men with royal connections. Hell, there might even be some old Europe money mixed in too."

Catherine stopped and put her hands on her hips. "Always the one with the sensible advice and a broad perspective. I *knew* there was a reason I'd hung out with you all these years."

"Why thank you kindly, little sister." Carmelita opened the door and reached for the light switch.

Both women suddenly froze as a startling and blood-chilling sound suddenly warbled through the apartment.

Catherine broke the silence after a few seconds. "No way!"

Carmelita closed her eyes and gently shut the door. "Oh, come on, not *now!*"

The younger sister kicked off her designer shoes and padded back into the apartment, where the tinny electronic ringtone was much clearer. "Yeah, it is."

Carmelita followed her sister. "We can't be at home all the time, can we?"

"*You* can tell that to Rosalita if you want."

Once again, both women stood still as they listened to the plaintive chirping of cheap electronics echoing through the opulent and tasteful Mediterranean apartment.

Eventually, Carmelita gestured towards a short hallway leading to the bedrooms. "It's your turn."

Catherine stamped across to a small but elegantly scrolled walnut table and reached beneath it. After a few seconds of grunting and face-pulling, there was a tearing sound as she retrieved a battered cell phone and hurriedly pulled off the duct tape securing it in place. "There go my nails, goddammit."

Carmelita pulled a sour face. "If this is some guy jacking off in a phone box again…"

Catherine rolled her eyes and pressed the green answer button. Holding the handset to her ear, she said nothing as she heard the line disconnect. She raised her pencilled eyebrows at her sister.

"Do you think…" Carmelita was cut short mid-sentence as the phone rang for a second time. After three chirps it fell silent once more.

A tense atmosphere descended rapidly as both women stood motionless, just staring at the scratched handset. That silence grew heavy and thick as they anxiously awaited the next development.

Both sisters jumped as the phone rang for a third time, its strangled electric call bringing with it a sudden rush of nervous anticipation.

Catherine swallowed hard and answered the phone once again.

This time she heard a smooth, deep, and educated male voice on the line. "Hello, my dear aunt. It's been such a long time since I called you."

Both women exchanged nervous glances before Catherine gave the prearranged response. "I'm sorry, but I think you must've called the wrong woman. Perhaps you should try again."

The voice on the line paused for a moment, then spoke clearly and deliberately. "I'm very sorry. I was trying to reach my aunt Margarita. I will hang up and dial again as you so wisely suggest." The line promptly went dead once more.

Catherine ended the call and looked at her sister, nodding slowly.

Carmelita motioned to her expensive evening dress and jewellery ensemble. "So *that* was a complete waste of time. You know I blew fifty Euros on my hair? *Fifty Euros!*"

Her sister nodded, making a similar gesture to her own exotic outfit. "We'd better get moving. Should we call Rosalita?"

Carmelita shook her head. "No time, and we've nothing to tell her yet. We'll just have to fill her in later."

"I don't like it. I feel kind of vulnerable when we're one short, but you're right." Catherine quickly removed the sim card and battery from the cell phone and placed all three items on the baroque style table. Reaching underneath once more, she prised a small, twenty-two calibre automatic free from its own nest of duct tape. After chambering the first round, she followed her sister hurriedly towards the bedrooms.

* * *

Within ten minutes, two of the three Moirae sisters were in the narrow street below their apartment, dressed in cheap, mass-market clothes which were a thousand miles and just as many dollars removed from the designer dresses they'd so hurriedly discarded.

Catherine stood by with a crash helmet in each hand as Carmelita started up the battered little scooter which always waited faithfully outside, come rain or shine.

Within seconds, both sisters were on the bike and weaving expertly through the meandering throng of commuters and tourists that milled around the countless cafes, bistros and street-food stalls crammed into Barcelona's achingly fashionable El Born district.

As the architecture began to thin out, so did the tourists and commuters, to be replaced by roving gangs of kids kicking footballs outside concrete apartment blocks.

Carmelita reached out and tossed the battered cell phone into a trash can as they slowed at some traffic lights, having disposed of the sim card and battery earlier on. She glanced at her cheap watch as they bumped up a cracked curb, weaving between some bollards and coming to a halt at the edge of a small
public square.

Their destination was a far cry from the fashionable awnings and elegant apartments of their home district. Although they'd only been riding for about fifteen minutes, this grey, brutalist version of a public space felt like a different country, a different world even. Weeds sprouted through cracks in the uneven paving, struggling for sunlight in the shadow of the surrounding tower blocks; while graffiti policemen, bankers and boxers gasped for breath behind an encroaching spread of sun-bleached posters and cheap, faded flyers.

Both women left their crash helmets on as they scanned the square for signs of trouble. Although it was early evening and the weather was warm, the place was mostly in shadow and fairly quiet, with just some old bloke feeding the pigeons and a group of teenagers skateboarding around a dry, cracked concrete fountain.

This was a place their well-heeled neighbours knew nothing about, but the Moirae sisters were only too familiar with those endless acres of concrete warehouses used to store surplus citizens who languished on welfare or struggled vainly in poorly paid and thankless tourist jobs.

In many ways, these forgotten corners of the great city were the true source of the sisters' strength. They knew such places intimately, and each fleeting visit renewed and reaffirmed their cold, unshakable conviction that they would *never* go back.

The payphone stranded near the dead fountain was already ringing by the time the sisters reached it, but nobody else heard that lonely call for contact, save for the army of bottle blondes pouting from poorly printed contact cards that fluttered and flapped in the warm evening breeze.

Catherine glanced around once more before removing her helmet and picking up the greasy receiver. "Yes."

The same educated voice crackled over the line, although this time it was somehow more distant and tinnier, as though somehow diminished by the payphone's public utility components. "I've lost my delivery."

Carmelita leaned in to follow the exchange, although she faced outwards to keep a watchful eye on the surroundings.

Catherine twisted her body to allow her sister to hear. "You should be more careful with valuable and volatile consignments. I assume you're taking every measure to recover your property."

"That's why I'm calling, out of courtesy, and to reassure you there is no cause for concern should you see my spotters in your genteel neighbourhood or even outside your apartment."

The sisters exchanged silent glances before Catherine spoke again. "There's no reason either of those packages should turn up in our neighbourhood."

The voice on the phone remained polite and professional. "I sincerely hope not, but missing consignments do have a habit of returning to their senders, one way or another."

Catherine's voice hardened. "Those packages were delivered in good faith and *exactly* as you specified. If you can't keep hold of two valuable items for more than a week then I suggest you review your security before bothering your suppliers."

There was a pause before the voice crackled down the phone once again. "In point of fact, I have only mislaid one package. The other has already been recovered; alas also, it was damaged beyond repair."

"Damaged? How?"

The caller sighed heavily. "Water damage. I'm afraid some of my movers were a bit careless during a delicate situation, but it's so hard to find good staff these days. Naturally, I'm very upset with them and in turn they're determined to recover at least *some* of the considerable losses we've suffered during this transaction. I assured them that you were reliable and acting in good faith, although you know how suspicious staff can be. Some of them went so far as to outright accuse you of covertly recovering your own merchandise in order to redirect it to another buyer."

Catherine bristled. "Now, just you wait a minute…"

The voice on the phone continued. "Let me put your mind at ease. I have placed you and your dear sisters firmly off-limits to all investigators, so once again you have my reassurance that my contractors pose no significant risk to yourselves, despite their rather brusque and martial manner at times. Of course, they are aggrieved at their own failure and are very keen to put things right, hence their commitment to keeping a watchful eye around your neighbourhood. Just in case."

"We'll be keeping watch too."

"I'm sure you will. Now, if you hurry, you'll still catch the second act, although you'll have to change first. Personally, I think your working clothes imbue a kind of spray-painted urban wisdom which you've worked hard to achieve and thoroughly deserve, although it's hardly suitable attire for the great and the good of this fine city. Goodnight, ladies, and do take care on the way home. You are not in the brightest or safest of districts."

The line disconnected.

Catherine replaced the handset, grabbed a tissue from her pocket and wiped her palm. "What do you think?"

Carmelita glanced around before taking a small flyer from her pocket and sliding it beneath the other adverts for French lessons tutored by unfeasibly busty courtesans with comically accentuated features. The flyer carried a new cell phone number to replace the one they'd just abandoned. "I think our friend should be more careful with his inventory, although I don't like the idea of merchandise just wandering around unsupervised. Anything could happen."

Catherine tossed the tissue onto the ground as the sisters walked back to their battered but well-maintained scooter. "There's nothing to connect the merchandise to us unless Kal squeals to save his own skin."

Carmelita nodded thoughtfully. "We could arrange a meeting to, you know, take care of the situation."

Catherine smiled ruefully. "I always thought the younger sibling was supposed to be the hothead. There's nothing to suggest anyone's looking in our direction but creating corpses without good reason would pretty much guarantee that happening."

The older Moirae sister donned her crash helmet and jumped onto the moped. "You're right, let's not make any risky moves unless we see a reason to. Come on, little sister, there's a whole battalion of eligible bachelors waiting to wine and dine us, and I'm really hungry."

Catherine shivered as the sun dipped behind a drab grey tower block, sending a chill shadow slicing across the tired and dusty square. She couldn't shake the sudden feeling that it was some kind of portent, a vague warning expressed by some supernatural means. She silently scolded herself as she jumped onto the seat behind her sister. Their client was the superstitious nut job, not them. All the same, Catherine knew she'd feel safer once all the Moirae were together again, although she didn't relish the idea of breaking the news of a stray to Rosalita.

The Nephilem

SUN IS SHINING
Chapter 2

Sunlight gleamed and glittered on a languid ocean as the ferry began its slow, lumbering turn towards the shore. The vibration of the steel deck plates all but vanished as the engines throttled down, allowing momentum to steer the large and unwieldy vessel as it inched towards its allocated berth. No hurry.

Hyienna reluctantly sat up and opened his eyes, blinking in the bright Mediterranean sun, despite his good quality if somewhat dated sunglasses. High up on the open deck, he yawned and stretched as he watched a general ripple fidget through the passengers scattered across the sun-bleached space, as parents gathered in children and retirees began packing away newspapers in preparation for disembarking.

Hyienna knew he'd soon have to move too, and that realisation elicited a vague and surprising frisson of resentment inside him. This was a nice place, a good place, a place of warm sun and calm seas. During their short time together, the ferry had become something more than just a big boat; it had come to embody thoughts of reunions and happy times, adventure and discovery.

As he watched his nameless companions begin trooping down towards the dusty car deck, Hyienna wondered which of those symbolic meanings would loom largest in the coming days. Reunion had called to him, and discovery was a certainty, while he fervently hoped for happy times and always daydreamed of adventure. Despite the very mixed feelings churning around inside him, he figured that the omens were generally good.

The weather was calm, the crossing had been easy, and a peculiar feeling of peace had crept through his soul as the short journey had unfolded. Maybe it was merely a matter of distance, of leaving his own life behind him, if only for a while. Whatever the case, he couldn't shake the feeling that his was an important journey, a life-changing journey.

He smiled and nodded at a young mother who was busy readying both herself and her child for departure.

The pretty young woman smiled back while her infant son stared curiously at him, having not yet learned the unwritten rules of interaction with strangers.

As he smiled at the kid, who clearly had his mother's eyes, Hyienna wondered how strange he must look to that small child from a small island. He removed his sunglasses, pulled a funny face and deliberately made himself cross-eyed, a trick he'd learned while he was still at school.

It worked, and the kid started to smile and kick his little legs around as infants have a habit of doing.

Mum joined in and whispered something in her son's tiny ear as she lifted him up and waved at the strange and silly Black man with funny eyes.

Hyienna found himself smiling back as a tiny hand pawed at the air, trying to mimic his mother's friendly gesture. He gave his own little wave of farewell as mum smiled once more and turned towards the steps leading down to the car deck, filtering in with the last few passengers as they clambered down to ready themselves for departure.

Almost alone on the open deck, Hyienna stood up as he watched mother and son disappear through a doorway. Cute little kid; couldn't have been older than three or four. It always amazed him to imagine how that tiny facsimile of a man could become a high-powered executive or maybe a hulking special forces operative in just a couple of short decades. It didn't seem possible, and yet the proof was all around him…

He quickly replaced his glasses and mentally reigned himself in. There he was again, dwelling on what kids might become as they grew to adulthood, cheerfully wandering back down the darkening trail of what might've been. Although the counselling hadn't really made him feel any better, it had at least taught him to look out for the warning signs of trouble inside himself. Children were always a possible trigger; the first link in a chain of thought that could quickly take him into a confusing, shadowy, and ever-shifting labyrinth of introspection, fruitless speculation and self-recrimination. The shrink had been right about that much at least, and the only sure defence against the shadows of the past was to concentrate on the sunlight of the future, wherever he could find it.

Taking a deep, calming breath, Hyienna forced himself to focus on the present by not just looking but really seeing the idyllic holiday island of Formentera as the ferry finally docked. Although it was less than an hour from Ibiza, the contrast was quite striking. Whereas Ibiza was an alcopop fuelled twenty-something partying hard into the night, Formentera seemed like a much more settled, stable, middle-aged kind of island. Hyienna at once detected a more measured kind of milieu as the ferry's hull squeaked against its wooden berth and the cables were secured. The place seemed a little slower and somehow more self-aware, which was no bad thing. Even the buildings seemed to be more grown-up and neighbourly, with the large coastal hotels spacing themselves out more evenly rather than jostling for space and fighting for prominence.

It was almost a shame to leave the deck and break the oddly reflective mood which had overtaken him, but he sensed that reflection was something he'd be getting plenty of in the coming days.

* * *

The hot Spanish sun flared brightly as Hyienna bumped his scooter off the ferry ramp and hit the tarmac of Formentera proper for the first time. Settling down into the seat, he took the chance to glance around quickly as the traffic slowly filtered into town and began to disperse across the island. If anything, his first impressions were reinforced as he noticed that Formentera looked like a typically Spanish tourist resort, although perhaps a little more rustic and better organised than the heaving mainland or the thumping party island he'd just left behind. At the same time the place exuded a kind of generic Mediterranean vibe shared by a large area stretching from southern France to the northern reaches of Africa.

He thought about Sarah and her boyfriend Solomon. The news

that Sarah had a boyfriend struck Hyienna with a feeling of bitterness. He had heard rumours and whispers about how Solomon could be a charming gentleman… to essentially any girl that came his way. Solomon had many assets, but fidelity was certainly not one of them. It was not a matter of if, but when, he would break Sarah's heart. It shamed Hyienna to take some hope from this grim future.

Eventually, he reached a busy junction, where gleaming storefronts jostled with more traditional and, well, Spanish looking streets as the traffic honked and weaved its way across a crowded stretch of tarmac. The directions he'd been given told him to turn right, so he went left, a move which he figured had been pretty much typical of his whole life generally and the last few years in particular.

He knew he'd have to find his way to the rendezvous soon enough, but Hyienna just didn't feel quite ready to meet that part of his own history; not on such a beautiful and carefree day as this. After all, there he was, on a Wednesday morning with no compunction to be anywhere or to do anything. It was a freedom that few were able to enjoy, even though the accompanying stress and financial worries were familiar to many. Still, he could be worrying about money *and* sweating in some office rather than worrying about money while driving around a beautiful Mediterranean island instead. He knew he had the best of it, or at least that was what he told himself.

As both the traffic and the architecture began to loosen up, Hyienna knew that sooner or later the road would lead to his true destination, but the only thing that felt right at that moment was movement. He couldn't figure out whether he was escaping from an unresolved personal past or just enjoying the feeling of riding into an unknown future. Whatever the case, he felt almost powerless to quell the urge just to keep moving and to find something new. Maybe it was a different kind of living and a different way of seeing things that he sought, or maybe it was just delusion and self-justification; yet another novel excuse for his not knuckling under and doing as he should.

In truth he didn't really care which was his true motivation as he rode through that scorched Mediterranean scrub, just letting his instincts do the steering.

He knew he was heading *somewhere*, but not knowing where that somewhere might be just added to the sense of freedom, whether that feeling of freedom was truly real or not.

* * *

Hyienna had been riding for quite a while, enjoying the sights and soaking up the laid-back island vibe when he first caught sight of it. At first, he thought he'd made it up in his head, but as he rounded a corner beside a grove of dry and thirsty looking trees, he realised he'd been right the first time.

It was a lighthouse.

He pulled onto the dusty verge, kicked down the stand of his scooter and stepped onto the deserted country road to take a better look. Shading his eyes against the mid-morning glare, he glanced at the incongruously tall structure perched peculiarly on the horizon, as though the gods of Olympus had misplaced a child's toy. He wasn't sure why that functional building had caught his attention so, but for some reason he just couldn't take his eyes off it. Maybe the fact it was easily the tallest structure for miles around held his attention, as though the fates had brought him to this very spot in order to convey some kind of deep, esoteric message that could never be spoken or written down.

Hyienna looked around and realised that he was completely alone for the first time in…well, he couldn't even remember how long. No cars travelled that cracked and sagging rural route and his only companion was the dust hurrying before a ceaseless Mediterranean wind, a desiccating breeze that dried and crumbled everything beneath its gentle yet unending assault.

Hyienna turned a slow, full circle as he observed the flat countryside around him. There was nobody nearby and nothing to break the monotony of dry, undeveloped scrubland interspersed with small orchards and distant flat-roofed farmhouses. There was just him, that lonely wind and his inner meditations on a distant lighthouse, a beacon erected to warn against danger. Was it a message, a metaphor...?

❀

Just hold it right there, my boy! Remember what the therapist said.
Hyienna took a deep breath for the second time that morning, reminding himself just how easy it was to fall into that endless fog of introspection, forever following phantom spirals of existential speculation…all leading nowhere except to unreliability and unemployment. That was something else the shrink had been right about, although she could offer no real help explaining why his brain was wired that way while everyone else just saw the world with pragmatic eyes. She'd told him it was just an abnormality of his psyche, as unpredictable and inexplicable as genius or being unusually tall. The medical experts didn't know how or why Hyienna was the way he was, only that the reality of his peculiar personal makeup meant that he had to be on the lookout for flights of fancy.

Despite the quiet warning inside him, Hyienna knew he'd be headed down the road towards that mysterious lighthouse the moment he was back on his faithful little two-stroke.

* * *

The scooter's battered seat squeaked reassuringly as Hyienna leaned back and looked up at the lighthouse. He struggled to fathom why it held his attention so, but it somehow seemed to stare back at him as he observed its silent, inscrutable lines picked out against the bright blue Mediterranean sky. He didn't know what he was waiting for; after all it was just a pile of painted stone and metal, yet still he expected something to happen as the breathless and sultry atmosphere prickled over his skin and inside his own head.

He'd expected to see more people there, given how the lighthouse was easily the tallest building on the whole island, at least from what he'd seen of it. There were a couple of tourists wandering around the base, looking out to sea and no doubt discussing big plans for their own futures as they escaped from wherever it was, they'd come from.

Hyienna watched them standing arm in arm, looking out to sea, and not for the first time did he envy those couples who seemed to have somehow found a solution to sharing a life together, at least for a while. It wasn't even the physical side of romance that Hyienna missed so much; it was something deeper, something more fundamental. It was just the idea of someone truly *knowing* that you were alive, to somehow bear witness to your hopes, dreams, triumphs, and failures. Maybe that was the secret to humanity's endless quest for romance; maybe it ran far deeper or higher than a purely biological drive. Maybe it was something almost spiritual; maybe there really was something to the whole soulmate idea. He wouldn't be at all surprised.

Leaving the couple to their private moment, Hyienna turned a slow circle, glad for his ageing designer glasses as a squall of warm Mediterranean wind picked up a handful of orange dust and sent it hurrying past him, leaving a dull film on his clothes, backpack and less than a pristine scooter. Some sort of bird twittered through a huddled group of stunted and wind twisted trees, but there was no sign of any other human life. Here he was, standing on an idyllic Mediterranean island with more of a future before him than he'd known for a while, and yet Hyienna felt uneasy for some reason, almost as though he were being watched.

Back to the lighthouse again. He knew it was irrational, but still he couldn't shake a feeling that the place was somehow meant for him, that this was where he was supposed to be at that particular moment.

As he looked again, Hyienna realised there was something wrong with the place in general and the lighthouse. The angles were odd, with a wide stone path cutting an oblique, almost diagonal course towards the front entrance. A strangely angled path shouldn't make any difference, but Hyienna saw it as a sign of some deeper and more esoteric design. After all, there was nothing around the lighthouse, so why not just lay the path straight up to the front door? It didn't make sense unless the architect was trying to say something unspoken with ageless stone. The more he stared at it, the more it seemed like the tall cylindrical structure was leaning over, moving and yet motionless at the same time. One moment it seemed to be gliding forward as though to crush him beneath it, yet a single blink later it looked to be leaning precariously over the cliff, ready to topple into the sea at any moment. The whole place exuded a weird kind of vibe, reminding him of an old movie where some kid's drawings came to life in the world of her dreams.

He swallowed hard, his mouth and throat suddenly dry as he thrust his hand into his pocket and grabbed a small, polished pebble of tumbled brown agate he'd bought from some cute chick at the hippy market back on Ibiza. Apparently, it was good for helping to stay grounded and steer the mind away from distractions…and it worked too, at least for him. He couldn't really vouch for some deep adjustment of spiritual vibrations, but it had still become his anchor when the tide of fancy threatened to sweep him away. Although therapy had been questionable in some ways, it hadn't been a total loss, and ideas like his pocket-sized anchor had saved him from slipping away into spirals of speculation more than once. Not that there was anything *wrong* with spirals of speculation, but he knew from bitter and hard-won experience how that glittering road of fantasy led only to darkness, just as chaos rode hard on the heels of that first unparalleled trip down the white powder trail.

With his hand wrapped tightly around his own personal rock, Hyienna deliberately tore his gaze from the lighthouse and kicked his feet through the dusty Formentera scrubland to make certain he stayed in the here and now. He gazed out across the idyllic blue horizon, where distant yachts and powerboats cut silent white wakes while huge commercial ships dissolved into the haze at the edge of the world, all working hard and heading somewhere…all except for him. No, wait, that wasn't true, he *was* heading somewhere, maybe for the first time in years, maybe ever.

With his equilibrium restored and his feet back on the ground, Hyienna replaced his pet rock in his pocket and smiled as he caught sight of what looked like an old kids' den, complete with crude skull and crossbones painted upon a decaying pallet. He looked around again to find there were no kids, adults, or anyone else in sight. Hell, for all he knew the kids who'd built that little pirate den might be his age by now, with their own kids worrying about skin cancer as they stayed glued to the Xbox or whatever they had these days.

He turned and glanced back at the lighthouse as it struck him, he was standing between two dusty relics from a bygone age. Hyienna was no maritime expert, but he'd heard that lighthouses were no longer necessary in the traditional sense, what with satellite communication and radio markers. Just like the old kids' clubhouse, it was another human experience supplanted and nullified by the rise of the microchip. Another signpost of ages and rites of passage made invisible, impermanent and digitised.

Hyienna idly kicked at the sun-bleached and crudely painted warning to strangers, only to see it fall flat and splinter at the merest touch. He stepped back suddenly as he realised that the decaying old pallet most likely *hadn't* been left there by kids after all, but by adults with a serious purpose. He backed away as the broken pallet tilted and slid into what looked like a deep fissure in the ground. Sand and pebbles clattered after it, sending up a cloud of choking dust as the rumble of falling debris grew steadily louder.

Realising the danger, Hyienna turned to beat a hasty retreat, but it was too late as he felt his left leg suddenly vanish beneath him. He instinctively lunged forward and grabbed at a tuft of brown scrub as his body slithered over the edge of a rapidly expanding chasm. He wanted to say *oh shit* as he slid backwards, but all he could manage was a strangled cough as the dust clogged his throat and he plunged into the darkness below.

* * *

Pain.

Pain and darkness. Those were Hyienna's first thoughts as his consciousness limped back after its sudden and unscheduled absence. Had he been dreaming? He grasped at the ghost of some nocturnal adventure involving an old woman on a riverbank, but the shadow cast by his subconscious mind faded away as he began to sense the light beyond his own eyelids.

As Hyienna's faculties slowly returned, so did his sense of his own experience, bringing his pain sharply into focus as it settled around both his leg and his head. Some sense of feeling slowly returned as he noticed a firm surface beneath his buttocks and back, jolting him into a

27

much more alert state as he realised, he was sat upright...sort of.

He blinked rapidly as he opened his grit filled eyes, wiping away the tears as his blurred vision began to show him some sort of orange light. At first, he wondered if he was concussed and simply seeing random colours and shapes displayed by his rattled brain, although his opinion quickly changed as he began to discern his surroundings.

He moved his arms and legs a little even though his left knee hurt like crazy. Hyienna began to think he'd had a lucky escape, although how the hell he was going to get out of wherever he'd fallen into was another question altogether.

He jumped and scrambled back against the wall as something large moved in front of his slowly clearing vision; then it was gone again.

"Just relax, my friend. You took quite a tumble."

He rubbed his eyes again, harder this time as he willed them to show him where he was and who was speaking. It was hard to see in the low light, but at last, the world slowly sharpened into some sort of order, although what Hyienna could discern made about as much sense as the blurred shapes and flashing blotches.

Unsure even of where his limbs were, Hyienna felt around and gingerly tried to push himself up with his arms. He felt sharp stones and rock under his palms for a second before he collapsed back down as a wave of pain and nausea robbed him of what little strength he had left. Some distant, rational part of himself seemed to be trapped far away, calling to him from the endless darkness of concussed confusion.

He knew he must have fallen pretty hard, and some distant alarm sounded way off in his stranded consciousness as some quiet part of him feared he might be seriously hurt.

Was that singing he could hear? He struggled to focus as some distant and alluring siren song hummed from somewhere close by. He tried to speak but his body simply refused to obey his commands. Oh God! Perhaps he really *was* hurt badly. It was an idea that he didn't want to face and yet knew he couldn't escape as that distant angel hummed right in his ear and the world stubbornly refused to settle into focus.

Suddenly something moved in the distance, a dark shape passing in front of that indistinct orange glow. Was someone *there* with him, wherever there was?

Hyienna breathed a long sigh as the pain receded and the edges of his vision began to darken once again. The humming stopped and for a moment there was an eerie, almost unearthly stillness before the dark shape reappeared, only this time much closer, only inches away, blocking out the orange glow and leaving just an ethereal outline of a woman dressed in some sort of shawl or blanket.

There were no features within those dark, dense folds of cloth, yet the figure seemed to stare intently at him, despite being little more than a deep and almost flawless shadow hovering just inches from his face.

Part of him was glad that he was so badly concussed; otherwise, the idea of a solid shadow rearing up in front of him would've been more than a little frightening. As it was, all Hyienna could muster was a drowsy curiosity as he stared at the woman who wasn't there and listened to her strange and urgent whispering. He tried to follow the words, but it was difficult to pick out one distinct language as her words tumbled forth in a stream of syllables that failed to form sentences, yet somehow elicited strange ideas from somewhere deep inside him.

Hyienna sensed he was hearing a story, some sweeping epic that turned around the timeless themes of life, death, and eternity. He wanted to hear more, straining to focus on the stream of ideas suddenly conjured forth into the empty and confused vessel of his conscious mind. He had to hear the ending, sensing some great and secret wisdom woven through that whispered, wordless tale; yet he also felt himself sinking back into the dark ocean of nothingness from which he'd so briefly surfaced.

If he'd been more awake, Hyienna guessed he would probably have screamed with terror as that impossibly dark, human-shaped hole in his out of focus world leaned closer still, extinguishing the last light of his brief awakening and leaving him alone with only that urgent whispering for a company in that silent, endless sea of the unconscious.

***

Time passed once again, and Hyienna found himself slowly drifting back towards the waking world a second time. The throbbing in his head and the pain in his knee hastened his journey back towards something resembling a sense of self-awareness.

Blinking rapidly, his eyes watered as he smelled a strong and unexpected scent. Was that disinfectant of some kind? Maybe he'd been asleep longer than he'd thought. Maybe he was in the hospital. Maybe that strange dream had just been a garbled and mixed-up mess of meaningless images, his synapses firing at random inside his shaken and shocked brain.

Maybe.

At last, his eyes began to focus and the throbbing in his head was complemented by a sharper antiseptic sting to match the smell in his nostrils. Whether by accident or design, that sharp odour acted much like smelling salts, clearing the buzzing confusion inside his head as the world finally flickered into focus.

He was underground, that was clear. Luckily, he hadn't fallen as far as he'd first feared, although it had still been enough to knock the wind out of him and render him senseless for a while. The bright morning sun streamed through a ragged hole above, picking out the dust swirling in that cool subterranean space.

Hyienna gingerly clambered to his feet, wincing as his knee complained but did its job by supporting him. He tried not to think about Alice in Wonderland, but he couldn't help it has he realised he'd somehow dropped into another world. He just hoped the inhabitants would be friendly.

An oil lamp burned on what looked like a makeshift table fashioned from a pair of tea chests, throwing its light across a chaotic collection of empty food cans, old bits of paper and what looked like discarded blister packs of pills piled high and spilling across the uneven stone floor.

Other shapes lurked in the shadows, maybe a bed and some more of those tea chests, although it was difficult to make out any details in the darkness. The one thing he *could* see clearly was the woman who raised herself out of what looked like a cheap garden chair.

"Err, hi." He said, feeling both foolish and frightened as he nervously broke the silence. He also tried not to think of the countless zombie movies he'd watched as the dishevelled figure shuffled past him in the semidarkness. He didn't know if she could even hear or understand him, but he thought better of speaking again straight away. Instead, he concentrated on seeing as much as possible lest he should have to make a sudden getaway, although he fervently hoped that wouldn't happen as he doubted his knee would be up to the task. As his eyes adjusted to the darkness and finally stopped watering,   Hyienna   began to make out dozens of mysterious symbols and glyphs, all scribbled on curling paper and pinned to the sides of tea chests and any other available surface. He didn't know their precise meaning although he recognised an astrological symbol here and there, or something he'd maybe seen in a movie somewhere. Maybe he'd watched too many movies.

Realising that his eyes wouldn't be much more use in the dim light, he turned his attention to his ears. Hyienna could hear the languid song of the sea echoing somewhere in the distance, seemingly from behind him. He figured it made sense because whoever the mysterious cave dweller might be, she sure as hell didn't drop into her strange subterranean home the same way he had. That meant there had to be another way in, or out.

There was a sudden scraping sound as the woman struck a match and lit another lamp. "That's better. Now I can see my knight in shining armour."

Oh crap, she's crazy! I hope I don't have to get physical. Hyienna instinctively took a deep breath as the cavewoman picked up her lamp and finally turned to face him. In truth he didn't really know what to expect, but in any event, he was still surprised at what he saw, and again he had to remind himself that he wasn't starring in any kind of straight-to-video, Wednesday night horror flick. She was tall, and her age was hard to determine, especially as the dim flickering light gave her sunken features an unsettling and cadaverous look when she smiled broadly at him. Hyienna noticed that although her hair was matted and her clothes were dishevelled, she still sported a full set of expertly worked teeth which seemed completely at odds with the rest of her unkempt appearance.

She swayed slightly as she shuffled forward, as though her painfully thin legs could barely support her. She wore quite a large skeleton for a woman, which made her obvious weight loss even more apparent and uncomfortable to look at.

Hyienna had no idea of who she was or what she might say and do next. In fact, when he thought about it, he had no idea of what *he* should say and do next either. In the end he just repeated himself. "Hi."

The cave-dweller changed course and reached out for her chair, lifting it forward and placing it carefully on the floor of the cave. She groaned into it and pushed some of the debris from the tea chests to make space for her second lantern. She seemed not to notice the empty medicine bottles and other detritus clattering to the floor as she pointed in Hyienna's general direction. "Sit yourself down; you're making the place untidy." Her voice was papery, thin, and tired sounding.

Hyienna felt a pang of sorrow as he glanced around and located another cheap garden chair. He couldn't believe that anyone could be living and suffering like this in the twenty-first century, at least not in Europe. For a moment he just considered grabbing one of the lanterns and finding his way to the sea, but both compassion and a sense of morbid curiosity prevailed over him.

For a moment, the two of them silently stared at each other; one with an expression of bemused befuddlement and the other looking as though she were studying a fascinating abstract painting.

It was the befuddled visitor who broke the silence. "Hi." He couldn't think of anything else to say as he stared at his unusual host, although he tried not to let the word *captor* enter his thoughts too much. At last, he concluded that the mysterious cave dweller was probably middle-aged, even though she moved like a very old woman. The lines etched into her features looked more like the work of pain and stress than the passage of time. The various medical detritus scattered around her makeshift hovel also supported that idea.

At last, she spoke. "I'd given up on you."

Taken aback, Hyienna blinked rapidly. "What?"

"Are you simple or something?"

He could immediately see the annoyance on her face, even in the poor light. She had large and even features typical of someone with African ancestry, and although pain and sorrow had done their best to dull her beauty, Hyienna could see that she had once been a handsome woman. Her large frame and features meant that she'd never have made the cover of Vogue, but he could see that she was nonetheless used to commanding the space around her, or at least she once had been.

There was a hiss of annoyance as the mystery woman spoke again. "I pray for salvation and instead I get a simpleton. Maybe that's my punishment; maybe *you're* my punishment."

"Do you...*live* here?" Hyienna tentatively asked. The simpleton jibe had kind of rubbed him the wrong way, but he figured that an unkind word might be the least of his problems.

She gestured around, her imitation jewellery glinting dully in the dim lamplight. "At least for a while, if you can call *this* living."

"Who are you? I mean what are you doing down here?"

A sudden spasm of phlegmy coughing rattled the nameless woman's frame and she angrily waved him back when he rose to help. "I'm the eldest of three, although I'm not the first to leave my sisters behind. That's the worst part of it, thinking of my beautiful baby sister, all alone out there."

Settling reluctantly back into his seat, Hyienna tried hard not to think of Macbeth's witches, but it was too late. "Do you need help? Do you want me to call someone, your sisters maybe?"

She leaned back in her chair, looking for all the world like some southern matriarch in a rocking chair on her porch. "What's your name?"

For a moment Hyienna was reluctant to answer, although he soon dismissed the danger of a confidence trick or some hard luck story. Besides, it wasn't like she'd sought him out; in fact, *he'd* dropped in on *her*, quite literally. "My name's Hyienna. What do people call you?"

"Hyienna?" She wrinkled her face as though there were a sudden bad smell in the air. "Angels should have names like Seraphim or

Auriel, or Diazepam. Still, you're here now and who am I to question?"

Hyienna smiled kindly at the obviously disturbed woman. "I think maybe you've got me confused with someone else. I'm just some poor sap who fell through a hole in the ground."

"Yeah?"

"Yeah." He slowly rose from his seat. "Look, I should best be on my way. I'm late for an appointment anyway."

"Wait!"

Very reluctantly, Hyienna turned back. He'd already decided he should call someone about a sick woman living in a cave, but he decided not to mention it directly to her. She was obviously half crazy and there was no reason to upset her. Besides, there was just something about her, something significant, although he couldn't put his finger on what it was. "Is there something you want?"

The woman rose again and shuffled across to a dark corner, re-emerging a moment later and clutching a small rucksack, kind of like an overnight bag. "You must take this."

Hyienna smiled indulgently. "I don't need anything, thanks, apart from maybe a lamp to find my way out. Christ, that's a point; please don't tell me I gotta *swim* to get out of here."

She groaned back into her chair. "Heroes don't swim unless it's with tridents or crocodiles or something. Anyhow, you don't look like much of a swimmer to me. It's funny, but I always thought you'd be taller; not for any particular reason now that I think about it, but you know how imagination can be. In fact, I'd be willing to bet your imagination's a lot more active than the average prole. Good, you'll be needing it in the coming days." The cave-dweller leaned forward and rummaged in the bag.

Hyienna felt his knees tremble and his blood run cold as his nameless host slowly unfolded what looked like a large square of fabric. He kept the word *fabric* fixed firmly in his mind, although in truth he had no idea of what he was really looking at.

The blanket, if that's what it was, almost defied explanation as it greedily sucked in every morsel the light around it and gave absolutely nothing back. Hyienna had read something about the darkest material ever created, and how it fooled the eye by looking more like a hole in the world than a regular object. That was certainly the impression he got as he stared at the perfect, flawless nothingness held casually between the old woman's fingers. He rubbed his head as a distant tinnitus whine started up from a place, he couldn't quite pinpoint.

The strange cave dweller said nothing, merely cocked her head and watched.

"What is this? Who are you?" Hyienna asked suspiciously as he began to feel oddly nauseous, as though he'd just reached the crest of a giant rollercoaster and was about to hurtle headlong into the infinite darkness that hovered between the old woman's hands. Was it his imagination, or was the world itself slowly bleeding into the edges that impossible portable hole?

Hyienna eventually turned away. The whole thing, whatever it was, was just so damned…disturbing!

The woman carefully re-folded her portable tear in the cosmos and placed it back in the rucksack. "If there were a Fate called Redemption, then I would be her; at least as far as *you're* concerned. Although in truth I've earned a different name for myself over the years."

Hyienna didn't really hear what she said due to a strange and sourceless whining sound which made the whole world seem somehow more distant and less real. He tried to think about what he'd just seen but his mind refused to latch onto the idea and stubbornly wandered off into nothingness. Eventually he was able to repeat himself. "Who are you?"

The dishevelled hermit smiled sadly. "Just a clever fool who couldn't see the danger around her; or who just didn't *want* to. Now I'm breathing borrowed air and I can travel no further, but I can at least help *you* to reclaim a part of yourself."

"How can *you* help *me*?"

"You've been lost for a long time, Hyienna, but at last you've found your way again."

"By falling down a hole? I was damn lucky not to break my neck!"

"Quests are never meant to be easy, that's why there's always a dragon or an evil wizard waiting somewhere along the road."

Hyienna had heard enough, and he'd been right from the beginning. The woman was obviously nuts and he was getting the hell out while the getting was good, even if he did have to swim for it. He'd already decided he'd call social services, or the cops, or *someone* once he'd escaped. After all, it wasn't right; a woman down here all on her own, and she didn't look well either. With his mind made up, he finally stood with a renewed sense of purpose. "Look, I don't know what your angle is, but I'm out of here."

"It wasn't your fault."

Hyienna stopped and turned back. "Excuse me?"

Lost in the darkness, the old woman's eyes gleamed like polished stones as she stared at him intently. "The child, the boy. There is no blood on your hands and no stain on your soul, yet still you suffer. You have carried another's burden for far too long, and now that injustice has brought you to me."

Although part of him knew it was a bad idea, a larger and more powerful part of him knew full well that the woman's words were just too much of a coincidence. Sure, Hyienna was mindful of all those head-shrinking sessions where he'd unravelled what was real from what was in his head, but that that was why he knew the hole in the ground was real, the cave was real, and the woman was real too… although he was far less certain about what she'd just stuffed into that small rucksack. Despite that strange and ominous doubt, he couldn't deny that the undisciplined thoughts in his head had brought him first to the lighthouse and next to this dark place, but surely *that* was all real too. "That's a pretty neat trick and I'm very impressed, but you were wrong about one thing; it was a little girl."

The woman frowned and tilted her head, seemingly confused. She rummaged in the pocket of her shabby coat and pulled out a tattered and dog-eared stack of what looked like tarot cards. She cut the pack once and turned over the top card before answering with a rasping chuckle. "No, it was a boy for sure, but you're wise to be cautious. Maybe you're not quite as hopeless as you look. Well, that would figure; after all, the greatest heroes never begin their trials as heroes. What would be the point of that?"

Hyienna picked up his chair and gently set it down on the other side of the makeshift table. "What's your name?"

"At last, he asks. Just call me Moirae, that's the name you'll need for this journey."

Hyienna racked his brains, trying to remember where he'd heard that name before, although the answer eluded him. Instead, he gestured around the cave once again. "What are you *doing* down here; hiding from something, someone?"

"You could put it that way, although both the Reaper and the Almighty found me long before I was called to this place."

"Called, how?"

She tapped the cards with a ragged fingernail. "The same way *you* were called, and for the same reason."

Hyienna jumped as a sharp digital beeping sound rudely disturbed the cool atmosphere inside the cave. He watched as Moirae rummaged among the debris on the floor, retrieving a cheap digital watch, a battered bottle of water and an equally battered packet of pills. She rapidly swallowed two of them, wiping her cracked lips with her sleeve. "Do you need help?"

"Too late for help now, and maybe too late for redemption as well. I suppose I'll find out soon enough." She paused, looking into the middle distance for a few seconds before she spoke again. "Do you know what the very worst of sins is?"

Hyienna was taken aback by the strange question, although he thought for a moment and answered just the same. "Murder I guess."

The old woman shuffled in her chair and took another sip of water before placing the battered deck of cards on the dirty makeshift table. "Many people say that, and they're all wrong. Sure, ending the life of another is something you'll have to answer for, but at least the repentant killer stands a chance of forgiveness. No, the very worst of sins is to carry the name of the Almighty in vain, or to put it another way, to use God's name to justify your own personal bullshit. There's no coming back from *that* one; the book says so."

"What are you trying to tell me?" Hyienna fought against a rising sense of destiny inside him if *destiny* could really be called a human emotion.

If she'd heard him, she didn't acknowledge his question. "I've committed nearly every sin you can imagine; violated nearly every commandment during my short time in this world. I've committed murder more than once and adultery more times than I can count. I've coveted just about everything I ever laid my greedy eyes on, and I made a ton of money and spread even more misery by bearing false witness. After all that, the only thing that *truly* terrifies me is that I did all those things in the name of a righteous cause, or at least I told myself that I did. You see, *that's* a sin that can never be forgiven. Don't get me wrong, I wasn't at the top of the ladder, but we all carried out the most grievous offences against both man and God in His own name. That's what I fear the most."

Not being much of a student of theology or much of a student of anything for that matter, Hyienna was at a loss. Sure, he had a pretty decent sense of right and wrong, but he knew nothing about mortal sin or any of that stuff or whether any of it was truly real or even mattered. After thinking for a few seconds, he opted for a more practical approach. "Look, I can tell that you need some help, so that's what I'm going to do, whether you like it or not."

She smiled a sad, winsome smile. "You're all the help I'll ever need. Besides, it's too late now and they cover their tracks well."

"They?"

A short, bitter laugh escaped her lips. "Well, it's more of a he, really. Don't know if he's the Devil himself, but he sure as hell works for him. You see, that's his best trick, he persuades you to do his bidding from behind his cloak of righteousness. I guess that's why they call him the Deceiver."

"Who, the Devil or the guy who works for him?"

"Take your pick, but at least I can draw some comfort from believing that he's just an evil man. That means he'll face his own same judgement sooner or later. If he's more than just a man then I'm well and truly damned, but I don't think so. Demons don't poison people any more than angels cure them; they leave all that stuff to mankind because it's not like we need their assistance to help or hurt each other. They know we're free to choose good or evil, so all they have to do is show us the way they favour."

Hyienna shook his head, trying to clear it of the fog whirling around inside his brain. "Poison? Are you saying you've been poisoned?"

"I was poisoned a long time ago, first my mind, then my spirit and then my body. Like countless fools before me, I was only too eager to embrace the means of my own end. All that's left now is my soul, and I fear the Dark One will eat that soon enough as well."

"You didn't answer my question. Are you trying to say that someone's poisoned you?"

"Who knows? It doesn't matter anyway, not now. All that matters is you're here at last." She tapped the small rucksack with her foot. "Just make sure this gets to where it needs to go."

Hyienna shook his head. "Look, I'm totally baffled by all of this. I don't know what the hell I'm supposed to do with some weird looking blanket handed to me, no offence, by some strange old woman living in a cave, dying in a cave, or whatever the hell it is you're *doing* in this cave. I don't understand any of it."

Moirae grunted as she leaned across and flipped over the top card of her tarot deck. "You soon will."

PARAMOUR
Chapter 3

Hyienna winced and cursed as his long-suffering moped bumped down another pothole. Throttling back, he pulled over to the side of the road both to look at his front wheel and double-check the house name spelt out in broken tiling on a sturdy but neglected perimeter wall. He sighed out loud as he read the words *Casa Santa Cruz* when he was actually looking for Casa Hermoso. He knew he was on the right road as a question to a bemused looking man on a tractor had confirmed it, so where the hell was Casa Hermoso? He'd checked every nameplate and mailbox for the last half mile, and he was running out of options.

The only other place he could see was clearly the peacock in the parade. Picked out in shimmering white cement, the sprawling multi-storey house in the middle distance looked more like one of those holiday rentals for unfeasibly large families rather than any kind of settled family home. With a smart red roof and clean, well-defined edges, it proudly expressed its modernity in contrast with the fading yet desirable and frankly much more homely looking houses he'd passed by on his journey along the coastline. Hermoso indeed.

He looked down at his front tyre again and stared for a moment before finally convincing himself that it was fine. He kicked over the engine once more as his eyes momentarily strayed to the small rucksack bungee across the pillion seat directly behind him. If it wasn't for that single piece of physical evidence, Hyienna would have thought the whole surreal subterranean experience was just the creation of his concussed brain. After all, it wouldn't be the first time his imagination had literally run away with him, but the proof was there, nonetheless. Maybe he should take another look, just to be sure…but then again maybe not.

Although he didn't really know why, Hyienna figured that poking around in that battered and innocuous looking bag for no good reason was not the smartest thing to do, and he'd gotten pretty sick of not doing the smartest thing. Besides, he still had to make an important rendezvous and he was already annoyed with himself for running late. That was an old habit he'd really wanted to avoid.

Hyienna set off down the cracked semi-rural road and soon arrived at some heavy gates guarding a paved drive leading to the ostentatiously tidy new-build on the block. Sure enough, there it was, Casa Hermoso, spelt-out in carved stone and leafed with gold. Hyienna felt a surge of some uncertain emotion run through him as he realised his cousin lived in what was easily the biggest and most expensive house in that neck of the woods. He was surprised at his own sudden and less than charitable reaction. Where had *that* come from? Was it jealousy? That was doubtful as Hyienna would be the first to admit that he'd never been especially interested in material things. Resentment? Maybe, but wasn't that just another name for jealousy?

Hyienna shook himself from his reverie and gripped the pebble in his pocket as he noticed the tiny camera lens subtly built into the intercom box beside sturdy looking gates. He reached out to push the button and jumped as he heard a mechanical clank and a whirring sound as the gates swung open with a speed and silence that could only be described as majestic.

It looked like somebody was home at least.

With a deep breath and a sudden sense of trepidation, Hyienna jumped back on his scooter and slowly rolled onto the smooth driveway of dark interlocking stones. It was a relief to be off the less than pristine municipal roadways, although the sudden silence and lack of response from the bike beneath him was oddly disturbing, as though he was suddenly sliding down an icy hill in the blazing sun.

He coasted down the gentle slope, giving himself time to take in the sights. All in all, it was quite a place, with a sprawling, informal yet carefully designed air about it as the house and gardens spread out over the dry and windswept countryside. Although it wasn't quite up to Bond villain standards, Casa Hermoso certainly wouldn't have looked out of place as the HQ of a cartel kingpin in some mid-budget Mafia movie.

Hyienna couldn't tell whether it was his long-anticipated rendezvous or the sheer pristine neatness of the place that was making him nervous. He felt naked, exposed and completely out of place as he pulled up on a large and immaculate turning circle and stared at the front doors that were clearly more about statement than function. Nobody was *that* big.

He killed the engine and took off his crash helmet, kicking down the stand as one of those ostentatious doors swung open and someone stepped onto the porch.

Hyienna lost his breath for a moment as he stared at the elegant and very chic woman framed by the doorway, looking for all the world like a model from some magazine dedicated to unattainable lifestyles. Her flowing white dress exuded a catwalk kind of confidence which was reflected and amplified by her surroundings. She looked at him coolly for a moment before the spell was broken and she waved her arm in an almost childlike manner before running down the steps to greet him.

Within a moment Hyienna found his arms wrapped around his little cousin in an embrace that was a greeting, an apology, a reconciliation and forgiveness all at the same time.

The two of them stood locked together in the hot afternoon sun with neither willing to relinquish the contact they'd missed for so long. Eventually Hyienna slackened his grip. He wasn't really sure why, but it just felt appropriate, what with his being a guest. It didn't make much sense, but it was how he felt so he just went with it.

For a few long seconds he just stared at the beautiful woman who stared straight back at him with those expressive brown eyes of hers. Sarah had always been pretty, but she had truly blossomed in this luxurious if somewhat harsh environment. Obviously, the rich surroundings agreed with her.

As he stood there looking mutely at the woman he hadn't seen for so long, Hyienna realised he'd completely forgotten what it was he'd been meaning to say on their first meeting after so many years. For the second time that day he was lost for words. "Hi Sarah, you look beautiful."

She smiled sweetly at the compliment, although her eyes were narrowed with concern. "Hey Hyienna, long time no see. You fall off

❦

your bike or something?" She reached forward and gently touched the bump on his forehead.

Hyienna smiled and inwardly winced, although the pain was more to his pride than anything else. "Yeah, damn potholes." He'd already decided not to mention his bizarre encounter earlier that day, at least until he had some idea of how things were going to play out. After all, it had been a long time and people could change, and not always for the better.

Sarah smiled ruefully and hugged him again. "Same old Hyienna. It's so good to see you again. We shouldn't have let it go so long."

Hyienna hugged her back, hoping that embrace would dull the sudden pain he felt as she summarily dismissed all that hard and agonising inner growth he'd endured with a single flippant, off-the-cuff remark. "Hey, it's as much my fault as anyone's. Still, we're here now and that's what really matters."

Sarah stepped back once again. "Where have you been?"

"To hell and back." Hyienna gestured to the impressive house and gardens. "Nice place; you win the lottery or something?"

She winked at him and beamed a broad, friendly smile. "Something like that. Come on; let me give you the tour." Without waiting for a reply, she grabbed his hand and led him up the wide front steps like an excited teenager.

Hyienna was happy to let her lead and the air was refreshingly cool in the wide and spacious hallway. It certainly was a relief to escape the glare of the mid-afternoon sun.

"Voilà! Welcome to Casa Sarah, and Casa Solomon too."

Hyienna wasn't really listening as his cousin reeled off a list of rooms and amenities, pointing excitedly this way and that. Her voice faded to a low murmur as he turned a slow circle in mute astonishment at the sheer opulence of his little cousin's home.

A tiled floor weaved an intricate pattern of interlaced geometry marked out in quarry red and gleaming white; a modern take on the latent Islamic influence found across that part of the world. In many ways the floor reflected the rest of the house as it branched off and soared upwards in endless acres of flawless white walls and gleaming glass. It was a pleasing if oddly oxymoronic style best described as a traditional modernist Mediterranean home. Furniture was sparse in that part of the house, allowing cool air to move freely and bestowing a settled and calm feeling on visitors. The occasional modernist painting or a discrete sofa nestling in a corner accentuated a smart yet homely feel; with those interior décor pieces appearing to be well made and most likely one of a kind.

Sarah always did have a designer's eye, although the house and the furnishings must've come from someone else's very deep pockets.

Hyienna was jolted out of his contemplative state when he realised the cousin, he hadn't seen for so many years had just asked him something.

"What? Sorry, I didn't catch that; too busy admiring your beautiful home." That should do the trick, she always responded well to compliments.

Sarah smiled warmly. "Yeah, I see you still have that laser focus you were so famous for. Come and meet the gang." She grabbed his hand and pulled him towards a heavy looking door leading off the spacious hallway. "Mind your step." The door swung open silently as she pushed it, immediately allowing a swell of hushed voices to escape from the spacious room beyond.

Hyienna took his cousin's advice and looked down, carefully negotiating the two gleaming tiled steps leading down into a spacious, airy room that he could best be described as a study, or a den, or some kind of lounge, or maybe all three combined.

It was a long, rectangular room filled with deep and comfortable looking sofas and chairs, interspersed with occasional tables and cabinets filled with what looked like archaeological artefacts. Hyienna caught a glimpse of an outdoor pool glistening beyond some billowing white chiffon curtains before his attention focused on a man and a woman standing in the middle of the room. Although they must've seen and heard the two arrivals, they simply lowered their voices so that their conversation couldn't be overheard.

❧

Although Hyienna thought it was pretty damned rude, they were not altogether successful in their attempt and he heard the woman talking about someone called Nathaniel, who sounded quite mysterious and important, whoever he was. Dressed in white in a similar fashion to Sarah she was certainly attractive, although her features were more angular and chiselled which made her beauty more statuesque and aloof when compared the radiant, smiling warmth of his recently reconciled cousin.

Sarah turned to Hyienna. "This is Solomon, and the good-looking one is Kate. Hey guys, Hyienna's finally made it."

Hyienna frowned as Solomon merely held up a finger for quiet as he wrapped up his hushed conversation without turning to acknowledge his guest. Dressed in crisp white shirt and equally crisp dark trousers, he was obviously used to being in charge.

For a moment Hyienna got the idea of some kind of religious cult in his head. It was a crazy notion, but there was just something about the way everyone was dressed and the odd air of deference which had suddenly descended. It was a strange idea, but it was made all the more persuasive when the conversation finally wrapped up and all eyes turned to fix firmly on him.

Hyienna wasn't sure if the women had noticed Solomon's challenge, but it was clear enough to him when the larger man cocked his head on one side and thrust his hands in his pockets as he observed his visitor with a mixture of curiosity and barely disguised amusement. Tall, gym honed and sporting the clean-shaven head of the classic Black man of action, Solomon was obviously someone with a exceedingly high opinion of himself.

Sarah clicked across the tiled floor and leaned up close against Solomon, wrapping her hands around his muscular arms both as a sign of affection and perhaps also as a way of laying claim. "Hyienna, I'd like you to meet Solomon, my fiancé. He runs the Island Scuba School, along with a few other businesses around the place. This here is Kate, a good friend of ours and someone who always seems to know what's going on before everyone else."

Kate was first off, the mark, stepping forward with a mischievous smile. "So, you're the long-lost link. Sarah's often talked about you."

"Only the good stuff I hope." Hyienna cursed his own social clumsiness as he gently clasped Kates' soft and manicured hand. God knows how many times a woman like her must've heard a lame reply like that.

At last Solomon spoke. "My girlfriend beat you up or something? She does that." His voice was deep, matching his imposing frame and weight bulked physique.

Sarah slapped Solomon's muscular arm. "That's fiancé to you."

"Sure, sugar; whatever you say." Solomon finally took his hand from his pocket and offered it to Hyienna.

Caught off guard but doing his best to look nonchalant, Hyienna disentangled himself from the smiling Sarah and turned to face the smirking, Solomon. "Fell off my bike on the way over. Damned potholes." He grasped Solomon's hand firmly and tried to contain the annoyance rising inside him as the larger man refused to let it go.

Solomon's smirk grew a little more noticeable. "So, you're Hyena."

"That's Hyienna."

"Yeah, right. I fell off my share of scooters when I was a kid, although I prefer four wheels and air-con these days. All the same, you can't beat the wind in your face on a hot day like this, even though it ruins your shirt." He eventually let go of Hyienna's hand and gestured upwards with his head. "Sarah will take you to the guest room and get you cleaned up." He winked before turning away and pulling a cell phone from his pocket, making it clear that the introductions were over.

Sarah quickly grabbed her cousin's arm. "Come on, you'll *love* the guest room."

* * *

Hyienna shook his head sadly as he packed his dusty travelling shirt into his small rucksack. This wasn't how it was supposed to have turned out, not at all. It was great to see Sarah after such a long time, but he knew he couldn't stay and risk getting into some kind of argument with her fiancé. Solomon was clearly a dick with some serious attitude, but it would do neither him nor his cousin any good to say so. Love is blind and all that stuff.

Still, on the upside, Sarah had certainly landed on her feet and Hyienna felt pleased that his cousin was living in such high style. In fact, the house was *so* spectacular that he'd half expected a large portion of it to suddenly fall down, as though it were some kind of elaborate movie set or a conjurer's illusion. It was all real enough though, as the tranquil view of Mediterranean reminded him as he stepped onto a small balcony sheltered by a wicker sunscreen. He'd had such high hopes for this trip; a long overdue reconciliation and an unexpected mystery to share as well. What *was* that thing, and how on earth did that old woman fit into the picture? He figured that locals like Kate would be a big help, so it was a pity he didn't know anyone well enough to trust them with something so downright bizarre.

There was a tap at the door, and he took a deep breath to hide the annoyance in his voice. "Yeah?"

"Sarah's invited you for drinks on the patio."

Hyienna smiled and shook his head ruefully as he recognised Kate's muffled voice outside the door. *Drinks on the patio.* It really felt as though he'd fallen into another world, maybe as some bit player in a Bond movie. He grabbed the little rock in his pocket as he realised it was the second time that day the world's most famous fictional spy had sneaked into his head.

He stepped back into the cool guest room, running his hand lightly over the heavy carved wood of the guest bed. It was an impressive piece of furniture, so God only knew what the master bedroom looked like. It was probably all gaudy gold and pointless gadgets if he'd got Solomon's number. Still, the guest room was pleasant enough and it was with a heavy heart he realised he couldn't stay there.

* * *

The sun glinted on brightly polished glass as Sarah regaled her cousin with yet another tale of Solomon's business acumen, which always seemed to end with her explaining how much money they were making.

Hyienna nodded politely now and then, but he'd got the idea a while ago. Solomon was good at making money and Sarah wasn't afraid to let everyone know about it. It seemed like they were *both* good at showing off.

Sarah had changed into a flowing halter necked white dress, while Kate had donned an expensive and chic looking trouser and blouse combo, which highlighted the dark tones of her seemingly flawless skin.

Solomon had changed neither his clothes nor his boorish manner as he directed the women to see to their guest's comfort, and by default to his own. He talked about new cars, which he enjoyed buying; scuba diving, which he was good at and entertaining, which he apparently excelled at.

Hyienna wouldn't have been surprised that Solomon was single-handedly working on a cure for cancer, which no doubt he would've been brilliant at.

Although the drinks were refreshing and the location was nothing short of beautiful, the more the afternoon wore on, the more uncomfortable Hyienna became. His discomfort reached a peak as Solomon started fishing for compliments. "So, Hyena, I hope the spare room is okay for you."

Hyienna swallowed down his anger as Solomon deliberately mispronounced his name for the umpteenth time. No doubt the man was absolutely hilarious after a few drinks, and no doubt that was something *else* he always told everyone. "It's very nice, very comfortable."

"Yeah, you'd struggle to find a hotel room as good as that anywhere on the island, so I guess you can thank your little cousin for being related to you. I guess that's your lucky break."

Hyienna could stand it no more. He drained the last of his very agreeable Sangria spritzer and made his move. "It's a beautiful room all right, great for someone who might be staying for a couple of days, but I'm not sure how long I'm going to be here, and I really don't want to take advantage."

Sarah's face fell. "Oh, that's okay…" She stopped mid-sentence as Solomon held up his hand for quiet.

❀

"Listen, if the man don't wanna be a burden then let him find his own way. A man should be self-reliant after all. Ain't that right, Hyena?"

Hyienna rose with all the calmness and dignity he could muster. "Thanks for your hospitality. Is there anywhere I can crash nearby?"

Solomon smirked. "Bad choice of words with that bone rattler of yours out front, my friend."

Kate, who'd made a good job of looking like a human ornament, finally spoke up. "Sure, there's the Green Lizard Tavern just up the road. It's a nice spot and Yaz will take good care of you."

Solomon winked. "Plenty of ladies to chase on that mean machine of yours too."

Hyienna thought he saw a flash of irritation in his cousin's face as he made his excuses and left the table.

* * *

Oh crap! Can't I just get the hell out of here without saying exactly what I'm thinking? Hyienna forced a smile as he descended the stairs to where his cousin was waiting. He'd seen enough of the world to know that a woman standing with her hands on her hips was never a good sign. The expression on her face wasn't all that encouraging either.

"Hey cous', I'm glad I'm not gonna get lost looking for you around here. So where do I find this Green Turtle place?"

"I can't *believe* you, Hyienna. You roll up here after all this time and pretty much the first thing you do is throw my hospitality back in my face. I knew this was a mistake."

Hyienna had been trying hard all afternoon, but he couldn't hold it in any longer. "Last time I checked, the word *hospitality* had nothing to do with letting some pumped up, corn-fed lounge lizard walk all over me." He gestured around the tastefully appointed hallway. "You might think it's worth it, but that guy puts no food on *my* table. And I'll tell you something else too, no way would the Sarah *I* knew put up with that kind of bullshit from a boyfriend, fiancé or anyone else."

Sarah sighed with exasperation. "Jesus, do you have to pick a fight with everyone just to prove a point, or are you just sore that Solomon's actually *done* something with his life?"

"All I can see is a jerk who mistreats the people he should care for the most." Hyienna made for the door. "Nice place you've got, I just hope it didn't cost you too much." He heard her say something else as he slammed the door behind him, although by that time he wasn't really listening. The whole day had been a disaster from start to finish, not to mention unbelievably weird. All he wanted to do was just get the hell out of that stiflingly clean, orderly, and ostentatious place and back to something resembling normality. If Sarah was happy then good for her, but her silence at Solomon's endless taunting had told him that she'd made her choice and was content to lie in the bed she'd chosen. Well, that was fine for her, but it looked like Hyienna just didn't match the furniture anymore.

He stamped across the smooth paved driveway to recover his dusty and somewhat battered scooter, which suddenly seemed to be all the more out of place in the sumptuous surroundings, like a guy in sneakers at a black-tie ball.

Oh, Christ Almighty, I can't bloody well believe this! Hyienna shook his head as he stared glumly at the flat tyre at the front of his scooter. He thought he'd got away with it, but it looked like that damned pothole had done for his ride after all. He took a quick look, but he couldn't see any obvious signs of damage, and he wasn't about to start messing around with his front wheel on the driveway.

Goddammit! Of all the bloody times! He stood up and wondered if he could maybe call a cab or even some kind of tow truck to get him back to town.

"Looks like you got yourself a flat there."

Hyienna whirled around as he heard Solomon's deep voice close behind him. In truth he didn't know if he was mad because he couldn't just tell the guy where to get off or because, once again, circumstances had conspired to make him look foolish in a place where he really didn't want that to happen. "Yeah, must've been that pothole on the way in."

Solomon thrust his hands into his pockets and stepped closer. "Well, that ain't going nowhere tonight. Tell you what, grab your gear and I'll run you over to the Turtle."

Hyienna hesitated.

Both Solomon's stance and expression softened, as though he could sense what the other man was thinking. "Listen, you don't want to pay no attention to me, I was just busting your balls as the Italians say. You know, I thought you were a bit of a pushover until you basically told me to go screw myself by staying at the Lizard. I like that; a man should have a little fire in his blood and some steel in his spine, even if he shows it in a different sort of way. In truth, I don't really care if you think I'm a jerk, you're a stranger to me, but you're Sarah's kin and I have to respect that. She's been through some tough times, and you have too, from what she's told me."

Still Hyienna hesitated.

Solomon gestured with his head. "Come on, we'll get your bike fixed first thing in the morning."

* * *

The coolness of the air conditioning left Hyienna feeling oddly detached as he watched the parched landscape from behind darkened glass. Solomon's Range Rover was a five-star ride, no doubt about it, but he found the high degree of separation from the outside world oddly disconcerting. It seemed as though the fully loaded vehicle was a means to escape from the world rather than a way to discover more of it.

That oddly unreal quality was made all the more unsettling by the sudden change in Solomon's attitude. He wasn't exactly acting like a best buddy, but his unexpectedly friendly demeanour was oddly off-putting. Hyienna didn't believe that it was all a big act, but neither did he think that Solomon had suddenly revised his attitude and thought of him as less of a loser because he didn't own a big house and drive an expensive car. On the other hand, Hyienna had seen enough of the world to know that wearing the suit didn't mean the tailor had been paid.

The slightly off kilter quality in the car was reflected in the way the larger man spoke as they rolled silently through the Formentera countryside. It was clear that Solomon knew a lot about history, especially that of the island and its people; and it was a knowledge which he seemed keen to impart to any audience he could find. It was almost as though Solomon wore that knowledge like he wore his clothes and his car, his research being just another accessory to show his standing in the world. The folktales and the impromptu history lesson were all very well, but they were relayed in a very detached and uninvolved manner, just as Solomon's prestigious vehicle left both of them detached and uninvolved.

It was a great effort for Hyienna not to glance back at the mysterious rucksack nestling incongruously in the rear footwell. It was also a great effort not to think that whatever was inside had cast a mysterious and less than benevolent influence on affairs. He tried to resist the idea that it had called him to that mysterious cavern by the sea, and he would not be released from its power until he had done its bidding; whatever the hell *that* might be. It was hard not to think of Tolkien's infamous ring of power, and once again he had to scold himself against his own tendency to over dramatise. No way was he going to reach into his pocket while he was sat next to Solomon. He'd never hear the end of it!

"Just a second, we need to pick someone up."

Hyienna looked around and realised he had no recollection of the route they'd taken or even where they were headed. He must've seemed a million miles away, which in fairness was a bit rude on his part, not that he cared very much.

He was surprised to see that they'd pulled up in front of an old church, complete with dusty graveyard and what looked like some kind of courtyard out the back. If it wasn't for the incongruous air-conditioning pipes running along the roof, the place could easily have passed for a Sergio Leone movie set with a little creative cutting and some tight camera angles to avoid the small cluster of more modern shops and houses that seemed to have sprung up for no reason beside the dusty highway. "Where are we?"

Solomon was keen to show off his local knowledge once again. "This is la iglesia de San Miguel. There's been a church on this site since at least the Crusades and maybe even longer, although the archaeology gets a bit jumbled, and the Vatican doesn't like having its sites disturbed."

"The Vatican?" Hyienna was intrigued, although he wasn't really sure why.

"Sure, it's Catholicism all the way in these parts, and its roots reach deep into the local folklore. In fact, they're kind of mixed together in a weird way around here; part religious doctrine and part superstition all at the same time."

"I see." Said Hyienna. He had to admit that Solomon's take on the place had been banging on the bull's-eye from what little he'd seen. Formentera *did* have a strange air about it. Away from the traffic and the tourist spots, there was a timeless quality, a feeling of slight disconnection from the rest of the world. Those air conditioning pipes were accepted as a compromise rather than embraced as progress.

Hyienna watched with curiosity and a little trepidation as a bulky figure emerged from behind the church and made straight for the car. Solomon was a big guy, but the man approaching was *huge*. He just hoped the newcomer didn't mind riding in the back.

As if on cue the big man adjusted his course slightly and climbed into the back of the Range Rover. He reached across to clasp Solomon's hand before looking at Hyienna.

Solomon spoke for both of them. "This is Hyena; sorry *Hyienna*, Sarah's cousin. He's headed to the Green Lizard. Hyienna, meet my bro, Seth."

Seth shook Hyienna's hand firmly but not too hard, even though it was a bit awkward. "Hyienna. I heard you were coming. The Lizard's a good spot and Yaz will look after you." Seth's voice was as deep as his biceps were wide and he was clearly not a man to be trifled with.

One of the first details Hyienna noticed was the large hammer of God tattoo on Seth's right arm. Picked out in intricate Celtic knot work, its impact was lessened as the black ink produced little contrast to Seth's own dark skin. However, rather than hiding the needle artist's fine work, that lack of contrast left the impression that Seth's body art was as much an integral part of him as the large limb it adorned.

It was as though he'd always worn that statement on his arm, and it did not escape Hyienna's attention that the big man didn't seem to be sporting any other body art or piercings. That suggested the tattoo was something special, something meaningful; a clear statement standing alone, rather than a single sentence lost in an incoherent hotchpotch of overlapping imagery. That single tattoo suggested a single-minded man, but although Seth was an intimidating figure, he did not project the immediate confrontational challenge of Solomon. Clearly a man with little to prove, Seth might be a great guy or a total jerk; there just wasn't enough information to make any kind of judgement.

With the introductions complete, Hyienna turned back to contemplating the darkened countryside through his smoked window and Seth settled back into his own seat, seemingly oblivious to the remarkable and perhaps even miraculous artefact hidden right beside his feet.

Seth's arrival seemed to suck all the energy out of the atmosphere, leaving it brittle in a way that made speech seem somehow impolite and even inappropriate.

The short journey to the Green Lizard was conducted in silence.

* * *

Hyienna found it difficult to sum up the Green Lizard in one word when he first clapped eyes on it. *Craphole* was his first impression, although he quickly realised, he was way off the mark as they got closer.

As they pulled into a dusty car park, it was clear that the Green Lizard had decided that its future was firmly rooted in the past, leading Hyienna to quickly revise his assessment of what turned out to be a little slice of rustic heaven as he clambered out of the air-conditioned Range Rover. Although his trip had been as comfortable as could be, he was nevertheless relieved to be back in the real world so to speak, with his otherworldly burden close at hand. Despite the obvious friction it had caused, he immediately knew his decision to stay elsewhere had been the right one.

Perched on a small rise overlooking the glittering ocean, this place was far more…connected to the world in a way that Sarah's beautifully appointed home was not. The rustic looking building had probably hosted fishermen, travellers, pilgrims and bandits over the years, although, like many buildings in the region it seemed to be of an indeterminate age.

Hyienna watched with interest as the two big men clambered out of the car, seemingly not bothering to lock it as they headed inside. Hanging back to get the vibe of the place and also to recover his bags, Hyienna was immediately charmed by the Green Lizard's faded holiday charms. He at once knew this was where he was meant to be, in readiness for the next stage of whatever journey or pilgrimage he'd stumbled into.

Just a short drive from the main road on the island's south side, the Green Lizard was nonetheless very quiet with no immediate neighbours. Smart chrome napkin holders glinted on half a dozen well-scrubbed Formica tables as they waited patiently for hungry visitors. A couple of soft drink machines lurked beneath a sun-bleached canopy festooned with fairy lights and wind chimes that twinkled and tinkled in the warm afternoon breeze.

It was hard to tell if the place was actually open for business, although Solomon and Seth seemed to have no such difficulties as they wandered straight through the brightly painted yet faded front door.

Hyienna noted an ageing but serviceable looking payphone on the wall as he stepped into the cool and somewhat dim interior of the Green Lizard Tavern. He immediately knew it was much more like his kind of place, with worn quarry tiles and a jumble of mismatched but scrupulously clean tables scattered around a small yet well-stocked central bar. He nodded to a couple of older locals talking over some sweating glasses of beer as the incomparable smell of home cooking permeated the atmosphere, adding to the Lizard's informal, lived in and welcoming feel. It was the polar opposite to Sarah and Solomon's immaculate show house, which although impressive, had made him nervous to even stand on a rug or sit on a sofa for fear of wrinkling some of those sumptuous fabrics.

That general feeling of informality seemed to affect everyone as they crossed the threshold, with Solomon unexpectedly reaching out to hug a woman who Hyienna assumed was the owner, or manager or something. Clad in a billowing and loose-fitting green dress, she clearly enjoyed Solomon's embrace, her fingers splaying around the back of his neck and head with an intimacy more intense than that of a simple friend.

Seth somehow perched his large frame on a narrow stool and reached into a small fridge at the end of the bar. Retrieving a cold bottle of beer, he briefly raised it in the owner's direction before twisting off the cap and taking a long swig. Hyienna didn't see him hand over any cash although he figured that places like the Lizard still ran on an informal tab system.

Finally breaking his long embrace, Solomon gestured for Hyienna to come over. "Yaz, this is Hyienna, Sarah's cousin from Ibiza. Hyienna, meet Yasmina, owner and manager of the Green Lizard Tavern. Best food, best beer and best beds this side of the island."

Yasmina smiled at Solomon before stepping forward and offering her hand. "Just call me Yaz. It's so nice to meet you, Hyienna. Any kin of Sarah's is welcome here." There was a genuine warmth to her manner and speech, although there was also another, more elusive quality that Hyienna couldn't immediately put his finger on. He began to wonder if there was something in the local water as Yasmina was also attractive, although there was an aspect to the earnestness of her demeanour that made him wonder about her. She and the Green Lizard obviously belonged together, and he could easily envisage a grainy image of her younger self popping up in some random photo taken at Woodstock…or with the Manson family.

Hyienna felt an immediate connection with Yasmina, although it wasn't really based on any kind of physical chemistry. It was more of a kinship of shared experience as he saw how sadness and sorrow had dulled those once bright and enquiring eyes. Yasmina could still put on a good show if she chose to, but a more guarded and cautious spirit now dwelled where once carefree abandon had been everything.

He realised he'd better say something rather than just smiling and staring. "Thanks, I appreciate it. Do you have any rooms? I'm thinking of staying for a few days."

There was that brightness, like a switch being flicked on when Yasmina felt needed. "Sure! Sarah phoned ahead and we've got you the presidential suite overlooking the ocean. Are you hungry? I can fix you something real nice, Mina and I are quite the cooks even though I do say so myself."

Before Hyienna could respond, Yaz called through a doorway and a young woman emerged in a cloud of good smelling steam. "Ermina, say hello to Sarah's cousin, Hyienna."

Ermina, who was younger and obviously related to the tavern's owner, beamed an excitable smile as she stepped forward to greet him. "It's so great to meet you, even though I thought you'd have been staying at Solomon's place." She glanced across to where Solomon and Yasmina had taken up position on either side of the bar.

Hyienna made his excuses. "Well, I don't know how long I'm gonna be staying and I don't want to be a burden to anyone."

Ermina glanced at Hyienna's lack of luggage. "Travelling light?"

"Yeah, I don't need much, and I figured I could pick up anything else I might need while I'm here."

Not deterred, Ermina glanced over his shoulder. "No car?"

Rescue came from an unlikely quarter as a Solomon chipped in. "Poor guy got a flat, so he left his ride at our place. Now I know you girls are going to take good care of Sarah's kin, which pretty much makes him my kin too."

Again, Hyienna noticed Yasmina's hand on Solomon's arm as she spoke. "Don't worry; you have the best room in the tavern, probably the best room on the island. We don't advertise and we like to keep things low-key."

"Just the way I like it." Hyienna confirmed.

Seth said nothing, merely sat quietly drinking his beer. For such a big guy he made a good job of being inconspicuous.

At last, Ermina changed the subject. "You hungry? I can rustle you up some ham and eggs or maybe a burger. It's a little early to start on the dinner menu."

Hyienna avoided the trap of asking whether there would be anyone around to order from the dinner menu. "I'll just have a beer for now, thanks." He picked up his bags and made his way to what he considered to be the best seat in the house. It was a small table around the corner from the bar and just beneath a small window with a brightly painted frame. It had been one hell of a day and he just needed to unwind and sit quietly for a while. He had an awful lot to think about and he couldn't figure out how he should feel about the first day of his Formentera adventure. To say it had been a rollercoaster was an understatement, and in truth he was feeling more than a little lost   and overwhelmed.

He flopped into a worn but surprisingly comfortable wooden chair and shrugged off his jacket, enjoying both the warmth of the afternoon sunshine through the window and the coolness of the shadows beneath the table. Hyienna knew straight away that he'd fallen on his feet in terms of accommodation as he gazed out through those small glass panes. He could see the glittering Mediterranean as well as a sweeping curve of sandy beach as it took a sharp turn towards some sort of inlet that vanished behind a nearby clifftop. That stretch of coastline was much like the tavern, being devoid of tourists and locals alike. In fact, he could only see one solitary figure standing down there on the beach, although he couldn't decide whether it was a local resident or some kind of visitor.

Hyienna jumped as Ermina appeared with his order, and never was a cold beer more greatly appreciated. "Quiet here." He remarked as she turned to leave.

"That's just the way we like it. We do get a few tourists passing through, mostly backpackers, although the bulk of our trade is local."

He thought it impolite to ask how the tavern could make ends meet, after all there must be a thousand things he didn't know about the place and how it worked. Instead, he just nodded and stared out of the window once more, playing a game in his head as he began inventing backstories for the lone figure standing on the beach. Maybe he was a famous writer escaping from the pressures of the world and dedicating himself to his next book, like the beginnings of so many good and mediocre horror movies. Maybe he was a retired intelligence operative, burying himself in the middle of a sunny nowhere as he tried to forget the things he'd done in the service of civilisation. Hyienna speculated that the lone figure might be some unconventional but brilliant sports trainer, come to test out some ground for his latest protégé to train in secret.

Ermina interrupted his daydreaming as she leaned across and looked out of the window. "Something cool out there?" She quickly lost interest as the man on the beach turned and walked slowly away. "That's just Nathaniel, don't worry about him."

"Local guy?" Hyienna asked, before wondering why he was inquiring about a random stranger standing on a deserted beach, although he remembered it was the same name he'd heard on Kate's lips when he'd arrived at Sarah's house. It was probably just one of those odd coincidences, although he couldn't shake the feeling that the mysterious figure on the beach was somehow intertwined with whatever the hell kind of mystery, he got himself wound up in.

Ermina sounded far less interested. "Yeah, kind of. Not sure if he was born here, although I heard somewhere that he's some kind of orphan; grew up in a church or something. I don't know, anyway, he keeps himself to himself and he's a bit of a strange one if you ask me."

Hyienna looked at the suddenly deserted coastline as Ermina joined the small group at the bar and loudly relayed the news that she'd seen Nathaniel on the beach again.

It wasn't really Hyienna's intention to eavesdrop, but the place was so quiet that he couldn't help but overhear the conversation taking place over the bar. He was no expert on psychology or body language, but from what he could see it was pretty obvious that Yaz and Solomon were good, *good* friends. He felt an immediate surge of anger when he thought of his little cousin being betrayed by a guy who was, frankly, more than a bit of a misogynist and a boor in the truest sense of the word. His first instinct was to raise the subject with Sarah, but then the pebble in his pocket and a sip of cold beer counselled caution. He didn't really *know* a single soul on the island, and certainly not anyone whose discretion he could rely on. Besides, Sarah had been happy to let her fiancé walk all over him in front of company, which made him wonder about the whole thicker than water idea.

The more he considered his position, the more Hyienna realised he was just a stranger who'd dropped into the lives of a bunch of people who'd known each other for quite a while. They had no reason to trust him and he sure as hell didn't know who he might trust in return. All he knew for sure was that his reunion with Sarah had not gone even close to the way he'd planned it, plus he'd ended up in possession of something that at least *appeared* to not be entirely of this world. Although the thing in the rucksack resembled a large piece of cloth, the word *blanket* just didn't seem to do it justice, whatever it was. Eventually he settled on the word *artefact*, much more fitting description, not that he was in a hurry to describe his discovery to anyone.

As he sat back in his chair and drank his beer, Hyienna came to the unexpected realisation that, probably for the first time in his life, he understood what the word faith really meant. He had no idea of what he should do tomorrow or even for the rest of the current day, so he had little choice but to have faith that the mysterious artefact would make its purpose known somehow. Besides, the Green Lizard's quiet rustic charm was like a soothing balm for his soul, calming his mind and settling his spirit in a way he'd not known for many a long and difficult year. Despite all the little intrigues and petty human jealousies, Hyienna knew that fate, Providence or whatever else it might be called had brought him to this place for a reason. He instinctively realised that reason would never reveal itself before the right moment. That meant he had time enough to enjoy a beer, discreetly take in the gossip and have faith that his adventure would unfold in the fullness of time.

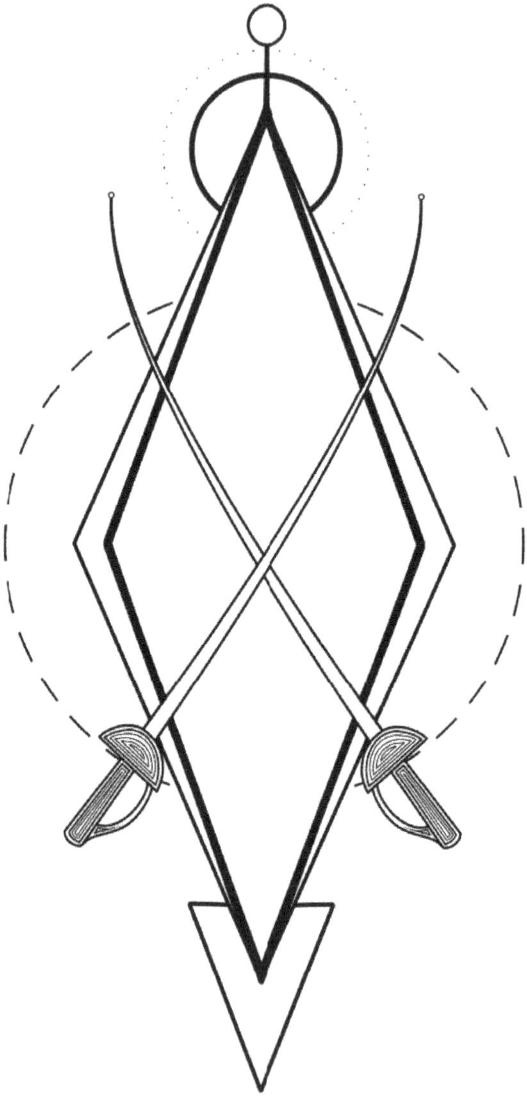

EXTENDED ABSENCES
Chapter 4

A rolling cloud of mist slowly melted and became a curtain, while a distant murmur of profundity slowly faded into the soft song of a Balearic breeze. Hyienna blinked rapidly as he desperately tried to capture the memory of that other place, lingering between the waking world and somewhere strange that sort of felt like a dream.

She was there again, the old woman, haunting those silent dark hours like a spectre of doom from some Dickensian ghost story. She always spoke, but Hyienna could never quite recall what she'd said by the time he'd fully woken. The notepad beside his bed was of little help as dawn's pale shadows quickly fled once the veil of the night was melted by the morning sun.

Hyienna rolled over and scribbled that thought down, even though it wasn't strictly speaking a part of his dream. He blearily flicked through the pages of his notebook, trying to discern some pattern or flash of inspiration from the catalogue of fleeting impressions that had haunted him since his arrival on the island. It had only been a few days, but he couldn't escape the nagging feeling that the topsy-turvy world of his nocturnal subconscious was a lot more clued in than the rest of him.

He sat up, his eyes immediately focusing on the battered antique wardrobe in the corner of his rustic yet very comfortable and homely room. There was an odd unreality to the idea that the greatest mystery of his unremarkable life rested quietly in a dark corner, just behind a couple of shirts and a pair of jeans he'd managed to bring across from Ibiza. Once again indecision paralysed him as he studied the patterns of the early sun as it dappled the room through cracked shutters and shifting curtains. What was stopping him? Why didn't he just march across his own room and pull that innocuous looking rucksack out into that bright Mediterranean morning? There was nothing and nobody to stand in his way, save for the frisson of fear that froze his very soul when he considered the unearthly mystery waiting in the wardrobe.

He had no rational explanation for his ideas, but Hyienna instinctively understood that it was forbidden, declared strictly off-limits by some unwritten edict, decreed by some higher authority that he didn't really want to consider too closely. Although the old woman had specifically given him the…*thing*, he knew he was merely a messenger, a caretaker, a courier tasked to take whatever the hell it was on the next leg of wherever the hell it was travelling to. Deep down, he already knew that the idea of a destination had no place in meditations on such an impossible darkness. This was something eternal, like the tides, the moon and the sun; it was something fundamental to everything a man could know, yet every contemplation revealed nothing that could be grasped by mere plodding rationality. The thing in the wardrobe was everything, yet it explained nothing. Despite the impenetrable metaphysical mystery in his charge, Hyienna was certain of one thing; he knew full well that endless spirals of introspection and speculation were the sure road to ruin, especially for him.

He was more than glad when the sounds of mundane humanity saved him from the supernatural when he heard a car approaching. Without really knowing why he was hiding, he rolled out of bed and stood beside the peeling balcony shutters, peeping out as soft chiffon curtains swayed in the warm Balearic wind.

Solomon's Range Rover glinted in the bright morning sun as it slowly, almost gingerly, rolled to a stop directly below. It was as though the driver didn't want to get dust on his paintwork, something which Hyienna could easily imagine.

He felt kind of awkward as he secretly watched Solomon clamber out of the driver's seat while Yasmina walked out to greet him. Hyienna felt even *more* awkward as he watched them embrace more like lovers than friends. He'd been hoping he was wrong about Solomon and Yasmina, as the last thing Hyienna wanted was to be caught in the middle of some unpredictable love triangle just as he was beginning to reconnect with his only meaningful relative. By witnessing proof positive of something he desperately hoped *wasn't* true, Hyienna knew he was screwed either way and there could be no good resolution to such a situation. He and Sarah hadn't spoken in years, and he had no right to go poking into her personal affairs. On the other hand, there was no way he'd be thanked when Sarah found out about the two of them and began to wonder how it was that Hyienna hadn't noticed anything.

Hidden behind those billowing white curtains, Hyienna silently cursed the pair of them as Solomon and Yasmina stood in a semi-embrace, discussing their respective futures. The meandering island breeze lifted fragments of conversation onto the balcony, whether he wanted to hear them or not. It was pretty clear that the conversation in the deserted car park was a well-worn and well-rehearsed one. The two of them clearly had some kind of history and it seemed that Yasmina wanted them to seize the second chance they'd been given, whatever *that* meant.

In the meantime, Solomon was doing what guys like Solomon always did. He was trying to have his cake and eat it too by placating his lover and explaining how it was impossible for him to leave his fiancé for this, that or some other bullshit reason. Although Hyienna didn't really know Solomon, he was completely unsurprised and more than a little angry to hear such a big strong man twisting and turning like a lightweight wrestler as he tried to turn her affections to his own advantage, even if that advantage stretched no further than the bedroom.

He'd heard enough. Hyienna left the window, sat on the bed and hurriedly donned some clothes before reaching for his lightweight boots, which weren't much good for keeping out water but had proved reliable against the dust and sharp rocks that seemed to cover most of Formentera's surface.

Solomon's early arrival clearly meant that he hadn't driven over for a cold beer or a good meal; the place was deserted and Hyienna sure as hell didn't want to be around if they decided to come indoors. It was clear that Solomon and Yaz were engaged in some kind of extramarital affair, even though neither of them was actually married. Still, at least one of them was pretty damn close to it though.

Hyienna quickly figured out that Sarah had to be told. She might well hate him for it, but he knew he had no choice but to cut his losses. Better to be hated for telling the truth than despised for complicity in a betrayal of the heart.

❀

With his mind made up, he opened the battered but sturdy wardrobe to retrieve his battered but sturdy jacket. Of course, he tried *not* to look at the worn and well-travelled rucksack nestling innocently in a shadowy corner, but he knew it was a forlorn hope.

Quickly throwing on his jacket, he pulled out the rucksack handed to him by the witch in the cave. *Witch* was a word that came to mind far too easily. There was very little weight to the bag as he set it on the bed and stared down at the otherworldly mystery contained in a creased chunk of cheap luggage. Hyienna's fingers hovered above the zip as he tried to convince himself that he should look inside, just to make sure that he hadn't simply imagined the whole thing and been irrationally frightened of some ordinary square of black fabric. But then if it *was* just a square of black fabric, why should he hesitate to simply open the bag? Once again, he pondered how there was nothing to stop him, save a nagging but insistent voice somewhere deep inside that warned such things were not for him. He had been entrusted with some great responsibility for a purpose as yet unrevealed.

Hyienna was surprised at the rush of relief he felt as he placed the innocuous looking rucksack back in the wardrobe and closed the doors. Feeling like a smoker who'd resisted temptation, Hyienna felt a sense of calm accomplishment as he picked up his bike keys and quietly let himself out of his sparse but rustically comfortable room. He quickly made his way down the stairs and into the silent and darkened bar area. Luckily, Yasmina and Solomon were still outside so he quickly made his way behind the bar and slipped out through the kitchen door.

* * *

The sound of distant laughter swirled in the warm ocean breeze as Hyienna watched the busy deck of a large yacht anchored just a few hundred yards offshore. It was a very impressive sight, but Hyienna had little doubt that it was chartered for the day. Pay the deposit, hope the cheque doesn't bounce and snap that all-important selfie before the prosecco runs out. Still, the beautiful people on board seemed to be having a good time regardless, and maybe that was all that really mattered.

He turned to see the familiar figure of his older cousin striding confidently along the quiet beach towards him. For a moment Hyienna could easily picture Sarah on that self-same slice of chartered heaven bobbing out there in the bay, imagining that she would feel right at home in such luxurious yet ultimately fraudulent surroundings. He smiled and waved as she drew nearer, silently admonishing himself and wondering how on earth he'd become so cynical and world-weary. Of course, he immediately answered his own question as he mentally ticked off a long list of things in life that seemed to be solid but had turned out to be little more than painted scenery and stage management. All show and no substance.

Hyienna couldn't help smirking as he glanced back at the boat to watch the beautiful boys and girls diving into the ocean and lounge on various inflatables that were probably meant to be ironic in some way. Sure enough, there on the deck stood a woman with long hair, a large sun hat and a camcorder in hand, panning it this way and that as she made sure to capture the hilarious inflatable flamingos, hamburgers and even a plastic desert island, complete with solitary palm tree.

He turned his attention back to Sarah, who looked quite the beach queen in a fetching skirt and blouse ensemble, casually carrying her shoes in one hand. Before he knew what was happening, Hyienna felt a broad smile on his face as he walked towards her.

They embraced warmly, although Hyienna was confused at the kaleidoscope of feelings that glittered and refracted inside him. He was glad to see her, but at the same time he felt an inexplicable sense of guilt, as though they were engaged in some clandestine or immoral activity.

He quickly stepped back, wanting to open up a little distance as the irrational feeling of guilt threatened to spoil the moment. "You're looking good as always. You'll have to tell me what your secret is." Once again Hyienna silently criticised his own weakness as he realised, he lacked the courage to tell his cousin flat out about Solomon and Yasmina. Maybe she already knew and didn't care, or more likely she would be angry at *him* for breaking such ill news and generally poking his nose in. Right there and then Hyienna changed his mind and decided *not* to raise the subject unless she asked him a direct question. After all, keeping quiet was one thing but lying to protect people to whom he owed nothing was way over the line.

He was surprised when Sarah linked her arm with his as and began to slowly stroll along the shoreline, but he didn't dwell on it too much. She seemed happy, very happy in fact, and he silently prayed that nothing would spoil the moment.

"So, what have you been up to at Yasmina's place? Apart from drowning in gossip and good food, I hope."

Hyienna suddenly wondered why he felt defensive; after all, he'd only been there for a few days and he'd spent his time just chilling out, thinking about the woman in the cave and walking on the beach. "You know how it is; I've just been finding my way around and doing a lot of reflecting."

Sarah nodded. "This is a perfect place for thinking, for reflecting. You know I've missed you these past years. It's been hard after everything that happened."

Hyienna opened his mouth and almost blurted out that it sure as hell didn't *look* too hard from where he was standing, but he thought better of it. Even that it was true, his saying so wouldn't change anything.

It was almost as though Sarah could sense what he was thinking. "I'm sorry for just up and leaving like that, but I guess we had to deal with everything in our own way. Sure, we have a beautiful home here and a good life, but that's not why I left."

Hyienna had tried to hold back, but the dam finally burst. "At least you *could* leave; the cops wouldn't let me go anywhere. Eventually they had to back off for lack of evidence, but that's just a fancy way of saying that we think you did something, but we can't prove it."

"Listen, Hyienna…"

It was too late though, Hyienna's reserve had buckled, and the torrent of pent-up emotions was streaming through, dredging everything up in its wake. "Actually, the police were the *least* of my problems. Do you have *any* idea what it's like to live with a cloud of suspicion like that following you around? Losing my job was just the start, bad publicity they said, but not even *that* was enough to get me off the hook. You know what happened the first time I walked into Big Freddy's bar after I was released?"

Sarah stopped walking and turned to face him. "No; what?"

"They gave me a round of applause and a great big cake. What the hell do you *think* happened?"

"But the police cleared you."

Hyienna gave a short, bitter laugh as he turned to gaze out across the glittering bay. "Oh well, I guess that's okay then. It didn't really matter that half the city thought I was some kind of crazed child abductor; no, a good word from the cops and everything was just fine...apart from the death threats and the odd sprint to escape a kicking, not to mention being completely unemployable basically forever. Yeah, I had nothing to do with whatever happened to that poor kid, but I've had to pay for it all the same. Hell, maybe I deserve it. Okay, so I never would've hurt the little tyke but I sure as hell did nothing to protect him either."

Sarah put her hand on his arm. "It wasn't your fault, everyone knows that."

Hyienna sighed heavily and let his head fall back. "He was just a toddler, and I was a grown man. Isn't that what we're supposed to do for toddlers, even if they're not our own? At the very least we're supposed to make sure they don't get kidnapped in the middle of the night by Christ knows who."

"I'm sorry, Hyienna, I never knew how hard it was for you. I hope we can put this behind us and move on, for both our sakes."

Hyienna shook his head sadly and gazed into his cousin's beautiful brown eyes. "You can never put it behind you. Every night I wonder if he's out there somewhere. I fantasise that he ended up with some rich and loving couple who couldn't have kids of their own, but that's something out of a storybook because none of us will ever know how it ended. One thing we *do* know is that life is no fairy tale."

There was silence for a while as both of them gazed out across the ocean, deep in thought. Eventually Sarah spoke. "If it makes you feel any better, I think about poor little Samuel every day too. At the beginning I thought it was going to drive me crazy. The worst part of it was how they even made me doubt you just for a minute. Just for a little while."

"And now?"

"Now I know that you weren't to blame for what happened, but I had a choice of falling into darkness forever or reaching out for the lifeline that Solomon gave me."

Hyienna spread his arms wide and turned a slow circle. "Some lifeline! Still, you always did have a great sense of style, so I guess an overbearing and boorish boyfriend is just fine, as long as he dresses well."

Sarah's chest rose as she took a deep breath, then fell as she let it out slowly. "Listen, I know how difficult Solomon can be, but that's only because he's had to struggle and work hard for everything he's got. He's an honourable man and he cares a lot about me. I really don't know what would have happened if he hadn't been there for me."

"Sure, well, none of us can change the past." Realising that his cousin just couldn't grasp the subtle difference between being depressed about a bad situation and being locked up as a potential child abductor, Hyienna quickly re-evaluated his plan to take Sarah into his confidence about whatever the hell was lurking in his wardrobe. Although it was so great to see Sarah again and reconnect, Hyienna felt even more isolated as he gazed at the collection of inflatables bobbing jauntily around the anchored yacht.

Sarah poked her little cousin in the ribs. "You're staring again. Don't be getting all deep and moody on me, it doesn't suit you."

He turned and smiled. "I'm glad you're happy. In the end, what else is there?"

Sarah seized her chance. "Speaking of happy, we're having a get-together on Saturday, and we'd love to have you over."

Hyienna hesitated.

Sarah pouted. "Now come on, Mr frowny face, it's not like you've got big plans or anything."

"Maybe I have a date." Hyienna retorted with mock indignation.

"You need a night off from drinking, walking and thinking. Well, from the walking and thinking anyway. Besides, Solomon and I won't be the only ones disappointed if you're a no-show."

Hyienna raised one eyebrow in his best James Bond fashion, a trick that never failed to make his cousin smile. "Don't think I know anyone else around here, well, not really."

She playfully slapped his arm. "You're too hard on yourself, you know that? *You* might not have a very high opinion of the impression you make, but you certainly had an impact on Kate."

Hyienna folded his arms and frowned. "Kate? Your pal? The one who looks like she's permanently modelling for some fashion catalogue?"

"You could have at least *pretended* you hadn't noticed her."

"Would you have believed me?"

Sarah feigned intense thought for a moment. "Probably not. Anyhow, that charming, dusty Charlie Brown act of yours must've hit the right spot because she's done nothing but ask me about you since you breezed back into my life."

"Now you're just teasing. That's mean." Hyienna scoffed.

"Suit yourself, but if you don't want to spend a relaxing evening with not one, but *two* beautiful ladies, why on earth did you bother coming here in the first place? You can shut yourself away in Barcelona just as easily as you can here." Sarah's forehead creased and her face fell, her tone suddenly becoming sombre. "Be wary of Kate."

Hyienna looked at his cousin quizzically, waiting until a strolling middle-aged couple had passed out of earshot before speaking again. "That's no way to talk about your friend. Do I sense a little feminine jealousy here?"

Sarah suddenly looked uncommonly thoughtful. "Kate's a beautiful woman; not only that, but she *knows* that she's beautiful and she knows how to use that beauty too. You know I dream about her sometimes, but the dreams are always odd, strange."

"You mean there's such a thing as a normal dream?"

She looked at Hyienna although her eyes seemed not to focus as her voice took on a light, distant quality. "Bewitching, that's the word. You know it's funny, even though Kate's been nothing but kind and supportive, I'm somehow afraid of her."

"Some friend." Observed Hyienna dryly.

"It's hard to explain. Kate is warm and funny and really smart too, yet I sometimes feel like I only know a tiny part of her. That sounds really weird; I don't want to make out like there's some kind of crazy bunny boiler just waiting to be unleashed, but there's something oddly wild and dangerous underneath all that grooming. It's like she can make anybody do anything, and she can make anybody fall in love with her, man, woman or child."

Hyienna tried to lighten the mood. "Hey, there's only room for *one* half crazy dreamer in any family, and I got the gig first."

Sarah continued as though Hyienna hadn't spoken. "A bewitching siren, that's her. I've never known anyone with as much personal power and charisma as that woman, but I sometimes wonder if it's all just to wreck passing sailors on the rocks. After all, if she is so easily loved, what value could it hold for her?"

"You're not doing a very good sales job here, big cousin. Don't you worry about Solomon with such a bewitching siren around the place?"

A smile spread across Sarah's face and suddenly she was back in the present. "I already know Solomon's in love with her, just like I am, but it's not like that. Like I said, Kate commands the affections of whoever she wishes, and I just don't want my little cousin getting hurt."

"Good job I've got you to look out for me then." Hyienna stared back out to the party yacht glinting in the bay.

"Kate is wonderful, but just be wary. She doesn't live by same rules that the rest of us have to follow."

Hyienna watched the inflatable island as it slowly separated itself from its plastic companions and began drifting towards the open ocean, as though pulled by a different current reserved only for itself. "Well, with all this drama and mystery, how could I say no? There's just one thing."

"Sure, what?"

"Just tell your fiancé not to call me Hyena. I know he's the kind of guy who likes to rip on folk, but he'd do well to remember that we'll be related by marriage one day."

"How wise you are, Charlie Brown."

Hyienna playfully elbowed his cousin. "You never know, I might beat you to the altar yet."

Sarah smiled, but the mirth quickly vanished from her face.

Hyienna wondered if he'd accidentally hit a raw nerve, but he didn't feel much like pursuing the subject. Like most things in life, the conversation with his cousin hadn't gone even remotely according to plan, which more or less fitted in with the grand scheme of his own uncertain course. Seemingly from nowhere, a mysterious and alluring woman had been thrown into an already chaotic and somewhat bewildering mix of experiences. Hyienna was mindful of his cousin's warning, but he figured he had little to lose by getting to know a beautiful woman. Besides, he knew nothing would come of it anyhow. His own backstory was the most potent anti-aphrodisiac known to man, even though he hadn't done anything wrong.

He glanced across at Sarah, who seemed to be deep in thought. Unwilling to break the silence, Hyienna looked out across the bay to where the cartoon island bobbed and twisted on its journey out to sea. If any of the beautiful people from the boat had noticed its lonely departure, they sure as hell didn't seem to care. After all, why should they give a damn about what happened to one cute, amusing but ultimately useless piece of plastic? It was a peculiar thing, but Hyienna suddenly found himself wishing the plucky little inflatable well as it began to fade against the bright blue of the ocean. It pained him to think that a lump of plastic swept out to sea had garnered more sympathy and goodwill than his own recent departure from a place that simply didn't want him around anymore.

Hyienna fervently hoped Formentera would be different.

SOLOMON'S PARTY
Chapter 5

Once again Hyienna tried not to think about movies as he paid the friendly cab driver and crossed the quiet road outside Solomon's house. Strictly speaking it was Solomon and Sarah's house, although that description didn't sit well as Sarah's fiancé didn't strike him as the sharing type. Still, sharing type or not, he'd been invited back to the house, and it was immediately clear that Solomon liked to throw a good party. Hyienna mentally checked himself as he silently speculated that Solomon saw it as more of a chance to show off than to extend any warm hospitality to family and friends. He silently remonstrated with himself and wondered exactly when he'd become so negative and cynical; before answering his own unspoken question. It was obvious really.

"Good evening, Sir. Can I help you?"

Hyienna blinked at the neatly dressed security guard outside the gate. He wondered how long he'd been standing there arguing with himself. Hopefully it wasn't too long, and hopefully it had been a silent dialogue. It wasn't always. "Hi, yeah, I'm here for the party."

The large man at the gate appeared neither sceptical nor impressed. "May I see your invitation please?"

Invitation? No one had said anything about an invitation. "Well, I'm Hyienna, Sarah's cousin."

"I see. Lucky for you she said you'd be dropping by." The guard put his hand in the pocket of his black jacket and a moment later the heavy steel gates of Casa Hermoso swung open.

"Thanks." Hyienna quickly walked onto the drive before the guard realised, he'd never asked for any sort of ID. A second or two later it occurred to him that the security guy wasn't *that* stupid and the whole exchange had been monitored by the camera mounted discreetly beside the gate. Hell, they'd probably watched him get out of the cab and stand in the road like an idiot before the guy at the gate finally spoke up.

Despite all that, he was in and walking down the smooth driveway, illuminated by small LED lights sunk into the surface on either side. Not too bright, they had the effect of deepening the shadows cast by the foliage rising above the low wall running the length of the drive. Burning braziers would've made the whole experience more atmospheric, but the lights did a pretty good job as Hyienna rounded the shallow bend in the drive and saw the house revealed in a blaze of light, which was expected, although the thumping reggae beat was a surprise. As usual, Hyienna hadn't really known what to expect, but the sounds reverberating in the warm evening were something altogether unexpected.

He stopped at the edge of the large turning circle and began picking his way through the cars carefully packed into the limited space, wondering what would happen if the first person to arrive wanted to leave early. Lucky, he hadn't driven over as there would be nowhere to park, plus his little Lambretta would've been distinctly out of place. He felt self-conscious enough already with his limited wardrobe and he hoped he wouldn't look too much the misfit when he stepped inside.

The heavy front door was ajar and there was no obvious security presence, although Hyienna had no doubt that the guy on the gate wasn't alone. Hyienna looked down at his boots, silently thankful that he'd decided to hire a cab and save them from that film of fine Mediterranean dust that endlessly swirled around the windswept island.

Well, this was the moment, it was now never. Hyienna wondered why he was feeling so nervous; he never used to be that way, but a difficult period in Barcelona had left its mark and he harboured a secret fear that someone would recognise him as the guy who was involved in that kid's disappearance. That hadn't happened yet, although the internet guaranteed it was just a matter of time. He just hoped he could at least make a few half decent acquaintances before the rumours followed him across the ocean.

Realising that he was once more standing in front of a door while debating with himself, Hyienna took a deep breath and grasped the polished silver handle. A blast of thudding music and laughter rushed out to greet him like a disembodied spirit, ushering him inside to join the party. A cloud of incense, cigarette smoke and what smelled suspiciously like ganja rolled past him and escaped into the warm evening air, a genie of joviality released into the quiet countryside.

For a few seconds he just stood there, finding his feet as he let his brain catch up with what his eyes were seeing. In truth Hyienna didn't really know what one of Solomon's parties might look like and he was finding it difficult to process mentally.

The hallway was a jumble of men and women lounging, leaning, standing, and talking in a haze of intoxicating smoke. Although the clothes were obviously different, the first thought that popped into Hyienna's head was one of oddly exotic bars from that old Blade Runner movie. There was a strange, almost indefinable eroticism in the air as Hyienna slowly made his way along the hall. Women smiled seductively as he passed while men nodded politely in greeting, despite the fact they were all strangers. Maybe it was all the weed smoke laying heavy in the atmosphere, but Hyienna felt like a gate crasher, a fraud expecting to feel the heavy hand of a security guard on his shoulder at any moment.

He slowly made his way along the hall, following the sound of the thudding bass he figured must be out the back near the pool…and hopefully the bar.

Having threaded his way through the long lounge and out to the pool area, Hyienna was relieved to spot what looked like a small wooden bar area complete with rustic tiled roof. He also spotted Kate standing beside it. They were still some distance apart, but Hyienna clearly saw her smile and raise her classic martini glass in his direction. If he didn't know better, he'd say that Kate was the real hostess of this lively party, keeping a benign yet watchful eye on her guests as she chatted to various partygoers as they refilled their drinks. Effortlessly elegant in a long white off the shoulder number, the glittering gems resting on her ample bust winked and glimmered as she moved, catching the attention of all passers-by. Curiously, even though it was clear that she knew nearly everybody, Kate never engaged in any long conversations; she merely exchanged a pleasantry or two before resuming her smiling vigil beside the bar.

Hyienna decided he needed a beer, plus Kate was only one of three people he even vaguely knew in the whole place, so the bar was his most logical destination. He could feel Kate's eyes patiently following him as he weaved his way through the revellers around the pool. As he made his way towards the bar, Hyienna couldn't figure out whether he was underdressed for the occasion. All the guys seemed to be in suit jackets and trousers of some sort, yet nobody paid any attention to his jeans and boots, or at least nobody made it obvious.

Kate's smile broadened to show her perfect white teeth as Hyienna finally reached his goal. For a moment he was trapped in indecision; all he really wanted was a cold drink on a warm night and he wondered if his choice of drink might make him seem like a bit of a rube. He toyed with the idea of asking the bartender for a glass of wine, but then figured that would just make him look like a guy in a leather jacket trying to blend in by drinking wine; and no *way* would he be able to carry off one of Kate's 007 martini glasses. Eventually he opted for the safer and more honest option of a beer straight from the bottle. He decided right there and then to just let Hyienna be who he was and let the chips fall where they may. At least that would make one small aspect of his life easy to manage.

Kate's smile beamed brighter still as she stepped forward and kissed his cheeks French style. She smelled good and Hyienna was more than a little relieved when she spoke first. "Hey there! Glad you could make it to our little shindig. So, what do you think?" She raised her eyebrows and smiled in not such a seductive but more of a playful manner, as though she was engaged in some sort of game.

Hyienna at once understood what Sarah had been trying to tell him on the beach. Although he was desperately trying not to think in clichés, he couldn't help it as the raunchy thudding of the sound system faded away, leaving just the two of them stranded between a beer and a martini while the world span away into a blur of distant colour and sound. He blinked rapidly, realising he'd better say something, but as usual he drew a blank when it really mattered. That had long been a problem for him. Hyienna knew he wasn't bad looking and neither was he socially awkward as such, it was just that, like so many guys, he felt cripplingly self-conscious around attractive women. At last, some words tumbled from his mouth. "I think I'm talking to the most beautiful and engaging woman here."

Kate's smile widened and she winked. "Right answer, Casanova." Hyienna mentally kicked himself for uttering such a hackneyed line, despite his thinking it was true. He couldn't even blame the booze so early in the evening.

The cheeky, seductive grin remained on Kate's face as she stared playfully at him. "So, know many people around here?"

He couldn't help smiling, even though he knew she was teasing him just a little bit. "Oh yeah, there's Jack the lion tamer over there, and on the way in I saw Jodie the ferret farmer."

Kate played along. "I'm glad Jack's here, lion tamers are so exciting, not like ferret farmers." She pulled a face. "So, you just gonna hang out with me at the bar all night?"

Hyienna shrugged. "It's a tough job but someone's got to do it." He immediately cringed inwardly, certain that his playful response had crossed some sort of invisible and unknowable line. Thus, he was more than a little surprised when Kate suddenly grabbed his hand and started pulling him towards the house.

"Well, if you're gonna hang out with me then you'd better come and meet some people. Let's see if we can find your ferret farmer." Kate winked and waved to a woman from across the pool as she steered him in that direction.

Hyienna just managed to grab his beer from the bar as he let himself be led into the fray. He knew it could be a bit of a bumpy ride socially speaking but it was too late for half arsed excuses, he was in it up to his neck.

* * *

Hyienna was relieved to see to see the house was becoming less crowded as he flopped into a vacant armchair. Taking a sip of beer, he watched the comings and goings around the pool through the white chiffon curtains that billowed in the cool night breeze. He had no idea what time it was and in truth he didn't much care. Finding out would be as simple as looking at his battered but reliable old watch, yet there was something oddly liberating about not knowing the hour.

He needed just to chill out and ground himself for a little while. At some point in the endless avalanche of introductions and shallow small talk, Kate had somehow turned into Sarah, which was an agreeable enough swap. It was good to see the old excitable Sarah again as he let her lead him around the place just as Kate had done, proudly introducing her little cousin to all and sundry. There was this guy who did something in banking, and that woman who ran a travel agent and so on and so forth. Everyone had been very polite and gracious, although Hyienna had never found mingling with strangers especially easy. Luckily his cousin knew it and so she didn't leave him dangling for too long before she made her excuses and dragged him off to meet the next knot of good-looking people. Hyienna just hoped none of them spoke to him again because they were just too many names to remember. It was a funny thing though, because the one name he *could* recall was that of Nathaniel, the mysterious guy on the beach below the Green Lizard Inn. It seemed like he was a bit of a local celebrity although nobody could quite explain why. He was some international man of mystery, or so it seemed; a man with a mysterious past who grew up in an orphanage, or escaped from political persecution, or maybe it was the law depending on who you were listening to. In fact, the mysterious man with sand in his shoes was such a talking point Hyienna was surprised he hadn't bumped into him at the party. He'd considered asking his cousin why the famous Nathaniel was not there tonight, but some peculiar and inexplicable instinct cautioned against it. He had no rational cause for thinking it was a bad idea to raise the subject, but he'd learned to trust his instincts since the tragedy in Barcelona, and that conviction had grown even stronger since the mysterious incident of the witch and the rucksack. *The witch and the rucksack;* hardly the title for a bestselling children's book, but it was the most appropriate description he could come up with on the spot. Once again Hyienna's mind wandered back to the mysterious bag of shimmering nothingness waiting patiently in the darkness of his battered wardrobe. *Waiting*…that was an interesting choice of words and one that was probably more appropriate in this case. He had no doubt that the thing that the rucksack was waiting for the right time make its purpose known to him.

Hyienna nodded and raised his half-drunk beer to a young man who walked through the lounge and out towards the pool. The man nodded and smiled in return but thankfully he didn't engage in conversation, because he was one of the many whose names were already forgotten. All Hyienna could remember for sure was that he was a lawyer of some kind; at least he *thought* that was the guy.

He laid back in the soft leather armchair and just let the sounds from the system wash over him. Clearly the party was starting to wind down as the music was a little more chilled out and the place was a little less crowded, although there was still plenty of enthusiasm to go around as the relaxing sounds of whatever fashionably obscure artist the DJ had chosen gently tapped and echoed around the modernist facade of Solomon's house.

Solomon! That thought was a strange one because it suddenly occurred to Hyienna that he hadn't seen the big guy all night. It struck him as rather strange as he figured Solomon would've been right in the thick of things. After all it was a perfect chance to show off his house, his wealth and his general coolness, which made his absence all the more inexplicable. Still, it didn't really matter because he was having a great time just chilling in his armchair, having been introduced to what felt like half of Formentera. He closed his eyes and the first thing he saw was Kate. Sarah had been dead right; she really was a strange, compelling and completely alluring woman. He hadn't spent much time in her company, but he understood exactly what Sarah meant when she'd told him that Kate could make anyone fall in love with her. *Bewitching*, that was the word.

Hyienna wasn't sure if he'd dropped off to sleep for a while before he noticed a change in the pitch and tempo of the voices around the pool. The general ebb and flow of conversation and laughter had been interrupted by a new, jagged tone of raised voices, several of them.

Curious and a little surprised, Hyienna rose from his chair and stepped through the open patio doors leading to the large and tastefully illuminated pool area. He heard the splash before he had time to focus in and figure out what was happening. However, it quickly became obvious as the partygoers rapidly made space for the three young guys who were squaring up to each other, plus a fourth who was cursing liberally as he clambered out of the pool with as much dignity as he could muster, which wasn't a lot.

Hyienna's eyes flicked across to the bar area, where he caught sight of Kate casually sipping her martini as she watched the confrontation with a strange mixture of interest and detachment that almost defied description.

It wasn't clear exactly what was happening, although Hyienna had long ago learned it was a bad idea to go diving into the middle of somebody else's fight. Despite that, he immediately started forward as he spotted Sarah rapidly making her way towards the young men who'd just graduated to the shoving stage. There were just seconds before the punches started, and by Hyienna's reckoning that would be the moment his cousin stepped into the fray to cool things down. He rapidly walked around the edge of the pool and had just reached the first corner when the conspicuously absent security made a shock and awe appearance.

Hyienna stopped and watched open mouthed as Seth and two other large guys waded into the young men and ruthlessly extinguished any hint of resistance. He saw Sarah's hand rise to her mouth as they both watched Seth drop the loudest of the group with a well-placed elbow strike to the side of the head. The young man just folded to the ground, while his buddy's protestations were cut short as Seth stepped forward and jabbed him hard in the solar plexus with the heel of his hand. The two remaining guys had already surrendered, but that didn't save them from being bent double by painful arm locks and marched out through a small side gate. Two more security guards suddenly appeared to pick up the gasping and the unconscious before bundling them out the same way. The whole incident was over in less than a minute, leaving the onlookers in a state of surprise and shock as the DJ cranked up a jaunty reggae beat to lighten the mood.

Hyienna glanced back towards the bar area and saw that Kate had barely raised a pencilled eyebrow at the whole incident; although Sarah was clearly upset as she spoke quickly and quietly to Seth. From where Hyienna was standing, there could be no doubt that Seth was in charge of security. He was the biggest of a bunch of already big guys while the black jacket rule didn't apply to him, his plain black T-shirt struggling to cope with his oversized biceps. Just like in the car, Seth's Hammer of God tattoo was clearly visible and once again it caught Hyienna's attention. Not for the first time it made him wonder about its significance as he knew that gym junkies like Seth were either heavily inked or didn't go in for that stuff at all. It looked like Solomon's security guy had made an exception for just this one special image, and Hyienna found that intriguing as he watched the exchange between Seth and his cousin from across the pool.

Sarah was very shaken, and while Seth wasn't exactly rude, neither was he especially interested in what she was saying. He had one of those inscrutable Secret Service vibes about him as he clasped his hands together and leaned forward to better hear her.

There was no trace of any disturbance or any of the protagonists by the time Hyienna had made it to the bar, save for a wet patch where the hapless guy had clambered out of the pool. He looked first at Sarah and then at Seth before he realised, he had no idea what he was going to say.

Somewhat unexpectedly, Seth came to the rescue by speaking first. His voice was every bit as low as his appearance suggested, although his words were pointedly directed towards Sarah. "A lady shouldn't have to see such things, but that's the fault of young men with too much beer and too little discipline."

Sarah's voice was quieter than usual. "Did you really have to hit them so hard?"

Hyienna was about to interject until he saw that Seth was preparing to speak once more. The big man holding what almost amounted to a proper conversation was such a surprise that Hyienna found himself

❀

waiting with bated breath, while his eyes once again focused on the incongruous tattoo adorning Seth's arm.

Solomon's head of security took a deep breath, and his voice softened a little, although it lost none of its intimidating bass tone. "I once watched a man bleed out on the street for the crime of telling some punk parked at the corner to turn his music down. We're only here for a short time before we are called, and that time is far more precarious than most of us will ever know. You have the right to disapprove, but everyone's still alive and nobody's seriously hurt. The rest is just noise."

Hyienna was somewhat taken aback by Seth's eloquence as he'd just assumed the big guy would be a monosyllabic Conan type. The strong African accent was also a surprise as he'd mentally allocated some kind of south LA patter to him as well. So much for assumptions. He was even more lost for words when he watched Sarah turn on her heel without a word. Once again, he was left just standing there without really knowing what to say or do, and once again Seth came to the rescue.

The big man stepped forward and spoke quietly. "Solomon sends his apologies. He's sorry that he hasn't been here to meet you or his other guests, but he's got some important business to take care of. In fact, he asked me to find you and take you to his office."

"And where is that?" Hyienna asked.

Seth wasn't waiting for a response, and he was already at the corner of the pool when he turned back and jerked his head, indicating that Hyienna should follow.

Hyienna didn't really feel like he had much of a choice, so he followed.

* * *

Solomon's private office was hidden upstairs in a quiet corner of the house, and it was pretty much exactly how Hyienna expected it would be. Although he didn't like to admit it, he did feel kind of like a big shot as Seth opened a large pair of double doors and ushered him inside.

Sure enough, there were enough abstract sculptures and leather sofas to make Solomon's office a perfect location for some end of season showdown from one of those unending daytime soaps.

Seth quietly closed the door and stood beside it. Although he could be surprisingly unobtrusive for such a large man, his unspoken message was clear. They were not to be disturbed and neither would anyone be leaving until the boss said so.

Solomon was on the phone, and he just carried on with his call as though he hadn't noticed anyone come in, even though he obviously had. "And that's it? Nothing else? What do you mean by weird? What *kind* of noise? So, it's not actually *making* a noise? But you just said it was. That doesn't make sense, it's either making some sort of sound or it isn't. Well, just take a quick look. I doubt very much if it's booby-trapped. Look, just do the job and do it properly. I don't understand; why can't you just open it up and take a look inside?"

Reminding himself that he didn't actually work for Solomon, and neither was he still at school, Hyienna settled himself on a comfortable black sofa as the King of Casa Hermoso laid down the law. He hadn't set out to listen; in fact, he began to wonder if maybe he was *supposed* to overhear the conversation.

At last, it seemed like King Solomon was wrapping up. "Look, I gotta go, so you just do what you're supposed to and get back to me later."   At last, he hung up and leaned casually against his oversized desk. Reaching behind him he picked up a heavy whiskey tumbler and took a sip, all the while his eyes never leaving Hyienna's. "Sorry I couldn't catch up with everyone at the party. Business, you know how it is. Can I fix you a drink?"

"Nah, I'm good thanks." Hyienna suddenly realised that he didn't know how many beers he'd drunk that evening. He wasn't seeing double or slurring, but neither was he stone cold sober. That was suddenly a disconcerting thought as he wondered if anyone knew where he was.

Solomon nodded approvingly. "A grown man should know his limits, unlike some of the kids around here." He shifted his gaze to the big man by the door. "I hear there was a little dust up just now."

Seth's shoulders barely shifted as he shrugged. "Nothing serious, just kids and booze, that's all."

Solomon took a sip of scotch. "I don't like having my guests unsettled like that. This isn't some Ibiza strobe club."

Seth said nothing.

Hyienna desperately wanted to turn his head and look at the big man behind him, but he thought it would make him look nervous, which was something he wanted to avoid because he actually *was* nervous. He felt a little calmer when he heard the door behind him quietly open and close as Seth resumed his security duties.

Solomon continued to stare for a few seconds before he tipped his head back, swallowed the last of his scotch and placed the tumbler carefully on the desk beside him. He tapped his fingertips together, looked down and sighed heavily before meeting Hyienna's gaze once again. "Look, I was out of order before. I know I can come on a bit strong sometimes, but that's only because I've had to fight for what I've got." He pointed to the door behind Hyienna's head. "Seth is just the same; in fact, he had a harder start in life than I did."

Hyienna felt he should say something. "He was pretty rough on those kids out there."

Solomon shook his head dismissively. "No, he wasn't. Seth knows what he's doing, and I trust him completely. I don't much like talking about people behind their back, but I'm pretty sure you've figured out that Seth is more than a little used to seeing violence. That's why he acts the way he does. The likes of you and me might think he's a bit over the top but in the end those kids have walked away with a few bruises and some dented pride, both of which mend pretty damn fast when you're young. Decisive action that *prevents* serious harm, besides, I won't tolerate people acting out and abusing my hospitality."

Hyienna could see some logic in Solomon's outlook, but he still wasn't convinced; neither could he think of anything useful to add.

It didn't really matter, as Solomon had already moved on to the next subject. "Look, I was out of order showing off like that when we first met, and I didn't try all that hard to talk you out of staying at the Lizard. Don't get me wrong, it's cute enough in a mumsy sort of way and Yaz sure can cook, but it's not really a long-term option."

"I like it well enough, and I'm not under anyone's feet." Hyienna could tell what was coming next, but he'd already made his mind up.

Solomon picked up his empty tumbler, for a second and put it back down again. "You can stay in the guest house for free as long as you want. Sarah's told me all about what happened in Barcelona. That's a tough break, one of the toughest, even though in the end you did nothing wrong."

"Well, that's not your problem."

"Not directly, but we're almost family now and a family has to stick together. No family, no security. No future." Solomon's expression brightened. "No decent wardrobe either. Why don't you make yourself at home here? You'll be able to stretch to more than two shirts."

Hyienna stood to leave. "Like I said, I like the Lizard just fine. It suits me."

Solomon raised his hands in a conciliatory gesture. "Hey now, don't get all ruffled, I didn't mean nothing by it. Hell, if I was riding a scooter with just a backpack, *I'd* only have two shirts as well. There's plenty of room for you here, your scooter and your backpack too."

Hyienna felt his own eyes narrowing. Was Solomon playing with him? He couldn't be sure, but the strange phone call and the unlikely mention of a backpack was more than enough to unsettle him. Whatever the case, it was just another reason to keep his cousin's fiancé at a safe distance. "Hey, I really appreciate the offer, but I'm very comfortable where I am. Speaking of which, I guess I'd better think about getting back."

Solomon just shrugged. "Whatever you say, buddy. How are you going to get back to the Lizard at this time of night?"

"Same way I arrived; I'll just call a cab."

The absent host of the party scoffed, putting his arm around Hyienna's shoulder as he pushed open the ostentatious double doors to his office. "Nonsense! I'll have one of the guys drop you off; you know it's actually a pretty short boat ride from here, straight across the bay. Just don't fall out or anything."

Several beers and a late-night were beginning to take their toll, and

Hyienna couldn't think of a good reason to refuse Solomon's generous offer of a free ride back.

* * *

Hyienna turned down his collar and shook droplets of water off it as a last distant rumble of thunder faded into the cool darkness of the night. He turned to the nameless security guy at the tiller of Solomon's private motorboat, his *runabout* as he'd called it. "What in the world was that?"

The nameless security guy didn't seem to notice that they were both soaking wet. "That's what they call a thunderstorm."

Hyienna let that little barb of sarcasm slide by as he was alone in a boat with a trained fighter. Instead, he looked up at the sky. "Where the hell did it go? Where the hell did it *come* from?"

Meteorological anomalies were clearly of little interest to the man on the tiller as he showed no sign of even having heard the question.

Knowing that he wasn't about to enjoy any kind of conversation about the weather, or anything else, Hyienna settled back in his seat and tried to ignore his wet clothes as the little motorboat bobbed briskly across the darkened bay. However, it had happened, the squall was gone just as suddenly as it had blown up, leaving a high moon shining down on the black surface of the water, twinkling in mesmerising ripples that spread out from the bow of the boat in a never ending chain of dancing lights. It was a staggeringly romantic moment and Hyienna felt a small pang of regret that he had no one to share it with, save for the immaculately turned out and robotically polite security guy Solomon had tasked with ferrying him home.

Hyienna ran the oddly mundane yet somehow strange events of the party through his mind. Every time he tried to focus on something someone had said, Kate's beautiful, alluring and unusually expressive face distracted him, leading his mind down a different path until he forgot what he was trying to remember in the first place. She certainly had a power of some sort, kind of like an overdose of charisma that just rendered the rest of the world dull, mundane, and grey. He smiled ruefully to himself in the darkness, thinking that he'd just conjured up the lyrics to some old Sinatra number. If not, it was pretty damn close.

In the end he abandoned his attempts to analyse the subtle nuances of his experience and focused on a single lamp shining defiantly on the approaching jetty. That feeble, yellowy illumination somehow seemed more homely and wholesome than the crisp, surgical LEDs that seared Solomon's immaculate and angular landing space. In truth Hyienna had no idea who actually owned that little rickety jetty on the quiet beach, but as it was almost directly below the Green Lizard, he'd just kind of assumed. Either way, he noticed that the guy steering the boat didn't seem to need any directions. Maybe it was a regular trip.

Hyienna thought back to the ferry ride from Ibiza as the little boat throttled back and began drifting towards its destination. Maybe he was just imagining patterns where there were none, but water had suddenly struck him as important in whatever story was unfolding around him. He'd arrived from the sea; he'd been entrusted with something very strange beside the sea and now he was returning to the closest thing he could call home via the sea. On the other hand, on a small island it was kind of hard *not* to involve the ocean in whatever was going on.

As his private water taxi drew closer to the shore, Hyienna noticed that he wasn't the only one who was out late and contemplating the water. The silhouette of a tall man, a *very* tall man slowly materialised beneath that lonely lamp as though someone was awaiting his return. Hyienna blinked rapidly as he tried to focus on the featureless figure standing motionless in that small pool of light. His head was almost grazing the underside of that single lonely lamp, but that would make him well over seven feet tall, if not taller still. Surely not! He glanced back at the guy on the tiller. "You seeing this?"

"Seeing what?" Was his less than helpful response.

Hyienna turned back and pointed towards the more clearly defined figure standing on the uneven boards. It must've been the beer or maybe a trick of the ocean's languid swell as the space between the lamp and the watcher's head was far greater than he'd first thought. "Never mind."

The mysterious silhouette finally acquired human features as the boat slid up alongside the jetty, its fibreglass body squeaking against the ancient car tyres hanging from the sun-bleached woodwork. Although Hyienna had never seen the guy up close before, he knew exactly who was keeping a lonely vigil out there by the ocean. He was surprised when Nathaniel smiled and reached down to help him out of the boat. Hyienna had grasped the outstretched arm and was standing on the creaking planks before he'd even had time to consider why a stranger might be helping a slightly drunk partygoer onto dry land.

"Saw you coming in." Nathaniel's voice was calm, measured and matter of fact. He spoke as though he was addressing an old friend rather than someone he'd never met before.

Hyienna didn't exactly feel unsettled, but neither was he completely at ease as he watched the boat pull away and vanish back into the darkness without so much as a cheery wave or a polite goodbye from the pilot. A few seconds ago, he'd been contemplating the more esoteric aspects of water, now he found himself standing on a crumbling jetty with a stranger who seemed oddly familiar. So, this was the mysterious Nathaniel, the source of so many rumours and whispers around Solomon's house. It was like the guy was some kind of minor celebrity, for reasons that were obscure at best. Nathaniel didn't appear to do very much, and neither did he seem to be socially active, yet it was his name he'd heard on everyone's lips as he'd passed them by earlier that night.

Nathaniel spoke again. "Had a good time? You look like it. Been swimming?"

Hyienna blinked as Nathaniel's features momentarily dissolved into a strange, featureless darkness, unnervingly like the endless ocean of black hiding in a cheap little rucksack close by. He knew he'd better say something. "Got caught in the thunderstorm out on the bay; the name's Hyienna." He stretched out his hand in greeting not because he was especially pleased to see the guy, but because it just seemed like the right thing to do.

Nathaniel reciprocated. "No storm here, but I've heard all about you. I'm Nathaniel, but I guess you already learned that."

"Sure. Well, it's nice to finally meet you face-to-face, although I've seen you down here on the beach quite often." Hyienna at once noticed that Nathaniel's hand was unusually soft and smooth, matching the rest of his dark and flawless complexion; at least that's how it looked in the dim light of the solitary jetty bulb. Up close it was pretty obvious why so many people, especially the women, were talking about him. Nathaniel was a good-looking guy; tall, muscular and with a difficult to define kind of brooding quality about him. With a knotted cravat and some riding britches, he could easily have been the aloof object of burning desire in some epic corset buster of yesteryear.

The mysterious Prince Charming of Formentera smiled with one side of his mouth. "Likewise, and I thought to myself, there goes an interesting guy with a lot on his mind."

Hyienna suddenly let go of Nathaniel's hand, hoping he hadn't been holding it for too long. "Yeah, how do you figure?"

Nathaniel turned towards the dark glittering ocean and thrust his hands in his pockets. "They say that life began in the ocean, so what better place to contemplate the really important questions?"

Hyienna just shrugged. "Hey, we all have questions, but are they really important to anyone else?"

"Depends, I guess."

For a few seconds both men stood staring into the darkness before Hyienna spoke once more. "Well, it's been nice meeting you, but if you don't mind, I'm heading off to bed." He didn't feel it necessary to mention that he was staying at the Green Lizard; somehow, he figured that Nathaniel already knew that. "You okay out here by yourself?"

Nathaniel continued staring out to sea. "Sure, I like the peace, the solitude."

"Yeah, me too. Well, I guess I'll see you again soon enough." He turned to leave.

"Lunch."

That single word stopped Hyienna in his tracks. It was just too incongruous. "Lunch?"

Nathaniel turned on his heel and looked straight at Hyienna. "Lunch, soon, you and I."

"Lunch? Why would we be having lunch? We're strangers, you and I."

Nathaniel's voice took on a quiet, thoughtful tone. "We're strangers both, not just to one another but to this place."

"Haven't met many people actually *from* Formentera yet." Hyienna hadn't really thought about it until he'd said it, but it was true, nonetheless.

"There's more to being a stranger than where you're from, but I have a hunch you know all about that anyway. Let's meet at La Mari Ses Roques later this week. We can have some lunch and figure out what we have in common."

"How do you know we'll have *anything* in common?" Hyienna asked, both a little perturbed and more than a little curious at the same time.

Nathaniel turned back towards the ocean. "We're both here, staring at the sea in the wee small hours, which means we're both here to reflect on things that are much greater than just ourselves. Settled and contented men do not stare out to sea all by themselves in the middle of the night."

"Well, I guess that's something. Maybe I'll see you for lunch after all; a lot depends on what I've got planned for later in the week. Good night then." With that Hyienna walked along the jetty and onto the rutted footpath winding its way up to the Green Lizard's car park.

Nathaniel said nothing more as the darkness swallowed him up once again.

LUNCH WITH NATHANIEL
Chapter 6

No, that wouldn't do either.

Hyienna sighed heavily and made his way back to the bed, pushing a teetering stack of designer bags onto the floor as he reconfigured the trouser and shirt combinations laid across his bed. Standing back, he wiped his forehead and took a long swig of ice water as he looked at the new options laid out before him.

It was hot, and Hyienna didn't want to turn up to lunch dripping like some over exerted builder on a double shift; neither did he want his companion to think he was making too much of a special effort. He glanced at his watch; still an hour to go so there was plenty of time to decide. Maybe he needed a woman's eye on the problem, Yaz was just downstairs, and he had no doubt she'd be happy to give her opinion on this or that outfit. But no, he couldn't ask her, the last thing he needed was more gossip; there plenty of that to go around anyhow, and that was *before* he'd agreed to meet a total stranger for lunch.

A big part of him was glad that Nathaniel's invitation had arrived some three days after their chance encounter on the jetty; if indeed chance had anything to do with it. If nothing else, it had given him the excuse to spend a couple of days upgrading his wardrobe, which on reflection was probably more a result of Solomon's cutting remarks than Nathaniel's invitation. Still, it had all ended up the same way, with Hyienna spending more than he should have in Sant Francesc Xavier's more swanky shops in an effort not to be seen in the same two outfits by everyone on the island. At least he'd have something to put in his battered wardrobe now…the wardrobe. As though part of a well-rehearsed ritual, Hyienna felt his eyes straying inexorably towards those scratched wooden doors, while his mind journeyed inside to consider the mystery that waited within. In truth a part of his mind was *always* anchored to the fathomless darkness handed to him by the woman beside the sea. One way or another, his inner and outer worlds had begun to revolve around that hub of nowhere-ness within a very short time. Like ink spreading across a newspaper, that bottomless blackness had seeped through every fibre of his being, subtly changing him in ways he could only glimpse in the grey twilight between waking and sleep.

Hyienna was surprised at how quickly he'd become accustomed to the strange dreams, despite their often opaque and disturbing nature. His eyes momentarily flicked to the notebook beside his bed as a fleeting image slipped past the lens of his consciousness…something about an egg or a gift, or maybe an egg *as* a gift. The river was always there when he slept, as was the egg, or at least he thought so. For a moment he considered scribbling down the word "egg" to see how it might fit into the jumble of other impressions he'd recorded on waking, but he knew it would come again. Whatever force had been emancipated when he'd taken possession of that battered rucksack, Hyienna instinctively understood that he was no longer fully in control of events. That was especially true in the nocturnal realm.

After a moment's hesitation he dismissed the notebook and focused once again on his new wardrobe. He knew he'd see the egg and the river again and again until the full message had been revealed. In the meantime, life went on and it was always a question of priorities. Hyienna knew that lunch was in about an hour while his mystical destiny would wait at least until tomorrow.

White. It had to be white really. One thing he'd noticed about Formentera was that white seemed to be the colour of choice for a large number of natives and long-term residents. It seemed to be more of a practical than a cultural thing, but whatever the case, Hyienna felt an unusually strong urge to blend in and to do things the island's way. He wasn't sure where his new-found fondness for conformity had sprung from as it certainly wasn't something he recognised in himself, but there was just something about the place, a timeless acceptance of life's great and sweeping cycles. Here, it wasn't just about Hyienna; it was about Hyienna, his surroundings and his place in the grander scheme, whatever that turned out to be. This was no time for rugged, confrontational individualism; it was a time for watching, waiting and learning. Yes, white it was.

His mind made up, Hyienna finally reached for the crisp, loose fitting white shirt he'd bought from a boutique with no name, just a big neon exclamation mark outside. His hand hovered for a moment before he changed his mind for the umpteenth time that morning. White was definitely the right choice, which left him in no doubt that Nathaniel would be wearing exactly that. Hyienna did wonder why he was thinking like a woman in terms of dressing but wearing the same colours as his male lunch companion was just too weird, although he couldn't put his finger on exactly why.

In the end he opted for a pastel turquoise shirt and a pair of plain and smart fitting black jeans, as anything else would be impractical for scooter riding. He quickly changed his clothes before he changed his mind again, then glanced at his reflection in the mirror and nodded. Before he could talk himself out of his wardrobe choice, Hyienna hurriedly slapped on some cologne and picked up his jacket. With one final glance at his chipped wardrobe doors, he stepped out onto the cool of the landing as he tried to stop the Miami Vice theme tune from looping round in his head.

* * *

Despite his wardrobe vacillations, Hyienna made it to La Mari Ses Roques with a few minutes still to spare. He was glad he'd left himself plenty of time as he didn't want to turn up looking too dusty and flustered.

The day had grown steadily hotter, and he could see the heat shimmering off several smart, well waxed cars as he made his way to restaurant's smoked entrance doors. Initially he'd been surprised at the number of people who were already there, but after a moment's thought he figured it made sense. Lunch was a big deal on the island, kind of like a local ritual or minor religion, and no more so than at La Mari Ses Roques. Arguably one of the best restaurants on the island, it was a place both to see others and, more importantly, to be seen.

The air conditioning washed its cooling welcome over him as

Hyienna stepped through the dated glass doors and presented himself to the maître d', a friendly young woman dressed in, surprise, a crisp white blouse and smart black skirt. Hyienna mentally checked himself, resisting the childish urge to shine the tops of his boots against his calves as he gave his name and reservation details. Glancing around, he wasn't entirely sure if he was overdressed or underdressed as the patrons' attire ranged from sharp business suits to casual jeans and shirts, although there was a notable and welcome absence of shorts and flip-flops.

If the maître d' had any opinions about Hyienna's sartorial sense, she kept her own counsel as she escorted him to a small but tastefully dressed table in the shade of an ancient grapevine winding around the open terrace.

Hyienna was glad of the shade as the day seems to be growing hotter by the minute. Although it would be cooler inside the restaurant's air-conditioned dining room, that somehow seemed a little artificial, divorced from the organic interaction that was about to take place. No, outside was just fine and he could keep cool with a nice glass of Jean Leon Chardonnay poured from the sweating bottle waiting on the table.

A waiter appeared from nowhere and removed the cork for Hyienna to go through the ritual of tasting the wine to show his approval, like he was going to send it back once it'd been opened!

"Aren't you going to pour me one of those?"

Hyienna looked up to see Nathaniel smiling down at him, wearing a white shirt. "Sure, and thanks for inviting me to lunch."

Nathaniel folded his tall frame into the seat opposite. "My pleasure. You strike me as a singularly interesting kind of guy, and I think we might have a lot in common."

Pouring his companion, a glass of cooling white wine, Hyienna settled back into his seat. "You make a habit of inviting strange guys out to lunch?"

"Not a habit exactly, but this isn't the first time. If life has taught me one thing over all these years, it's that the further I stray from my instincts, the further I stray from my true self as well as good fortune. I think that applies to most people, except those with really terrible instincts. Now *my* instincts are pretty good, and they told me you were somehow important and hopefully a new friend. We could all do with a few more of those."

Hyienna tried to remain outwardly nonchalant, although his mind was racing with possibilities and speculation regarding the strange burden he'd recently been handed. Surely this meeting was too much of a coincidence. "The last person I mentioned fate to just got up and walked out, sticking me with the bill."

Nathaniel chortled. "Serves you right too. Still, I have a good sense for these things, and you strike me as a man with a story."

"We've *all* got a story, so what makes mine so interesting?" Hyienna briefly wondered if word of his difficulties on the mainland had already leapfrogged ahead of him.

Nathaniel just shrugged. "Like you said, we've all got a story and I have a sense for the unusual."

"I'm unusual?"

"There's no need for false modesty here." Nathaniel picked up the heavy looking menu and opened it. "You know, this is probably the best seafood restaurant on the whole island."

Hyienna picked up his own menu. "Good job too because I could eat a whole whale right about now."

* * *

Hyienna didn't order himself a whale but settled instead for what was easily the finest paella he'd ever had the pleasure of eating. Cooked with the freshest ingredients straight from the quayside, it was quite obvious why the restaurant had such a great reputation. It was also clear why Nathaniel had such a strange reputation. For a man who was curious about other people's stories he seemed to be highly reticent about his own. Apparently, he'd grown up in an orphanage somewhere or other and he'd lived in Barcelona for a while, although he'd been very vague about his foster parents. He'd even had a brother way back, but apparently, he'd died in some sort of accident when they were just kids.

In truth, Hyienna wasn't very surprised that his lunch companion didn't want to dwell on that subject, other than to say his brother had drowned and how he missed him every day. That must have been rough, to grow up without natural parents and *then* to lose your only sibling. He could only imagine what that must've been like. All the same, Hyienna was left with the distinct impression that he was having lunch with a man who boasted a mysterious and no doubt very interesting past. Hell, maybe it was even a sinister one, although Nathaniel didn't seem like the sinister type. Still, Hyienna's own experiences had taught him the folly of judging a book by its cover, especially as this was just the latest in a chain of strange events that had befallen him since he'd set foot on this beautiful yet secretive island.

"You got room for dessert? You know the lemon mousse is really excellent here, and not too sugary if you're watching your figure."

Hyienna had no doubts about the lemon mousse, but somehow it just didn't seem right to be ordering dessert on a stranger's tab. It's not like it was business expenses or anything. "No thanks, I'm good, although a glass of water wouldn't go amiss."

Nathaniel duly summoned the nearest waiter and ordered a bottle of Pellegrino before turning back to the table. "So, what are you going to do with your time here? The days are long, and this place has a brooding quality that gets under your skin if you spend too much time in your own head. I think most islands are like that."

Although nothing had been said, Hyienna realised that Nathaniel was done with talking about his past, not that he'd been especially forthcoming to begin with. "So, how do you keep busy?"

True to form, Nathaniel answered without actually saying anything. "I have more than enough to occupy my time. In fact, you might say I'm on kind of a vacation, getting away from it all so to speak."

Hyienna tried again. "Okay, so what do you do when you're *not* on vacation and getting away from it all?"

Nathaniel grinned. "I collect people. That is, I collect stories."

"Is that why we're having lunch, so that you can collect me?"

Nathaniel's eyes sparkled darkly. "A lovely lunch for whatever story you want to tell. Seems like a fair deal if you ask me."

Hyienna couldn't really argue, in fact he kind of felt like he'd short-changed his host by being so vague about his reason for being in Formentera. On the other hand, Nathaniel was still a stranger and lovely lunch or not, Hyienna had no intention of sharing his true reasons for escaping to the bright yet pensive Formentera. Instead, he just asked another question. "So, what are you, a writer or something?"

"I do write a lot, although whether that makes me a writer is more of a philosophical question."

At last, Hyienna had to admit they'd reached a strange kind of conversational stalemate. Nathaniel wasn't prepared to elaborate on pretty much anything, while he himself didn't want to get into the details of his recent experience in Barcelona. In fact, a part of him couldn't shake the nagging suspicion that Nathaniel already knew all or part of his story, and that was his real motivation for inviting a total stranger to lunch. It sort of made sense, although why Nathaniel would be interested in the story of some random loser afflicted by a streak of bad luck was beyond him. It wasn't like Nathaniel was the gossipy type, in fact his tight-lipped approach to his own story marked him out as quite the opposite.

"Hey, you okay there?" Nathaniel cocked his head and waved his hand across the table.

Suddenly Hyienna was back in the moment. "Oh, sure. Sorry about that; I just kind of zone out sometimes when I'm thinking." He resisted the temptation to reach for the little rock in his pocket.

Nathaniel didn't seem ruffled. "Don't apologise. Thoughtful men are a vanishing breed, and you should never be sorry for who and what you are."

"Who and what we are isn't always all that great."

"Maybe not; but it's real, it's true and that's what really counts."

Hyienna was about to ask if a violent criminal should be true to *his* nature or whether he should try to change his ways, but he noticed that Nathaniel seemed to be off on his own kind of daydream. He watched curiously as the man who'd brought him to lunch mouthed something under his breath as he stared at the entrance doors to the terrace.

Hyienna followed his companion's gaze and immediately saw that Nathaniel's attention was firmly fixed on a man who'd just emerged from the restaurant.

Dressed in a crisp white linen suit and matching Panama hat, the new arrival was obviously used to commanding both the space and the people around him. His vibrant blue hatband and matching pocket handkerchief were clearly designed to catch the eye and make an impression before a single word was spoken. His dark, almost polished ebony skin gleamed in sharp contrast against his crisp white cuffs as he clasped the maître d's hand warmly between both of his own. Whoever he was, this was clearly a man of substance and one who took both himself and his appearance extremely seriously. Not only that, but the restaurant knew him well and took him seriously too.

Alas, the situation had spun out of control before Hyienna had the chance to utter a word. He found himself turning back towards an empty chair as Nathaniel crossed the terrace to engage with the new arrival. The tinkle of glass and the shocked gasps of patrons told Hyienna that the two men weren't just exchanging pleasantries, even before he'd managed to swivel round to see what was happening.

When he finally *did* turn round, it took Hyienna a moment to take in what he was seeing. He hadn't really known what to expect when he'd met a stranger for lunch, but not once had it crossed his mind that his companion would end up in a full-blown fight with some well-dressed pensioner.

The stranger's seniority clearly meant nothing to Nathaniel as he pinned the older man up against the ancient vine, dislodging glasses and cutlery as he pressed his attack.

Despite being significantly older, the man in the linen suit was still quick and threw up a guard which prevented Nathaniel from gaining a hold around his throat. The older man's lip curled into part snarl, part sneer as he locked eyes with his attacker.

Hyienna was instinctively on his feet within a second and pulling at Nathaniel's shoulder. "What the hell? You trying to get us kicked out or something?" It was as though he wasn't even there as both men pointedly ignored him while they exchanged greetings of hatred in some unfamiliar language.

Hat man scowled with an expression that almost defied description as he growled in some sort of African dialect. Although much older than the angry Nathaniel, there was something about him that counselled caution.

Neither man made an impression on Nathaniel as he leaned forward and spoke his own incomprehensible words.

The African accents reminded Hyienna of the way Seth spoke and he wondered, no he *knew* there was some sort of connection. He glanced around to see the maître d' and a waiter hovering nervously on the sidelines. La Mari Ses Roques was hardly a sawdust bar, so the staff were no doubt wondering whether to intervene or to let the altercation run its course.

When Nathaniel finally spoke in English, his voice was low and measured, betraying a deep, cold fury. Bad blood didn't even come *close* to describing his tone. "I'd heard a rumour that you were dead. I almost let myself believe it, but the world's not that lucky."

Although Hyienna had no knowledge of who the man in the hat might be, he could tell that the ageing patriarch's eyes had seen things incomprehensible to him and viewed the world in a way so alien that they could well be from different planets. Above all, despite having no clue about what had just been said, Hyienna understood that the man in the linen suit was not someone to be trifled with.

Now the hat man switched to English too. "Every man possesses a finite amount of luck, and some much less than others."

Hyienna jumped as Nathaniel lunged forward again, this time managing to grab the older man by the throat and pushing him further into the foliage. "Give me one good reason why I shouldn't break your scrawny neck right goddamn now!"

There were more audible gasps from the assembled diners and the hovering waiter started forward as yet more glass and cutlery clattered onto the worn paving stones. In fact, the only one who *didn't* seem angry or afraid was the man who appeared to be in the greatest danger.

Hat man deftly grabbed Nathaniel's wrist with both hands and twisted free as he stared defiantly into the younger man's eyes. "You think you understand loss; you think you understand suffering. You think my life belongs to you, when the truth is that yours belongs to *me*. Your brother traded all his future days for yours and now you squander his gift with your own selfish vendettas. You will never be the end of me, providence will *not* permit it."

Hyienna grabbed Nathaniel's elbow. "Hey, I just came here for some lunch, not get mixed up in whatever mess this is."

Nathaniel turned and fixed him with a steely gaze. "Nobody's *asking* you to get mixed up in my affairs." With his grip broken, he finally turned away and stalked off across the terrace, quickly vanishing into the darkness of the restaurant.

Awkwardly stranded in no man's land, Hyienna was intensely aware of the older man's eyes fixed firmly on him as he watched the immaculately dressed stranger straighten his tie and settle the linen jacket on his slim shoulders.

With his wardrobe back in order, the patriarch looked curiously at Hyienna. "Your friend should know the folly of carrying such anger inside him."

"Look buddy, he's not really..."

The recent arrival adjusted his hat and sat stiffly at the ravaged table. "It is not wise to break bread with someone who is not your friend."

"He could be a business associate." Hyienna cringed inwardly as he wondered why he was even justifying himself to a complete stranger.

The old man waved a long bony finger up and down. "You are not dressed for serious business, even though your clothes are new." Although his English was flawless, the strong African accent remained.

Hyienna was about to make a Sherlock Holmes quip, but he just couldn't shake the feeling that he shouldn't antagonise the well-dressed stranger. Although he was no musclebound scrapper like Seth, Hyienna knew he would have no problem picking up where Nathaniel had left off and wringing the old guy's scrawny neck. At the same time, he instinctively understood that some terrible retribution would befall him if he even *considered* such a rash action. Besides, they were strangers, and he had no idea what may have passed between this man and his now departed lunch companion. Nathaniel's long dead brother had been mentioned and Hyienna was at least wise enough not to step in the middle of *that* mess.

Clearly used to being in charge, the immaculate luncheon guest beckoned a relieved looking maître d' across the terrace. "Please convey my apologies to Señor Mario. I had a mind for a large tuna steak when I arrived, but now I think I shall just take some of your excellent lobster bisque and be on my way. Oh, and please add this young man's bill to my account."

The maître d' nodded and turned to hurry away, but Hyienna reached out and touched her arm. "That's okay, I'll settle of my own account."

Caught between conflicting instructions, the maître d' looked nervously at the man in the blue tie.

The man in the blue tie gave a small, almost imperceptible shake of his head.

With the casting vote finally settling the matter, the maître d' hurried off.

Still awkwardly stranded in the middle of the terrace, Hyienna was again unsure of what to do next. He glanced around and noticed that the other diners were studiously staring into their plates once more. They obviously knew better than to pry too deeply into the affairs of the man in the Panama hat.

The man in the hat seemed oblivious to the broken glass and crockery at his feet as he leaned forward and righted a salt seller which had fallen over. "You should really learn to pay more attention to those around you. At any given time, the man in front of you can be your greatest friend, and also your greatest danger."

Hyienna hoped he hadn't been standing there like an idiot for too long. "I'm sorry?"

The man at the table wore an expression somewhere between interest and amusement. "Since you have neither the wit nor the manners to ask, my name is Kal and I assume that you are Hyienna, not that you have given me your name as yet."

The alarm bells immediately started ringing in Hyienna's head. "How do you know who I am?"

"This is a small island, a fact which makes such things very easy to guess."

"Right. Well, I think I'd best be on my way."

Kal shook his head sadly. "You will give yourself indigestion running around like this. Come, sit; perhaps take a little cheese and let your meal settle."

"Thanks, but I think I've already outstayed my welcome."

Kal waved his bony finger again. "Where I come from, food is not taken so lightly, perhaps because it was harder to come by in those days. In any case, food is a central part of the cycle of life. Without it we cannot live, and so other things must die in order to sustain us. In fact, food is the hub of life's wheel, where all things are eating or being eaten. You young people simply shovel it down like coal into a furnace, which is why you are all so out of balance these days. You should let the wonderful food Chef Mario has prepared for you do its work before you go hunting once more."

Hyienna had heard more than enough to convince him that Kal was a man best enjoyed from a healthy distance. He wasn't quite sure how the immaculately dressed visitor had gained his strange attitude towards food, although he was certain hat he didn't want to hear *that* story. Besides, whatever Kal and Nathaniel had been mixed up was heavy stuff by anyone's reckoning. "Well, I'll try to bear that in mind next time I eat. I'll see you around, Kal."

Kal flashed his large set of immaculately white teeth. "Yes, you will."

SKULD
Chapter 7

The tiny electronic chirp was incongruous, yet oddly normal as Hyienna gingerly peeped through his wardrobe door. He couldn't remember why the mob was so angry with him, although it had made perfect sense just a moment ago. He had an inkling that their rage was something to do with his luxurious house, although he didn't remember stealing anything. Despite all that, he still knew he'd done wrong somehow.

There it was again, that upbeat digital warble, only this time it was closer. What *was* that?

For a moment he thought about stepping outside to investigate, but he knew for sure the old woman would see him straight away. She was the worst.

Once more the otherworldly chime intruded on Hyienna's nocturnal fears, filling him with a blend of hope and annoyance as it broke his concentration. Through the crack in the door, he watched his home slowly fade into darkness as the noise of the mob was drowned out by that increasingly shrill and insistent tone. It sounded like a phone, in fact, he suddenly remembered it was *his* phone, calling to him from the limitless darkness between waking and sleep.

Within a single breath the dream was gone, obscured orange glow of a new dawn as Hyienna blearily opened his eyes and waited for all of himself to exit the realm of night.

Once motor functions had been restored, he rolled over and clumsily fumbled for the handset, cursing silently at his own stupidity for not switching it to silent before going to bed. "Yeah?"

The voice on the line was playful, contrived…and female. "Hey sleepy head; haven't gotten you up, have I?"

Hyienna shook his groggy head to clear it. "Kate, that you? What's up?"

"I'm an early riser y'know."

"Well good for you." Hyienna was torn between continuing the conversation and making some excuse to go back to sleep. In the end the decision was made for him.

"So, what are we doing today?"

He groggily looked at his phone and found it was a few minutes past six. "Are we doing something?"

"Only if you want to." If it was possible for a voice to pout, Kate had just managed it.

Rapidly waking up, Hyienna played along. "Wouldn't be right to disappoint such a beautiful lady. So, what's on your mind?"

"Bikes."

"Bikes?"

Kate's voice was part seductress and part little girl. "Sure, silly; everyone rides bikes around here. There's no better way to really get to know the island, and it's good for the legs too."

Hyienna sensed his cue. "Hey, it's impossible to improve on perfection."

"I know, but perfection's pretty high maintenance and that means plenty of bike work."

"You know I don't have a bike, unless you're planning a trip on my little Lambretta."

Kate's tone changed from a pout to a wink. "Well, that sounds like a lot of fun, but today it's pushbikes. Yaz has got a few stashed in that old barn out the back."

Hyienna stifled a yawn. "Oh yeah, I think she mentioned something about that."

"There you go, sport. It's still early so we've got time for some breakfast and a few miles before it gets way too hot. Just head for Sarah's place and you'll see that outcrop on the coast road. I'll meet you there in a couple of hours."

The phone went dead and Hyienna let himself fall back onto the bed. Part of him was pleased that he'd be spending some time with the alluring Kate, while part of him was slightly annoyed at being wide awake so early in the morning.

* * *

The breeze on his face was just the antidote to the previous day's peculiar and unsettling events, almost blowing the ever-present image of that mysterious rucksack out of Hyienna's mind as he cycled Formentera's cracked coastal road. Almost, but not quite.

It was getting warm again, but Hyienna didn't mind too much, especially as he was letting Kate set the pace up ahead. It allowed him to hide how out of shape he was, as well as giving him the opportunity to appreciate the athletic curves hard at work just a few feet in front of him. He was pretty sure that Kate knew full well that the glittering Mediterranean wasn't the only view he was admiring, and he also knew that was probably her plan. He recalled Sarah's cautionary talk and in truth he wasn't sure if he was just being taken for a ride. He knew full well that some women got a kick out of toying with the men around them, and his easy-going nature had always made him a prime target. Still, at least he'd grown wise enough to know that he might be led a merry dance and that was fine by him. In truth there was only one way to find out and besides, Sarah had been dead right. No way was he in love, but Hyienna could see how easy it would be for anyone to fall hard for Kate. There was something very alluring in her free and easy manner, coupled with a self-assurance rooted so firmly that she said exactly what she was thinking at any given moment. Kate was trouble, that much was certain, but Hyienna figured that whatever happened, it couldn't be worse than anything he'd been through before. He was quite happy to sit back and see where the threads of his new adventure might lead him, confident in the knowledge that they would all tie together somehow or other.

At last Kate pulled off the road and into a dusty layby at the crest of a long but mercifully gentle incline.

Hyienna followed close behind, grateful for some respite.

She grinned as she balanced her pitch-black sunglasses on her head. "Hope I wasn't too rough with you."

Hyienna leaned his bicycle against a sun bleached and graffiti scarred picnic table, while his eyes were drawn longingly to a battered old mobile snack bar selling ice creams and cool, freshly squeezed orange juice. "Well, I'm a bit out of practice but I'll soon get the hang of it."

"They say you never forget once you've learned how." She winked mischievously and headed towards the time-worn little snack wagon.

Being a Wednesday morning, the rest area was all but deserted, save for the two of them and the man who squeezed orange juice and crushed ice for thirsty passers-by. There was only that constant island wind and the clatter of the snack wagon's battered diesel generator to break the tense, sweating silence as orange juice was rapidly squeezed, swallowed, and squeezed again.

Hyienna mopped his face with the bottom of his T-shirt as they walked to a low, cracked wall separating the safety of the layby from the hazardous rocky cliffs and outcrops on the western part of the island.

For a few minutes they both sat silently, drinking in the glittering sun as it sparkled on the calm of Mediterranean, broken only by the occasional foaming wakes of powerboats and jet skis.

Eventually Hyienna broke the silence. "You know, I'm glad you called me this morning, even if it *was* stupidly early."

Kate seemed to be studying the tiny speck of a sailing boat as she dabbed at her neck with a small towel she'd produced from somewhere or other. "I tried calling yesterday but I couldn't reach you."

"Well, you know how the signal is around here." Hyienna immediately wondered why he was being evasive about the previous day.

Kate raised one pencilled eyebrow. "You were out of range *all* day? Don't tell me you spent the whole day in bed."

"I should wish."

She nudged him playfully with her elbow. "International man of mystery, huh?"

"Well, I *could* tell you what I was doing, but then I'd have to kill you." Hyienna frowned seriously, happy to play along.

Kate pouted. "And I thought I was bicycling with an honourable man, yet here I am all alone with an utter scoundrel."

"A bounder."

"A cad."

Hyienna imagined himself holding a martini glass and put on his best bounder expression. "Well, I guess you're not the only one in demand around here. If you must know I was having lunch with a friend."

Kate suddenly looked crestfallen, and it was impossible to tell if her expression was feigned or genuine. "A lady friend?"

Too late did Hyienna realise he'd been outplayed and checkmated. "It could've been, but it wasn't."

Seemingly satisfied, Kate turned back to the middle distance. It was a while before she spoke again. "I can't see you having lunch with Solomon *or* Seth; in fact, I don't see you as the lunching type at all, so who is this mysterious stranger whose claim on your time rivals mine?"

Hyienna knew the struggle was over, so he just went with it. He had nothing to hide and so he wondered why he was feeling nervous about revealing his whereabouts. "If you must know, I had lunch at La Mari Ses Roques with Nathaniel."

For a few seconds Kate was silent, although a crease had appeared above her right eyebrow. "*The* Nathaniel. How did you end up having lunch with him, and what did he want?"

Hyienna thought for a moment. "You know, now you mention it, I'm not really sure if he wanted *anything*, although he said something about collecting people's stories or some such."

"Did he now? Well, it looks like you're settling in and making new friends."

"Yeah, I guess he's an okay kind of guy. Do you know him?" Hyienna couldn't shake the feeling that Kate wanted to say something specific, as though she already knew a great deal more about the mysterious Nathaniel than she was letting on.

"Only by reputation. A lot of people think he's kind of stuck up, aloof."

"And you?"

Kate bent down to tighten her shoelace. "All I know is a lot of people seem to have a pretty strong opinion of the guy, one way or another."

"Yeah, I saw that yesterday."

Kate straightened up and started walking back towards the bikes.

Hyienna followed, suddenly very conscious of the fact that she hadn't questioned his last remark. It seemed so unlike her not to be nosy, and he began to wonder if she already knew all about the trouble between Nathaniel and Kal at the restaurant. In truth he desperately wanted to ask her about the mysterious and well-dressed man, but some ill-defined instinct told him it was a bad idea. He sensed a change in her, a slight distance which hadn't been there before the subject of lunch with Nathaniel had come up. "Hey, why don't we all have a drink together?" He had no idea why he'd said that.

Kate threw her leg over the saddle and made sure her foot was firmly on the pedal. "Well, Nathaniel's very charming in a brooding poet kind of way, but he's too remote for me. I've got my eye on a different sort of guy altogether. Although, now that you've brought it up, I think Nathaniel's much more Sarah's type." She fixed him with a stare and winked that mischievous smile of hers.

Hyienna instantly felt his own smile return. "Really? I don't think Solomon would be too impressed."

A dark and surprising chord of contempt entered Kate's usually smooth and often playful voice. "Solomon doesn't own Sarah, *or* me, despite what some people say."

Hyienna said nothing as he didn't want to be the instigator of any relationship troubles. He and Sarah had only just reconnected after such a long separation, and he didn't want to rock the boat. True, he didn't have much time for Solomon, but Nathaniel was a complete unknown and *both* men had been involved in trouble in the short time he'd known them. Besides, his cousin was a grown woman and Hyienna knew that poking his nose into stuff like that was a sure-fire way to get it bitten off. He mounted his own bicycle and prepared to follow Kate back to the Green Lizard.

"Say, wouldn't it be great if Sarah could just bump into you guys sometime real soon." With that, Kate was off down the hill at a brisk pace.

Hyienna knew he'd just learned the true reason for their rendezvous, and what's more, he knew he would do exactly as the bewitching woman on the bicycle was about to tell him.

* * *

For the second time that day, Hyienna's dreams were interrupted by the tinny electronic warble of his cheap mobile phone. He tried to hide his irritation as he answered, but he wasn't sure if he'd done a very good job.

The voice on the line was familiar, even though he hadn't heard it all that often. "Hey man, it's Nathaniel. How you doing?"

"Fine, I guess. Things okay at your end? You left pretty quickly yesterday." Hyienna massaged his aching legs. Maybe it had been a mistake to just plonk himself on his bed after all that exercise.

"Yeah well, it was either that or get myself locked up. Listen, I just called to apologise."

"Screw that! Who *was* that guy?" Hyienna picked up his watch and saw it was a little after midday. He turned his back on the wardrobe.

There was a long pause on the line before Nathaniel spoke again. "*That* guy is weapons grade bad news, just stay away from him and don't fall for the wise old man routine either. Kal is as ruthless and cold blooded as any man alive. Where he comes from, you don't get to the top without leaving a lot of holes in the desert, understand?"

Hyienna didn't understand much of anything, but he instinctively knew Nathaniel was telling the truth. "Hey, I never got to thank you for the lunch. It was really great, although the last course was a bit sour."

Nathaniel sounded contrite. "Listen, that was a real screw up and I'd like to make it up to you."

"Really?"

"Sure, just let me know what I can do."

Hyienna couldn't help smiling as it was just too perfect. "Well listen then, are you free this evening?"

* * *

"Hey, you gonna lurk in that cave all day?" Sarah's voice was muffled by the battered but solid wooden door.

"Yeah, come in." Hyienna quickly glanced around and was relieved to see that he hadn't left any underwear lying about.

Sarah stepped into the room, striking as ever in a pair of expensively frayed designer jeans and a loose-fitting green blouse. The afternoon sun streaming in from the balcony bathed her lithe figure in an almost ethereal glow, while the alluring aroma of jasmine filtering in from the trellis work made for an altogether magical moment.

"You, okay?" Sarah raised one eyebrow and dropped the opposite side of her mouth in a quirky way only she could manage.

Hyienna was suddenly jolted out of his reverie. "Yeah, I was just thinking how someone kidnapped that pretty young girl I used to know and replaced her with this truly beautiful woman."

Sarah's response was typical. "And I was wondering who'd replaced my lovable cousin with such a smooth-talking charmer."

Hyienna couldn't help smiling because it was just like old times; except that life had moulded them into different people who'd somehow arrived back at the same place. "Must be those fatal charms of mine that brought you running over here a little bit early. I'll be with you in just a second. You got your swimming towel?"

Sarah dropped her large shoulder bag on the floor and perched on the corner of the bed. "Sure thing, boss."

Hyienna leaned on the edge of the dresser as he put on his trusty battered boots. "So, how's things?"

Sarah rubbed her temple. "Always a laugh a minute at Casa Hermoso; especially when Kate floated along in such a great mood. What on *earth* did you do to that girl? No, never mind."

"I'll have you know I was the perfect gentleman, although it's kind of hard to be a dastardly cad on a bicycle. Still, I hope Solomon's okay with me fraternising with his harem like this."

"I'm just gonna treat that like a joke and not get pulled out of shape because you've managed to insult me, my fiancé *and* a close friend all in one sentence. That's pretty good going, cousin." She frowned and raised a long index finger to her ear.

"Well, I'm sorry; I didn't mean anything by it." Hyienna knew he had a big mouth and could sometimes put his foot in it, but he and Sarah had always had a great relationship; more like a bromance than anything else. All the same he wondered if he'd accidentally hit a raw nerve.

"Just forget it." The irritation in Sarah's voice was quite obvious.

"You okay, hon? I was just joshing, you know me."

Sarah only seemed to be half listening. "Yeah, sure. You got any aspirins?"

Hyienna made a conscious effort not to look at his wardrobe. "No, but I'll eat my hat if Yaz hasn't got some stashed away behind the bar. Come on, let's get out of here. I'm sure you'll feel better for some fresh air."

"Yeah, sure." Sarah stood up and made for the door, still rubbing her forehead above her right eye.

* * *

"Wow, I wasn't expecting *this!*" Sarah stopped dead on the small jetty below the inn.

Hyienna grinned and hopped into the powerful rigid hulled boat he'd rented for the day. He knew it was a little childish to show off, but there was a small part of him that wanted to stick it to Solomon, just a little bit. "Pretty cool huh? Now all I've got to do is not crash this beast and get my deposit back."

Sarah whooped with joy and hopped into the boat. "Take me away from all this!" She flounced to the bow and theatrically shaded her eyes with her hand as she gazed out to sea like a carved wooden figurehead.

Hyienna smiled. The old Sarah was back again, and he knew perfectly well why. "How's the head?"

"Much better, thanks. Like you said, a lungful of fresh air solves all kinds of problems."

"Great! Now hold on tight and I'm not kidding." Hyienna fired up the powerful outboard motor and cast off the moorings. Hurrying to the seat in the centre of the boat, he sat at the wheel and gently opened the throttle. He momentarily wondered if he should've opted for something smaller as he felt the boat rise out of the water like a thoroughbred horse straining at the reins. Throttling back, he let the boat pick up speed before gently accelerating again. Within a minute the little jetty was a speck behind them as they sped across the calm glittering sea, framed by the orange orb of the afternoon sun. Hyienna made sure to note of every aspect of the experience, resolving to commit the sights and sensations to the deepest and most protected part of his memory. This was one of those times; one of those rare occasions when some ordinary schmuck found himself in a situation worthy of some fanciful Hollywood movie. He figured that such experiences were kind of like Warhol's fifteen minutes of fame; everybody might get one or two of them in their lives, so it was important to immerse into each of them as fully and completely as possible. When else would a guy like him get the chance to experience something like *this?* Screw the money and screw tomorrow as well; *this* was what mattered, speeding across an impossibly beautiful ocean with a lovely lady sitting proudly at the bow, the wind blowing freely through her hair. The only thing that might make it even better would be a lover sitting up ahead, but perhaps the rekindling of an old and dear friendship was just as important, maybe more so in the grand scheme of things.

Sarah turned and gingerly made her way to the centre of the boat, shouting above the roar of the engines and the whistling of the wind. "So, where are we going, hotshot?"

Hyienna glanced past her. "You'll see soon enough." He grinned as he made a slight course correction and began to ease off on the throttle as the ocean became steadily more crowded with boats of all descriptions. The exhilarating journey had been far too short for his liking, but they were almost at their destination. "Hey, just scream if I'm about to run anyone down."

Sarah's voice floated back as she returned to the bow. "You always were the responsible type. You're good if you hold this course."

Hyienna throttled back further still and let the boat drift under its own momentum. "Aye aye cap'n." Eventually they bobbed to a halt about fifty yards off the coast of S'Espalmador, if *coast* was the right word for a glorified sandbank. He threw out the small anchor and looked around. For once it seemed like the hype was deserved as it sure was a beautiful place. It was just a shame that its reputation as a posers' paradise was equally well deserved. The boats bobbing in the tranquil blue waters were as sleek and shiny as the people parading on the beach and lounging on the pristine white sand. *Parading* was definitely the right word as Hyienna could easily imagine those same beautiful people promenading along some tree lined Victorian avenue in some other life long gone. The more things changed the more they stayed the same it seemed to him. Still, at least his hired boat didn't look too out of place among the ostentatious yachts and sleek powerboats. His rigid hulled craft was a hulking muscle car among the preening dilettantes and that was just fine by him.

"Are we swimming from here or what?"

Hyienna was jolted back to the present by the voice of his cousin. "Yeah, I guess. I don't know what the rules are around here."

"Okay then." Within seconds, Sarah had discarded her clothes and stood ready in a white backless swimsuit, somehow sexy, classy, and just plain beautiful all at the same time. Within another couple of seconds, she'd vanished into the cool clear water as her lithe form sliced through the surface in a well-rehearsed and perfectly executed dive.

Hyienna wasn't able to keep the grin from his face as he stripped down to his jaunty swimming shorts and launched himself into the untidiest and poorly executed flop of a dive he could manage. What's more, he suddenly didn't give a damn whether the posers on the decks of their yachts thought he was some kind of uncouth lout. In fact, he rather hoped they *did* think that.

* * *

"You know what this place needs?" Hyienna squinted up at the flawless blue sky. It was still too bright despite his new sunglasses. He closed his eyes again and let the warm sun and the equally warm sand wrap him in a blanket of contentment.

Sarah's voice filtered across to him. "Don't say a waterslide!"

"I had no intention of saying anything of the sort! What sort of slob do you think I am? I was *going* to say this place needs a hotdog stand."

Sarah sat up and looked at her cousin. "So, you think the smell of frying onions would add to the ambience?"

"You betcha! Onions, ketchup, the works!" Hyienna grinned as he thought of it.

Sarah pulled a face. "You've got no idea where that stuff comes from."

"Hotdog heaven if you ask me." Hyienna also sat up and raised his arms in praise to hotdog heaven, just to rub it in.

Sarah couldn't help smiling. "You've always been a culinary heathen."

"And well fed for it."

Sarah lay back against the warm white sand once more. "Solomon used to bring me out here. The whole champagne on the beach routine."

Hyienna wasn't a bit surprised. He thought about making a wisecrack about anchoring the boat to Solomon's ego, although he kept his own counsel.

Sarah yawned and stretched. "So, are we heading back? I think we're done swimming."

Hyienna sensed it was the right moment. "Sure, but there's something I want to do first. Something touristy."

Sarah looked over the top of her sunglasses. "Well, I'm sorry, but I don't think they sell oversized sombreros here either."

"You know me so well. In fact, I'd really like to take a look at these famous mud baths."

"Seriously? You worried about your complexion or something?"

Hyienna camped it up a bit. "Well, a boy's got to take all the help he can get."

Sarah was hesitant. "I don't know."

"Ah come on! I'll even buy you an ice cream."

Sarah feigned a swoon. "You sure know how to sweep a girl off her feet."

Within a second Hyienna was grabbing his cousin's hand and pulling her towards the low sand dunes behind the beach. "You know it makes sense."

"Listen, you can schlep around in the goo if you want to, but I like this swimsuit."

"I thought you girls were all about rubbing seaweed on yourselves and eating mud, or is it the other way round?" Hyienna scratched his head theatrically.

"Funny boy. At least the poor girl who's fool enough to marry you will have plenty to laugh at."

Hyienna winked. "Well come on then, let's get filthy."

"Okay but remember what I said."

* * *

"We must be going the right way." Hyienna whispered childishly as they passed a group of young revellers who looked distinctly dirty.

"I wish I'd brought my towel." Sarah observed as she stepped aside to let the last of the group pass them on the narrow path.

Hyienna ran to the top of a low rise and posed, chest out and right leg bent. "This healthy outdoor living is bringing out my inner Hercules."

"More like your inner ten-year-old." Observed Sarah as she joined him at the top of the ridge.

Hyienna looked down at the expanse of black volcanic mud. It was clearly a popular spot, with innumerable holes and footprints where the beautiful people had partied and shot selfies of themselves. Nearly everyone was gone, save for a single figure covered from head to toe, lying deathly still on the ground just beside the dark, gooey expanse. It was just at that moment when the absurdity of Hyienna's situation finally hit him. Here he was, doing the bidding of a virtual stranger in the hope of little more than a smile of appreciation. *Dammit!* Sarah had been right all along; Kate really was some kind of witch or expert manipulator. Either that or *he* was even more dumb and desperate than he thought he was. For a moment Hyienna toyed with the idea of just fessing up and coming clean about the true reason for the whole facade. After all, Sarah wasn't stupid, and she must know that something was up, even though she'd played along so far.

"Hey, dreamer boy, don't tell me you're wimping out over a little bit of mud."

Hyienna jumped as his cousin nudged him in the small of his back. "Hell no, it's just different from how I imagined it would be."

"Life is pretty much like that."

Hyienna nodded before suddenly sprinting the last few feet and launching himself headlong into the large and oily looking expanse. It suddenly struck him that he had no idea how deep the mud might be or whether there were rocks at the bottom. Either way, it was too late, and he just had to trust to luck as he contacted the cool, clammy darkness. The world vanished in an instant and it took him a few seconds to orientate himself and realise that his head was still well above the surface. In fact, he was able to easily stand as the mud was no deeper than knee height. It was still a confusing experience because, unlike water, the mud continued to cake his eyes and obscure his vision even though he was standing up and listening to Sarah's muffled laughter as he unclogged first his eyes, then his ears and nose. Okay, so diving in headfirst might not have been the smartest idea he'd ever had, but there was no harm done and he'd amused his cousin.

It took Hyienna a minute to get the hang of walking in that unyielding prehistoric soup, but he was soon lumbering towards Sarah in true B movie style.

She screeched with alarm and laughter as she tried to escape but it was too late. Within a minute she was captured and slung over Hyienna's shoulder. "I'm warning you, Hyienna! Don't you dare!"

"Ugg! Swamp creature like pretty lady!" He deliberately slowed down, bending further as he lumbered towards the sticky glutinous mass, enjoying the screams of his helpless victim as he clamped his arm tightly around her legs.

Sarah screamed something unintelligible as uncontrolled giggling and threats of retribution formed an ululating screech as she kicked her feet to no avail.

"Honey, we're home!" With one final heave, Hyienna dived back into the mire, only releasing his squealing cousin when he was certain there was no chance of escape.

Water and mud sprayed high into the air as their combined weight carved a deep groove in the primal sludge.

Hyienna rolled onto his back, wiped the mud from his face and started to laugh as he made an angel by flapping his arms and legs.

"You're such a dick, Hyienna!"

He choked as a large globule of mud hit him square in the face. "You know, you're never going to sound angry if you keep laughing all the time." He sat up, still chuckling and looked across to where his cousin was sat just a couple of feet away. She'd fared better than he thought, with mud splashed all up her left side but far from completely covered. Alas the white swimsuit had suffered significant staining and he knew he'd be in trouble for that. All the same, he couldn't help noticing that her body was still shaking with suppressed laughter as she sat with her arms crossed and wearing her meanest, angriest expression. "Hey, looks like you missed a bit."

Sarah screeched again as Hyienna lobbed a large handful of mud, hitting her square on the chin and running down her front, both inside and outside her swimsuit. "Ewww, you're so gross, Hyienna. No wonder you're still single."

"Hey, Shrek lived in a swamp, and *he* married a princess, so there!" He glanced at the figure at the edge of the mud bath and saw that he hadn't moved so much as a muscle that he could see.

At last Sarah gave in with a rueful smile and began plastering the thick dark mud up her long, willowy arms. "Didn't like this swimsuit anyway."

Hyienna let his head fall back and he gazed straight up at the blue sky once again. It would be light for a few hours yet, all the same he thought they'd better soon think about heading back. He wasn't exactly the salty sea dog type, and he was uncertain how well he'd fare trying to navigate at dusk.

"Hey, swamp boy. Wanna give me a hand over here?"

He turned his head to see Sarah struggling to reach the centre of her back with her sticky, mud covered hands. However, help was already close by as the previously motionless man by the side of the baths had begun to move. As if on cue, he walked quietly up behind her and began to apply a thick layer of mud to Sarah's exposed back.

Momentarily confused, she glanced across at Hyienna before starting and scrambling to her feet we she realised it wasn't her cousin close behind her. Her expression quickly changed from alarm to curiosity as the tall man silently raised his hands and wiped the mud from his eyes and face. Sarah's features quickly turned to a strange combination of wonder, delight and some other, almost inexplicable emotion as Nathaniel's face was finally revealed.

"Oh my God, it can't be you!" Her voice was weak and breathless she stared dumbfounded at the man standing just a couple of feet in front of her.

Nathaniel said nothing; neither did he move as he stared back at Sarah.

"It *is* you."

Again, he said nothing and scarcely moved.

"*It is you. It is you; it is you, it is you!*" Within a second, Sarah had flung her arms around Nathaniel's neck and buried her face in his mud-covered shoulder. "It's you, it's *really* you!"

Nathaniel wrapped his arms around her and pulled her into him.

Sarah's words tumbled out along with years' worth of pent-up feelings and regret and the bitter reminder of what could have been. "I thought I'd never be with you again. Are you really here with me right now? This isn't just a dream?"

"If it is…," said Nathaniel. "…it's one I hope to never wake up from."

At last, Sarah stepped back, tears washing the mud from her cheeks. She opened her mouth to speak and then closed it again. Then she tried a second time, placing her hand on the flat of her stomach. "You were right there." She whispered, staring up at Nathaniel with a dreamy, almost mesmerised expression.

Nathaniel cocked his head curiously.

Sarah said nothing more, merely reached out, grasped his face in her hands and kissed him tenderly, giving no thought to the thick volcanic mud covering them both.

Hyienna could tell that he'd outstayed his welcome. He'd done everything that Kate had asked of him in reuniting the lovers he hadn't even known *were* lovers. He knew that she'd be pleased and so he wondered why he was feeling so upset and hurt, desolate even. He couldn't bear to see Sarah and Nathaniel in their heartfelt and passionate embrace.

As he quickly walked back towards the beach without so much as a word of farewell, Hyienna struggled to understand his own feelings. He knew he wasn't jealous, because despite Sarah being a very attractive girl, their relationship had never been about any of that stuff; in some ways it was much deeper. Perhaps it *was* jealousy after all, but not of the kind felt by spurned lovers. Maybe it was much more like that of sibling who believed his parents favoured the other child. Whatever the true source of his feelings, Hyienna knew that they sucked. All he wanted to do was grab Nathaniel and tell him to keep his hands off his cousin, but it wasn't as though he wanted her for himself, at least not in that sense. It was all very confusing. All he knew for sure was that the more he thought about the situation, the angrier and more upset he became.

Hyienna scrabbled in the pocket of his shorts for his little rock, mentally anchoring himself to the present moment, but that only made his feelings both stronger and more inexplicable. In the end he hit upon exactly what he should do. Nathaniel must've gotten himself *onto* the little islet somehow or other, so he figured that he and Sarah could get themselves off it by the same method. He was out of there.

* * *

"Here, you look like you could use another."

Hyienna jumped a little as Yasmina placed his second cold beer on the bar. "Sorry, what?"

Yaz smiled as she began switching off the lights behind the bar. "You look like a man who's trying to figure out something really important. You guys always have that same expression."

"Yeah, I guess I'm a little distracted." Hyienna reached for his wallet.

Yaz shook her head. "That one's on the house. Besides, you're not distracted, in fact you wish you could think about something other than whatever's bugging you. If there's one thing, I've learned about men it's that they really *can't* think about more than one thing at a time."

Hyienna smiled and nodded as he realised that Yaz was probably right.

She opened the till and removed the cash left inside. "I spend a lot of time behind this bar, watching men, and if there's one thing, I know for sure it's that whatever's eating you up inside, you've got to deal with it one way or another."

Hyienna couldn't really think of anything to say, mostly because he knew that she was exactly right about everything and therefore no response was needed.

Yaz stuffed a few notes into the pocket of her flowing dress and yawned. "Well, I'm off to bed. Don't drink the whole bar and remember to switch the lights off when you come up." She tapped the switch panel by the door as she vanished into the darkened kitchen.

Alone with his thoughts, Hyienna picked up the fresh beer, raised it to nobody in particular and took a long swig. Leaning back against the bar, he let his mind wander as he considered exactly what the hell kind of mess, he'd gotten himself mixed up in. One thing was certain; he should've heeded Sarah's warning about Kate more seriously. In truth he'd silently scoffed at the idea that she was some kind of witch but sitting alone in a darkened bar with his whole life probably about to unravel again, he had to consider the possibility that she did indeed possess some kind of strange compulsive power which ran far beyond the average feminine wiles. What the hell had he just done?

He glanced nervously towards the darkened car park as headlights gleamed off the windows before vanishing into the night. It wouldn't have surprised him if those lights had suddenly come blazing up to the front doors, accompanied by a furious Solomon and his formidable henchman. What would he say when that time inevitably came? Maybe he could plead ignorance or stupidity; at least one of those excuses would be honest.

Hyienna placed his little rock on the bar and stared at it as he took stock of just how big a fool he'd been taken for. First of all, he'd let himself be talked into some kind of stupid relationship game like some acne ridden lovesick teenager. That was bad enough, but it also seemed that everyone on the island knew a lot more than they were letting on, at least to him. Solomon, Seth, Kal, Kate, Nathaniel and even Sarah were all interconnected by some web of intrigue that still he couldn't map out or rationalise. He was especially upset with his cousin as it was painfully obvious that she and Nathaniel were an awful lot more than just acquaintances past. Kate must have known it and probably Nathaniel too, which at least explained why he'd agreed to Kate's peculiar plan involving S'Espalmador and its mud baths. The whole thing was absurd, but the most ridiculous part was how he'd just blithely gone along with the entire farce without ever stepping back and wondering what it was all about.

Hyienna knew he'd been played, but he also knew that wouldn't cut much ice with Solomon when he came asking questions about his fiancé. Of course, he could always bring up the big man's obvious dalliance with Yasmina, but Hyienna doubted that would count for very much. He'd met the likes of Solomon a hundred times before, and such men viewed ideas like morality and decency as weapons to beat others with, not rules to regulate their own behaviour.

If it wasn't for one inescapable fact, Hyienna could easily have dismissed life on Formentera as the shallow shenanigans of a bunch of isolated people with too much time and money on their hands. He felt his eyes inexorably being drawn to the ceiling while his mind focused on his room above and the impossible, no, *magical* nothingness waiting inside that cheap nylon rucksack. More than ever, he sensed that whatever unnatural thing he'd been charged with protecting, all the secrets he was slowly discovering revolved around that one central point. What had begun as a mystery had become a distinct danger. He knew that Solomon wouldn't let a little thing like rank hypocrisy get in the way of a beating when he discovered that he'd been the architect of Sarah and Nathaniel's reunion. Hyienna also knew that Kate would walk away scot-free from the whole debacle. Kate always walked away scot-free from everything.

Nobody was playing a straight game, which meant that nobody could be truly trusted with the one piece of information that he alone was privy to. Whatever else happened, it had become increasingly clear that destiny, fate or whatever other names it might have, had placed that strangest of artefacts in his possession for a good reason. It, therefore, followed that he was charged with that mystical item's protection until such time as it could be taken to its proper place.

Hyienna had thought that the Green Lizard was a safe enough location for such a timeless wonder, but now he knew that things were far deeper and more complex than he'd initially thought.

He drained the last of his beer and glanced up again at the ceiling again. It was a quiet moonlit night and Hyienna knew it was no accident that he was still wide awake while everyone else slept. It was the perfect time to act.

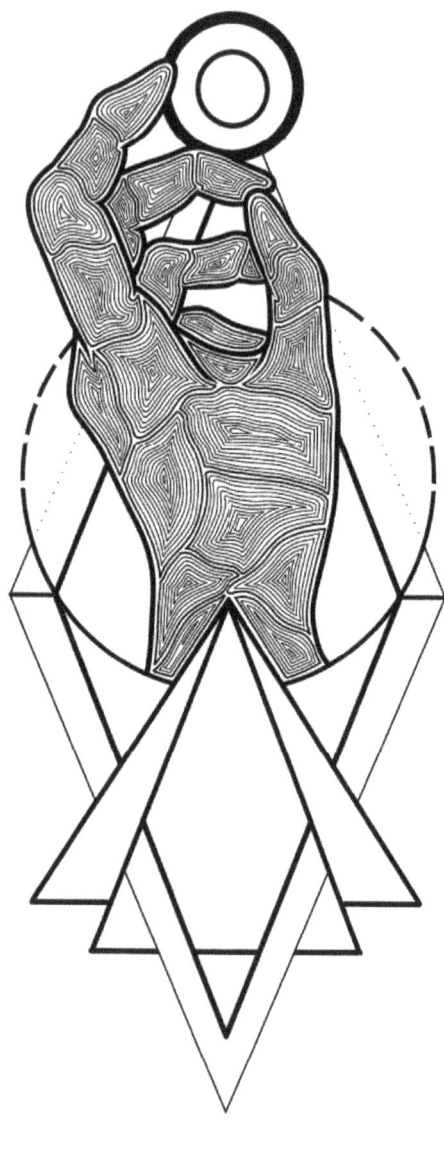

TWICE REMEMBERED, ONCE LIVED
Chapter 8

"Stop the car, stop the fucking car! I can't breathe in here!"

"Just hang on…"

"Now Nathaniel! Stop this fucking car right goddamn now!" Sarah lunged from the passenger seat and wrenched the steering wheel towards a dusty layby, populated by a scattering of picnic tables and some battered old snack wagon.

"Jesus Christ!" Nathaniel stamped on the brakes and the car slewed to an untidy halt in a cloud of dust and a clatter of small stones. "You trying to get us both killed?"

Sarah was out of the passenger door before Nathaniel could finish his sentence. She began pacing like a trapped animal, muttering to herself as a torrent of guilt, regret and fear washed her away and left her scrabbling for the shores of reason. "Do you know what I've sacrificed to be here with you? Oh Christ, what have I done? What have *we* done? Why did you come back into my life? No wait, why should *I* come back into *yours*? We've done it now; he won't just let this go, he can't."

Nathaniel stepped out of the car, grateful that there was nobody else around save for the man from the snack wagon, who seemed to be conspicuously absent. "What's wrong?"

Sarah rounded on him in a fury of sharp nails and even sharper condemnations. "What's *wrong?* Are you crazy? No, maybe you're not, but *I* sure as hell am!"

Nathaniel held up his arms to fend off the worst of the blows and waited till the fury subsided a little. "I know this is going to get bad before it gets good..."

Sarah took a deep breath and clenched her fists in an effort to stop them from shaking. "You don't *know* him; you don't know what he's capable of. What's even worse, I don't know what *you're* capable of either."

"Me?"

"If I want to be spoken to like a child, I can just call my fiancé. Just what the hell are you mixed up in?"

Nathaniel frowned. "I don't know what you're getting at."

Sarah pointed a shaking finger down the empty road. "*That car;* and don't you damn well dare ask me *which* car, the car that's been following us for the better part of an hour."

Nathaniel said nothing as he looked back at the deserted stretch of tarmac.

Sarah calmed down a little and placed a hand on his forearm. "Listen, you can be the big hero if you want, but you've got no idea how much trouble we could both be in. Solomon's worked hard for everything he's got, including me, and he knows how to fight to keep what's his. I know he's hurt people before, and as for Seth…" She trailed off, unwilling to finish the sentence.

Nathaniel looked down and gently stroked a tear from her cheek. "Listen, I'm no movie tough guy, but I've seen enough of this world not to be rattled by the likes of Solomon."

Sarah turned away with a sigh of exasperation. "When I saw you again it seemed like a dream. My knight, my lover had sought me out, just as I'd sought *him* out. I even let myself believe we could just turn away from everything and start again."

"Well, you should know all about *that*. I've still got your lovely note, you know, the one where you told me you would seek the verdict of the ocean. That was very poetic by the way."

Sarah looked down at the ground as the tears started again. "You've every right to be angry, but the truth is I did what I said I would, and I nearly didn't make it."

Nathaniel's tone was weary and bitter. "I guess Solomon's fancy house and shiny car convinced you that life was worth living after all. Pity I couldn't do it with patience and understanding. So much for poetry."

Sarah sniffed and wiped the tears from her eyes, turning her back on her old flame and gazing out across the ocean. "Maybe I'm not the woman you thought I was. I tried to tell you I'm not any kind of earthbound angel, but I think you'd fallen for some romantic notion of who I really am. The truth is I'm not some abstract idea but a real person just like you, and just like you, I can screw up hugely. Besides that, you were always too wrapped up in your own troubles to really see mine."

Nathaniel rolled his eyes. "I tried everything I could to help you, but in the end, I had to make a choice. Sure, you can hate me for leaving if you want, but here we are still, after everything that's happened."

Sarah continued staring out to sea. "After you'd gone, I felt like the last plank was kicked out from under me. In case you were wondering, I really did try to end it more than once with pills, by drowning; hell, I even tried jaywalking once, but something always happened to stop me. One of the biggest things to stop me was Solomon. I still don't know what he saw in me, but whatever it might've been, it was enough to make him propose."

Nathaniel's eyes narrowed. "And you agreed, on one condition…"

"That's right. I told him I wanted to make a fresh start, put everything behind us and move to Formentera, the place where they hang the fish from the trees."

"You really *said* that to him? You used those words? Jesus!"

"I did it because I could, and he would never know it was the dream we'd shared, the song we sang in each other's arms. He will never know how I swore I would come here or die trying."

"Well, maybe you'll get your wish after all, because when Solomon finds out he only moved here to help fix his fiancé up with an old boyfriend, I reckon he'll do the job himself."

Sarah's voice was low and thoughtful. "Maybe you're right. Maybe that's what I deserve, and maybe *you* should've taken me seriously when I said I wasn't some magic spell to end all unhappiness. I'm just a woman, as foolish and fickle and messed up as the rest of my kind."

Nathaniel watched as the man with the battered snack wagon reappeared and promptly began packing up, clearly favouring an early finish to hanging around on the off chance. "So, just what the hell are we *doing* here?"

She turned and gently touched his face. "I've dreamed about finding you again every day, every night since you left, but now that we're together again I'm afraid."

"Afraid of what?"

Sarah pushed hard against Nathaniel's chest. "I'm afraid of you!"

Nathaniel looked puzzled. "Me; why?"

She shook her head with exasperation. "You've been the centre of all my hopes and dreams for so long now, but I could cheerfully murder you with a baseball bat right here in this car park. You *really* have no idea?"

"How can *I* frighten *you?*"

Sarah ran her fingers through her hair and growled with frustration. "Depression, suicide attempts and a crazy scheme to follow you here with an even crazier fiancé in tow. I was a normal girl before I met you with your brooding mystery and flights of romantic fancy. I could've been happy, but now all I have is this ache inside me that's terrible when I'm with you and even worse when we are apart. I've done crazy things, insane things, dangerous things to keep myself close to the source of my madness, and you ask me how I frighten you?"

Nathaniel watched as the little snack wagon coughed into life and clattered away in a cloud of roadside dust. "I don't know how to fix any of this. All I know for sure is that we're meant to be together. I know I've kept secrets, but sometimes the secrets are better than the truth."

Sarah shook her head. "If there's one thing all this madness has taught me, it's that secrets are *never* better than the truth. If we're going to stand a single chance in this screwed up world, then the only place to begin is with the truth."

Nathaniel nodded slowly. "Okay then, no secrets, but you might find out that *I'm* not the man you thought I was either."

Sarah took a deep breath. "Okay then. Who is Kal?"

For a moment Nathaniel was silent. "Why start with that question?"

"Oh, I don't know, *maybe because he'd been following us in his car*

for over an hour, and don't even *try* to tell me you didn't notice."

"How do you know Kal, have you met him?" Nathaniel sounded genuinely confused.

Sarah sighed and clenched her fists once again, trying to hold onto her temper. "Christ, how many times do I have to tell you this is a small island? Word of your little bust up last week has gotten around. No, I've never met Kal, but that doesn't mean I don't know who he is…so who is he?"

Nathaniel took Sarah's hand and led her to one of the chipped and sun-bleached picnic tables. He waited till they were both seated before speaking again. "I've known Kal for a very long time, but even now I'm not really sure who he is."

"You're not making sense, Nathaniel."

"I know, I know, just listen and I'll try to explain." He paused again as he gathered his thoughts. "I've already told you I had a pretty strange kind of childhood."

"The orphanage, right?"

"In fact, there were a couple of orphanages; the first was St Gemma's when we were younger and then the second, where Kal was in charge."

Sarah smiled. "Do you know that's more than you've told me the whole time I've known you?"

Nathaniel continued. "St Gemma's was a pretty standard affair, run by the church and a bunch of nuns who were more fearsome than any nightclub bouncer I've ever seen."

"Yeah, they have a reputation."

Now Nathaniel smiled. "St Gemma's was really strict, but at the same time it was safe and me and Benjamin were mostly content with our lot. Even though it was heavy on the religious side they taught us well, they fed us well and generally things were okay. I know there's a lot of horror stories about these places floating around nowadays, but that wasn't really our experience."

Sarah pressed him gently. "Do you realise that's the first time you've mentioned your brother's name?"

"Really?" Nathaniel sounded genuinely surprised.

"Yeah; you said you had a brother, but I never knew what his name was."

Nathaniel looked thoughtful for a moment before continuing his tale. "So that was mine and Ben's life, at least for the first decade or so. I remember it was just past my twelfth birthday when I saw a woman walking into the office one day. That was unusual because she wasn't a nun or anything; in fact, she was pretty glamourous. I remember her because we rarely saw outsiders. Anyway, it turned out that she represented this special school that me and Benjamin had been selected for."

"Selected?" Sarah raised her eyebrows.

"Yeah; I don't remember doing any tests or anything but before we knew it, Ben and I were packed off to the Trinity Foundation School. All the nuns seemed very excited, telling us how lucky we were to be going to such a prestigious place."

Sarah sighed sadly "It must've been hard leaving everything you'd ever known, just like that."

"It was, but it wasn't like we had a choice. Still, we thought we were heading to a new kind of school with maybe a bit more freedom, but we had no idea what was waiting for us."

Sarah squeezed Nathaniel's hand. "Kal." She said softly.

He nodded. "Yeah, well, to cut a long story short, Kal was the man in charge of Trinity."

Sarah's eyes widened.

Nathaniel quickly continued. "When I say he was in charge I don't mean he was there day-to-day, but he owned the place, and he called the shots. Every now and then he'd come by with sweets and little gifts. He'd talk to me and my brother, and the other kids too, telling us how very special we were."

She took his hand gently in both of her own. "It's okay, I get the idea."

Nathaniel shook his head, almost angrily. "It wasn't like that though, really. Okay, so he was, *is*, a really strange guy, but not in that way. In fact, he always made sure we were safe and well looked after. And the guys who *did* run the place never left us alone with strangers."

"Sounds like they did their best for you, so what went wrong?"

There was a long pause before he continued. "Ben and I had spent our whole lives in those two institutions, and for the most part I suppose we were happy enough. Looking back, I think we got a better than average education, but it all came at a price. We weren't exactly prisoners at the school, but we weren't exactly free either. Sure, we could go out and about, but there was always a chaperone, always somebody watching and making sure we didn't spend too long with the kids on the outside."

Sarah didn't really know what to say, having had no experience of such things.

Nathaniel continued; seemingly keen to tell his story at long last. "It was weird too, a complete reversal of St Gemma's. Back there, all the teachers had been women, nuns, while at Trinity they were all men, and they were all African too; I mean *African* like Kal is, complete with same accent and everything. The deference they showed to that man was bordering on…no, it *was* creepy. It was like he had some sort of power over them."

There was a silence while Sarah thought about what she'd heard. "Another church, or another branch of the same church I guess."

"Yeah maybe, although I'm pretty sure they weren't any kind of official church. Whatever the case, those guys were a lot sterner than the nuns, and that's saying something. There was talk about them having been in some army or militia somewhere, but I never managed to find anything out for sure."

"So, it was a military academy?" Sarah sounded confused.

"No, it wasn't; just a bunch of rumours spread by kids. All the same, I can't help thinking those stories were based on *something*, judging by the way the teachers handled us."

Sarah placed her hand on his cheek. "My poor baby, they must've been so rough on you."

There was another pause while Nathaniel marshalled his thoughts. "It was kind of like that and yet it wasn't. As long as you did as you were told and tried your best in class the masters were really great, like kindly old uncles or big brothers; but if you did wrong then wow, did they ever freak the fuck out. It was real Jekyll and Hyde stuff. As long as you behaved then everything was cool, but if you crossed them, it was the belt, if you were lucky. So that's how it went on, with Ben and I trying to keep our heads down and more or less avoiding a beating for breaking the rules."

"Didn't anyone ever come to check up, like the church or the government?"

"Sure, they did, but we knew better than to cross the schoolmasters, let alone the man in charge. Anyway, that was my life and Ben's too; sure, it could be rough at times, but everybody knew where they stood."

Sarah nudged him along gently. "So, what happened next?"

Nathaniel just shrugged. "Nothing specific, I just hit my teens and started discovering things like girls and music, the usual sort of stuff, I guess. Being educated about the great big world out there wasn't enough; I wanted to see at least a little bit of it. Besides, I could tell something was up at Trinity Academy, but I couldn't put my finger on what it was. Maybe it was all in my head; maybe *I* was the one who'd changed by noticing more and more things outside of myself. Either way, I started to act up and even sneak out when I could."

Sarah's eyes widened. "Yeah, I can imagine how *that* went."

"I got away with it a few times, or so I thought, but they weren't fools and eventually I was found out. Sure, the beatings were bad but that was just part of the deal, and it didn't really scare me. What *did* scare me were the rumours about what had happened to kids who'd played up in the past. Thinking back, I don't know if any of them were true, but I can't say there was nothing to them either. The worst part was the effect it had on Ben. He was only ten and he really believed his big brother might just vanish one night and never return. He stopped eating, he couldn't sleep, and he even started to wet the bed, which was something he'd never done before. Of course, that incurred the wrath of the schoolmasters and things just went from bad to worse. I tried to protect him but there wasn't much I could do. In the end I realised the only way to properly look after my little brother was to get the hell out of there, so that's what we did."

Sarah swallowed, almost afraid to ask the next question. "Is that how Ben died?"

Nathaniel took a deep breath and paused before continuing, glancing up and around the empty parking area as though ensuring he couldn't be overheard. "We'd only been in Barcelona for a couple of days before they found us. We'd kept a really low profile, but we must've been spotted and tracked to our hideout by the river. That was typical of them, to move in when everything was nice and quiet. Anyhow, the first we knew about it was when we spotted Abioye, one of the schoolmasters. We tried to run but the bastards had been watching us for a while and they had us surrounded. The only way out was to swim, so I just jumped in and told Ben to do the same. It was only when I'd made it across that I realised he wasn't with me. I never really saw what happened, in fact the only thing I *did* see was Abioye and one of the others diving around in the middle of all that murky water. I guess Ben had gone under and they were trying to find him. Before I knew it the rest had split up, with some staying on the bank and the others piling into a car to chase me down again. I could either stay or run, so I ran."

Sarah was quiet for some time as she considered Nathaniel's harrowing tale. At last, he'd answered so many questions about himself, although one still remained. "So why is Kal here, now?"

"I don't know, but whatever he wants, it won't be anything good." Nathaniel's eyes began to shine with silent tears of grief.

Sarah paused again before she spoke. "We should go to the police, they'll help you."

"No!" He grabbed her by the shoulders, staring intently into her eyes. "Promise me you'll never do that! I mean it, Sarah!"

She wrestled free from his grip, rubbing her aching shoulders. "Jesus! What's got into you?"

Nathaniel's words tumbled out in a torrent of emotion as the dam finally burst. "You don't know what he's capable of, the others, there are still other out kids there."

"All the more reason…"

"*No! Listen to me!* You think I haven't already tried that? He's protected by…well; he's protected in ways we'll never understand. You think there were no questions after Ben died? Nothing ever came of it though, just a troubled boy and a tragic accident. All that's left of my brother is a number, a statistic, a name buried in a dusty file somewhere." The tears finally welled up and spilt silently down Nathaniel's cheeks. "Don't go chasing some phantom called justice because there's no such thing, not in this world."

Sarah pulled his head to her breast as he began to sob quietly, his tears moistening her soft flesh as she ran her slender fingers through his hair.

Nathaniel breathed Sarah's perfume deeply, pressing his head to her chest as he listened to her heart beating strong and steady. He spread his fingers across her back, pulling her body closer to him as he felt the softness of her breast against his cheek. He felt her hand tighten on his head as she pushed him further into her chest and his lips brushed the soft, feminine swelling of her breast.

Sarah softly murmured encouragement as she subtly guided him to her rapidly hardening nipples. She felt confused yet still she knew that Nathaniel was the only thing she wanted, right there in that dusty layby above the ocean. Her body ached and quivered at his touch, and she silently thanked the fates that she'd been born a woman.

As Nathaniel's agony was scorched by the flames of sudden desire, he needed no further urging from his lost love as he rolled his thumb over Sarah's hardened nipple and squeezed her breast. His other hand glided down to the small of her back as he pulled her closer to him, his arousal quickly climbing to match hers. Within a second his lips had found her mouth and he tasted not just her warm, moist body, but something far deeper and more profound, an essence of some inner truth expressed in the very cells of her lithe form. Suddenly his mind was filled with a torrent of ideas that swirled around the central pivot of his want for her. Life, spirit, truth and something profound yet impossible to vocalise filled his mind as his hands searched for the hem of her skirt.

Sarah was ahead of him, and Nathaniel swallowed hard as her hand somehow found its way inside his jeans and gripped him tightly, as though testing his hardness, his fitness, his worthiness to lay claim to her body. She'd always been a sexy lady but there was something less refined, more urgent and more primal in her than he'd ever sensed before. She whispered something in his ear, but lust slurred her words as she suddenly swung her leg over him, straddling him right there in broad daylight. He assumed nobody was watching, although it was too late anyway as she skilfully shifted her hips and suddenly, he was inside her. She hadn't even waited for him to undress!

Again, he heard the urgent, wordless whispering as she dug her fingernails into his back and pushed her hips forward, refusing to back off as she hungered for every single part of him.

Nathaniel felt both eager and powerless as Sarah put herself squarely in control, moving against him with a rhythm guaranteed drain him dry in the shortest time. Her expertise paid off in less than a minute as he was unable to hold back. The shockwaves rocked both their sweating bodies as every muscle in Nathaniel's body tightened before he slumped back, empty and spent.

In turn, Sarah dug her fingers into him for a few seconds longer before she began to relax, the rhythm of her hips slowing as she descended from the dizzy heights of ecstatic, animal fulfilment.

Neither of them spoke as they stayed locked together, panting from their exertions and trying to find the strength to separate.

Nathaniel ran his fingers through her hair and gently kissed her ear, wondering who the familiar stranger in his arms really was.

WHAT IS, IS COMING INTO BEING
Chapter 9

Hyienna stared into the deep shadows of the hole, while the hole stared back, taunting him with its inscrutable silence. Turning away, he looked up at the lighthouse bathing in the warm glow of the rising sun.

The tall tower was solidly the same as it had been just a few weeks before, whereas *he* had changed significantly. It was almost as though the building sensed the subtle shift in his consciousness, its polished windows seeming to squint down at him with an air of disdain and disapproval.

Hyienna hunched his shoulders against the early morning chill and tried not to entertain ideas of being watched from above. He'd thought about what he was going to do, and he knew had no rational reason to feel guilty, not that the thinking had eased his conscience one little bit.

The worst crime he could be committing was trespass, and even that wasn't especially clear; all the same he wanted to get it over and done with before the tourists started showing up. Too many awkward questions.

Satisfied that nobody was watching, Hyienna quickly reached into his rucksack and extracted a length of stout rope. He'd found it in a tool shed behind the Green Lizard and he figured nobody would miss it for a few hours. He quickly tied one end around a stack of pallet planks he'd wedged firmly across the mouth of the opening. With half a dozen lengths of wood tied together, Hyienna was pretty confident they could hold his weight. After throwing the rope down into the hole he picked up the other rucksack, trying to ignore the subtle but definite whine that settled somewhere deep in his ears.

Looking back over his own shoulder, Hyienna silently told his mystical burden to take it easy before gingerly leaning out and testing his weight on the makeshift anchoring point. Confident that he wouldn't immediately be cast into the abyss, he tested his construction a little further by sitting on the beams and dangling his feet over the hole. It would have been much safer to acquire a boat and enter the cave by sea, but that might attract too much attention.

Checking his small LED torch was secure in his pocket, he gently lowered himself off his impromptu platform and hung there for a moment, listing for creaking and cracking sounds. Satisfied at last, Hyienna quickly let himself down the rope, hand over hand until he felt the solid floor of the cave beneath his boots.

Within a second, he'd flicked on his torch and cast it around the cool subterranean space. "Hello, hi. I guess I'm back again. The disc of white light passed over the rock walls as he turned a full circle.

It became clear that the cave was empty. In fact, not only was the space empty, but it had been *emptied*. There was no trace of any makeshift furniture or piles of detritus scattered throughout that silent, echoing space. If it wasn't for the odd piece of litter lurking between the cool damp rocks, there would be no reason to think that anybody had ever lingered there. The only other hint of recent habitation was a trace of incense hanging in the damp atmosphere.

Hyienna had no idea where the old woman had gone to, but he was pretty sure she hadn't just upped sticks and moved by herself. There was no way she could have climbed out through the roof with all her worldly possessions, which meant she must have left by boat.

Picking his way towards the sound of the ocean, Hyienna wondered who might have helped the mysterious woman to leave her lonely encampment, or perhaps to escape it.

He followed the wall of the cave around a shallow bend until the floor became little more than a narrow ledge that vanished into the ocean. He started and almost slipped into the water as his torch beam picked out a figure standing in the shadows close to the water. "Hello."

There was no reply, in fact there was no sign of life at all, and it took him a moment to realise why. Cautiously stepping closer, Hyienna shook his head ruefully, as he realised, he'd been talking to a painting; a piece of lifelike street art hidden far away from any street. From a distance the painted outline was quite convincing, while on closer inspection it was just plain disturbing.

Hyienna quickly felt for his little rock as he caught himself glancing over his shoulder at the rucksack waiting patiently on his back. Ignoring the whine in his ears, and why the word *waiting* had suddenly popped into his head, he slowly stepped forward and cast his torch beam over the life-sized image. It didn't take him long to conclude that it wasn't any kind of generic outline, but a very deliberate and accurate depiction of one particular person, the very person he'd expected to see when he'd lowered himself down on that rope.

The silent shadow painted straight on the cave wall was unsettling enough, but the stack of neatly folded clothes at its feet whispered formless tales of dark designs and deeply esoteric ideas.

Hyienna turned a slow circle, casting his lamp over every part of the cave as he tried to shake off the uncomfortable impression of eyes staring at him from the shadows. He could see nothing, but still the feeling persisted.

Shuffling forward, he gingerly looked over the rocky ledge and into the dark swirling water as it rose and fell with the heartbeat of the ocean. This must surely be the place where the old woman had begun the next leg of her mysterious journey, and the treacherous descent only confirmed his suspicion that she couldn't have left the cave without help of one kind or another.

He turned his attention to the pile of shabby clothes, complete with worn sneakers and the old woman's dog-eared tarot pack carefully placed atop the neatly folded stack. Hyienna had only met the woman once, and under the strangest of circumstances too, but that was enough to tell him that the cave dweller would never have abandoned such a central part of herself, unless she knew she would not be returning.

Crouching beside the ledge, he shone his torch on the dark slippery rocks but could find no sign of blood or scuff marks, in fact there was nothing to suggest that the old woman had departed her subterranean world in a violent manner. That discovery should've been a comfort, but it just made him feel all the more uneasy. If she'd really departed of her own free will, then why would she leave her clothes symbolically stacked like that? On the other hand, it seemed unlikely that she'd been coerced in some way as there was no evidence of a struggle. Besides, why would some kidnapper bother to tidy the place up, paint a picture and neatly fold her clothes before leaving?

There was still a third possibility, one that accounted for the old woman telling him she didn't have long left. With her voluntary declaration in mind, Hyienna reckoned it was entirely possible that she'd decided to depart the mortal realm while she still had some semblance of control over her affairs, such as they were.

Once more he stared into the black, fathomless waters that were never warmed by the light of the sun, much like the impossible emptiness in the cheap rucksack on his back. He stood mesmerised and unblinking as the black waters rose and fell, reaching up towards his feet before slumping back and gathering the strength to repeat the cycle. Slowly he slipped the rucksack off one shoulder and then the other, holding it over the dark ocean's swirling surface. Nobody would ever see him, and nobody would ever know. It would be so easy; just open his fingers, turn on his heel and climb out of the cave. All he had to do was let go of that cheap nylon strap and he would be relieved of a burden and a mission he had never even wanted, let alone understood. Maybe *that* was why he'd felt the urge to return to the place where it had all started. Perhaps deep down some unconscious part of him knew that the mysterious witch was gone. Perhaps the impossible blanket had called to some quiet and hidden part of him, urging his return to the cave so that it might follow its rightful owner into the peaceful darkness.

But if that was the case, *why couldn't he just let go?* Hyienna thrust his hand into his other pocket, feeling for his little rock as he felt perspiration between his fingers. He could hear nothing but the rhythmic breathing of the ocean, yet somehow, he understood that the rucksack was imploring…*ordering* him not to let go. He could hear no words and not even the tinnitus whine that so often accompanied such encounters. No shadows flickered on the walls and no terrifying apparition suddenly materialised close by, yet there could be no doubt that the little nylon rucksack was deadly serious. Although imparted in a manner that defied description, the warning that an abyss far deeper and darker than the cave awaited him if he turned his back on his obligations.

There was also a second warning, it too unformed and wordless, and Hyienna couldn't figure out whether this one emanated from the uncanny burden he carried or from somewhere deep within his own psyche. Somehow, he knew that all the things he'd quit and walked away from in his life had shepherded him towards this moment. Now it was up to him whether to back down or stay the course, but he knew that a wrong decision would mark a turning point in his life. It would be a decision he could never recover from in *this* world, never mind what might lay beyond.

Reluctantly he slung the rucksack back over his shoulders and wiped his sweating palms on the front of his jeans. He turned to examine the uncomfortably neat pile of threadbare clothes at his feet, suggesting a singular finality to the arrangement that confirmed his fears without revealing direct evidence. The witch was gone, and he was all alone with his burden; no map, no guidance and nobody to advise him as to what to do or where to go next.

Except maybe…

Hyienna squatted to look more closely at the worn deck of cards stacked neatly beside the late cave dweller's shoes. He kept his hands well clear, as though he were studying some exotic insect or a beautiful but dangerous reptile. Had they been left specifically for him? Was the old woman *really* smart enough to know that he'd come back? How could, he be sure?

He cast his torch slowly over the silent bundle of clothes once more. He wasn't really sure what he was looking for, but he was all out of ideas and so he figured that Providence, or intuition, or *something* might offer some clue as to where to go or what to do next.

The answer wasn't long in coming and he swallowed hard when the beam of light inexplicably flickered as it passed over the worn tarot deck. Coincidence? No, it couldn't be. That torch was dependable, and it had never dimmed like that before.

Desperately hoping that he wasn't repeating old patterns of self-delusion, Hyienna steeled himself, reached forward and flipped over the top card. He didn't have any clue how to interpret the cards, but he figured he might see something meaningful if he was on the right track.

Hyienna hadn't really known what to expect before he turned the card over, but he was jarred to find himself face to face with the figure of the Fool, about to step right off a mountain top. He didn't know what all the symbolism meant, but the Fool's bundle tied to a stick and carried over his shoulder was just too much of a coincidence, while he was pretty sure that the small dog at the man's feet was trying to warn of impending disaster.

He picked up the card and stared at it, feeling as though he was handling something forbidden and yet perhaps essential to helping him navigate whatever might lie ahead, a stolen map of a hitherto uncharted region.

At last, he overcame his indecision, threw a mental nod towards the departed cave dweller and picked up the rest of the deck, quickly pushing them into a roomy pocket in his jacket. They fitted perfectly.

His purpose fulfilled, Hyienna took one last look at the bundle of clothes and painted silhouette. Although completely lacking detail, it was still an intricate work that displayed the contours of clothes and the mysterious woman's unkempt hair. In fact, the more he studied it, the more it resembled a kind of life-sized stencil rather than some artistic interpretation. Curiously, he found it reminded him of the inexplicable blackness he'd been unable to cast into the ocean. He wasn't sure why as the pitch, or paint, or whatever was daubed on the wall reflected the light as it emphasised the contours of the cave, rather than just existing as an uncanny blanket of blackness.

He reached forward to touch the freshly painted shadow, quickly snatching his hand back as his fingertips became damp and sticky. He rubbed his fingers together and gingerly sniffed at the black tar-like substance clinging to his hands. Surprisingly, it didn't actually smell anything like tar, instead exuding a strongly herbal, almost sweet aroma that cut the back of his throat when he breathed in too deeply. Hyienna had no idea what the substance was, and he really didn't *want* to know either. He quickly rubbed his hand against the rock wall, then the leg of his jeans as he tried to remove the stubborn, staining substance from his hand. The strange glutinous paint was both oily and sticky at the same time, making it almost impossible to remove entirely without the aid of soap and water.

Making a mental note to wash his hands as soon as possible, Hyienna swept his torch around the cave one last time before making his way back to the rope. He'd dropped into the underworld with the intention of returning the rucksack to its previous keeper, but instead he was climbing back up with more than he'd brought down. Not only that, while his added burden was small, it was something central, something intimate to the identity of the woman who'd gifted him the…whatever it *was* in his rucksack. He guessed it really was his rucksack as there was nobody left to return it to.

Taking a deep breath, Hyienna grasped the rope and began the arduous climb out of the darkness and towards the light.

❈

SARAH'S SMILING
Chapter 10

Hyienna stopped and took a deep breath, slowly turning a full circle as he let the quiet of the countryside envelop him in its cool, refreshing embrace. He idly scuffed at the cracked and dusty road; his boots the only man-made sound he could hear save for a murmuring bassline filtering out of the gathering dusk. As he drank in the gathering darkness, he reflected on the unlikely events which had overtaken his life during the past few weeks. It had all been so very strange at first, but now everything seemed to have settled into a sort of stable inertia. He and Kate had continued their flirtatious non-affair while Sarah had become a lot more distant, although a significant part of him was quite glad about that. Hyienna really didn't want to be around when the whole thing inevitably blew up.

He let his head fall back and he gazed up at the darkening blue of late evening. Venus glimmered and winked from afar as a welcome breeze gently pushed the sun below the horizon. High season was winding down, although it would still be a good few weeks before Formentera settled down for her winter slumber. All the same, the evenings were just that little bit cooler and the heat a little less cloying after dark. In truth Hyienna preferred it that way as it certainly made for more comfortable sleeping, not that the subtle change to the atmosphere had any effect on his cycle of oddly insistent and endlessly recurrent dreams. He already knew there was only one solution to *that* problem, although he was surprised to still be left without a clue as to the mysterious rucksack's rightful place.

As was his habit, he reached into his pocket for his little stone of safety as the memories of those dreams crowded around him. The old woman was always there, as was the river; and there was something about a boat and something lost, but he could never quite piece the fading impressions together once he'd awoken. The only thing he

❈

was certain of each morning was a nagging sense of guilt, as though some incorporeal part of himself was urging him to *do* something. The problem was, after all those weeks of mystery, secrets and low-level drama, he still had no understanding of *what* it was he was supposed to do. He'd hoped that moving the rucksack would've helped him sleep a little better, but it had made no difference; in fact, he wasn't entirely sure it hadn't made the dreams *more* vivid and imbued them with a greater sense of urgency. Maybe that subtle change was all in his head; it was becoming harder to tell perception from reality, a problem which was especially dangerous for him.

Hyienna shook himself from his reverie and stepped onto the dusty track leading off the empty road. Coloured lights glinted in the darkness ahead while the thrum of distant music beckoned him to join the party.

He hadn't travelled more than a few paces off-road before he stopped dead, instinctively dropping to a crouch as he squinted into the gathering darkness ahead. He willed his eyes to gaze just a few feet further as he tried to discern the dark figure waiting on the path ahead. Was that somebody standing by the undergrowth, or was the ever-changing light of the falling dusk conspiring with his overactive imagination? After squinting a little more, he shook his head ruefully and stood up. There was nobody there, and in fact it wouldn't have been especially strange if somebody was there. After all, he was heading to a social gathering, so why shouldn't somebody else be arriving by the same route? Y*ou've got to get a grip on yourself, my lad. You're jumping at shadows and seeing things that aren't there; and you know very well where that could end up if you don't calm down.*

He took a deep breath and forced himself to walk straight forward like he owned the path, smiling to himself as he remembered another party where he'd recently arrived on foot. Although in some ways the situation was similar, any outward resemblance was entirely superficial; in fact, the experience was more like a mirror image or a polar opposite. The broken down, crumbling wall marking the drive and the rutted, unfinished roadway were a stark contrast to the antiseptic angularity of Casa Hermoso. Solomon's home was a statement, a subjugation of the surrounding countryside and an expression of the will to dominate.

By contrast Nathaniel's place, if it had a name, was more a study in benign bohemian neglect; being at once rooted in and slowly being subsumed the surrounding countryside. The place suited the owner and given the choice, Hyienna would definitely have chosen this house over Solomon's. Plus, it was just a short walk from the Green Lizard, which made him wonder why he hadn't seen Nathaniel in there at least once or twice.

Hyienna looked around as he realised, he'd stopped walking again. There were no shadowy phantoms blocking his path this time and he knew he was just stalling. He was already late yet still he dawdled, fearful of what might lie ahead. It was true that he didn't care for Solomon, but that wasn't really a justification for his assisting the man's fiancé to begin an affair with an old flame. The worst part was waiting for the explosion that must surely come.

Taking a deep breath, he steeled himself and marched determinedly forward once more. If he was lucky then he could maybe meet some new people and keep a low profile, before slipping away early with a headache or nausea or some such. Hyienna silently scolded himself for his pretty forlorn and frankly effeminate plan, but it was the only thing he could come up with.

Slowly the quaintly sagging roofline of Nathaniel's house revealed itself against the darkening sky. The whole place was pretty much how he'd imagined it, although it was bigger than he thought it might be. The rambling old farmhouse exuded the same informal chipped paint cosiness that made the Green Lizard so very homely and welcoming. The uneven structure was the kind of place that invited visitors to kick off their shoes and stretch out rather than to admire it politely and listen to its owner's personal manifesto for entrepreneurial success.

The old farmhouse's welcoming informality winked and shimmered in the glittering multi-coloured lights festooning the trees dotted around what had once been some sort of courtyard. The music was very different to Solomon's place too; with the raunchy beats of Solomon's pool party replaced by something with an altogether more traditional vibe of a Spanish guitar and modern electronic bass escaping into the lengthening shadows of the dusty countryside.

At last, he made it to what passed for the front turning circle, with the chaotic jumble of vehicles providing another stark contrast to the regimented organisation of Solomon's hospitality. Whilst you did as you were expected to do at Casa Hermoso, here at Casa Nathaniel, people just kind of showed up and did whatever. This was a place to actually chill out and socialise as opposed to somewhere to *be* seen. This was a place of true leisure, not a place of endless work cunningly disguised as a place to play. Arriving at Nathaniel's house felt much more like a social pleasure than a social chore, not that the informal atmosphere did anything to calm Hyienna's nerves.

The chink of glasses and the smell of freshly cooked food reached out to greet him as he followed a trail of flickering tea lights along a cracked and uneven path running past the house. The dancing candles soon led him through a crumbling farmyard wall, although the last time Nathaniel's place had produced any kind of commercial crop was anyone's guess.

Hyienna felt much more at home wandering through the informal jumble of tables, chairs and assorted garden furniture. Just like at Casa Hermoso, he didn't really know anyone, but that didn't seem to matter very much. Nobody was keeping score and that informal anonymity was something of a relief.

It wasn't long before Hyienna's nose led him to a soot blackened pizza oven belching out fragrant wood-smoke and the even more alluring odours of sizzling mozzarella and freshly cooked sausage.

"Hey buddy, great to see you!" A grinning Nathaniel thrust a glass of cold sangria into Hyienna's hand before deftly retrieving a tray of good smelling pizza slices from inside the oven. "Have some food, relax, or go nuts; it's all good at Granja de Cosecha."

Not wanting to be rude, Hyienna helped himself to a slice of fresh pizza and made for a vacant table at the edge of an uneven space that had become an impromptu dancefloor. Quickly grabbing a napkin from the dispenser on the table, he tried to look as cool as possible while eating his delicious but unruly pizza slice. As he wrestled with a long string of tasty mozzarella, it suddenly struck him that he really didn't care if anyone was watching. His usual self-consciousness just melted away as Nathaniel's wonderful food took charge and he realised that nobody was paying attention anyhow. It was a different crowd and a very different vibe that was far more in tune with his own ideas of kicking back and chilling out. Yeah, he could get used to this.

As Hyienna settled back into his seat and wallowed in the relaxed and friendly atmosphere, it suddenly struck him that despite hanging out on an idyllic holiday island, this was the first time he'd really felt completely at ease since he'd first set foot on Formentera all those weeks ago.

He jumped a little as a bottle of beer appeared on the table in front of him and a cute girl with crazy corkscrew hair smiled and winked. "Compliments of the chef." She jerked her head towards Nathaniel's snorting pizza oven before disappearing into a haze of wood smoke that drifted across the dancefloor, turning Nathaniel's guests into ethereal ghosts as they danced and shimmered in and out of sight.

Hyienna drained his sangria and picked up the beer, raising it in a silent toast to the girl who'd smiled into and out of his life just like that. Although they didn't look much like each other, she kind of reminded him of the pretty hippy chick who'd sold him his brown agate anchor back on Ibiza. He patted his pocket, content to know that his little slice of solidity was in its proper place, although he felt no need for an enhanced connection with the "real" world…whatever that actually meant. He took another sip of beer and yawned, leaning further back in his chair and stretching his legs out, letting his senses become entangled with the twisting threads of incense and cooking smoke drifting across the exquisitely neglected farmyard. Just like Nathaniel's pizza, the whole place was a little slice of heaven and right then and there it was all he needed in the whole wide world.

* * *

Slowly Hyienna regained his sense of his own being as the distant hum and chatter of the party pierced his consciousness, while a sudden brightness turned the dark and distant world unexpectedly red. For a moment his befuddled mind was trapped between waking from surprisingly deep sleep and not being quite sure of where he was.

He swallowed hard and sat up, blinking against the bright LED headlights rudely swooping across the dancefloor, turning revellers into moon dials as their shadows swooped and twisted across the uneven stone of the crumbling courtyard. Hyienna glanced at his watch and was surprised to find he'd only been asleep for a few minutes, even though it had felt like much longer. He'd even dreamt about something or someone, and some water.

He shaded his eyes as the headlights came to rest on the driveway beyond the house. They were quite high in the air, so he knew exactly who'd just arrived, especially when the lights stayed on for an unnecessarily long time.

At last, the lights blinked off and Hyienna closed his eyes again, luxuriating in his dark anonymity for just a little longer. He knew he only had a few minutes left before the new guests found him, and anything could happen after that.

Sure enough, it wasn't long before Solomon's deep voice interrupted the music. "Hey there; we stopped by the Lizard, but you were already gone. Getting a head start on us, huh?"

Hyienna yawned and stirred from his peaceful half-slumber, a little resentful but knowing this was a conversation that couldn't be postponed any longer. He smiled and raised the beer that Solomon had placed in front of him. "Thanks. So where are the ladies?"

Solomon flopped into the chair opposite and jerked his head back towards Nathaniel's magic outdoor oven. "Hobnobbing with the great man himself."

Hyienna sensed an invitation to talk. "But not you?"

Solomon took a swig of beer. "Hey, I don't want to say anything amiss, but…"

Hyienna completed Solomon's sentence. "But you're going to anyway."

There was a pause as Solomon took another gulp of beer, seemingly weighing up what he should say next. "The guy always looks like he's thinking one thing and saying another. His expressions don't match his words and I don't like guys with agendas."

Hyienna just shrugged. "He's a writer, which means he's only half with us most of the time. Besides, everybody has an agenda, benign or otherwise."

"Hey, no offence. I mean, I know he's your buddy and all, but just bear in mind you don't know him that well."

"And you do?" Hyienna raised his eyebrows.

"Not really. We don't tend to move in the same circles, but you know how the girls are with these creative types."

Hyienna made a conscious effort not to narrow his eyes. Did Solomon know something, suspect something, or was that just a chance remark? He decided to play it safe, although he was secretly dreading the possibility that Solomon might ask him a direct question. It was hard to know whether the truth or a lie would be worse in that situation. "Well, the man makes a mean pizza, so no wonder everyone wants to be here."

"You telling me you're here for the food? Is *that* why you've been hanging around with Nathaniel so much?"

Hyienna seized his chance for misdirection and camped it up as much as he could. "Why Solomon, you never struck me as the jealous type. How long have you been hiding these feelings?"

At last, one side of Solomon's mouth rose in a slight smile. "Very funny, wise guy. And here I was thinking that personal success and a good fitness regime were important to the ladies; but maybe it's all just pizza in the end." He nodded to someone on the dancefloor who'd recognised him.

Now it was Hyienna's turn to smile. "I guess chefs are never lonely. Everyone loves good food."

Solomon rose and turned towards the dancefloor, winking as he did so. "Say hi to Sarah, when she can tear herself away from Mr cheesy slice over there."

Hyienna raised his beer to Solomon's back as the big man quickly vanished into a fog of incense, wood smoke and ganja. Only when he was sure that Solomon was otherwise engaged did he dare look across to Nathaniel's cooking station. Sure enough, there he was, talking to Sarah as if they were just old friends. Well, he guessed they were, but they were so much more as well.

As though sensing Hyienna's scrutiny, Sarah turned, blew him a kiss and mouthed something that looked like *thank you*, but he couldn't be sure. He knew she was thanking him because she thought he was covering for her, which he supposed he was. Still, the question of what he might do if Solomon asked him a direct question nagged at his mind and dampened his mood.

Suddenly Hyienna's world went black as a pair of hands were placed over his eyes, although Kate's spicy perfume and the soft weight of her bosom against the back of his head somewhat gave the game away. The hands were quickly removed, and Kate's immaculately manicured hand placed yet another bottle of beer on the table beside him. He watched her sashay around the table and take up the seat previously occupied by Solomon. "I could get used to this; everyone's bringing me beer today."

Kate toyed with her trademark martini glass. "You look like you could do with a drink, honey. I thought you were about to crack under questioning." She inclined her head slightly behind her, indicating that she was talking about the recently departed Solomon.

Hyienna drained his rapidly warming beer and picked up the cold one Kate had just brought him. "I'm just starting to wonder if I've made a big mistake."

Kate shook her head. "You didn't make anyone do anything, so what do you care?"

"I don't like lying to people, even if I haven't done that yet."

Kate broke into a warm, almost maternal smile. "We're all liars, every last one of us, so there's no need for false piety. Solomon's a stranger to you and you're just protecting your cousin. Nathaniel and Sarah were going to do what they were going to do anyway, regardless of whether you were around. All we did was oil the wheels because, to put it bluntly, my friend had become a real pain in the ass with all her lovesick moping about. Look at her now; doesn't she look so much happier?"

Hyienna glanced across to Nathaniel's cooking station, noting that both he and Sarah were conspicuously absent.

Kate placed a hand on his arm. "Don't you go fretting about things that aren't your concern. Sarah's happy and Solomon's too busy impressing women he barely knows; so why sweat any of it?"

Hyienna couldn't help smiling as Kate winked that knowing, naughty wink of hers. Once again, she'd managed to make him feel both completely helpless and yet wonderfully free from responsibility all at the same time. "So, I should just do nothing?"

Kate stood up, smoothed down her dress and held out her hand. "No, my cute boy, you can dance with me."

***

Fragrant blue cigar smoke twisted into the night sky, a dark shadow briefly flickering across the face of a bright, nearly full moon. Hyienna leaned back against the tumbledown compound wall and nodded appreciatively at the stogie lodged between his fingers. It had been a long time since he'd smoked anything, but it just seemed as though kicking back and enjoying one of life's simple vices was de rigueur at Nathaniel's place. Besides, it would have been rude to refuse the cute girl with the crazy hair. He made a mental note to ask Nathaniel about her habit of wandering around and just handing stuff out to people. It was a nice idea, but he hoped she could afford it.

He took another drag on his cigar and looked out across the darkening scrubland, the lights from the house behind him lengthening shadows and enhancing contrast to imbue the scene with almost supernatural hue. Whilst it made the sandy scrub close by that much brighter, it was offset by the deeper shadows further away. That dense darkness at once drew his mind back to the nothingness waiting for him in that cheap, nondescript bag. He quickly reached into his pocket for his little agate anchor, not trusting himself stay put rather than floating away on a cloud of introspection fuelled by alcohol, tobacco and second-hand ganja smoke.

Glancing at his watch, he stretched, yawned and began to think about making his way home. It was a little after three in the morning and the party was winding down. Sure, the music was still playing and there were plenty of folk about, but most of the dancing was done and little knots had formed around different tables as old friends and new acquaintances chatted and drank through the small hours. He didn't really know anyone that well, especially as Solomon had taken Sarah and Kate home about an hour ago. Solomon seemed to be in good spirits, but still Hyienna couldn't shake the idea that Sarah's fiancé was feeling him out, trying to see if his suspicions about her were well founded. Sure, he'd gotten away with it for one night, but Hyienna knew full well that the situation would come to a head, and probably sooner rather than later.

He jumped as he heard a footstep close behind him.

"Hey relax, don't die of a heart attack on my property." Nathaniel grinned, with his own cigar clamped between his teeth. "Puts the idea of cigarette girls in a whole new light, don't you think?"

Hyienna breathed out heavily. "I guess, kind of a nice touch really. She a friend of yours?"

"Yeah, she's a good kid. She just wants to make everyone happy and she's way too pretty for her own good. I try to keep her out of trouble."

"Maybe it's yourself you want to be keeping out of trouble."

Nathaniel stepped over a low point in the wall and raised his eyebrows. "Am I in some kind of trouble?"

"Don't get cute. You know what Solomon will do when he finds out about you and his fiancé."

Nathaniel's stare hardened. "There's no reason for him to find anything out."

Hyienna was surprised to feel his patience slipping. "You know, you're either incredibly arrogant or unbelievably stupid. Now Solomon might be arrogant too but he's not your average fool. He won't need me to tell him what's blatantly bloody obvious to everyone."

Nathaniel's expression softened again. "Yeah, you're probably right, but there's no need to worry. It's not your problem."

"You know you're the second person to say that to me this evening."

The host grinned. "Then I guess I'm not the only smart boy in the neighbourhood."

"Who said it was a boy?"

Nathaniel was silent for a moment as he looked up at the moon. "Fair point, and you're probably right about Solomon. Someone once said in a movie that some things have to end badly, or they wouldn't end at all."

Hyienna also looked up at the night sky, thinking how peaceful, serene and remote it seemed in comparison to the undignified scramble of the countless daily lives playing out below them. "Listen, I'm not much for telling people what to do, but if I've learned just one thing in this world it's that you can't just keep repeating the past. It never ends well."

Nathaniel gestured towards the stars. "*Those* patterns have been repeating for billions of years, and none of us would be here if they hadn't been. Repetition is a necessary condition for anything... *everything* to exist in the first place."

Hyienna blew out another plume of cigar smoke. "That might be a fine outlook for some distant galaxy, but it's not much of a philosophy for people. You can't move forward if you're always looking behind you; you're bound to come to grief sooner or later."

Nathaniel was silent for a few seconds. "Well, my cigar smoking philosopher, we can speculate all night about what has been and what might be, but I can tell you something that's certain in the here and now."

Curious, Hyienna turned to face him. "Oh yeah, what's that?"

"Sarah was smiling all evening. Now *that's* the truth." Nathaniel clapped him on the shoulder and wandered back to the party.

Hyienna took another long drag on his cigar as he thought about what Nathaniel had said Hyienna took another long drag on his cigar as he thought about what Nathaniel had said. Suddenly he found himself squinting into the darkness once more. Was someone out there?

PSALM OF LAMENT: YASMINA
Chapter 11

The orange glow of a bright new day painted the world in black and watery grey as Yasmina placed her wicker basket on the ground. Reaching out for her coffee which waited on an old stump of wood, she took a sip and closed her eyes, drinking in the cool quiet of the summer morning. It was always a struggle getting out of bed so early, especially as she seldom slept well. All the same, she was glad that she'd made the effort on a beautiful day like this.

The dawn belonged to Yasmina; a time when she had the whole world to herself and that world shrank to contain only her, the thoughts in her head and the Green Lizard's famously clean and crisp white sheets.

Hyienna had gotten back very late, not that she minded especially. He could keep the night and she would have the morning. It seemed like a fair trade.

She watched a tiny bird swoop low through the dry and dusty undergrowth, twittering the first tentative chords of a new dawn. She often wondered what it must be like to be a little bird, flying here and there, able to flee from all danger and free of regret. Sometimes Yaz felt as though she knew nothing *but* regrets, the weight of them pressing down on her soul to leave it permanently crushed, scarred and misshapen.

The knowledge that many people would kill to start their days in such a manner couldn't completely chase away the shadows that waited in the wings, ready to swoop in and turn even the brightest summer morning to a darker shade of melancholy. If only things could be different. If only she'd told him…if only.

She sighed heavily and picked up a freshly laundered sheet from the basket by her feet. Her laundry routine had become something of a ritual, and she missed the wet days when she couldn't hang sheets out before six in the morning. In truth it was better to be doing something useful rather than just lying in bed, kicking over the same old regrets, the same old emptiness born of the past as well as the same old uncertain future.

Maybe one day she *would* do something different. Maybe one day she'd wake up and make the call, just like that. Maybe she'd drink too much and blurt it out one evening, telling Solomon everything. Maybe.

Why was happiness always ethereal while anguish was an all too real and constant companion? Why did it have to be that way? Why did she hide the truth, even from her own sister?

She quickly grabbed another sheet to distract herself from the bitter yet directionless anger she so often felt welling up inside. Why did *she* have to be the other woman? Why should Sarah be living the high life at Casa Hermoso while she rose with the sun to hang her sheets? Why?

She let the second sheet drop back into the basket as she felt a hot tear well up in her eye. Why should she hide? Surely Sarah must suspect something, so why didn't she say anything? If it was her man carrying on behind her back, she'd be setting things straight right away. Nobody would be taking Solomon away from *her*, so why did she let herself play second fiddle, happily waiting for whatever scraps of affection he could spare, either in or out of the bedroom?

If only he knew; if only she could find the courage to tell him.

She gazed out across the tranquil glittering ocean as she tried for the hundredth, no, the *thousandth* time to summon the courage to just tell the truth. Perhaps one day she might find some untapped reserve of strength hiding somewhere in the corner of her aching soul; some new way to square the circle of love, fear and regret…perhaps one day.

Once more Yasmina felt her eyes drawn to the surface of the glittering ocean, her mind drifting away on a gentle current of daydreams, suppositions, and heart-warming speculation. She wondered where Samuel might be today, what he might look like or even what his name might be. Would he remember her, and would she even know *him* if they met face-to-face on some far-flung day? Who might he be? *What* might he be?

Yaz felt her heart begin to sink as her mind refused to let her idle daydreams wander unchecked. Even *if* he was out there somewhere, she would never find him now and there was a more than even chance he wouldn't even remember that little apartment in Barcelona. So long ago now. Maybe it was better just to let that part of her past, that part of herself, drift out of focus and into the shadows of history, just another story of a bereft mother and a missing child. Supposing she did find Samuel someday; what then? What right did she have to go barging into some stranger's life as though she was entitled to something in which she'd played almost no part?

She finally looked away from the sparkling sea and up towards the faded green shutters of the Lizard's sun-bleached exterior. Try as she might, she couldn't imagine Solomon moving into such a humble if charming abode, while the idea of her becoming the first lady of Casa Hermoso seemed equally far-fetched. Maybe this was as good as it got, and she would have to be content with a part-time lover rather than a full-time companion. Deep down she knew that a mistress was not a natural role for most women, but still she found it impossible to make the break. Without Solomon she would have nothing left of Samuel, save for some fading memories and a crumpled Polaroid photo.

All the same, it wasn't right to keep Solomon in the dark about something so important, but she felt sick with fear every time she tried to pluck up courage to tell him that they'd had a son together. How would she even *start* a conversation like that after all this time? Why should he believe her? Having lost her only son, the thought of also losing his father was more than she could bear, so she drank at night and hung her sheets in the morning, trying to live each day as though it held some meaning greater than merely sleeping long enough to see another sunrise.

Yaz angrily threw another sheet over the line and tried to ignore the headache that was beginning to form over her right eye. It was often there, brought on by alcohol and stress most likely, although this morning it seemed particularly bad, almost buzzing inside her skull as it threatened to blossom into a full-blown migraine.

That was all she needed! Still, Ermina could step in if it got really bad, *if* she could stop yakking and actually get something done for a change. Yasmina was a woman, and like most women she liked to talk, but Ermina even wore *her* out with her insatiable appetite for idle rumours and trivial gossip. It was a bad habit that would lead her little sister out of her depth one day.

Yaz hurriedly pegged out the last sheet and picked up her basket, wanting to get out of the sun before her headache got any worse. She turned towards the back door of the inn, squinting against the flashes of light and blotches of colour that were the outriders for one of her famous belting migraines. She was well used to them, although she hadn't actually had one in a while. The symptoms were pretty predictable although this time there was something else, something unusual, a strange kind of hum or buzz accompanying the blotches and the dancing flickering lights behind her eyes.

She stopped and rubbed her forehead, trying to focus on the strange noises that seemed to emanate from inside her own skull, yet drew her in a very specific direction. Was she hearing things, or was she hearing *something?* It was hard to tell one from the other.

Putting down her basket, she made her way towards the tumbledown stables which had long since been converted to general storage. For a moment she thought the sound was coming from the shed, until she realised that the strange vibration was emanating from some place near the cliffs, just beyond the peeling wooden fence marking the boundary of her property.

She ducked under the sun-blasted wooden rail and promptly stopped. She wasn't sure if migraines caused hallucinations, but that distant buzzing hum had somehow evolved into a very distinct sound, a sound that she and all mothers knew only too well.

It was the sound of a child crying.

It couldn't be not out here surely? On the other hand, it wouldn't be the first time some kid had got lost or…*oh God, the cliffs!* Her headache forgotten, Yasmina ran towards the cliff edge, careful not to slip on the loose stones and dry dusty earth as the ground began to tilt downwards.

"Honey, where are you? I can hear you, just hold on."

Puzzled, she looked around, searching for the source of the sound. It was close, but she still couldn't see anything. "Don't worry, I'm here. Can you wave your hand?" She slowly walked towards a parched and wind-dried patch of scrub. "It's okay, it's okay. Just take it easy, I won't hurt you." She reached out and parted the tinder dry foliage, fully expecting to find a small child huddled beneath it.

The crying promptly stopped.

Confused and concerned, Yasmina walked around the edge of the scrub and looked in at a different angle. "Don't be frightened, honey. You're safe now."

Nothing.

She swallowed hard and felt the hairs on her neck stand straight. Something was very wrong, and she had to fight against a sudden urge to back away, return to the inn and pretend the whole thing had never happened. Why was she even feeling like that? What kind of woman, what kind of *mother* would turn her back on a frightened child? She pushed through the gorse, aiming for what looked like a dark shadow at the base of a large, flat rock.

Sure enough, she soon found herself peering into a small void beneath the smooth stone, probably caused by water flowing down towards the cliff edge. "Don't be frightened, honey; I'm here." Yaz reached into the darkened hole and felt something soft. Taking a firm grip, she pulled what she thought was a terrified child out into the early morning sunlight.

The object of her search was much lighter than she'd anticipated, meaning that she soon ended up on her backside as the result of pulling way too hard. She barely noticed the sharp stones and gorse branches that she stared mystified at the small rucksack that somebody had obviously hidden beneath the rock.

She stood up and looked around again but still there was only silence. "Honey, can you hear me? Can you shout out?"

Nothing; only the restless breeze hurrying through the parched undergrowth.

❦

Laying down flat, she reached under the rock once more, her hand searching every part of the void beneath, but there was nothing else.

She turned her attention to the rucksack, wondering if she should open it or just put it back where she'd found it. After all, it wasn't unheard of for smugglers and criminals to leave stashes of illegal cargo or cash payments close to quiet coastal locations. It wasn't a huge problem in Yasmina's neck of the woods, but it wasn't like it had never happened either.

After minute's deliberation she decided she had to open the bag. She certainly didn't want to be accused of complicity if someone *was* using her property as some sort of stash house. As she looked a little more closely, the mysterious bag seemed kind of familiar, but she couldn't place where she might have seen it. Most likely it had been carried in by a patron, but she couldn't be certain.

She reached out for the plastic clasp, wondering why her hand had begun shaking and her back was suddenly soaked with sweat. She hesitated; overcome with a sudden wave of fear that she couldn't really account for.

Get a grip, girl! What would your sister think if she saw you shaking at the sight of some tatty old bag? Just open the dam thing first and then figure out what needs to be done.

She withdrew her hand, swallowed hard, then quickly reached forward again, un-buckling the simple clasp and throwing open the top before she lost her nerve again. For a few long seconds she just sat there, staring in mute incomprehension as she tried to comprehend what she was seeing, or rather *not* seeing.

At last, she remembered to breathe, taking a long, gasping lungful of air as she stared into...into...*what?* What *was* she actually looking at? She rubbed her eyes and tried to keep them focused as she stared into the impossible dark nothingness somehow contained within the nylon walls of that little knockoff rucksack.

Shaking her head to dislodge the buzzing whine in the centre of her skull, Yaz gingerly reached forward, snatching her hand back as her fingers contacted...something. She put her other hand to her chest as she felt her heart beating against her ribs, forcing herself to breathe slowly and she tried to still her shaking fingers. It was hard to remain focused on that strange, buzzing emptiness as it tricked the eye and blurred the vision, defying the mind tried to map out the division between something and nothing...except that the nothing was actually *something!* She could touch it, she could feel some kind of cloth against her fingertips as she reached into that endless blackness and grasped a handful of infinity, bringing it out into the sunlight and staring mystified at the hole in the world that wavered in the breeze right in front of her.

The blanket, for want of a better word, defied all rational description as it remained completely impervious to the bright dawn sun, that infinite darkness swallowing every point of light that dared intrude on its surface.

Yasmina just stared, mesmerised as her forearm completely vanished behind the impossible nothingness she held in her hand, its edges erasing the world and then restoring it as the nothingness moved and rippled just like a blanket would. She barely registered that her migraine was at full force as she stared unblinking into...into, what should she call it? Was it a trick, an illusion, something magical? Perhaps it was the doorway into another world, perhaps some wonderful place or maybe an endless plateau of pain and suffering? There was no way to know anything as she willed the impossible object to reveal some hint as to its true nature and purpose.

Yasmina would never know whether the change had come from within her or whether the impossible blanket was some kind of dark mirror, drawing out and reflecting the deepest depths of her own pain, loneliness and despair. The shift in her consciousness was subtle at first, so subtle that she barely noticed her own thoughts slowly moving towards her long-lost son. It was true that she thought of Samuel every single day, but this was different somehow. Just like the wavering emptiness before her, the thoughts in her mind also defied description, as though somehow that endless inky blackness was drawing those ideas and memories from some deeply hidden wellspring inside of her.

Yasmina felt her face begin to burn as the thoughts of her long-lost son became sharper and clearer, crowding in on her and clamouring

❀

for ever more space on the screen of her mind as images and sounds rushed faster and faster. Fond memories and long forgotten moments merged into a growing cacophony of uncontrollable and unbearable melancholy.

She could hear herself sobbing freely, yet she was strangely detached as she watched her little boy's life stretch out in a single instant, from the day he was born until the day he vanished. He was right there, she could see him, hear him and even smell him as the tornado of images crowded everything out and drowned her mind in one single, unifying thought. *Samuel!*

* * *

"Sam!" Yasmina winced and put her hand to her chest, gasping against the sharp pain that knotted tightly inside her ribs. Her mind raced as she struggled to breathe. *Is this a heart attack? Can't be I've only just turned thirty! What's happening to me, where am I, where's Sam?*

At last, she drew a ragged, shuddering breath and pushed hard with the heel of her hand as the agony began to subside. Finally, her breathing steadied a little and she slumped back onto the bed.

The bed! She sat bolt upright again, wincing at the pain in her head and chest as she looked around her darkened bedroom. Sunlight streamed between the curtains to charge the heavy, thick and sultry atmosphere.

Confused, she lay back on the bed and grimaced as she realised her whole body was bathed in a sheen of perspiration. For a minute she listened to the thudding of her heart slowly subsiding to a steady beat. When she was satisfied that she wasn't actually suffering from a heart attack, she gingerly swung her feet off the bed and sat up again, not trusting her legs to hold her weight as she tried to figure what was happening.

Slowly the recollections swam back into focus as she saw the image of that impossibly dark fabric in her mind's eye. Everything was hazy after that, with flashes of memories that seemed impossible, yet were as real as the crisp white sheets she'd hung on the line that morning. She felt tears welling up in her eyes once again as she thought of Samuel; his laughter, his childish embrace and even his smell were still with her as though he would come running through the door at any moment.

But it wasn't true though; she knew he was gone and somehow that strange encounter with the rucksack had left her *knowing*, not feeling, that her little boy was truly absent. It was difficult to vocalise or even express as a rational thought, but some force, some *power* had showed her that little Sam no longer dwelled among the living. He wasn't out there somewhere, living some other life because he'd actually passed away some years before.

However, that dark and desolate knowledge was tempered by the understanding that Samuel's passing was not the end. Somehow his essence and maybe the essence of others continued in some strange way that defied description. Samuel was gone and yet he was somehow *not* gone. It was truly heart-breaking to know that she would never see him or hear his voice again, yet the promise of something beyond the mortal realm filled her with a peculiar melancholic calm.

She looked at the clock and was shocked to see it was the middle of the afternoon. She'd lost several hours to that darkness, that *thing* hiding beneath the rock beside the cliffs. Yasmina had no memory of where she'd been or how she'd arrived in her bed, or whether if she'd been anywhere in *this* world at all.

It was all too much, and she already knew that she would learn no more from her strange encounter with something truly otherworldly. She'd unwittingly stared into the abyss, and the abyss had offered up the answers to her deepest, darkest questions. The constant crushing weight of uncertainty was replaced by the searing pain of finality.

Samuel was dead, but there was more to the grave than just the cold dark earth. Perhaps that barbed comfort might let some sort of healing finally begin.

Perhaps.

Yasmina turned onto her side and silently wept.

THE RIDING IN OF AUTUMN

Chapter 12

Solomon yawned and flexed his toes as he stretched out on his leather sofa. It wasn't exactly the most professional demeanour, but it was Sunday, and Sundays were set aside for relaxing and off-the-books business. On this particular Sunday he would be doing both at the same time.

He wasn't looking forward to the upcoming exchange, but he knew he couldn't put it off any longer. He'd let too many things slide already and it was time to start taking control. Maybe he was just putting two and two together and getting five, but he'd learned to trust his instincts over the years, and those instincts were keeping him awake at night. It was time to act.

He sat up and straightened his shirt as the office door opened and Seth filled the doorway, looking oddly incongruous in a gaudy Hawaiian shirt, blue jeans and battered straw hat. Solomon made a conscious effort not to smile as for some reason that old straw hat made him think of a faithful old donkey plodding along in the sun, although Seth was nothing of the kind. A tank painted bright pink was still a tank after all.

Seth stepped forward and closed the door behind him.

Solomon rose and crossed to the small bar area built into a dark wooden cabinet. "Coffee?"

Seth didn't move. "No thanks, I'm good."

Solomon shrugged as he poured himself a cup. Seth never accepted coffee, let alone alcohol, but it never hurt to offer. It was just good manners and good business. "How was church?"

"It was good. There was a really thoughtful sermon on divided loyalties; you'd have enjoyed it."

"Yeah well, I like my churches quiet, you know that." Solomon always fell back on that line if the subject of church came up. It also happened to be true that Solomon *did* much prefer churches when there was nobody in them. After all, they were interesting places crammed full of history, mystery and folklore. He'd often wondered if he could be a religious man; not that he considered himself irreligious, but like so many people he just really didn't know what to make of all that stuff.

"Is there a problem?"

Seth's deep bass voice jolted Solomon from his introspection. "No problem, just a delicate situation."

Seth clasped his large hands together; his signal to show that he was paying attention.

With his coffee prepared, Solomon crossed back to his desk and perched himself against it. "I need you to make some discreet enquiries for me."

"Sure, no problem. Who's the subject?"

"Our creative culinary friend, you know, the one who seems to be everyone's best buddy all of a sudden."

Seth's face remained inscrutable. "Nathaniel? Is there something going on?"

Solomon looked thoughtfully into his coffee. "Maybe; maybe not. You must've heard about his run-in at the restaurant by now."

Seth's nod of confirmation was almost imperceptible.

Solomon continued. "Seems like he and Kal have some history, and it's not a happy one."

"Am I missing something?"

Solomon shot the big man a rueful look. "Come on, Seth; you can't play the big dumb mule with me. Kal's got some heavy connections, which means Nathaniel might have some heavy connections too."

Seth spread his hands as he spoke. "He's a writer. Writers know all kinds of people."

"Yeah maybe, but the trouble is I can't find a single thing written by him, and if he's using an alias, he hides it well. Not only that, but his house is also registered to some sort of trust and as far as I can tell, he has no legitimate source of income."

Seth's face moved noticeably for the first time as his eyebrows rose.

"He doesn't look like kingpin material if you ask me."

"You're probably right, but there's *something* about that guy. Nothing about him adds up and that makes me nervous."

With his instructions issued, Seth turned to leave. "Sure thing, it'll take a few days to get the initial info together. Trawling deeper will take longer than that, you know how it goes."

"Just bring me what you've got when you get it and I'll figure out if we need to dig further."

"Sure thing." Seth stepped back through the double doors and closed them quietly behind him.

Solomon stared at the doors, wondering if the big man had bought his story. There was no reason why he should doubt it, after all it was at least half true. Seth was a smart guy though, despite his musclebound jarhead routine. He was certainly smart enough not to question his employer's motives despite what he might think personally. Solomon consoled himself with the fact that it didn't really make much difference either way. Seth was reliable and very discreet, he just wished he could say the same about his own fiancée.

* * *

Nathaniel frowned as he watched Sarah glance nervously at the window for the hundredth time. She'd been jumpy all night, her eyes flicking back-and-forth as the glint of headlights passed along the main road. The sparse traffic was barely visible from the farmhouse, but nonetheless she kept her nervous vigil as she tried to look relaxed and pretend, she was enjoying her meal.

At last, she put down her knife and fork, her tasty Caesar salad only half eaten. "Sorry, I'm just not as hungry as I thought I was."

Nathaniel patiently reached for the wine bottle as Sarah emptied her glass in two large gulps. "You know, you're gonna fall over if you keep chugging this stuff like it's beer." He poured her another large glass.

She giggled nervously and took another mouthful. "Sometimes I wish he'd just come storming in right now. At least it would be over." She sighed and cast her eyes around Nathaniel's rambling home. You know, this place is beautiful, like something out of a dream. It's like I've been here forever, like *we've* been here forever. I always knew you could make it work, and I always knew I'd bring you trouble if we ever met again."

He placed his napkin on the table, picked up his wineglass and wandered across to the window. "Well, there's no Range Rover tearing down the drive tonight, which is a good thing because we've got a lot of catching up to do." He crossed the large open-plan space to a comfortable-looking sofa positioned in front of a dark and silent TV set, patting the back of it as he invited his long-lost love to join him.

She was there in seconds, her head nuzzling into his chest. "This is all I ever wanted, I'm so happy but I'm so scared it could all just end at any moment."

Nathaniel took a sip of wine and stroked her hair. "Sounds pretty much like business as usual. Step out the door one morning; car crash, heart attack, aneurysm, violent crime, stupid accident, you name it. Anything could end at any time, just like anything new can begin at any time."

"It's not the same. A sudden heart attack is nothing like knowing that sooner or later Solomon's going to find out that his fiancée's cheating on him, if he doesn't know already."

Nathaniel conceded. "Yeah, you're right, bad analogy."

She looked up at him, her eyes wide and moist. "Why don't we just pack up and go? Why can't we just leave?"

Nathaniel's expression changed, becoming more thoughtful and introspective. He gestured around his charmingly neglected rambling farmhouse. "This is my *something*, the something I created for me, and now for us. I don't know what's going to happen, but I'll be damned if I ever choose between you and nothing again. Other people can manage both and I want the same thing as everyone else, dammit."

Sarah persisted. "But surely you could sell this place. Must be worth a fair bit."

"Like I said, it's worth a lot more than just money." Nathaniel drained his glass and stood up, thrusting his hands into his pockets. "Right about now I'm supposed to do the whole big-hatted Texan millionaire routine, telling you how I came here with nothing but the clothes on my back and five bucks in my pocket. I wish I *could* say that it would be a great story, but the truth is a lot more complicated."

"I don't understand." Sarah frowned with confusion.

After a long silence, Nathaniel took a deep breath. "I thought you were dead, and looking back, I think a part of me died that night too."

"What night? Talk to me, Nathaniel."

He crossed back to the table and grabbed the wine bottle. He refilled both their glasses, shaking the last drops out before placing it on the cracked and rustic wooden mantle. "You know very well what night; it was the last night you and I spoke."

Sarah was quiet for a few seconds. "I looked for you, honestly, I did. Where did you go? I know you quit your job."

Nathaniel chortled into his glass. "I didn't quit, I was fired; I mean they must've fired me at some point."

"You're confusing me, what happened to you?" Now Sarah took a sip of wine.

There was another long silence as Nathaniel considered his words. "I was skipping work that night, sloping off just to call you because I was worried."

Sarah nodded. "I remember."

Nathaniel continued. "I could tell you'd been down for some time, and you were getting worse. I just couldn't reach you, and I'm pretty good at reaching people most of the time. You'd just drifted so far away I thought it was too late. All that talk of the ocean and feeling like you were drowning; well, what was I supposed to do?"

Sarah said nothing, not wanting to interrupt her lover's confession.

Nathaniel continued. "So, I forgot about my work and set out to prove there's no future in nihilism. You can probably guess how *that* went. I got to your place, but you weren't there, just a half-finished email explaining why it had to end."

Sarah gently took Nathaniel's hand. "I spent that night wandering the streets, wondering about the finality of the end, wondering if the abyss could be anything other than darkness and peace."

Nathaniel gave a short, bitter laugh. "I guess we nearly found ourselves in a romantic movie, maybe if I'd turned right instead of left, I'd have bumped into you as the music swelled, but I didn't. I just kept wandering different streets, streets I'd never seen before."

"I looked for you, I mean later, but the restaurant said you never came back, and I didn't know where else to go. Why would you never tell me where you lived?" Sarah reached for a box of tissues on a low coffee table and dabbed at her eyes. "What happened; where did you go?"

For a while Nathaniel said nothing as he stared into the empty dark fireplace. "It's hard to explain, but I didn't go anywhere. I remember it was getting light when I wandered into a bar and, well, you can imagine how *that* went. Maybe it was some kind of psychotic episode, I don't know, but I wasn't thinking straight. You left your life behind and that's all *I* wanted to do as well. I guess I could lay on some shrink's couch for hours while he lectured me about how I was dealing with suppressed trauma and all the rest, and he might even be right, but it wouldn't change anything that's happened."

Sarah persisted, albeit gently. "So, where *did* you go?"

"Like I told you, I went nowhere. Maybe I just wanted to follow you into the darkness, and I didn't have the courage to admit it to myself. I don't know, all I'm *really* sure of is that I wanted nothing from this world after you'd left it. In a nutshell, I spent my time wandering the streets, drinking and debating with the other lost souls who live in the shadows."

Sarah swallowed hard, her voice trembling as she asked her next question. "And you did all this just because of me?"

Nathaniel sighed heavily. "I don't think so, but I guess believing you were never coming back was the proverbial straw and I just couldn't take anything else, not on top of Trinity College and Benjamin and all the rest. Maybe some part of me just wanted to go back to where I felt safe and anonymous as the tourists and the commuters passed me by. I don't think I'll ever know for sure why I acted that way, and I guess it doesn't really matter in the grand scheme. Now I'm here and so are you." He smiled at last. "Hey, maybe we'll get that rom-com ending after all. Maybe we were just playing out the first act back in

Barcelona. Maybe."

Sarah blew her nose and stood up, crossing slowly to the small, tiled kitchen area, where she reached into a rustic wooden rack and extracted another bottle of wine. "But you're here now, *we're* here now, so something must have changed. Something must have happened to get you back on track. I mean this might not be a palace, but it sure as hell isn't a shop doorway either." She began fiddling with a corkscrew.

Nathaniel's response was soft and matter-of-fact. "Father Mullen happened."

Sarah finished twisting the corkscrew and brought the bottle across for Nathaniel to open. "Well, life with you is never boring, my love; and I guess this is the part where you tell me who the heck Father Mullen is."

Nathaniel popped the cork and poured them both another large glass. Sitting back on the sofa, he turned his wineglass in his fingers before speaking. "Father Mullen saved my life, probably twice. He was the one who reached out to me after Ben died. I was a real mess back then, just some-snot nosed teenager with no home, no family and no future. When I wasn't stealing buns from bakeries, I was chalking poems on walls and sidewalks. Tourists used to give me bits of change and I managed to get by; but I was existing, not living. Then one day this tall Irish priest strolled by and gave me five euros for one of my poems. That was Father Mullen. After that he came by almost every day with the same deal, a new poem for five euros. I didn't trust him much at first, especially with *my* history, but over the weeks we got to talking and I told him how I'd grown up at St Gemma's and then transferred to Trinity. Of course, I left out some important details, like Ben, but all the same he never seemed to judge me."

Sarah rubbed her forehead. "Wait a minute, just back up a second. How old were you when you first met this, Father Mullen?"

"A little over fifteen."

"And you'd been living rough in Barcelona for how long?"

"About six months, give or take."

She took a sip of wine as her forehead creased with concentration. "So, what happened to Kal; what about Trinity College?"

Nathaniel just shrugged. "No idea really. I spent the first few weeks constantly looking over my shoulder. Every cop and every guy who looked like he might be from Trinity made me nervous, but after a while I started to realise that nobody was interested. Maybe Ben's death scared them off but I'm not really sure. All I know for certain is that nobody came looking after that day, even though I would've been pretty easy to find. After all they found Ben and me quickly enough the first time around."

"What happened then, what changed your mind about this priest, Father Mullen?"

"By the time autumn blew through I was ready to hear Mullen's offer of a bed and a place at, you guessed it, yet another institution. Of course, I'd had it by then and I told him so. Then he offered me a compromise, a spare room in his apartment and some paid work to go with it."

Sarah took another sip of wine. "What, like some sort of housekeeper?"

"Keeping the place clean and tidy was part of the deal, but that wasn't what I was being paid for. You see, Father Mullen suffered from some sort of neurological disorder. Apparently, it was pretty exotic, and I never did catch its proper name, plus he made it clear the subject was off limits. He did a good job of hiding it although his speech was affected sometimes. On a bad day he'd get the shakes and he struggled to do things with his hands, like writing. He used to have really bad nightmares as well, and he started seeing things towards the end."

"The end?"

Nathaniel raised his hands. "Hey, let's not jump ahead just yet. Anyway, that was my life, at least for most of my teens. I'd look after Mullen's place, which was pretty easy, and I'd transcribe these notes and tape recordings he used to bring back."

"What was *that* all about?" Sarah cocked her head, curious.

Nathaniel began circling the room, pacing slowly. "Despite his health problems he travelled a lot, and quite often without his collar. I asked him about that, and he said the church sometimes worked undercover, just like cops. Anyhow, he used to bring me all these tape recordings and handwritten notes of people telling their life stories."

"I'm no expert, but that all sounds pretty strange for a priest. Didn't he have a parish or something?" Sarah asked with a puzzled tone.

"He couldn't do regular church duties because of his health, so he had other work instead. Yeah, maybe it was strange, but it was all fairly mundane from my viewpoint. Just a collection of biographies."

"Whose biographies?"

"I never really knew. Oh, sure there would be names and places like a city or a town, but there were never any really specific details. Father Mullen just said it was a history project for something called the Mormon Foundation, although the stories came from far and wide and didn't seem to be connected. Sometimes they were in English and sometimes you could hear two voices, the storyteller and an interpreter. I remember hearing Spanish, Japanese I think, and what sounded like Russian. Plus, there was every English dialect you can think of. After a while, taking care of Mullen's apartment and writing up the notes he brought me became my routine, and you know what, it was just fine."

Sarah's response was slow and thoughtful. "Okay, so how long did *that* go on for?"

A little over four years, but then things started to get kind of difficult. "For starters, Mullen was just getting older and sicker. His shakes were getting worse, and he'd started drinking heavily by that time. Yeah, I know, a drunken Irish priest; but I have to tell it like it was. Now I don't know if it was the booze or the illness or the medication, but he started hallucinating."

"You mean…"

Nathaniel nodded. "Yeah, he started seeing things that weren't there, even talking to them sometimes."

Sarah's eyes narrowed. "What *kinds* of things?"

Nathaniel was silent for a while, his lips pursed as he considered his response. "Angels, demons, ghosts, the past, the future, all of it. He always said there were two worlds, the visible and the invisible, overlapping and constantly colliding. He claimed it was his job to glimpse the invisible and to bring the message back to others."

Sarah stood up as she was jolted by a sudden memory. "Wait a minute, you said he was tall, did he have a big bushy beard?"

Nathaniel nodded.

"Oh my God, I knew him! Well, I knew who he was. He used to do a kind of circuit around Barcelona. He used to just point at random people and tell them stuff about their lives, stuff he couldn't possibly know unless he'd followed them for months on end. Everyone thought he was crazy, but I remember one day he called out to some random guy in a business suit and said something about his father's old sea chest. The thing I remember most is how the colour just drained from that man's face. He didn't hang around either, nobody ever did."

Nathaniel poured himself some more wine and topped up Sarah's glass. "Yeah, he got around. Anyhow, I don't know exactly what happened, but he suffered some sort of break or episode and he ended up in hospital for quite a while. In fact, they flew him all the way to Rome to take care of him."

Sarah frowned as she thought back. "Yeah, I seem to recall he just kind of vanished one day, before we met, I think. Rome huh? I guess crazy old Father Mullen must have had some serious pull with the church."

"You're telling me! It isn't every day you get a visit from a full-blown cardinal."

Sarah's eyes widened.

"Honest to God. I hadn't seen Mullen for a couple of days and so I started ringing around the usual places, cops, hospitals and such. I was almost at the end of my list when there was a knock at the door and there he was, Cardinal Buttoni, complete with dog collar, Italian accent and even a red scarf around his neck. To cut a long story short he told me that Mullen was in good hands in Rome and that I was to look after his place while he was gone. He seemed to know all about me and all about Mullen's work as well. I suppose it figures really. He told me that I was to call his office if I had any problems, he even gave me his card." Nathaniel crossed to a sturdy if battered sideboard and rummaged in a drawer. After a few moments he handed a creased and worn looking business card to Sarah.

"Wow! I had no idea that cardinals have business cards." Sarah held the card incredulously between her fingers. "So, this is kind of a Vatican hotline?"

"So, the man said, but to be honest I've never had a good enough excuse to call it."

Sarah placed the card on the coffee table. "Then what became of Father Mullen?"

"He just came back, just like that."

She blinked, surprised by Nathaniel's reply. "But you said he was ill."

"So he was, but he got himself juiced up with some sort of fancy treatment in Rome because he just turned up one day." Nathaniel's eyes fell. "It was really embarrassing too because it was about a month after I'd lost you, or at least I *thought* I had. I was in a real state then, constantly drunk and thinking about ending it all myself. Most of the time I never even bothered going home. The idea of comfort seemed just…well, unworthy somehow. The Foundation had sent me some work, but I just chucked it all in a pile and left it. The whole world could go to hell in a handcart as far as I was concerned. Then Mullen just turned up one day, as though he'd just returned from one of his jaunts to collect somebody's story."

Sarah shook her head and held up her hand. "Wait a second, back up. Was he okay? I'm no doctor but I'm pretty sure that's the sort of thing they can't cure."

Nathaniel looked down at the carpet again. "No, they can't. Basically, he'd received first class care in Rome which I believe involved some sort of experimental medication. He'd volunteered for some research project on the condition that he could come home. Apparently, the trade-off was that he'd feel much better for longer, but he'd deteriorate faster at the end. So that was the decision he'd made, and from my point of view he didn't arrive a moment too soon. That's how Father Mullen saved my life a second time. He squared everything with the Foundation and told me I could stay as long as I liked, on two conditions."

Sarah reached for the wine bottle. "I'm guessing the first was that you stopped drinking, at least to excess."

"Right, and the second was that I did one last transcription job, one last story to tell."

Sarah's response was quiet but matter of fact. "Your own."

Nathaniel nodded slowly. "Obviously we'd talked over the years, so he pretty much knew the story, but he said the Foundation was interested in my life's history. He also said it would be good for me, a kind of therapy and exorcism rolled into one."

"So, you did it?"

"Of course, I did it, why wouldn't I do it? You know it's funny, but I took my time, and I *almost* enjoyed the experience, what with trying to find some new meaning in my life and taking care of the one man who'd been there for me when the whole world had cast me aside."

Sarah gently put her hand on his shoulder. "I'm guessing that Father Mullen passed away eventually."

"Not long after I'd finished my last assignment. A part of me wonders if he was just holding on to make sure I'd finished the job. Whatever the case, being a priest, he had no family, so he left me everything."

Sarah was quiet for a good while as she digested Nathaniel's story. At last, she spoke softly. "So that's how a man can vanish and go nowhere at the same time. No wonder you'd never take me to your place."

"Yeah, sharing an apartment with an ageing priest just invites too many questions, even if he was in Rome at the time. I was very wary back then and I couldn't exactly erase his presence from the place. I still am wary I guess, it's just that I can't risk losing you again."

She rested her head on his chest. "I don't know about karma, God's great plan, chance or any of that stuff. What I *do* know is that we've somehow managed to find each other through all the chaos and the pain and I'll never let you go again."

Nathaniel stroked her hair gently. "You'll have to be getting home soon, your fiancé will wonder where you are."

THE RIDING IN OF WINTER
Chapter 13

Solomon leaned back in his chair and took a long, deep breath. Damn, that woman could cook! He drummed his fingers on the battered tabletop as he let the expectation of an excellent meal both relax and fill him with anticipation. Whoever said that the surest way to a man's heart was through his stomach must've known a thing or two after all. He'd have scoffed at such an idea just a few years ago, defaulting to his reductionist outlook of physical prowess and material success. Maybe it was just age, but perhaps for the first time, Solomon began to *kind* of see why so many of his fellow men sought solace and security in the simple pleasures of hearth and home.

Maybe it really was an inevitable by-product of the ageing process, as inescapable as greying hair, or an increased world-weariness. After all, Solomon had never imagined himself settling down, yet here he was engaged to be married. Okay, so the fact that he was in another woman's kitchen still marked him out as a serious player, but he could no longer deny at least a small measure of empathy for family men.

He smiled as his mistress bustled in with a basket of bread. "Smells good, what's cooking?"

Yasmina smiled back. "Something special; after all, it's a special evening."

Solomon watched appreciatively as she sashayed back into the kitchen. He couldn't think of any particular reason why it should be a special meal. It wasn't anyone's birthday or anniversary, at least that he was aware of. All the same, Yaz did seem different somehow. He couldn't put his finger on exactly what it was, but his often-needy mistress seemed more composed, more together, more…present than he'd ever seen her. For a moment his blood ran cold as he wondered if she might be pregnant. After all, pregnancy often had that kind of ill-defined effect on a woman as her systems geared up to fulfil their most fundamental biological role.

However, after thinking for a minute or two, Solomon dismissed the idea as both of them were always very careful in that department. All the same, that thought had left a nagging doubt that something was definitely up.

The door to the little private parlour swung open again and in she floated once more, accompanied by a plume of good-smelling steam as she placed two dishes of hot vegetables on the table.

Solomon instantly recognised them as the same solid yet tasty offerings that Yaz and her sister knocked up for the Green Lizard's patrons. It was all good though, and he wasn't about to turn down a fine meal with a sexy lady. Of course, it meant that Ermina was running the place for the evening, and would no doubt be running her mouth for the rest of the week.

With candles lit, Yaz bustled out again, leaving Solomon to wonder why Sarah never questioned him more closely about his evenings with Yasmina. Maybe she never asked because she didn't want to hear the answer, or maybe she just understood that he was the kind of guy who needed more than one woman in his life. Deep down he knew he'd have to break it off with Yaz, and sooner rather than later. After all, he was looking to get married, and he knew that he should at least make *some* effort to be faithful. He'd miss her of course; Yasmina was simple and free and uncomplicated, even though she was a little clingy from time to time.

At last, the food arrived, and Solomon felt his mouth water as Yasmina reappeared with a perfectly cooked steak sizzling on a hot plate, the steam from some fresh pepper sauce quickly filling the room with its hunger-inducing fragrance.

"That smells really good." Solomon playfully slapped her on the rump as she turned to place her own grilled chicken on the table and take her seat.

Yaz giggled as she slid seductively into her chair and picked up her wine glass. "Here's to a bright future, built on a solid past."

"Sure." Solomon raised his glass at her somewhat cryptic toast before unrolling his napkin and picking up his cutlery. "You planning on building something bright on something solid?" He knew Yasmina well enough to realise that she had something to say, but it was different this time. More than once, he'd had to untangle himself from her desire for them to be a public and permanent item, although that didn't seem to be what she was thinking as she took a small mouthful of grilled chicken.

Yaz waited a few minutes before she spoke again. "You know, despite all the time we've shared together, there's one thing I've never asked you before. Do you *believe* in anything?"

Solomon swallowed a large chunk of steak, surprised by the strange question. "You mean like God or something?"

"Sure, if you want to put it that way. I guess what I'm asking is, do you think there's more to this world, this life, than what we can see and hear, and maybe even just think about?"

"Never really thought about it." Solomon didn't want to get into a lengthy conversation about strange and supernatural things. It was weird enough when Seth went off on one from time to time.

Yaz fell silent again as she chewed her chicken, then she changed tack. "You know you mean all the world to me, Solomon Vaughan; but *your* world is just   too small."

Solomon wondered if this was a lead into some kind of breakup speech. He hadn't seen anything like that coming and he knew he was pretty good at reading women. All the same, Yaz had been acting strange of late so nothing would surprise him. In fact, the only unexpected turn of events was that his mistress might dump *him*, which was something he'd never envisaged happening. "Something wrong; what happened?"

"Nothing's wrong, my dear, gorgeous, troublesome lover. Things *have* been wrong for a very long time, but now everything's been made right."

Solomon raised his eyebrows, maybe she really *was* about to dump him after all.

Yaz reached for her glass of wine and took a long sip. "You remember when we first met?"

❁

"Sure, it was the best midnight swim I've ever had." Solomon couldn't help but smile at the memory of their impromptu liaison in the ocean. It seemed like a very long time ago.

Yaz smiled coyly as she carefully placed her wine glass on the table. "So, I guess you must remember what you did after that night."

So, there it was, it looked like Yasmina was mad because he never came back for more. That was pretty standard for the women he'd known, but still he wondered if this was just a warmup for some sort of explosion. It wouldn't be the first time. "Hey, listen, I'd already made a whole bunch of plans and there was a whole bunch of people relying on me. Anyway, you know what happened. I took my diving school to Sharm el-Sheikh and came back to Barcelona when my visa ran out. I've told you that before, so what gives?"

A half-smile played on Yasmina's lips as she daintily chewed on another small piece of chicken, taking her time before she finally answered.

"Same old Solomon, that's just typical of you."

"What's typical?"

She leaned back in her chair, gently swinging the long stem of her wine glass like a pendulum. "Solomon Vaughan; so handsome, so confident. What it must be like to walk in those Italian shoes, to know that men admire you and women adore you; well, most of them anyway. You have everything a man could desire, a beautiful home, a loving fiancé, plus a devoted and discreet mistress. Always pushing forward, wanting more, knowing that you deserve it; always looking ahead and never looking back. Well, you can't can you? One glance over your shoulder and you may catch sight of the wreckage, despair and destruction you've left in your wake."

"Just wait…"

Yasmina's tone hardened as the muscles in her face stiffened. "Kiss the girls and make them cry, because you just know they'll come running right after you. I suppose I can't blame you really. That kind of power would be enough to turn anyone's head, but all the same I'd hoped you'd at least have thrown a word of curiosity my way."

Solomon closed his eyes as he realised his mistake. She had a point, even though she strangely seemed to think he owed her something. All the same, it would be a shame to split up over something so trivial, especially with Sarah acting so strange lately. No way did he love Yasmina, but he couldn't deny he'd be sad if she broke it off. "Okay, so you got me, guilty as charged."

"All this time and you never *once* thought to ask. You're not a bad man, Solomon Vaughan, but boy are you shallow."

"If you want depth, go date a philosopher."

Yasmina clasped her hands together beneath her chin as a muffled burst of laughter erupted from the distant bar. "I care for you deeply, Solomon, you know that. I wish that just once, you'd have been interested in *my* story."

So, the mistress was feeling unloved and unappreciated. It was understandable and also easy to fix. "Well, I guess I should've listened to your story long before now, but it's never too late."

Yaz shook her head sadly, although her expression was a peculiar blend of curiosity and certainty. "It's far too late for some things, like your son, for example."

Solomon tried not to spit out his steak. He knew Yaz was a bit of a dreamer, but he'd never figured her for that kind of by-the-numbers scheme. "So, let's hear it then."

"I'll never forget how strong and handsome you were, like a Greek God from an ancient tale of love, betrayal and heroism. I wanted you that night like nothing else I've ever wanted, and I've never regretted my decision."

Here it comes, thought Solomon. "But…"

"There is no but, at least there wasn't straight away. Okay, so a part of me always knew you would take me and then leave me behind as you have with so many other girls. I'm not mad about that as I can make my own choices and I always knew who you really were. But when I found out I was carrying your child it became a very different situation."

Solomon opened his mouth to demand proof of Yasmina's earth-shattering claim, then closed it again. Better to let her spin the whole unlikely yarn before he decided what to do. He was surprised to find

❁

191

that what bothered him most was saying goodbye to Yaz's steaks, and she cooked a mean steak. Hell, maybe she was right, maybe he really *was* shallow after all.

Yasmina stared at her philandering lover intently. "Wow, you really *didn't* know that, did you? I thought maybe you would've found out, as I know how keen you are on doing your homework. You know, I was about to say how sorry I am to just drop it on you like this, but that's not true. Sure, it might be a surprise to *you*, but this is something *I've* lived every day for years now, so my empathy is in pretty short supply."

"So where is this child then? Haven't seen any kids around here." Solomon folded his arms defiantly and leaned back in his chair.

"*Samuel!* His name was Samuel!" Yasmina spat out her son's name, her voice quivering with barely controlled fury.

Solomon tilted his head. "Was?"

Yasmina drained her wineglass in two large gulps. "Yeah, he died."

"I guess that means you don't have to prove he ever existed."

Yasmina's knuckles whitened for a few seconds before she breathed out and pushed her shaking hands hard onto the table. For a moment there was a tense silence before she stood up and crossed to a small sideboard next to the kitchen door. She quickly extracted an old candy tin and dumped it on the table, scratching the surface and rattling cutlery.

Solomon swallowed nervously. "What's this?"

Yasmina's response was calm, cold, flat. "It's your son."

Deciding to play along, Solomon opened the box and peered inside. To his surprise it was virtually empty, save for two folded pieces of paper. He took them out and laid them side-by-side on the table, his steak all but forgotten. His frown deepened as his eyes flicked first from a Spanish birth certificate and then to a Barcelona police report.

The room was silent, save for the muffled conversation from the distant bar and the nervous tapping of Yasmina's fingernails on the stem of her wineglass.

At length Solomon re-folded the papers and tossed them back into the box. He ran his hands over his face before he spoke again. "So, let me see if I've got this right. You're telling me that the kid in that birth certificate and the police report are the same. You're telling me we had a son together, but you never bothered to mention it until now. Not only that, but this so-called son was kidnapped while he was still a toddler. *Then* you're telling me the police couldn't track down any significant suspects, save for some hapless schmuck they ruled out early on."

For a moment Yasmina continued tapping on the stem of her glass. "You know, they say love is blind, and it must be true because I've only just realised how much of a callous bastard you really are, Solomon Vaughan."

Solomon bristled. "Yeah well, this wouldn't be the first time someone's tried to gouge me one way or another. I thought maybe you were different, but I guess I was wrong about that."

"You mean different from your fiancé?"

He shook his head sadly and stood up. "I'm outta here but call me if this non-existent son of mine ever shows up. I'd be curious to meet him."

The tapping suddenly stopped. "Don't worry, Samuel won't be turning up to cramp your style. He's dead, so I guess that gets you off the hook."

Solomon frowned. "No death certificate in that there box. I'm pretty sure you need to have one of those if someone's died."

"There is no death certificate, and there's not going to *be* a death certificate. Ever!"

"Why is that, because he's not really dead, or because he was never really alive in the first place?" Solomon recoiled as Yasmina's wine glass shattered against his forehead. "Jesus Christ, woman! You could've taken my eye out! Damn, I'm bleeding!" He pulled out his handkerchief and dabbed at the blood pooling above his right eye.

Yasmina's tone was scornful as she picked up her plate of chicken and salad to launch it at her lover. "I guess now you'll have to think up another new lie to tell your wonderful, devoted fiancé." She threw the plate as hard as she could.

Solomon ducked and quickly glanced behind him as the plate shattered against the wall. "You're crazy! You're out of your mind!"

Yaz snatched up the bottle of wine. "I must've been crazy to think you'd *ever* give a damn about anyone but yourself."

The door opened and Ermina poked her head in. "Hey what's all…"

"*Get out!*" Yasmina screamed at her sister.

Ermina didn't need telling twice and hurriedly closed the door, leaving the two of them alone again.

Yasmina pointed a shaking finger at the door. "Now I have to apologise to my sister, the only person to have stood by me through this whole sorry mess." She slumped back into her chair as though all her energy had suddenly been expelled via her outburst. She looked for her wine glass and laughed bitterly when she realised it was in a thousand pieces. "And to think I followed you here, hoping for…actually, you know what, I don't know what an earth I *was* hoping for. They say that losing a child is a traumatic thing and women tend to go a bit crazy. Well, I guess I went plenty crazy, but now I can see clearly again." She stared hard at her lover. "Your son, *our* son, lived and died without ever seeing his father's face. You're no man, you're nothing. You're just a horny teenager who got lucky, and that's all you'll ever be, Solomon Vaughan. Well, you might have a shiny car and that concrete cube you call a house, but the Green Lizard is *my* place and you're not welcome. Get the hell out of here, and don't you ever *think* of coming back. And by the way, you can tell that trained gorilla of yours not to come sniffing around either. Not one of you empty people will ever frighten or impress me again!"

Solomon looked at the blood on his handkerchief and pressed it back to his forehead. "You're crazy! You're fucking insane!" He made quickly for the door lest another piece of crockery should fly in his direction.

Yasmina listened to Solomon's receding footsteps as the tears finally welled up. "Damn you, Solomon Vaughan! Damn you for making me love you!"

THE RIDING IN OF SPRING
Chapter 14

Hyienna took a swig of beer and stared morosely over the dark, brooding ocean. The first breeze of early autumn whipped the surf into small glittering peaks illuminated by a huge harvest moon. It was truly a magical sight and Hyienna knew full well how fortunate he was to be sitting on a quiet clifftop and enjoying such a perfect evening. Not only was the evening perfect, but his relationship with Kate was blossoming by the day; plus, Nathaniel was good company and was fast becoming a friend. Even Solomon seemed to have backed off a bit, going so far as to make an indirect mention of some work coming up, maybe. All in all, things were working out pretty well on Formentera…so why the hell did he feel so damned anxious all the time?

Try as he might to think himself into a positive mood, Hyienna knew that things were anything *but* rosy. The life-changing mystical experience he'd hoped for was still stubbornly absent and he lacked the knowledge of how to look for it. He stared morosely at the rucksack leaning against the wall of the shed, the warm yellow light from the Green Lizard's windows falling gently on its unremarkable outline. It would be so easy, just pick the bloody thing up and heave it off that cliff, straight into the sea. It wasn't the first time he'd thought about abandoning the…*thing* before changing his mind. In fact, it had become something of a ritual.

Lost deep in introspection, Hyienna started and almost dropped his beer when a shadow suddenly blotted out the light from the windows behind. He jumped a second time as the light suddenly picked out Kal's unmistakable outline not ten feet away. Dressed in a white suit and panama hat, he seemed to shimmer in the cool autumn darkness as he leaned nonchalantly on his walking cane. "Drinking alone?"

The question was strange, almost paternal, and it took Hyienna a couple of seconds to formulate a lame response. "Can I help you with something?"

Kal strode forward a few paces, his polished shoes silent on the sandy soil as he gazed out to sea, not five feet from the mysterious rucksack. "The ocean is filled with wisdom, if we have but the will to hear it."

Three beers in, tired and confused, Hyienna was in no mood for philosophical conversation. "Is there something you want?"

The man in white continued to stare into the darkness. "I think it's high time we had a talk."

"What do *we* have to talk about?"

Still Kal did not move. "I grew up beside the ocean. My mother was the daughter of an angler; she used to tell me all kinds of stories, folk tales I suppose you would call them. My favourite was about an old woman who finds a magic egg. Remind me to tell you it someday."

Hyienna's blood ran cold as he heard Kal describe the recurring dream he could never quite remember. "Who *are* you?"

At last, Kal turned, placing the end of his stick into the soft ground as he leaned his weight on it. "I am the man who can help you with your troubles. I am the man who can show you the right road." He gestured theatrically with his stick, first this way, then that.

Hyienna made a point of taking a long swig of beer, chiefly to give him time to think. "Why should you help *me?*"

"Call it Christian duty if you like. I see a man who is lost, and I feel compelled to show him the way."

"And I'm lost?"

Kal's jovial expression fell from his face as his stick planted itself back into the earth. "You have no idea where you are or where you're going. In fact, you don't even know *who* you are."

Finishing his beer and making a conscious effort not to look at the rucksack, Hyienna did his best to sound casual. "Listen; whatever bad blood there is between you and my friend, leave me out of it."

The older man cocked his head curiously. "What makes you think Nathaniel is your friend?"

Hyienna didn't really have a good answer, but he also knew he wasn't obliged to provide one.

Kal pointed with his stick once again, this time towards the back of the inn. "When I was a boy, our only light came from oil lamps. Despite the cost, we kept one burning at night to ward off the evil spirits prowling the darkness. Today I find myself in this world of light and aeroplanes and electricity. I still marvel that anyone can hop on a big metal ferry and be here within a couple of hours. Alas, all the time and distance in God's creation cannot separate us from the things we have done or failed to do."

"If you have a point, Kal, now would be a good time."

The man in the white suit shrugged innocently. "Sometimes it's better to just get everything out in the open so the healing can begin. That is why you are here, yes? To heal?"

Hyienna felt his eyes narrowing. "It's best not to go poking into people's private affairs."

A snort of derision escaped from Kal's mouth. "Or you will do what? Beat me up? Shoot me? Call me a bad name?"

Once again Hyienna had no answer.

Kal leaned forward on his stick once more, his eyes unblinking as he stared at the younger man. "Besides that, why do you imagine that your affairs are private? It takes a great deal of care and vigilance to go unnoticed in this ever-shrinking world."

"You still haven't told me why you're here."

"To hear your confession."

Hyienna blinked at Kal's matter-of-fact, yet spectacularly strange statement. After a few seconds he recovered. "You don't look like a priest, and anyway I'm not the churchy type."

Kal took a deep breath and gazed up at the night sky, the light from the Lizard's windows illuminating his polished ebony features in an oddly disconcerting way. "Church or not, priest or not, Providence has laid out certain rules for us to follow, and we transgress them at our peril."

"Well, if you wanna go knocking on doors and spreading the good word, go right ahead. I've done nothing wrong and even if I had, what makes you think I answer to *you?*" Hyienna rose and turned to head back to the Lizard.

"You failed to protect an innocent, and after *that* you failed to help the king's men serve justice. I will not burden you with the full chain of events, just know that your reckless behaviour has forced me to take the most drastic action."

"Bullshit! We've never even met before."

The man in white remained a picture of paternal patience. "Nonetheless, your foolishness has caused me, regrettably, to violate the Fifth Commandment. Now even *I* am unsure as to whether the situation can be contained. The damage is great, and the costs will be high regardless of the outcome. Through no fault of my own, I am now outside of Divine law. Whilst this is not a hopeless position as many may believe, it will take more than a few half-hearted Hail Marys to restore equilibrium."

Kal's words rooted Hyienna to the spot. He felt his fists clenching and found himself striding towards the man in white before he realised what he was doing. He tried to grab Kal by the lapels, but the older man was faster, deftly deflecting his attack and sidestepping out of reach. "Just who the hell *are* you?"

Kal stepped back further. "A wise man always knows his friends from his enemies."

"What does *that* mean?"

Although already intense, Kal's stare deepened still further. "It means that not one of your so-called *friends* is what they appear to be, but then neither are you."

"Now look…"

Kal held up his hand. "Please do not insult my intelligence with claims that you have done nothing wrong. I know why you left Barcelona and in truth I don't blame you for that. It must be a terrible burden, waking every morning and wondering if this is the day somebody will discover your secret."

Hyienna opened his mouth to fling an insult, then closed it again as he considered his position. After a few seconds he spoke. "Look, I don't really know what your game is, but all the same I'd appreciate it if you kept this quiet. Yeah, I've made some big mistakes in my life, but I never hurt anyone. Believe me, the police were camped out in my ass with a microscope."

"I *do* believe you, I most sincerely do, which is why I am concerned for your well-being now. I am not the only man on this island who knows how to check on things; it's only a matter of time before your cousin's fiancé and his musclebound friend find out about your unfortunate past. I know you are blameless, at least in the legal sense, but do you *really* think others will see you the same way, or stay silent?"

Hyienna slumped back onto the sand and reached for another beer. He knew the strange man in the sharp suit was right, just as he knew he'd been chasing a foolish fantasy to think he could put the past behind him so easily. "You still haven't told me what you *want*, Kal. Why did you come over here? It's not like you're my friend."

Kal idly drew a shape in the sand before speaking again. "I am a better friend than you know." He reached into his tailored jacket and produced a thick white envelope.

"What's that?" Hyienna asked suspiciously.

"Call it a gesture of faith, or perhaps a token of goodwill. Despite what your *friend* Nathaniel may have told you, I am concerned for your welfare. You've stumbled into something beyond your reckoning and here is your way out. This ferry ticket is good for six months, and there's some cash to help you find your feet at your new destination."

Hyienna eyed the envelope. "Are you telling me to get the hell out of Dodge? What happens if I don't?"

Kal shrugged. "You will come to no harm by my hand, but there are others I cannot speak for."

"Who are *you*, Kal? Why should I trust *you*?"

Kal paused for effect. "Has anyone on this island, apart from me, given you *anything* freely, with no strings attached? Even your loving cousin merely used you to re-kindle an old affair."

Hyienna opened his mouth to speak but Kal held up his hand once more.

Kal continued. "Her fiancé will no doubt seek you out when he discovers that your friend is sleeping with his wife to be. Then there is his especially large associate."

Once again Hyienna made a motion to speak but Kal beat him to it.

"Oh yes, I know who he is, and I assure you he is every bit as dangerous as he looks, in fact more so." Kal stopped and gazed up at the sky for a few seconds. "It isn't your fault, you are a babe in the woods, the new boy in the city. Everyone is playing you for a fool and you don't even know what the game is called."

"Kate never asked me for anything, and neither has Nathaniel." Hyienna mentally kicked himself as he justified his actions to a man, he knew nothing about, other than his name.

Kal tapped the envelope with a manicured finger. "*This* is something real, the rest is just meaningless words lost on the wind, forgotten the moment they are spoken."

Much as he hated to admit it, Hyienna knew that Kal was at least half right. Although Nathaniel was good company, he was more interested in his affair with Sarah, which left *him* feeling more than a little pushed away. On the other hand, Kate was a growing part of his life, although he was acutely aware of how close to Solomon she was. Could she be playing him? He didn't think so, although Kal's words had an uncomfortable ring of authenticity about them. Could it really be true, could he really be *that* naïve?

Kal stepped closer, holding out the envelope. "You've disturbed a delicate balance here, my young friend, and I wish to help you right the many wrongs you have left behind as you've blundered through this world."

Hyienna slowly reached forward. "But I can leave when I want, right?"

Kal moved the envelope away from Hyienna's grasp. "On one condition."

"What condition is *that?*"

"Why I've already told you, confession."

Hyienna shook his head with exasperation. "I don't even know what that means."

Kal's voice softened a little. "Although the Lord is pleased by his church, He does not need it. A true confession from a sinner is worth a thousand sermons to the pious."

Hyienna stepped back, regretting his earlier decision to indulge the crazy and somewhat unsettling old man. "Okay, you're freaking me out now. Maybe you should just be on your way. I won't tell anyone you were here."

Kal tapped the envelope again. "A fresh start, a new life if you want it. All I ask in return is you tell me everything that happened in Barcelona."

Hyienna's eyes narrowed. "You sound like you already know something."

"Yes, I know a great deal, but knowing the picture is different from completing the puzzle."

Hyienna was about to begin his story when a thought suddenly struck him. "Hey wait a second, why should *my* story interest *you?* We never met till that bust up at the restaurant, right?"

"That is true, but like I told you, you're in the middle of something you don't understand. Now I'm offering to wipe the slate clean. Nobody else will offer you safe passage, I can promise you that much."

Hyienna finally came to a decision. What did it matter if he filled in a few blanks that Kal may or may not know anyway? After all, the guy had a point. He'd not been treated with much respect since his arrival at Formentera. Plus, when had anybody ever offered *him* something, strings or not? "Okay, so what is it you want to know?"

Kal slid the envelope back into his pocket. "Just tell me the tale of how you came to be here, or rather, how you came to follow your beautiful cousin to this mystical island."

It took a moment for Hyienna to think of where to begin, then the obvious answer struck him. In fact, it was a question. "So, I guess you know about the kid?"

"I do."

"Just so you know, I really did have *nothing* to do with it."

"I know."

"The police cleared me."

"I know."

"It's just that, well, people get the wrong idea, they read half a story and think they know the rest."

"I know that too. What I do *not* know, is how you came to be *in* that apartment in the first place, and *that* is what you can tell me."

Hyienna relaxed a little. "Sarah's always been a strange girl. There's just something…bewitching about her. We used to be really close once, but then I guess life just kinda happened; boys and girls and jobs, the usual things."

Kal nodded. "Of course. Go on."

Hyienna continued. "It takes a long time to gain a little self-awareness, and I guess it took *me* longer than most people. By the time I realised I had no plan for my life I was just kind of drifting, with no career and no real family to speak of."

"If a man commits himself to nothing, then nothing will commit itself

to him."

Hyienna nodded. "Ain't *that* the truth. Still, it was Sarah who stood by me and, little by little, drifted back into my life. I don't think there was ever anything more than friendship between us, and besides, her life was just a mess of guys that I could never keep up with. Don't get the wrong idea, I mean, she's always been a decent girl…dammit, what am I trying to say here? I mean that she enjoyed the attention from guys, and she got plenty of it."

Kal smiled. "I think that is why the good Lord has arranged for guys to chase girls, and not the other way around. Just imagine this world if men possessed that same power."

"Yeah, I guess you're right. In any case I was glad to have my cousin Sarah fighting my corner. Lack of focus leads to drift, you see, and I'd fallen in with the drink and drugs crowd. It's not like I had a serious problem, but I've gotta be honest and say I was hardly Mr Reliable either. So, Sarah became my rock, and I guess I became hers too. She helped me to gain a little self-esteem and I helped *her* to control her need for endless attention. At least I thought so."

"How did you help her?"

Hyienna considered for a moment. "Not sure really. I guess I just made her laugh, and I was the only uncomplicated guy in her life."

"Sounds like you were good for her."

Now it was Hyienna's turn to smile. "Yeah, I was, at least for a while."

Kal's intense stare returned. "But…"

"But then something happened, she met this guy, a mystery man. She'd always been pretty open about her life, but that changed all of a sudden. When I asked her about it, she got really defensive, said he was a guy with a difficult past he was trying to leave behind."

Kal raised his eyebrows. "So naturally you were concerned."

"Well yeah, I mean, who wouldn't be? I thought maybe she was mixed up with some slick talking conman or something." Hyienna trailed off.

"Confessions are meaningless if they are easy, Hyienna. Clearly you are not proud of what you did."

Hyienna was quiet for a moment as he considered what to say next. "Cowardice is a lot like bravery, at least in the way it takes many different forms. Now I'm no hardened tough guy but I can look after myself in the bar if I need to. I might not be a *physical* coward, but I've always been an emotional one. Maybe it's all connected to my lack of drive, but I just couldn't find the courage to stand up to Sarah, even though I could see this relationship was taking its toll. Maybe it was none of my business anyhow, she's a grown woman after all. All the same, I wanted to be sure she wasn't getting herself into some sort of trouble, so I started tailing her."

"And how do you feel about that now?"

This time Hyienna didn't need to think about his response. "Are you kidding me? I feel terrible. I violated my cousin's trust, my friends' trust and poked into parts of her life where I simply didn't belong. I guess that was the first domino in the line that ends up with the two of us talking right here."

Now it was Kal's turn to look thoughtful. "There is a kind of fate to our lives, not so much a plan as a pattern, or a template if you will. The artist may become a sculptor or a painter or perhaps even a writer, but he will never become an engineer. This is why I offer my hand to you. I do not presume to understand the intricacies of the grand design, but I recognise the workmanship when I see it. You were destined to come here, one way or another. Providence commanded it."

Hyienna thrust his hand in his pocket, his fingers quickly closing around his little rock. He'd become suspicious of such quasi-mystical talk as it had led him down some very dark roads in the past. All the same, that didn't mean none of it was true. "Yeah, maybe you're right. At first, I thought she was dating this guy called Solomon."

Kal seemed surprised for the first time that night.

Hyienna nodded in confirmation. "Yeah, the same one, only they weren't an item at the time, I think. Still, that discovery led me to another of Solomon's many conquests." He saw Kal's eyes flick towards the back door of the Green Lizard. The man obviously knew a lot more than he was letting on and Hyienna just hoped he'd kept quiet. Yasmina had no idea that he knew anything about her, and he thought he'd done well with his pretence. All bets were off if she ever heard the tale he was recounting in the back yard. Okay, so he had nothing directly to do with her son's disappearance, but that counted for nothing with a grieving and obsessed mother in the mix.

Kal waved his manicured hand to attract the younger man's attention. "I have been told I am very perceptive, but not so much as I can hear what you are thinking."

"What? Where was I? Oh yeah, so I figured out this kid was Solomon's baby, and let me tell you *that* made me mad as hell because I thought he was homing in on Sarah at the time. Well, I guess he was, but at least it doesn't matter for *that* reason."

"But it should matter for other reasons?" Kal enquired.

Hyienna felt a sudden flash of irritation. "You want to hear this or not? In fact, why the hell am I telling you *anything?* I must be mad."

Kal's voice dropped lower than usual. "You know nothing of these people you surround yourself with, and yet you share yourself freely with *them*. Why am I different?"

Hyienna was rapidly having second thoughts. "Yeah, well, maybe this whole thing was a mistake. Listen, Kal, or whatever your name really is; you just go in peace, and we'll pretend this whole thing never happened."

The man in white sighed sadly. "I can pretend, and you can pretend, but I doubt very much that the poor broken proprietor would be able to pretend as well. I'll wager she possesses reserves of strength we can only imagine, and I shudder to think what her knight in shining armour and his iron-pumping friend might think should they learn the truth."

"You threatening me, Kal?"

"I have no need to threaten you. You are already in more danger than you could even begin to conceive, so witless you are as to notice none of it."

Now it was Hyienna's turn to shrug. "Doesn't matter anyway, you seem to have figured it out. There I was, about to spill the beans on Solomon's kid to my cousin when I first met Crisanta, Samuel's babysitter. We hit it off straight away and it was good, at least for a couple of weeks until the poor kid up and vanished from right under our noses when she was supposed to be looking out for him. Hell, I wasn't even supposed to *be* there."

"But you did not know this had happened?"

"No, not straight away. I still thought it was *Solomon's* apartment, so I was gone in the early hours. In any event I'd just made up my mind to come clean to the cops, but Crisanta must've beaten me to it. They questioned me for hours on end, days in fact. I think they really wanted me to have some connection to the abduction, and some of their other unsolved cases."

Kal obligingly filled in the blanks. "But they could find no evidence against you because you were not guilty. I suppose it made sense for them to not splash your name all over the papers, or they would surely be dealing with another murder."

Hyienna laughed bitterly. "Yeah, and to think I believed that would be the end of it, that nobody would ever find out. Shows what *I* know."

Kal was silent, his face inscrutable as he thought about what Hyienna had told him. At last, he spoke. "I do not believe you have had any meaningful influence on events, for better or worse. All the same, you would be well advised to use that ticket sooner rather than later. Your shortcomings are stupidity, naïveté and carelessness, but I would hate to see something more serious added to your suffering. If you possess *any* wisdom at all, you will catch the next ferry to the mainland and leave this place behind. You do not belong here." With that he pulled the creases from his sleeves, handed the envelope to Hyienna, and walked away without another word.

Hyienna watched as the man in white dissolved into a ghostly grey smudge before vanishing into the darkness. Opening the envelope, he discovered that Kal was a man of his word as he saw a significant amount of cash as well as an open ferry ticket. Immediately his eyes strayed to the innocuous-looking rucksack still resting against the peeling shed. Kal had made no mention of anything otherworldly, yet Hyienna had no doubt he was well versed in all things esoteric.

With his ticket in one hand and anchor in the other, Hyienna looked up at the bejewelled night sky as he searched for answers. It was only then he realised he was standing beneath a velvet blanket of perfect blackness. He could see no stars, and the glowing harvest moon had completely vanished. The sky was a flawless nothingness that mirrored the impenetrable darkness hiding in that cheap nylon backpack. In fact, if it weren't for the illumination from the nearby bar, Hyienna wondered if he would be able to see anything at all.

He shivered as he picked up the innocuous looking bag and quietly made his way back to the Lizard. He didn't really understand from whence his conviction came, but he knew that both the man in white and the unnatural darkness above were harbingers of some great yet hidden danger.

Answers were coming, and Hyienna knew nothing would be the same after they arrived.

The Nephilem

THE RIDING IN
OF SUMMER
Chapter 15

Hyienna watched the heavy gates of Casa Hermoso click shut, before turning his attention to the house ahead. It was still early, before seven, and the watery dawn washed the colours from Solomon's already soulless and non-descript abode.

He took a deep breath of crisp, cool morning air and wished he still smoked. This was the perfect place for a thoughtful cigarette, the perfect place to dawdle and dally for just a little longer. It was the perfect place to just put off, well, what exactly? He wasn't sure, but for some reason he couldn't quite fathom, he was nervous about confiding in his girlfriend. True, they'd only been together for a short time, but his reluctance to share didn't bode well for the future. He couldn't even pinpoint a reason for his reticence. Maybe it was just worldly cynicism creeping into yet another part of his life, or maybe it was something else.

Leaning over the handlebars of his moped, Hyienna stared at the glass and concrete block at the end of the swept sloping drive, hoping it might reveal some hidden secret that he'd missed on previous visits. Alas, the house was as implacable as ever, sleeping on in the early morning, just as those within slumbered in designer rooms filled with overpriced abstractions.

If Seth or any other heavies were around then they were keeping their heads down, not that he was any kind of intruder. In fact, Hyienna's increasingly frequent visits had made him something of a regular fixture, or maybe just a strange curiosity, a compassionate case taken on by the beautiful people.

On reflection, Hyienna realised that he couldn't figure out whether he was liked, loathed, or barely tolerated by the speedboat and sangria set. His growing relationship with Kate was pretty obvious, yet nobody had really mentioned it, at least not directly. Perhaps such a lack of interest wasn't all that surprising. After all, his own cousin and Nathaniel were too loved up to notice anything outside the bedroom, while Solomon vacillated between suspicion and philandering, sometimes by the minute. As for Seth, Yasmina, Ermina and the rest, they were either too polite or too self-absorbed to raise the subject in conversation. At times Hyienna caught himself wondering whether he wore some strange cloak of invisibility, similar to that which taunted him from inside that cheap nylon rucksack, the thing which he could neither discard dishonourably, nor pass on with great ceremony.

All of that was plenty weird enough, but now the mysterious Kal had paid him a visit and suddenly none of it was funny, if it ever was. Hyienna knew he was in danger, and he wondered once again whether he should've accepted the dapper man's offer of a free ferry ticket and a pocketful of cash. He didn't want to think about what the alternatives might be.

Whatever the case, he knew he was out of options and so he let his scooter roll down the drive under its own weight. He was glad he'd killed the engine before the gates opened as it seemed more than just rude, it felt just plain wrong to disturb the wondrous quiet of the early dawn. It was just him and the birds, while a big part of him wished it could stay that way.

Far too soon he coasted to a stop outside Solomon's ostentatious front door, yet still he was reluctant to kick down the stand and climb off. For a moment he felt as though his trusty scooter had become a different kind of anchor, keeping him safe from the swirling currents of the unknown. Sure, he and Kate had been getting on very well and there was definitely some chemistry there, but this was a whole other level. This was serious, life-partner kind of stuff and although he liked Kate very much, it was way too soon to know how she would react when he told her the news. She could be sympathetic, understanding or just plain mocking for all he knew. Suddenly he understood why he dawdled so.

At length, Hyienna's fear of looking shifty outweighed his

nervousness about asking for help and he stepped off his scooter. He was more than a little glad that he didn't need to enter the main house as he made his way round to a small side gate and let himself in. Not for the first time did he wonder if he'd been demoted to using a service entrance, but it had become routine all the same. He would text Kate and she would make sure the gate was open. In truth, he was more than happy to avoid both Sarah and Solomon for most of the time he was with his new girlfriend. Although Solomon had mellowed a little, he was still hard work. It was more difficult to quantify the change in Sarah, but it was there for certain. She'd become a great deal more introspective and absent minded since hooking up with Nathaniel, and Hyienna figured that if *he'd* noticed, her fiancé must've noticed too. He didn't want much out of life, but Hyienna prayed daily that he'd be nowhere in the neighbourhood when *that* can of worms inevitably spilt over.

Despite his growing list of problems, Hyienna still smiled and shook his head ruefully as he clicked open the side gate and stepped into the shady cool of the poolside patio.

He immediately saw Kate through the glass of the pool house, lounging on a recliner and leafing through one of those glossy magazines that were entirely unintelligible to the average guy. She didn't look up, so he took the opportunity to enjoy her figure as she flicked through articles discussing the ten most desirable table lamps, or some such. She must've been aware of his arrival because Solomon's security system was top notch, plus the pool house had kind of become their unofficial domain within Casa Hermoso. It was the closest thing to a guest house after all.

Although the view was ever so appealing, Hyienna's attention was drawn to a vacant couch as he tapped on the glass door and stepped into the pool house.

Kate's smile of welcome rapidly evolved into a frown of concern as she tossed her magazine aside. "You look like crap, honey, what you been up to?"

Glad to finally feel a little safer, Hyienna flopped onto the waiting couch and pulled a nearby throw over himself. The chill morning had seeped through his clothes on the journey over and he felt strangely cold inside. "I didn't get much sleep, any really."

She pulled a theatrical face. "Those party girls been keeping you up all night, babe? Hope they left some for me."

"Yeah, well, I don't like to disappoint." Hyienna's half-hearted joke trailed off into a yawn as he grappled with a wave of fatigue.

Kate stayed quiet, as though sensing he had something to say.

"Guess who came by the Lizard last night."

She thought for a moment. "By the look of you, I'd say it was our international man of mystery again. He sure can put that red wine away."

Hyienna let his head fall back, studying the shadows on the ceiling. "Man of mystery yeah, but you got the wrong one. *My* visitor was much better dressed and more than just a bit creepy."

Kate visibly stiffened. "Kal? *Kal* came by the Lizard? Really?"

"You know, I've met some strange people in my time, but that guy is off the scale."

"I'm surprised he would lower himself to be seen in a place like the Lizard, I mean, he's even more full of himself than Solomon."

Hyienna smiled ruefully. "Well, I guess he was half seen anyhow."

There was silence for the better part of a minute as Kate waited for Hyienna to speak again. Eventually it became clear that he needed a prod. "Hey, don't you fall asleep on me now."

Hyienna snored theatrically.

Kate threw the nearest cushion at his head. "Well."

"Well, what?"

Kate searched for another cushion, but none were in reach. "Well, what did he want?"

"Why would he want anything? What do you know about him anyhow?"

Kate sucked in her cheeks and spoke through half-gritted teeth. "I know he's not the kind of man to even open his eyes if there's nothing in it for him. So, what would *he* want with *you?*"

Stifling another yawn, Hyienna sat up. "Any aspirins in here? I had a beer or three too many last night."

Rolling her eyes, Kate stiffly rose and stalked across to a small but well-stocked drinks cabinet. Rummaging inside, she quickly produced a tall glass of ice water and a bottle of pills. With a manner more akin to a nurse than a girlfriend, she crossed back to Hyienna. "Take these."

Hyienna grinned, despite his tiredness. "Yes nurse."

Kate's usually confident and mischievous expression was replaced by one of concern. "I'm serious, honey. What would a man like Kal want with you?"

Sensing the change, Hyienna swallowed the pills and gratefully drained the water. "He said he wanted my confession."

Kate said nothing as she drummed her manicured fingers on her arm.

"Yeah, that's pretty much what *I* said. I mean, he doesn't strike me as your average dog-collar type. More of an eye for an eye kind of guy if you ask me."

Kate shrugged her shoulders in exasperation. "Well, what did you do?"

"I gave it to him, what do you think?"

"You *what?* Do you have any idea of the kind of man he is?"

Hyienna was somewhat perturbed by the sudden change in Kate's demeanour. "I'm guessing there's something I need to know."

"Wrong! There's something *I* need to know." She leaned forward, touching his face gently. "You know, I do really like you, Hyienna. I wouldn't want to see you get yourself into trouble."

Hyienna was about to tell her exactly what kind of trouble he'd already got himself into, when some inner instinct cautioned against it. Maybe it was time he got some information back, rather than just spreading it around all the time. With his decision quickly made, he opted for his usual humorous deflection. "Too late for that, I've been bewitched by this dark and irresistible goddess." He reached forward.

Kate quickly moved out of range. "I'm serious, Hyienna! Kal is not the kind of man to fuck around with, now what did he say?"

Surprised by the strength of Kate's reaction, Hyienna settled back onto the sofa. "Not that it matters much, but he said something about my being responsible for his taking a life. Well, violating the Fifth Commandment is what he actually said. Then he said it all started in Barcelona."

There was silence, broken only by Kate's nails tapping on a nearby table top. "What did he mean by that?"

"I don't know, and I sure as hell wasn't going to ask him either. You just told me Kal is not a man to fuck with and I believe you, *boy* do I believe you. Just meeting the guy is enough to give you PTSD, although you seem to know a lot about him. Who is he, I mean really?"

Kate ignored the question. "What happened in Barcelona, Hyienna?"

"Why does everyone think something weird happened in Barcelona? Can't a guy just choose a change of scene?"

"Stop screwing around, Hyienna! You're in the middle of something here, and if you're not careful it'll be the end of you. There's been enough trouble already and Kal isn't the kind of man to go fishing on the off-chance. He doesn't make wild guesses and he doesn't make mistakes either. If he sought you out, then he must've had a damned good reason."

Hyienna felt his hackles rising as his self-control slipped away. Before he knew it, he was off the sofa and pacing like a caged animal. "Just what the hell *is* it with this place?"

"Hyienna, I don't…"

"*Oh, shut up!* Wherever I turn on this goddamned island it seems that everyone's got some kind of hidden agenda, and that includes *you!* I came to this place looking for some answers, but I guess that just makes *me* a bigger fool than I thought I was. Right now, I feel like the guy from the movie who's been set up right from the start."

If Kate was angry or upset, she never showed it. "Hyienna, honey, listen to me. Nobody's set you up, I promise, but you need to understand that you can't walk fresh into something and expect to become a player just like that."

"A player? What the hell does that even *mean?* Why can't anybody just give me a straight answer?"

Kate folded her arms. "You're just so damned selfish, aren't you? Sarah was right, you can't see past the end of your own nose and you're too narrow minded to understand anything that doesn't involve you directly."

"*I'm* selfish? I'm not the one who's shacked up with my cousin and his fiancée, whatever kind of cosy arrangement that is. Come to think of it, where *do* you actually live?"

At last Kate softened a little. "Listen, I know that things seem really strange, but you have to believe me when I tell you it's for the best. Had it ever occurred to you that your ignorance protects you from Kal, and others like him? Had that thought ever once entered that beer and booty obsessed brain of yours?"

Hyienna tried not to smile but he failed, although he was suddenly at a loss for words.

Kate gently pushed him back onto the sofa and perched on the arm. "Listen, there are a ton of good reasons why people aren't always upfront with folks they don't know so well. Besides, sometimes the truth is so far out there it might just as well be a lie. One thing I *can* tell you is that if Kal's taken an interest, you'd better be on your toes."

"You still haven't told me who he is." Hyienna observed.

"You still haven't told *me* what happened in Barcelona." Kate countered.

Hyienna started to rise. "Look, I should go."

Kate was having none of it and gently but persistently held him down, covering him over with the throw and stroking his hair. "You've had a tough night, it's not easy dealing with something like that. Just relax and get some sleep, you're safe here."

Hyienna murmured some sort of protest, but within seconds his breathing had changed, and he was fast asleep.

Kate gently kissed him on the forehead and stood up, looking down curiously as he began to mumble and move his legs, almost as though he were swimming.

She crossed to the drinks cabinet and poured herself a stiff vodka. Dropping ice and sloshing a little soda into it, she closed her eyes and gulped the fiery liquid down as the sound of sirens filled her mind.

Glancing across at her sleeping boyfriend, she tried to dismiss the idea that he could possibly know anything about Carmelita's tragic end. It couldn't be true, surely not. Surely the man mumbling on the couch couldn't be the missing link, could he? Could this bumbling but rather cute and engaging guy be the unwitting first cause, a hapless prime mover in a bewildering sequence of events that led to her sipping liquor early in the morning?

It was a fantastical idea, but on the other hand, she was wise enough to know that there were no such things as coincidences, at least not like that.

She took another mouthful of vodka as the sirens melded into the memory of horrified onlookers crowding around Carmelita's horribly mangled body. A freak accident, the enquiry said, just a stolen car driven by a nameless joyrider. Just another coincidence.

She glanced out at the early morning sun glistening on the surface of the pool. How she missed Rosalita's lateral wisdom at such times. She used to scoff at her sister's mystical bent, but what she wouldn't give for some of that otherworldly insight right now. Why did *she* have to be the one left behind in this world? Lost, adrift, without even her real name for comfort.

Still, Kate knew she'd been spared for a reason, just as she knew it would all be over soon, one way or another.

YOU CAN'T SEE WHERE YOUR EYES CAN'T FOLLOW

Chapter 16

In the subconscious, Hyienna slept, hoping to find in his dreams the respite this tortured reality would not afford him.

But it didn't. Instead, he felt lost, running from an unseen danger, like the demons of Barcelona that would not let up. Whether in life or in dream space, Hyienna was always running.

Formentera was supposed to be the promised land that would wipe the red from Hyienna's ledger, offer him a fresh start. But as he revisited the land in his dreams, the echoes of Barcelona came from within, straining against the surfaces. Was this all Hyienna would ever amount to? A foundation formed from poor judgment and reckless decisions? Always being forced to take the cautious life and never knowing contentment?

And everywhere Hyienna turned, he could see Kal standing there, his face inviting and friendly. "If you possess *any* wisdom at all, you will catch the next ferry to the mainland and leave this place behind. You do not belong here." Kal's words ricocheted through his subconscious, a logic that Hyienna found strangely inviting. At times he felt like a blind man, wandering through a forever-unfamiliar landscape.

But as he wandered through the dreamspace, Hyienna realised that the blindless was forced on him by no one but himself. He wanted to treat his former self as a separate entity, to put an unspoken divide between the man he was and the man he wanted to be. But the past was forever upon him, tainting everything he had wanted to make for himself in Barcelona.

His thoughts turned to Nathaniel, a man who seemed cloaked in mystery. Every time Hyienna assumed that he had a bead on the man, a new layer of fog rose up around him, clouding Hyienna's judgment.

As Hyienna's mind drifted, trying to find a focus for the trepidations he was facing, Nathaniel became an increasing focus in his mind; just what did he know about the man? Hyienna remembered when he sighted him out on the beach, how he could have been everything and nothing at the same time. No matter how Hyienna had tried to fit Nathaniel into his preconceived notions, he always found himself concluding that Nathaniel was a man out of time, and he didn't belong in Barcelona, any more than Hyienna did.

And then he flashed to the meeting at Solomon's party, where Nathaniel had put him at ease with his apparent altruism. It took a lot for Hyienna to trust a man. He had once heard the expression, "You allow a man with a dark past into your life, you end up inheriting all his debts."

But Nathaniel was different. Hyienna knew that the moment he first laid eyes on him. If there was a darkness about him, it was a darkness that Hyienna was willing to invite. But during the lunch, that first glimpse of Kal, the way he had been able to instantly recall details the man had not been privy to, as though Kal was greeting an old friend.

Then there had been his longing for Sarah. It was while he had been making the final preparations to help Nathaniel through his courtship that he had first noticed a deep sense of longing in Nathaniel, as though he had a hole in his heart that he felt only Sarah could fill. He watched this confident man turn into a school boy, stumbling over his words. And then that mud fight where Hyienna had actually seen the hold Nathaniel had over Sarah.

Hyienna wanted that kinship for himself. And he wondered if that was what had pushed him to tell Nathaniel not to repeat the past. Was he doing it out of a sense of concern for broken souls? Or was he doing it because deep down, there was still a part of him that wanted to lash out and hurt Sarah? Part of him felt that he should have pushed Nathaniel harder. But he needn't have bothered. He could tell that the two were locked onto a collision course.

He was dreaming again, this time of an egg, being passed around like a precious jewel between women. The dream was a peculiar one as Hyienna seemed to be playing no part in the proceedings. He only acted as an invisible overseer watching the entire display.

There was one woman that stood out; a robed woman who was speaking frantically. Hyienna couldn't place the words she was speaking, but the women surrounding her were cowed. One of them even seemed to be pleading. But the robed women would not be silenced. And as she spoke, the sky darkened above the land.

But before Hyienna could see the outcome of the woman's proclamation, he was hurled out of the land and into consciousness again, now in his own bed. He realised that he was drenched in sweat, a tidal wave of neurosis having overwhelmed him.

He opened up his dream journal and scrawled in uneven handwriting what he had dreamed before the memory vanished from his mind. Comparing that with all of his other dreams was a difficult task. He felt that he was being gifted separate pieces from separate puzzles, but he had no idea how to fit them all together.

I can't go on like this, he thought to himself. He couldn't go on living in a world of half-truths. He needed answers.

***

Early in the evening, Hyienna walked swiftly down the streets of Barcelona, wishing he had an item of clothing that would conceal his face, possibly a hat or a scarf. Of course, such clothing would only serve to draw unwanted attention to him. Given the time he had spent in Barcelona, it was probable that a few people knew his name and face, but he didn't want to take the risk of being discovered. What he was going to do required stealth.

As he walked, Hyienna glanced out of the corner of his eye at the people passing by. People paid him little mind, but as far as Hyienna was concerned, they were all enemies waiting to be made.

The day before, with Sarah and Nathaniel otherwise preoccupied, Hyienna had made his excuses, feigning an illness, and had gone about looking through contacts. He already knew that Barcelona was home to many traders, but today, he was looking for someone in the information trade.

The source had been difficult to come by and the individual in question had questioned whether Hyienna really wanted to be put in contact with this individual. To speak with this man would be tantamount to opening Pandora's Box.

But he needed to move forward. And now, it felt like a price worth paying.

He arrived at a bar located on the edge of the city called the Catalan Lounge and entered.

The bar was sparsely populated and looking around at the characters. A man whose skin was shrivelled up, streaks of jet white hair. He looked as though he might predate the whole city. There was a woman present who was dressed in a smart business suit, keeping to herself, but making her distaste present. It was clear she didn't want to be caught dead in a place like this.

Hyienna had heard whispers about the Catalan Lounge. He had heard that it was a place where if you wanted the unattainable in life, you had to be willing to dance with the devil.

He considered ordering a drink, but he didn't want to risk announcing his presence any more than he already had done. He just sat in a corner of the bar and waited for his potential benefactor to make an appearance.

Fifteen minutes passed. People came in and out of the bar, but no one came over to Hyienna's table, clearly there on their own business and with no intention of mixing socially.

Hyienna wondered if he had the right man. Wondered if there had been some mix-up in the appointments. Or maybe he had gotten the wrong bar.

As he pondered whether there was somewhere else that he needed to be, a soft voice whispered in his ear, "Well, I'll give you points for punctuality, my friend."

Hyienna almost jumped out of his seat, prompting the surprised reactions of a few patrons, who quickly went back to their own business.

Hyienna looked up at the man who had spoken. He was a tall Black man in dreadlocks, wearing a jet-black trench coat. Underneath, Hyienna could see that he was wearing an open shirt underneath, and a gold chain with a variety of jewels was dangling around his neck. "A pleasure to meet you, Hyienna" The man's voice was so soothing and soft Hyienna felt as though he was having his ears wiped with silk. Then Hyienna remembered that this man had never set eye on Hyienna in his life.

"You… you're late" was all Hyienna managed to say.

"Oh, quite to the contrary, my friend," said the man. "I was here from the beginning. I like to hang back. Sometimes, sat there alone, the weight of their decisions hanging over them, people realise what is expected of them and make the smart decision to get out of dodge."

"And the ones who stay?" said Hyienna, daring himself to ask.

The man smiled thinly. "You're still here, aren't you? That's a sign that you're hungry." He paused, looking Hyienna up and down. "And you look positively dehydrated." He clicked his fingers in the direction of the bartender. "My good man" he announced. "Could you trouble us for two Calimocho?"

The bartender nodded and went about preparing the drinks. Hyienna staggered, embarrassed. "Please, let me get this."

"Hey, it's my treat. Some people say you should keep business and pleasure separate. I respectfully disagree; I prefer the philosophy that says 'the only business in life worth doing is the one that brings you pleasure.'"

"And who said that?"

"Me" said the man simply, holding out a hand. Hyienna took it reluctantly.

"I'm… I'm sorry, I just realised I don't know your name."

"People call me the Stream. Information flows through me like a river. It travels down certain routes and always gets to where it needs to go."

"Right" said Hyienna slowly. "Does that mean you're good with computers?"

The Stream looked Hyienna up and down as though he had grown a third eye. "No" he said, then added. "Shall we get started?"

Hyienna sat down in his seat while the Stream eased himself into the spare one. Before Hyienna could say anything more, the bartender came over with the two drinks. "That was quick" noted Hyienna.

"Helps to have friends in high places" purred the Stream. Hyienna hoped that he wasn't talking about this place, looking around at the decaying paint, the décor that looked like it belonged to the last century. He was still taking in the place when he realised the Stream was holding his drink in the air. "Cheers" he said. And not wanting to offend, Hyienna clinked his glass, taking a small sip while the Stream downed his drink until it was half-empty.

"Interesting story behind the Calimocho, you know" said the Stream, setting his glass down on the aged table. "It's not actually native to Barcelona or Catalunya. It was popularised by university students who were on the lookout for a cheap beverage, while still trying to kid themselves that they had something resembling class. During the 1970s, it was known as Cuba Libre del pobre, which essentially translates as 'the poor man's drink'. Apparently, vendors in the Basque Country realised that their wine had gone bad and mixed it with cola to mask the sour taste. And now, we seem to have appropriated it into our culture." Hyienna detected a veil of disgust in the Stream's tone.

"I'm sorry" said Hyienna. "Is there a point to this story or am I supposed to guess."

The Stream leaned over the table, staring into Hyienna's face with piercing eyes. "This city has a habit of collecting strays. Those who live here long enough will be able to swallow up the taste as though it were tap water. But those who recoil… they still have the stench of the outside on them… and you, *amic*, you have the essence of Barcelona bouncing off of you."

Now Hyienna was beginning to lose his patience. He couldn't tell what the Stream was getting at, but he was certain it was something derogatory, a show of superiority intended to take a stab at Hyienna's ignorance. "With respect, Stream…" Even as he said the word, it clashed with his tongue, as though it didn't fit the man. "…I didn't come here for a boozing lecture. I came here because I was told you might be able to help me with something. Something that has been troubling me for some time and possibly, something that only you can help me with." He threw in a touch of flattery in the hope that that would make the Stream more willing to aid him.

"You have been pointed in the right direction," said the Stream.

"So, you are a private detective?"

"I have been known to dabble from time to time. I have always been good at finding out the information that everyone is desperate to keep hidden. They think they can cover their tracks and bury their secrets in bottomless graves. But I adore the challenge." He smirked, memories of successful past cases flashing before his eyes, reflecting both confidence and triumph.

"How do you go about finding this information?" asked Hyienna wearily.

The Stream tutted. "Come, come, *amic*. You know better than to peek behind the curtain. A magician never reveals his methods."

"I need to know because I don't want to get involved in anything illeg-"

"Illegal?" The Stream cackled slightly, a scratchy sound that sounded like nails against a stone floor. "If this information you wanted was easily accessible, we wouldn't be having this conversation. I'd be telling you to perch your ass in front of a computer and get Googling. The only other alternative is to go up to your quarry and ask him for the information. But I'm guessing he wouldn't tell you. Possibly because he figures you might weaponize it against him?"

Hyienna gulped. He had tried to be sparse beforehand with the information he had sent out so that it wouldn't be traced back to him if no candidates for the job came forward. But he was both impressed and unnerved by how much knowledge this man brought to the table. He was now certain that the Stream was the right man for the job... but he was still unsure of whether that was a good thing.

"So, let's start from the beginning" announced the Stream. "What is your beef with this gentleman? Did he cheat you? Does he have a woman you would rather have on your arms?"

Hyienna couldn't be sure as to whether the Stream was making very accurate guesses or was just showing off his demonstrated knowledge. Either way, Hyienna reached into his bag and pulled out a handmade dossier on Nathaniel that he had prepared. He pulled it open to the first page. "Now, to start with..."

The Stream chortled. "Oh, that's cute. I'm serious, that is truly adorable."

Embarrassed, Hyienna said, "I thought that-"

"You can put that thing away. You won't be needing it" said the Stream assuredly.

"What?"

"I'm serious. Just tell me what your problem is with this guy, what you need to know, and I will take it all in."

At first, Hyienna thought – and hoped – that he was joking. But the Stream was looking at him now like a poker player who all, but knew he had the winning hand. "But how will you take it all in?"

The Stream raised an eyebrow. "My ears?"

"You don't need-"

"Hyienna, we live in an age where information is alarmingly easy to pilfer. That's how it always ends up in the wrong hands, armed by people with no idea how to use it properly. Like a toddler being gifted a loaded gun."

"I really feel for your sake, it might be easier if I just read out…" said Hyienna, his eyes going down to the dossier.

The Stream's smile slipped. "I can understand that this may be a bit unnerving for you. You aren't sure of the direction you're headed in, you feel like you're going to hurl yourself into the abyss along the way. You probably have an abundance of doubts, but my competence should *not* be among them.

"So, start from the beginning, tell me everything you know about this man. And leave no detail out whatsoever. The more I know, the better equipped I will be to do my job. But…" he held up a hand before Hyienna could speak. "There are a few ground rules; you never ask me how I got the information. No contracts being signed. I've already told you about my feelings regarding paper trials. And this is a one-and-done job. No follow-ups, no check-ups, no extensions. When I have handed over the information to you, we will never see each other again, do you understand?"

Overwhelmed by the certainty in the Stream's voice, Hyienna nodded slowly. What else could he do?

And so Hyienna began. His words came hesitantly at first as he struggled to properly articulate them, uncertain as to how much information he should provide. But as the conversation progressed, he relaxed in the Stream's presence and spoke at great length about all his encounters with Nathaniel, the impressions he had gotten, the blank spots that needed filling in. And though he was reluctant to do so, he also included Sarah in the equation, if only so that the Stream would be better prepared for the job he was going to do.

As Hyienna spoke, the Stream said very little. He simply nodded or grunted as an affirmation that he was taking in all the details. It wasn't until three-quarters through the conversation that Hyienna realised the Stream had never once taken his eyes off him. He was staring directly at him. Hyienna had once heard that the eyes were the windows to the soul and he wondered if the Stream was looking into Hyienna's soul itself, determining whether it would be worth catching.

When Hyienna had finally finished telling his tale, the Stream blinked for what seemed to be the first time in a lifetime and leaned back in his chair. "I see."

"I need to find out where his parents came from" said Hyienna. "I need to know what kind of background he has and what kind of shit he's gotten himself into."

"And what about Sarah? I would ask what would happen to her. But I think a better question would be, 'what would you like to happen to her?' But I think we both know the answer to that, don't we?"

Hyienna was right. He did know the answer. In his idyllic dreams, he wanted to see Sarah help him towards his second chance. But given how interlinked she was with Nathaniel; would she spend countless nights lying with Hyienna wishing that he was Nathaniel.

"This information isn't going to be easy to come by" warned the Stream. "You realise I'm going to have to turn over every stone in Formentera, don't you?"

"I've got money, I can pay you" said Hyienna, which was technically true. He did have some money saved up, but would it be enough to buy the Stream's services.

"Don't bother getting your wallet out" said the Stream, as if sensing Hyienna's thoughts. "That's not the kind of currency I trade in. Remember, I'm the Stream. I'm a natural part of life watching nature take its course."

"So, what do you want in return?"

And then the Stream smiled and Hyienna knew that there would be no going back from this point onwards, dreading that he was locked onto a collision course to hell. "Just the guarantee that you will put the information to good use. Be here in two days."

And with that, he downed the remainder of his drink and left the bar, leaving Hyienna to contemplate exactly what had taken place.

***

For the next few days, Hyienna barricaded himself in his room, not daring to emerge. He knew that when he finally did come out, the world around him would be changed forever. The people would be less trustworthy, the buildings would not promise a safe haven and the light in life would be a lot dimmer. If he was going to step out into a changed world, he wanted to be mentally prepared for it.

He took those precious hours trying to think about Sarah, envisioning a hero narrative in which Nathaniel would be revealed as a swine, a man undeserving of Sarah's love and these revelations would cast him from her life altogether. Sarah would of course be crushed by the bitter betrayal and would look for comfort, finding it with Hyienna, helping the cousins finally mend the bond that had once been broken.

It had occurred to Hyienna that in order to reforge one bond, he had to destroy another. Life was not without its little ironies…

***

Hyienna returned to the Catalan as scheduled, and unlike last time, the Stream was already seated waiting for him. "Whatever happened to 'keeping the customers waiting'?"

The Stream shook his head. "Only works the first time, *amic*."

Hyienna sat down at the table while the Stream stared at him blankly, apparently not considering that Hyienna was expecting him to speak. "Well?" asked Hyienna, suddenly impatient. "Did you find out what I wanted to know?"

"Oh, I most certainly did," said the Stream. "Your friend Nathaniel has the most colourful background; I'll give him that."

"And? What exactly is his background?"

"Ooh" said the Stream playfully. "You're eager to find out, aren't you? Like the kid who can't help wandering downstairs to peak at his Christmas presents."

"Look, stop dicking me around" snapped Hyienna. "I asked you to do a job and-" He stopped, realising what he was saying, and perhaps even more worryingly, who he was saying it to.

The Stream never raised his voice. That was the scariest thing of all. "I think you're probably forgetting who you are speaking to" he said in that silk-soft voice. "Just remember, that one day, you might find yourself on the receiving end of an information trail. And I could just as easily turn your life upside down if I wanted to. I am not some subordinate that you can badger with oh-so-specific instructions. You think I'm irritating now, as your eyes and ears? Imagine me as your enemy."

Hyienna did and having been blessed – or cursed – with a vivid imagination, he did not want to think about the havoc the Stream could wreak on his life if he wanted to. "You're right" he admitted. "I'm sorry, it won't happen again."

"Glad to hear it" said the Stream, giving a smile that was far too wide for his face. "Now, before we get into the nitty-gritty, I have got to ask you; are you absolutely sure you want this information?"

"Why would I change your mind?"

"Because it's always the same" said the Stream, unable to keep the self-satisfied smirk off his face. "Everybody wants to know the in's and out's… until they know the in's and out's. Even if you feel like you know what you will do with this information – good intentions and all that – but it's like lighting a wildfire in the middle of the forest. You have no idea what it how that information will toxify everything around you. You will find it polluting your thoughts and dreams. And the bags already show that you're not a heavy sleeper, so you find out this, you can easily kiss goodbye to any beauty sleep."

As the Stream lay all this out for Hyienna, the reality was starting to dawn on him, and he discovered that he had his hero narrative all wrong. There was a very good chance that Sarah would end up hurt by the revelations and she could easily blame him for bringing that hurt into their lives.

Hyienna had always believed that the more darkness one is exposed to in life, the more it shapes and redefines how we view the world. And he knew that his world was on the verge of being changed forever. He felt as though he was going to get all those exposures that adults had tried to shield him from as a child, to help him retain that innocence just a little bit longer.

Finally, he said, "Tell me everything" knowing that inside, he was hurling himself into an abyss from which there would be no escape.

The Stream spared no detail, laying out everything that he had learned, where he had learned it and the general timeline of events with Hyienna hanging on every word. He didn't keep track of how much time had passed since the Stream had started talking. It was as though all the minutes had melded together as Hyienna's new reality was reforming and re-establishing itself.

Finally, the Stream concluded, having said everything he needed to say and gave a deep breath, leaving to wonder how the man had been able to keep his pace for as long as he had. It was not possible for any human to maintain that momentum…

…unless, of course, the Stream wasn't human.

The Stream rose from his seat. "That's all I have to say on the subject. I am sure you will conclude as to what is right. Everyone else does… eventually." He patted Hyienna on the shoulder and Hyienna felt as though he were being stung by a scorpion. The Stream's neutral tone made it impossible to tell whether it was said earnestly or mockingly.

"Good luck."

***

Hyienna had told Nathaniel that they had needed to speak at the farmhouse. Now. No negotiations, no rearranging.

It was a long journey down to the farmhouse, lasting a good few hours, giving Hyienna plenty of time to ruminate on how he would approach the matter. Would he try to approach the subject as one friend confiding in another? Or would he go in aggressive and vindictive? He imagined Solomon would favour the latter approach.

Hyienna looked around the farmhouse, picking up on sensations that he hadn't noticed before. The squelching beneath his feet as he walked across the land and the stench of livestock hanging in the air like a bad omen. Why hadn't he noticed any of this before?

He had told himself that it was because Nathaniel had worked so hard to blind him, to pull the wool over his eyes. But even that justification felt weak. He knew that based on what the Stream had told him, Nathaniel's lies were not that well-thought out. All it took was a small tug to start the unravelling.

"What brings you out here?" There it was. That sense of comradery. The idea that they were equal men. Nathaniel walked towards him, smiling, seemingly oblivious. Hyienna wanted to punch it off his face more than anything. He couldn't understand how this man could maintain that smile on his face on a daily basis without once betraying the darkness beneath it.

"We need to talk" said Hyienna.

"I figured as much," said Nathaniel. "You going to tell me or are we going to have to play 20 questions?"

For a moment, neither man spoke. And it was clear that a bomb was about to detonate. The only question was who was going to light the fuse.

In the end, it was Hyienna. "I know what you are, Nathaniel."

Nathaniel's smile didn't falter. "What are you talking about?"

"I know where you come from. I know all about Kal, about your brother, about your whole life up to this point. I know that Moirae is on the island and you're probably the one responsible for her being here."

With each word, Nathaniel's smile faded. By the time Hyienna had finished speaking, he looked as though he had aged a decade. "How long have you known?"

"I only just found out."

Fearing the worst, Nathaniel asked, "Did Sarah tell you?"

Hyienna's eyes widened. "You mean, Sarah knows?"

"Yes, I told her." Said Nathaniel, disheartened by her seeming betrayal. Though he silently thought to himself that he hadn't told her the whole truth. He wondered if she would have been so willing to embrace him if she knew all the facts. Taking in Hyienna's confusion, Nathaniel realized that Sarah wasn't Hyienna's new source of information. Not that that reassured him. "Only a few souls know the whole story so how did you get hold of it?"

"I have my own resources" replied Hyienna, not feeling comfortable with dragging the Stream into the mix. He was already unnerved at the supernatural prowess with which he had acquired the necessary information.

"Are you even going to deny it?" asked Hyienna. "Talk me out of it. Tell me none of it is true."

Nathaniel stumbled where he stood and for a moment, Hyienna thought he was going to faint.

"I can't. You know, for the longest time, I hated knowing all those facts about myself. I thought that by not mentioning any of it, I could put some separation between the boy I was and the man I am now."

Before he had time to consider what he was saying, Hyienna instinctively offered, "I can relate to that." He found himself thinking about the babysitter he had loved and the child that had gone missing under her watch, wishing that any kind of denial would separate him from that tragedy. But he knew it would always be set in stone no matter what he did.

"In some ways…" said Nathaniel, walking forward until he finally came to an old milking stool and sat himself down on it, no longer having the energy to stand. "…in some ways, it feels good to get it all out in the open. It takes so much to lie to people, to convince people that your life is perfect and that you have it all together, only when inside, you're coming apart at the seams. You have no idea how much it relieved me to be able to tell Sarah."

"What?" Hyienna's jaw could have hit the floor.

"We talked a while back. She wanted to know things about me. And you know your cousin. She has a way of wearing you down eventually."

"Yeah, don't I know" said Hyienna, bitter that he had spent the last two days musing on the morality of bringing Sarah up to speed on Nathaniel's past, the potential cost to himself and their relationship… only to find out that she already knew.

As these thoughts occurred to him, it became increasingly apparent that this wasn't a criminal mastermind sitting before him determined to ruin lives; this was a broken man trying to pick up the pieces of his fragmented self. Hyienna felt a stab of shame for allowing himself to be so caught up in the pursuit that he had shed so many of his key values like a snake sheds its skin. He was glad that there were no mirrors lying about because he didn't think he would recognise himself.

Hyienna pulled up an old box made of rotting wood and sat next to Nathaniel. "How did it happen, Nathaniel?" he asked softly, trying to take a sympathetic approach.

"The orphanage at St. Gemma's… I used to hate that place, always looked back on it with hardened eyes. But with the benefit of hindsight… I would have gladly taken that place over the horrors that followed later in my life. There are times when I sometimes forget the details and I know that is just me wanting to forget. Sometimes, the only way for wounds to heal is if you just pretend, they're not there. I'm sure you know what I'm talking about."

"Only too well" said Hyienna grimly.

"You know, we all lose our innocence over time" mused Nathaniel. "As we get older and the shelter of adults falls away, we start to see the world as it truly is and we feel the need to either adjust to it, or let it kill us. I knew that I'd have to lose my innocence to survive one day. But I never thought it would be snatched away from me at such a young age."

"By Kal?" asked Hyienna, double-checking. Nathaniel nodded slightly. "You know, I'm normally on the fence about the existence of

God and religion. But I think you can make a very good case for that man being the devil."

"That's exactly what I think," said Nathaniel. "He didn't seem like it at first, always giving us sweets, telling us how special we were. But then I realised, that that's the devil's signature trick, he lures you in, appeals to you before reminding you what you've let yourself in for.

"Now, Ben…" Nathaniel smiled at the memory of his brother. "Now, Ben obeyed the rules, but there were times when he could be outright defiant. For example, stealing food supplies and then sharing it with the kids. He always knew that he was in for the belt, but he had also proved himself useful to the traders. Boys like Ben didn't come every so often. He was physically capable, and he had a great mind about him, even for a kid. You know, he was younger than me, but it often felt like he was wiser than me at least. I learned a lot from him.

"You see, experience does an odd thing to the view of your world. We were sold as babies, never knew a proper life, and never knew what it was like to have a home, loving parents, or a family. So, we didn't really know what we were missing out on. In some ways, I guess that made it easier for us to cope with our own circumstances. We figured that this was as good as it got. But as we got older, we dared to dream. But unfortunately, dreams can't be monetised, and the school wasn't shy about reminding us."

Hyienna dreaded to hear where this conversation was going. "Did they… beat you?"

Nathaniel shook his head vehemently. "No, nothing like that. We were basically like prized racehorses."

Despite the seriousness of the conversation, Hyienna raised an eyebrow. "I was under the impression a racehorse needed to be broken before it could reach its potential."

"Ha, bloody, ha" said Nathaniel, appreciating the moment of levity before he was flung back into the past.

"I still think back to the day when we escaped. To be honest, I had given up on the idea of getting out of there a long time ago. You only know how shitty life is when you've only got your own death to look forward to. But Ben was adamant that that wasn't going to happen to him. You see, he would always keep this scrapbook, he'd take pictures and newspaper articles and stick them in. They'd always be about places around the world, and he would mark them and talk with me after lights out about how one day he would go and visit them all. Of course, me being the pessimist I am, I couldn't see any way out of it. But I indulged him, because when it's little kids, you need to have something to look forward to.

"In fact…" Nathaniel's eyes welled up as the memory of that fateful day stirred in his mind. "…it was Ben who persuaded me to do a runner, ushering me out in the middle of the night. I'm still amazed that we managed to get as far as we did without anyone spotting us. We were almost clear when we heard someone… Ben suggested we split up, saying that if one of got caught, then at least the other one would be free. I managed to find somewhere to hide behind a barrel. And then the lights went up all around the area. And I could hear the captain speaking. He couldn't see where I was, but he was banking on the idea that I could hear him. And I did. I heard my brother being beaten within an inch of his life. And you could tell it was bad" said Nathaniel, shuddering. "Whenever Ben was being punished before, he would always keep a very tight-lip. He would never let the captains have the satisfaction of seeing him in pain. But he was screaming that night and it was like nothing you've ever heard. It haunts me still. To this day, I have no idea what they were using on him to cause him such pain. I couldn't bring myself to turn around and look at him. The captain got out a gun and told me to come out on the count of five or he would put a bullet through Ben's eye. I swear, those five seconds feel like an eternity was passing. And I was about to come out when I heard Ben shouting to me, 'Run'.

Nathaniel's eyes welled up as he relived the moment that would change his life forever. "So, I ran. I only got to about five steps before I heard the gunshot. I didn't need to turn around to see what had happened."

Hyienna looked on, horrified by the story and feeling nothing but sympathy for Nathaniel. In hindsight, his attitude was a miracle in itself, that he lived through such darkness and yet still fight like hell to avoid that dark path.

"And I've been running ever since. I've tried to make a new life for myself ever since. I thought that if I could put as much distance between me and the past, I could make it work. But at the end of the day… I left my brother to die. No matter how I try to dress it up."

Hyienna felt an urge to comfort Nathaniel. "You were just a boy. If you had gone back to them, you might not have ever gotten another chance to escape."

"Maybe not" said Nathaniel, drying his eyes. "But there are times when I can't help thinking of what life would have been like if Ben had lived, if I had actually gone back. I know I've made a big deal of showing off to Sarah, coming across as the big man on the island. But really, all of this is for Ben. I still have his scrapbook with me, and I'm working my way through it, trying to do all the things in my life that he would have done had he lived. That's the deal I make with him every day.

"Sometimes, I like to daydream about how things should have gone. If Ben had lived, grown up to be a man, gotten a chance to sample the good things life has to offer." Nathaniel looked proudly at Hyienna. "I like to think Ben would have been a lot like you as an adult."

Hyienna could tell that the comment was coming from a very personal place, but he knew it was meant as a compliment; perhaps the highest compliment he had ever been paid. "You're setting the bar kinda low there" he said graciously. "But I appreciate it all the same."

Neither man spoke for a moment, Nathaniel far too drained from reliving his trauma and Hyienna was trying to make sense of the story. Even though he had heard it all from the Stream, hearing the facts details with such an emotional charge by Hyienna brought a whole new light to the proceedings. He could see that Nathaniel was not his enemy, not some schemer, simply a man trying to move forward from his mistakes, only for the past to constantly drag him back.

This prompted Hyienna to move forward onto a difficult subject, one that he did not relish, but nonetheless felt needed highlighting.

"There's the subject of Kal. What are we going to do about him?"

Nathaniel put his head in his hands. "Honestly, I don't know. That man has laser vision. Once he gets something set in his sights, he will not stop until he gets it. You could put a mountain worth of concrete between Kal, and his prey and he would still find his way to his prey."

"I don't know" said Hyienna, thinking back on the information provided by the Stream. "I think he's already got his hands full with the Moirae"

"Shit" said Nathaniel grimly. "The vindictive triage of bitches responsible for selling children into slavery and the ones that put me and Ben into Kal's crosshairs. Kal would have really pissed them off. They will stop at nothing to get what they want."

"So how do we stop them?" asked Hyienna. When Nathaniel wasn't quick to respond, Hyienna said, "Don't go holding out on me, man. If these people really are the devils in human form, you make them out to be, then we're all in the same shitty, sinking boat. And I'm pretty sure they will kill anyone who tries to get in their way."

"Hence why I'm not telling you," insisted Nathaniel. "The last thing I want is to see other people getting punished for my mistakes. I've already done that once with Ben. I can't afford to go down that route again."

Hyienna scoffed. "Sorry to burst your martyr bubble, Nathaniel, but I'm already guilty by association. As is Sarah and-"

"There is no way to stop them" said Nathaniel bluntly.

"What?"

"If there was a way of stopping them, do you think I would have spent all of my adulthood and most of my childhood putting as much distance between me and them as possible? They won't be stopped. They can't. Not until they have what they want. The best thing you can do is hand it over to them and pray that you don't incur any collateral damage."

Hyienna thought over the words provided by the Stream, trying to find a solution among the cluster of facts only recently thrown in his direction. "Well," he said with shaky confidence. "We're just going to have to face her together. We need to look out for each other, Nathaniel, now more than ever. For all our sakes. If the Moirae approaches either of us, the other needs to be alerted. I know you seen them as invincible witches, but they can still be taken out. They need to be. That's the only way you'll ever be free of the past."

"You seem very confident for a guy whose never even met them" observed Nathaniel.

"Maybe, but it helps that I know what they are after; your child."

Now it was Nathaniel's turn to be confused.

"But… that's not possible" he stammered. "I haven't got one."

The Nephilem

GOING TO BARÇA
Chapter 17

Solomon allowed himself to sink below the water, into the blue-green oasis, the only place that seemed to offer any calm at that point in time.

He was supposed to be taking a group of tourists out into the waters in half an hour but was in a mind to blow them off.

It was in tranquil moments such as these that Solomon found himself contemplating everything in his life that had brought him to this moment.

He found himself thinking back to his dinner with Yasmina, thinking about what she had said to him.

It couldn't have been true. It couldn't be. He was all too familiar with the baby trap, the sure-fire way to tie you down. He told himself that it had been her way of putting his balls in a lifelong vice. It was often the case with women, fluttering around him like bees around a beehive. But sooner or later, they wouldn't be content with fleeting honey. They'd want the whole hive. And Solomon wasn't willing to give that part of himself. And Yasmina was the latest in a long line of women who were coming up with creative reasons why he should put himself on hold for them.

But what if it was true? Those six words ricocheted around Solomon's head over and over. He remembered the scraping rawness of Yasmina's emotions, remembered how she had spoken at length about their – her – son, thought Solomon, trying to shake her poisonous words from his mind.

The tears that had flown from her eyes, flowing down her beautiful face. That had not been mere acting. Those tears had come from a very real place. And the level

Thinking hypothetically, Solomon tried to imagine if the kid had indeed been his. Given the lifestyle he led, Solomon wouldn't have been too surprised if there was a squadron of Solomon Juniors running around.

He tried to imagine the type of father he would have been. Would he have been attentive, teaching his child the tricks of the trade, how to stay afloat in a world that constantly threatened to pull you under? Or would he have seen the kid as an irritation and been looking to cast him off the first chance he got.

Solomon had once heard a friend of his say that despite our best intentions, we all end up turning into our parents. Solomon would never find out if that had been the case. He had never really known his father, who seemed to have disappeared from the earth altogether, a non-entity in young Solomon's life.

Attempts to query his mother on the type of man his father had been, were sternly deflected. In all the years growing up, Solomon had never once heard a single utterance about his father.

From an early age, he had had a vivid imagination and with his mother unable to fill in the gaps. Sometimes, he imagined that his father was an important man; a hero who had been forced to leave his child to take up arms in a conflict far away from home. But as he grew older, and his bitterness over leading a fatherless childhood continued to gestate, Solomon wondered if his father had been a bad man, and that they might have been better off without him. The exact moment he changed his stance on his father came as a young man was watching the footage of the Almeria anti-immigrant riots. As he saw the flashes of brutality for the first time, saw what people were capable of under the worst possible circumstances, he gradually saw his father as a symbol of evil, as though trying to tell himself it was a good thing, he wasn't a part of his life.

Not that it stopped his mother from finding a string of boyfriends. They had all varied in age and occupation, some had come across as decent people, others only treated his mother as a means to an end, discarding her once they had done what they had wanted with her.

But the most consistent thing linking all of these men was that none of them ever tried to step into the role of father, if only briefly. They gave polite interest to Solomon whenever he was expected to interact with them, but they had never tried to nurture him, never seen him as anything more than an obstacle they needed to maneuverer around to get to his mother.

As he grew older, and the trappings of innocence fell away, Solomon found himself loathing everything about his life. Particularly his town. Solomon had been raised by his mother in the town of Rupit I pruit. As a boy, Solomon had loved walking down the cobbled streets, feeling a sense of comfort that comes with familiarity. But as Solomon grew older and blossomed into maturity, he began to feel the trappings of his environment; the whole town felt like a relic, a part of history that had been abandoned and left to decay. His mother had lived in Rupit I pruit her entire life and had never made any plans to venture beyond the confines of the town. But Solomon was determined to have experiences for himself, to know that life could take many exciting forms. But what?

The answer had finally come to him when he was sixteen, when he had ventured out to Saint Sebastia, one of the longest beaches in the country. He remembered swimming out into the infinite sea, feeling a surge of freedom like nothing else in his life. As the waves lapped against his body, he swam hard, determined not to let yet another force master his life.

And then Solomon had seen a tourist drowning; presumably, an inexperienced swimmer who had swum out too far. Solomon had dashed out into the sea and pulled the tourist – a young boy about four years younger than Solomon himself at the time – back into the shallow water.

Of course, this heroic act caught the attention of several attractive young female tourists, who were eyeing him admiringly. It was the first time Solomon had ever found power in his body and physique. His charm wasn't as well developed back then, but that didn't matter. Courage attracted women like a magnet.

And one of them had shown their appreciation for him that night, making love on the far end of the sandy beach, far from prying eyes. The girl had looked at him and seen a knight in shining armour. But when Solomon looked into her eyes, he saw himself triumphant, realizing the power he possessed over life and women. That day had pushed

Solomon into his current lifestyle, the adrenaline rush that came with scuba diving, every majestic breaststroke, a rebellion against higher forces wanting to control him, and the hedonistic conquests he enjoyed in the arms of many women.

Now he had taken to living life at a breathless pace, moving from one conquest to another. Partly was because of his belief that there were 'plenty of fish in the sea waiting to be caught', as well the unspoken truth that if he slowed down for introspection, he would worry how much like his father he was becoming.

He thought about his impending marriage to Sarah. He had never pegged himself as the settling-down type. And many of his friends had joked that maybe Sarah would make an honest woman out of him. Indeed, he had found a certain calm when he was with her, a sense of peace.

But it wasn't in Solomon's nature to embrace peace. He only felt at ease when he was dancing in the fire. And that was what he had found when allowing himself to get enthralled by Yasmina. There was an untameable fire burning in her belly that had attracted him to her. A darkness that couldn't be quelled.

Solomon wondered if he would ever stop his philandering ways, whether he could indeed settle down and play the role of the family man. He hadn't had a father who taught him about the importance of a man providing. So, what was there to stop him from making the same mistake? What if someday, Solomon himself would become a ghost in his child's life? Would the sins of the father become the sins of the son?

He pushed the thought to the back of his head as he returned to the surface. He had offered for Sarah to join him for a swim, but she had declined. Solomon wondered if Sarah had her own secrets. Maybe one day, some good-looking man would turn Sarah's eye.

That's what had started him about Nathaniel; there had been this allure, this enigmatic quality of a man who had seemingly come from nothing and was now worth everything.

He knew a lot of this was down to the enigma surrounding Nathaniel. Everyone in Formentera knew Solomon and his reputation. But Nathaniel was a man cloaked in mystery. Solomon had hoped that

Nathaniel would fall prey to 'small island mentality, with the residents rejecting him on the grounds of not liking what they didn't understand. But instead, they seemed to have embraced the outsider as though he had been one of their own from the beginning. And the man could certainly be charming when he wanted to be. Solomon had caught wind of Nathaniel's measure tone, able to simultaneously disarm you and put you at ease.

No. Sarah was loyal to him and him alone. Her feelings for Solomon were far too strong for her to even consider letting another man into her life.

***

Sarah threw her arms around Hyienna, enveloping him in a hug as he stood on the doorstep of Casa Hermosa.

Hyienna hadn't realized until now just how much he needed that hug. The past few days had been a whirlwind of emotion for him. He was still reeling from the revelations surrounding Nathaniel. Everything he thought he knew was being called into question. Solomon, Nathaniel, the Stream… it was too much for Hyienna and for now, he was grateful to find comfort in the arms of his cousin.

But even so, he felt the ground beneath them tremble considering what he had learned about Nathaniel. He wanted to be an ally to the man to guide him through the darkness, but he wondered how infectious that darkness would become.

"Well, this is nice" said Sarah, taken aback by the affectionate gesture, but leaning into the hug, nonetheless. "So, what's this in aid of?"

"I just wanted to see you" said Hyienna breathlessly.

"Love the gesture," said Sarah. "But you hug as though this is going to be the last time you ever see me."

Though Hyienna wouldn't say it out loud, it had crossed his mind that sense of foreboding, the possibility that he would hear that Sarah had been in an accident or fallen prey to another's evil. Everything in life felt so fragile, like foundations turned to glass, easily shattered by

Exquil

outside forces.

"I'm glad you popped round" said Sarah, finally pulling away from the embrace. "There was something I needed to ask you about…" She paused, trying to carefully measure her next words. "…I found something. A rucksack."

Hyienna blinked, staring at her blankly as though those previous two words had just bounced off of him. "What?" he asked, a half-whisper.

"I found a rucksack" sighed Sarah. "And there was a blanket inside."

"I…" Hyienna stammered, knowing that every second of hesitation that passed would only harm his eventual answer. His first instinct was to lie, to tell her that he had found it discarded on the beach, but with Sarah, he felt that his capacity for deception was lessened in her presence. But every time he tried speaking the truth in his mind, it sounded more and more ludicrous with each attempt. Somehow, Hyienna didn't feel he could get Sarah to take him seriously with, "An old woman in a lighthouse gave it to me."

Instead, Hyienna zeroed in on the other key revelation that had arisen. "How do you know about it?" He was sure he had kept it tucked away out of the reach of unwanted hands.

Now it was Sarah's turn to be on the offensive. The circumstances under which she had discovered it were most dubious at best.

She remembered paying a visit to Yasmina at the Lizard, hoping to have a chat with her about her complicated feelings for both Nathaniel and Solomon. She would have liked to have spoken to Kate about the issue, but she knew that if she confided in Kate, then by nightfall, the whole island would be caught up in the drama. And Solomon was known to be a possessive man, especially when it came to people, he felt were his. If he assumed that Nathaniel was trying cause a row in Solomon's house, Solomon would beat him black and blue.

So, she had gone to Yasmina to try and speak to her. But when she had got there, Sarah had been forced into a role reversal, with Yaz as the hysterical one and Sarah as the calm and collected one.

Yasmina had been inconsolable, her words incoherent, the words, "Samuel" and "dead" were only a few of the words that Sarah had been able to pull from the incoherent babble. Sarah had tried to soothe her, but to little avail. It was though she had just been hit with the full force of a lifetime of suffering.

She was pointing at something in the corner. A rucksack. And inside it, a small, worn blanket that looked like it had once belonged to a child. Sarah only had to remove a fraction of it from the bag for Yasmina to begin bawling again.

Sarah remembered looking at the blanket, almost transfixed. And as she looked, she was sure that she heard whispers coming from it. But as soon as she stuffed it back into the rucksack, the whispers ceased.

"I don't understand" said Hyienna finally.

"Whatever it was somehow managed to knock Yaz for ten" said Sarah, trying to sound rational. "I couldn't do anything for her. The way she was reacting to that thing… I'm trying to think of a better word than abnormal."

And Hyienna thought to himself, *that's because the contents of that rucksack were definitely not normal.* But he couldn't tell Sarah that. "So… how can I help?" asked Hyienna, wanting to make himself useful.

"I wondered if you would speak to her" pleaded Sarah. "You're good with people and I'm pretty sure she will take to you."

Hyienna was coming to the weary realization that everyone was now treating him as a human confessional, someone to confide their deepest, darkest secrets to. "Look, Sarah. I'd love to help, I really would. But… I wouldn't even know where to start." For starters, he cursed himself for not doing more to conceal the rucksack. If he had, perhaps Yasmina would still have her wits about her.

"She needs this" insisted Sarah. "She's an innkeeper, so she has a very public presence in Formentera. Two people came in looking to book rooms around the same time I was there. She only had to start screaming about someone called Samuel and it scared them off. Everyone on the island will think she is going mad. And from what I've seen, they have a point."

Before Hyienna could say anything else, he heard the sound of an irate voice in the distance, which he quickly recognized as Solomon's. He braced himself, waiting to receive a verbal beatdown…

❦

…but when he turned around, Solomon was venting whatever frustration had been built up over time. "I told you not to call me" he was saying in exasperation, not even acknowledging Hyienna's presence as he pushed past them into the house. "I told you I am not falling for your phantom-kid bullshit." Suddenly conscious of his partner being within earshot, Solomon slammed the door behind him and began speaking in hushed terms. "You say anything to her, and I swear to God, they won't even find what's left of you."

Leaving Solomon to his conversation, Hyienna asked Sarah, "Was there anything else abnormal about Yaz?"

Sarah raised an eyebrow. "You'll have to be more specific."

Hyienna tried to recall his own experiences with the rucksack, recalling when he wanted to hurl it into the ocean, if only to rid himself of the burden, only for a voice to ring out in his voice, imploring him to keep hold of it. The voice alone should have been enough to startle him, but he remembered trying to throw the blanket, mustering every ounce of will in his body, and yet his muscles failed to act in accordance with his thoughts, as though an unseen force had taken hold of him, acting like a puppet, imploring him to keep hold of the dangerous object. He wasn't sure what kind of danger it would bring, but he knew he was dealing with something that was not a part of this world. He had thought that he had successfully concealed the rucksack, chiding himself for how easily Yasmina seemed to have stumbled across it.

He needed to be able to speak to someone about it, to find out what he was dealing with. If this was to be his cross to bear, he wanted to know what kind of burden he was carrying. Something told him that he was carrying more than a faded blanket. But he knew with utmost certainty that if he went back in search of the old woman, he would not find her.

He could always contact the Stream again. That man seemed to have his fingers in many pies. But he felt as though the Stream would be an elusive figure, never one to put the puzzle together for Hyienna, but more content to watch from the shadows as he struggled to put the pieces together himself.

Something was coming for him. What it was, he couldn't explain, but based on Yasmina's explosive reaction, he wondered if he had painted a target on all of their backs.

For her part, Sarah searched Hyienna's face for answers, but found none. She was interrupted from her thought process by a buzzing of her phone. She reached into her pocket, taking it out and looked at the notifications.

It was from Nathaniel. 'I want to tell Solomon about us.'

Sarah felt her entire world darken in that moment. She had worked tirelessly to keep her two worlds separate, and now they were in danger of colliding. Sarah didn't respond immediately, but she could tell that Nathaniel was stood on the other end, waiting expectantly for a confirmation. She tried to keep herself composed.

She still wasn't sure how she felt about Nathaniel, hadn't considered what any future with him might look like.

When she was comparing Nathaniel and Solomon alongside one another, she thought of them in regard to how they seemed to treat her. She knew right away that while Solomon could be affectionate with her, she knew that he likely saw her as a trophy, a prized possession that he could show off and make him feel elevated among the people of Formentera. He often spoke at great length about her beauty. But how long would that last? How many years – or possibly even months – of happiness would they enjoy before Solomon would start thinking of the countless female tourists he could be bedding?

And what about children? Solomon had shown no outward interest in starting a family and Sarah had struggled to entertain the idea of herself as a mother. She remembered once having a dream many years ago in which she had a baby, and rather than feel the typical maternal pride one normally felt, she felt a strong sense of revulsion.

And in the world of the dreaming, time seemed to speed up, the baby grew into a toddler, then into a child, then into a teenager and finally into a beautiful woman who resembled Sarah…

…who had aged rapidly, her skin growing more wrinkle and loose, her hair grey and matted. Her body had started to decay into dust when

Sarah woke up with a start. The idea that having a child would drain any youth from her had scared her off the notion of having children for a long while.

But while the future laid out with Solomon seemed somewhat dismal, she had trouble envisioning what lay ahead for her and Nathaniel. She knew that the whole island would treat her as a pariah and would ostracize her. She trusted that Nathaniel would be able to provide for her, but she wasn't sure whether he loved *her*. Whenever he looked at her, there was no mistaking the tenderness in his eyes, but it always felt as though he was looking through her. He had spoken at length about the time that they had shared together in their younger years, and it made Sarah wonder whether he was seeing her or an idealized version of her that she couldn't hope to live up to.

And when he looked back on their memories together, Sarah noticed that Hyienna seemed to gloss over some of the more negative aspects of their time, and on the very few occasions Sarah had drawn attention to them, he had dismissed them or pretended as though he hadn't heard them. It gave Sarah the impression that he was only capable of looking on their experiences through rose-tinted glasses.

"Anything to be alarmed about?"

Sarah snapped out of her pensive trance as Hyienna spoke up.

"Oh, nothing" she said, not wanting to involve Hyienna at this point. Not down to a lack of trust. She already knew that Solomon would crucify Hyienna if he had even an inkling of his involvement in the proceedings.

She needed to think about this. If this was going to be the start of the next chapter in her life, she needed to make sure the right mechanics were put in place.

Without looking up at Hyienna, she quickly typed in, 'Come to the mainland with me first, then we'll tell him.'

Admittedly, this wasn't a long-term solution. She knew that she was just kicking the issue into the long grass until she had time to think of something more permanent.

"Hey, guys!" The sudden sound of the new voice almost made Hyienna keel over. It was Kate. "So, anybody want to tell me why you're gathered outside the front of the house?"

"Just wanted to let Solomon finish up a call," said Sarah.

For his part, Hyienna avoided making direct eye contact with Kate. The last time she had seen him, he had laid himself bare, told her things that he never thought would pass his lips to anyone. And from what he understood about Kate, passing information to her was tantamount to loading a weapon and waiting for her to fire, where it would no doubt ricochet and destroy his life. He had originally chalked this down to Kate being a gossipy hen, but he could see the danger in her.

"What's going on in there?" asked Kate.

"No idea," said Sarah. She knew there was a 50/50 chance that Kate would later come by the information by herself.

Solomon finally exited the house, rubbing his face and shoving his phone into his pocket. "Sorry about that, bit of business that went sideways." Nobody believed him for even a second, but no one seemed willing to contest him.

Solomon surveyed the gathering outside his house. "So, what brings you all down my way?"

Hyienna was about to speak up when Kate interrupted. "I was looking at taking Sarah out for a bit of shopping, have a girly day out."

This was certainly news to Sarah, who looked at Kate and mouthed, "What?"

"Oh, come on, girl" scoffed Kate. "I've seen the contents of your wardrobe. If you're going to make an impression with the locals, then you need to dress like you belong in this century."

Solomon chimed in. "She's got a point, sweetheart. When I take you out for a night on the town, I want to be able to show you off to everyone. I'm proud to have you on my shoulder, so you need to look the part."

The plan made sense to Sarah, and at the very least, it would give her time away from Solomon and Nathaniel, time to gather her thoughts.

What was the worst that could happen?

***

They had made it to the harbour with five minutes to spare before the ferry took off for the mainland. Solomon had accompanied them, as though he wanted to see Sarah off, to verify that she was going where she said she was going. Kate had assured Solomon that she would be keeping a close eye on her. Something about the way she said it sent a chill down Hyienna's spine.

This wasn't exactly how Hyienna had wanted things to go down. He still felt as though there were so many things left unsaid between him and Sarah. Feeling as though he may never get another chance, he tapped her on the shoulder, halting her.

He leaned close, whispering into her ear, "I've found something through a local…" He paused, trying to find the right words to describe the Stream without it sounding too far-fetched. "…search agency." He wondered, momentarily, whether he was betraying Nathaniel's trust, but given that Nathaniel had already informed Sarah of his troubled past, he pushed those fears to one side. "When you get a chance, go to the Barcelona library."

Sarah looked at him quizzingly. "Hyienna, I will not be caught dead in a library."

"I'm serious, there are things you need to find out. And…" He looked at Kate, who was talking with Solomon. "Be careful what you tell Kate. The woman's got the loosest tongue of anyone I know."

"So, what am I supposed to be looking for?" asked Sarah, noting the seriousness in his voice.

"It's about Nathaniel. Where he came from. Look in the records." But before Hyienna could say any more, Solomon and Kate stepped forward. "Anyone would have thought you were trying to steal your cousin away from me."

"Perish the thought" said Hyienna, suddenly realizing how his pulling Sarah to one side must have looked to the others.

"Come on" said Kate, taking Sarah by the arm. "Unless you fancy paddling to the mainland."

She ushered Sarah onto the ferry just in time.

Hyienna and Solomon watched as the boat pulled out, Sarah and Kate getting smaller and smaller as they waved to each other.

There was something about this goodbye that left a disturbing feeling in Hyienna that he couldn't quite shake off… a sense of finality…

"So, while the ladies are taking care of themselves, what are your plans, my friend?" asked Solomon, patting Hyienna on the shoulder with such force, Hyienna thought his entire shoulder was going to cave in.

"I think I'll look at getting back to the inn" said Hyienna, suddenly feeling the need to be alone again.

"Well, I tell you wait, I've got nothing better to do, I'll give you a lift."

"Oh, I wouldn't want to impose" implored Hyienna.

"Trust me, Hyienna, you'll collapse from the heat before you get back to the inn. No, I insist."

There was a forcefulness in Solomon's voice that put Hyienna on edge. And he did not want to run the risk of saying 'no.'

***

Hyienna was grateful that he took the drive, feeling the sweat dripping down his skin. It was so hot that he could even feel the wind in the air.

"I can wait an eternity for the 'I told you so'" said Solomon smugly.

Right now, Hyienna didn't want to give him the courtesy, his mind focused on Sarah and Kate.

"You know" said Solomon, not taking his eyes off the road. "Unless I'm mistaken, I think you will have been in Formentera for the better part of a year now."

"How time flies" said Hyienna tonelessly.

"Is the place everything you wanted it to be?" asked Solomon.

Hyienna looked back on his near year in Formentera, thought about the relationships he had established in that time, the forces he had come into conflict with, and the mysteries that had yet to be solved.

"It's grown on me" Hyienna finally said. And there was no sarcasm in his words. For better or worse, Formentera felt like a part of him now, and he felt as though he was spiritually bonded to the place. Even if he decided to pack up and leave tomorrow, he imagined he would always carry the island around in his soul like an unwanted weight.

"I imagine it would have gone down a lot smoothly without me getting involved," said Solomon. He sighed. "Look, Hyienna…" Hyienna noted that Solomon was taking care not to mispronounce his name. "I know we didn't exactly get off to the best start. More my fault than yours. I know I came at it a little heavy with the big 'I am. Can't have made it too easy to settle in."

Hyienna seemed taken aback by how forthcoming Solomon was being. "You may not believe this, but I was once like you."

Hyienna fought the temptation to roll his eyes. Was there anyone on this island who wasn't trying to outrun something or someone?

"I know what it's like to come from very little, to want to be able to find your own place in the world, not being content with playing the hand life deals you. I think that's the thing about Formentera. It's an island of strays and lost souls."

"No apologies necessary" assured Hyienna graciously.

"No, please, let me" insisted Solomon. "I've been on your case a lot when in all honesty, you were the one I needed to make a good impression with more than anyone."

Of all the things Solomon had said to him, this was the one that took Hyienna by surprise the most. "How did you work that one out?"

Solomon shrugged. "Because soon we're going to be family. I'm going to be marrying your cousin."

That is assuming you'll stop doing all your thinking with your dick, Hyienna wanted to say, but chose not to.

"I know I am probably not ideal husband material. But I generally love Sarah. She makes me want to be a better man."

Hyienna fought back the urge to laugh. Knowing his cousin as he did and her flighty nature and desire for the finer things in life, he figured she would make Solomon want to be a richer man.

Solomon continued. "I'd travelled down here a few times, often on holidays. When you compare it to the rest of Spain, it's not much to boast of. It has the necessities, making for a mundane paradise, but offers little more. When I was a kid, I always felt like I didn't belong in my own little town. I wanted to get out in the world, see everything sample all the cultures."

"So, what made you stick around Barcelona?" asked Hyienna, genuinely interested.

"Time lends a certain clarity" admitted Solomon. "I felt like this whole area was a part of me, and I wouldn't shed it, no matter how much I tried."

"I suppose I've got to ask" said Hyienna, moved by Solomon's honesty and yet at the same time, wanting to get certain things off his chest. "Why Sarah? I'd be lying if I said I didn't know you had a reputation."

Solomon shrugged dismissively. "News travels very fast."

"So do you from the sounds of it" dared Hyienna.

But Solomon kept his composure. "Fair play. But I generally want to make it work with Sarah. That's why I agreed to move to Formentera in the first place."

Hyienna felt a pang of guilt knowing that the only reason Sarah had wanted to move to Formentera was so that she could be close to Nathaniel. But that guilt faded at the reminder of Solomon's philandering nature.

And then, as if he had read Hyienna's mind, Solomon said, "It's your friend Nathaniel I'm concerned about."

"How so?"

"Well, look at everyone on the island, everyone is trying to pretend they come from something better, we're all hiding things, but Nathaniel seems to have it down to an art form. He has worked tirelessly to integrate himself into the island and the culture and the people. And in my experience, the more you claim to belong, the more you're hiding."

Knowing that he was now sitting on an explosive truth about Nathaniel, Hyienna shifted uncomfortably in his seat.

"And I've notice he's been spending a lot of time trying to catch Sarah's eye."

Hyienna tried to relax, knowing that because Nathaniel had buried his tracks so deep, the Stream was the only one likely to be privy to the information. And Solomon was hardly likely to have come across him.

"But I was put in touch with a friend in high places."

Hyienna gulped.

"There's been a lot of conflicting information regarding Nathaniel. They say he was a bit of a church boy. Some say that he is a self-made man. Some have even said he is God's gift to the island. *I* say he's full of shit. You can tell with the way he uses the local language like a parrot."

Hyienna tried to play it down, making out that he knew less than he actually did.

"Everyone has secrets, you pull the thread hard enough and my, my, how it unravels."

"What did you find?" asked Hyienna hesitantly, knowing that he would not like whatever came out of Solomon's mouth.

"My man knows a social worker who works for a judge. And apparently, he arranges closed adoptions."

Hyienna blinked. "I'm sorry, Solomon, you're going to have to come back to Earth and pick me up."

"Think of it like a regular adoption, only difference being that the biological parents' records are either sealed or wiped out altogether. It prevents either the kid or the parents from ever being able to find one another."

"I'm pretty sure that's illegal."

"You'd be surprised," said Solomon. "Everything that's now legal was at one point illegal. If there's one guarantee about the system, it's that it always finds ways to work against you while calling it legal. You take you and me, for example. You wind the clock back a few decades, you and I would have been treated no better than cattle."

Trying not to think about those last words, Hyienna pressed on. "What has closed adoption got to do with anything?"

"Closed adoption is perfectly legal in some areas. Nuns get a lot of mileage out of them, taking kids that have been born in less-than-ideal circumstances. If the parents say, are a pair of bastards, then it's in everyone's best interest that the child keeps away from them. And apparently, Nathaniel's records are sealed off. So, whoever he used to be in his previous life must have been quite damning."

Knowing both the details of Nathaniel's backstory as well as the fact that Solomon was disturbingly close to the truth, Hyienna tried to divert Solomon's attention away from the negative. "Look, I won't deny that Nathaniel probably has a few skeletons in his closet. But you want to be careful, Solomon. You don't want to make the mistake of confusing secretive with dangerous."

"You know, you're absolutely right" said Solomon, to Hyienna' s brief relief. "I'm a man of principle. I like to know if I'd dealing with a dangerous man. Hence the reason for this trip."

Hyienna suddenly felt an urge to jump out of the car. "What little trip?"

"I know that Nathaniel has been trying to worm his way into Sarah's knickers. And I know that *you* have been at least party to it."

Hyienna opened his mouth to speak, trying to think of anything to say that might absolve him of any blame.

"Now, I could thump you, and believe me, I considered it. But given I didn't do much to endear me to you to begin with, I can understand why you might have kept a tight lip."

This surprised Hyienna. He had pegged Solomon as the type of man who would stumble into a situation with fists flying.

"Truth is," said Solomon. "I need your help."

"My help?"

"You have been getting closer to Nathaniel more than anyone. For whatever reason, he trusts you more than anyone. If shit ends up hitting the fan, and believe me, it's looking more and more likely, I will need someone with me to help sort Nathaniel out. I don't know why he trusts you, but whatever the reason, he'll let you get closer to him. If I went into this myself, he'll see me coming a mile off, he'll be working to cover his tracks. At least with you, he'll be willing to let his guard down."

Hyienna chuckled nervously, not liking the idea of playing the agent in Nathaniel and Solomon's war. "I think you overestimate my importance in relation to him."

"No, I don't think I do" said Solomon, unwilling to hear anything that didn't fit with his logic. "He trusts you, and I need to use that trust to safeguard myself and Sarah. I know I'm not exactly Romeo, but I love Sarah. I *know* that in my heart. Now, Nathaniel, I know enough to know that he's dangerous. And he has Sarah in his sights. So, I need to protect her."

"I'm not sure what you're asking of me" said Hyienna.

"I'm asking you to help me keep her safe" said Solomon firmly. "You've not got a woman in your life, have you, Hyienna?"

"Last time I checked" said Hyienna dryly.

"Well, if you did, and you felt she was in a situation where she was dancing very close to the sun, would you honestly tell me you would stand by and let it happen? Or would you start working out how much heat you'd be willing to bring your way to save her?"

Hyienna could see Solomon's point. Although he couldn't help, but wonder if Solomon's knight in shining armour attitude was less because he was concerned for Sarah's safety and more because Nathaniel was encroaching on what Solomon considered to be his?

"So, where am I supposed to fit into this little soap opera?" asked Hyienna, unable to maintain his sarcasm.

Ignoring the comment, Solomon said, "We're going to meet somebody who knows a bit more, someone who can clue us in on all the details."

It was in that moment that Hyienna felt himself hurling into an abyss, feeling as though he had lost control of the situation and was never going to get it back. "Who are we going to see?" he croaked out.

Solomon smiled thinly. "That would be telling."

"And you couldn't tell me any of this man to man? You had to put up this façade of male bonding?"

"Hyienna, if I had outright asked you to help me, you would have said no and sided with Nathaniel."

Hyienna nodded slowly, reluctantly seeing the logic.

"When we get there, hopefully we'll be getting some answers."

"And what about Sarah?" asked Hyienna. "What are her thoughts on all this?"

"Oh, she doesn't know," said Solomon. "I figured if she knew, she'd try and warn Nathaniel. I needed her out of the way, if only for a few hours while I sort out this situation. When Kate said she wanted to take her out for the day, I figured, 'why not?' Perfect excuse. And there I was thinking I would have to spin a tapestry of bullshit."

Hyienna couldn't help but be impressed with Solomon's Machiavellian thinking. "Have you thought about how Sarah will take all of this?"

"Oh, she will get over it" said Solomon dismissively. "You know the type of things your cousin wants in life. You honestly think Nathaniel can provide her with all of that? Let's say, Nathaniel is revealed to be bumping shoulders with some really bad people. Best case scenario, they arrest Nathaniel and seize all of his assets, leaving her without a penny to her name. Worst case scenario, they decide to take Nathaniel out of the picture and make an example out of Sarah. And I will not have that.

"There's something else too…" He hesitated, not sure how to say what he was about to say. "…I think Sarah might be pregnant."

This made Hyienna bolt upright in his seat. "What?"

"All the signs are there. She's eating a lot; she's got morning sickness. She told me a few days ago."

"And how do you feel about it?" asked Hyienna.

Now, Solomon looked ashamed. "If I'm honest, I didn't react in the best of ways. I told her that neither of us were ready to be parents, that we'd be putting our entire lives on standby, so… I told her she should get rid of it."

Hyienna choked back his anger, listening to Solomon carry on.

"And it's not just our own issues. You look at all the demented shit that can happen around here. Would you really want to raise a child on an island of uncertainties?"

Having been on Formentera for nearly a year, Hyienna's opinion of the city had changed drastically, and he no longer saw it as a place of salvation. "No, I guess not."

"Exactly" said Solomon. "We'll go there, here this guy out, and depending on what he tells us, we'll be taking it from there."

Knowing he had no way out of the situation, Hyienna reluctantly accepted his place in the situation. "Fair enough."

"And there's something else" said Solomon, taking his eyes off the road to look directly at Hyienna. "I found some information on you too, my friend."

ZARAGOZA
Chapter 18

There was a faint wind in the air, whipping at Sarah's exposed skin. It was rare to get a wind in Barcelona, especially around the summer. She was used to feeling the light touch of the sun radiating from her. She wasn't dressed for this weather. And considering she had been about to use Solomon's credit card to buy a few sundresses, she may have to rethink what she was doing.

Kate, on the other hand, didn't seem bothered by the chill. If anything, she seemed to welcome it. She gripped the rails and that was when Sarah saw for the first time what must have always been there. Hunger. Her expression was a lustful one, as though what was in her heart's desire was almost upon her.

Sarah didn't have time to ask her before they were about to dock at Barcelona.

When they had set off on the trip, Sarah had been planning to all, but max out on Solomon's credit card for clothes and beauty treatments until she came back looking like royalty.

But over the course of the journey, Hyienna's words had worn her down. The urgency in his voice had unsettled her.

She figured it was to do with Nathaniel, who she instantly knew would object to him looking through anything to do with his past life. She remembered the confession he had given her about his past. She could see that it had taken a lot out of him, that he had scraped the bottom of his soul to recall that part of his life.

But as she looked back on the memory of Nathaniel's confession, new details appeared in her mind. The more she thought about it, the more she felt as though Nathaniel was holding out on her. As though there was a depth to his words that he was trying quite hard to avoid reaching.

Apart of her wanted to leave well enough alone. Sarah knew that Nathaniel probably wouldn't take kindly to her poking around.

She could just go on meeting Nathaniel, gaining security financially from being with him. But could she really risk it all? Throw away everything that Solomon was providing her all for the sake of a man who could just as well be her undoing?

No. She needed to be sure.

"So, where are we hitting first?" asked Kate. "I've been told on many occasions I have a sparkling personality and I could do with the jewellery to match."

"Actually, Kate…" asked Sarah, suddenly realizing how dependent she was on the woman for her mission. Kate had shown all the signs of a trustworthy companion, a shoulder to cry on when needed, someone who offered sage-like advice when prompted… but there was always the possibility that Kate might weaponize her mission against her, report it back to Solomon. When he heard what she had been planning… well, Sarah didn't want to try too hard to picture his reaction.

Should she try and abandon Kate to set off on her own? Or should she trust Kate with this dangerous knowledge and risk it all?

Finally, she decided.

"I think we're going to need to take a little detour, Kate."

If Kate was puzzled by the sudden change in plan, she did not show it. "What kind of detour?"

She went through the multiple options in her head, trying to think of the one that sounded least far-fetched. But none emerged. "The library" she managed.

"The library?" repeated Kate. "I never had you pegged as a bookworm."

"There are some things I need to look at. And… I'd prefer it if Solomon didn't find out. From anyone."

"What's that supposed to mean?" asked Kate in a playful manner, but with just enough edge for Sarah to take her seriously.

"I mean, I would really appreciate it if our little detour wasn't the talk of the town."

"Sarah, you make me sound like some kind of gossipy hen. Your secret is safe with me" said Kate reassuringly. "So, do you want to tell me what it is we're looking for?"

"I can't." But before Kate could protest, Sarah added quickly, "I can't because I'm not even sure what we're supposed to be looking for. So, I think we need to take it, one step at a time."

"Fair enough. So, what's the next step?"

"We're going to need a car," said Sarah. "I really don't fancy walking down to the library, especially not in these shoes."

"Well, if my memory serves, there should be a rental about twenty minutes away from here" suggested Kate.

Now Sarah was visibly wincing, as though it pained her to say the next few words. "There's just one thing, though. I may need your help with the cash."

Kate raised an eyebrow. "Girl, you've got Solomon's credit card on you. You're practically Miss Moneybags."

"I know, but the stuff I need to do, I'd rather Solomon didn't find out. He'd go apeshit."

"I'm starting to feel like you're asking a lot, Sarah," said Kate. "I mean, I love you like a sister and all, but I'd rather not go up against Solomon."

"He doesn't need to know, I promise. The less he knows the better."

"OK" said Kate simply and Sarah couldn't help but wonder if Kate had always intended to help her and had just decided to drag the dilemma out for the sake of it.

The two made their way to the dealership where Kate paid in cash for a rental. It wasn't much to boast of the car was well used, the leather seats that had once glistened in the sunlight were now faded and torn in some places. And it looked as though it had been years since the car had had a decent paint job. For Sarah, who had been used to getting the best of everything in life, it was quite a downgrade. But it was the best that they could afford with Kate's money, and it wasn't like they wanted to be noticed on this little endeavour.

Sarah drove the car towards the library, the two sitting in silence all throughout the journey. In truth, Sarah was surprised by how easily Kate had been persuaded to take part, she thought she'd have to do everything short of threatening her to get her compliance. In fact, Kate had seemed quite eager to part with her money and accompany Sarah on this journey.

It was almost as if she had a personal stake in this mission.

They finally arrived at the public library, pulling up a few blocks away.

Sarah had never been to this part of Barca before. She thought back to all the time she had spent in Formentera. An island that felt as though it got the best of everything in life, the slice of life that everyone wanted to remember.

But this part of the island, with its ancient, crumbling buildings felt like a relic people wouldn't mind forgetting.

They both walked into the building, with Sarah visibly taken aback by the lack of hustle and bustle.

The library was great and vast, with rows upon rows upon rows of books. Sarah almost wondered how such an old building had been able to contain such a vast source of knowledge. Looking around, Sarah eyed no more than eleven people sat in various places, their noses in their own books, looking for their own source of enlightenment.

Sarah felt a wave of heat in the room, causing her to sweat mildly. "Didn't think it'd be so hot in here" she remarked, trying not to let the discomfort ruin her complexion. "Don't they know how to open windows around here?"

"Would you like me to ask around for an axe?" asked Kate, one eyebrow raised.

"Can I help you?" came a voice alarmingly close to Sarah, causing her to jump out of her skin. The woman was young, in her early twenties at a guess, dressed in a black shirt with a cardigan, the seemingly dated sense of fashion betraying her youthful features.

"Yes, you can" said Kate, taking charge. "We're looking for birth records, going back at least two decades. You think you might be able to help us with that?"

"Of course, I can," said the librarian. "This way, please."

She took them through a doorway, down a circular staircase, where Sarah shivered at the evident chill. "Apologies for the temperature"

said the librarian without turning around. "We don't usually get visitors down here."

"It shows" muttered Sarah under her breath as the walls around her became increasingly stonelike, reminding her that they were moving further and further away from civilization.

"Do you mind my asking what it is you're looking for?" asked the librarian. Noticing Sarah's immediate apprehension, she quickly added, "It will help to improve the service I provide to customers."

"We're trying to track down an old family friend," said Kate.

"So, this must feel like coming home to you," said the librarian.

"Yes" said Kate. "You could say that."

At the bottom of the stairs, the librarian gestured to a stack of shelves, which contained moth-eaten cardboard boxes. "Like I said" said the librarian, a little embarrassed. "Nobody's come down here in a while."

"No shit," said Kate.

"Right" said the librarian. "That's me. If you need anything, just come up and get me. I hope you guys find what you're looking for." And with that, she left them to their search.

The two women browsed through the boxes listed in alphabetical order. To say that there was no order to the records would be an understatement. It looked as though papers had been shoved haphazardly into a folder before being thrown into the box. On several occasions when Sarah and Kate were taking out folders, they had to take care to prevent any papers from spilling out onto the stone-cold floor.

"You know" said Kate, not taking their eyes off the papers. "There's always the possibility that we won't find anything."

"How do you mean?" asked Sarah, running her finger over the papers trying to find anything that would stick out.

"Well, assuming that Nathaniel's adoption was… off the books, so to speak, it's not likely to turn up here of all places."

"How would you know?" asked Sarah, turning to Kate. "You an expert in back-alley adoption?"

"It's what anyone would do" said Kate defensively.

Sarah was about to probe the subject even further when, out of the corner of her eye, she noticed something on one of the folders. Nathaniel's name printed out in capital letters.

"This should be it" said Sarah, feeling triumphant.

But when she opened the pages, something alarmed her.

"What is it?" asked Kate, trying to get a better look.

Sarah showed her the file.

On practically every page, black bars blocked out words, phrases, sometimes even entire paragraphs. Where it not for the picture on the front of a young Nathaniel and the accompanying name, there would be nothing to suggest that this was Nathaniel's file.

"What the hell?" muttered Kate, taking the file from Sarah and looking over it. "Looks like your man has his fair share of skeletons in his closet."

"There's got to be an explanation for this," said Sarah. She thought that Nathaniel had told her the entire truth when they had shared that car ride, that he had borne his soul.

As if reading Sarah's mind, Kate said, "You know, I'd ask him to explain this away, but somehow, I get the impression he would button up."

"These are adoption papers," said Sarah. "Whatever Nathaniel was involved in, surely, he can't have done it himself. He would have only been a kid."

"And he couldn't tell you the whole truth?" asked Kate. "When men like that promise a confession and only tell you the half-truth, which means the whole truth will consist of some pretty shady shit."

"Excuse me?"

Both Sarah and Kate whipped around, feeling a desire to keep their secret hidden. The librarian was stood at the bottom of the stairs. Even though she maintained a polite posture, at a careful glance, Sarah could tell that the woman was shaking slightly.

"I couldn't help overhearing your conversation" began the woman.

"And here I was thinking we were surrounded by thick walls," said Kate.

"The adoption records…" And now the librarian was struggling to keep the shakes out of her voice. "…they were taken from here about a week ago."

"Taken?" asked Sarah. "What do you mean, 'taken?'"

"Someone wanted to know where they were, told me that it was a matter of life or death."

"And you just gave them to him?" asked Sarah disbelievingly.

The librarian looked down at her shoes, being unable to face not just the two women, but the lapse in her judgment. "He didn't seem like the kind of man one says 'no' to."

"Do you have any idea where we might be able to find this man?" asked Sarah.

"I couldn't say" stammered the librarian.

"Look" said Kate. "Why don't you and I have a little girl-talk in private? See if we can get to the bottom of this?"

She wrapped her arm around the librarian and led her away. Sarah began to follow. "Shouldn't I be listening in to this?"

"Yes, we could really do with you coming down on the poor girl like a ton of bricks." Softening, Kate said, "Trust me, Sarah, I have a way with people."

And Sarah was left to ponder what that way might look like as Kate and the librarian ascended the stairway.

She returned to the pile of papers on the desk, trying to restore order as best as she could.

As Sarah sat down, she felt a jolt in her stomach and her hand instantly went to her belly.

She wondered if this was where it started. She had heard that the pains always start off quite minimal before they progress with each month of pregnancy. She did not feel particularly enamoured at the idea of having this thing inside her eating away at her physically, taking away all of her strength and wreaking havoc on her body. She remembered as a child glimpsing the stretch marks on her mother who had apparently been quite the beauty before childbirth had taken its toll on her.

She knew that it was unfair, and it was not the fault of the child. It was not right that a child should be held accountable for the mistakes its parents made.

But Sarah wasn't even sure of the child's parents.

One reason she had been torn between the worlds of Solomon and Nathaniel would be because she had no idea who would be the father of her child. Solomon had already made his decision on the matter quite clear, and she imagined he would have a tough time changing his mind.

With Nathaniel, she had seen the way he had looked at her, a love that was unconditional, unbreakable, there was nothing superficial. Sarah didn't doubt that he would care for their child no matter the circumstances. But what kind of life would their child have? To have the child would mean coming clean with Solomon. And she knew that he was not a man to be wronged. His word carried a lot of sway with Formentera, and he could easily paint her as a ruined woman.

When she felt for her stomach, she didn't just feel a little life growing beneath her skin, she felt a ticking clock. If she planned to carry this pregnancy to term, it would only be so long before her belly started swelling and termination would not be an option.

She tried for what felt like the hundredth time to resolve the issue of the child's paternity. She remembered making love to Nathaniel shortly after their eventful car journey. She should have used protection, but she was swept away in the emotion brought on by Nathaniel's confession…

…and shortly before that, Solomon had come to her that one night, begging for companionship, but silently holding out for more, the way men do when they feel entitled to something and don't want to have to ask. Sarah herself had had quite a lot to drink that night. They had melted away into each other's arms.

There was a four-day difference, making it nigh-impossible for anyone short of a witch doctor being able to tell the difference. She had heard that there were tests that could be done to determine the baby's paternity, but from what she had heard, they were quite intrusive procedures, and there was no guarantee that they wouldn't damage the baby's health.

Even discounting the medical risk, she would not be able to have that kind of check-up without alerting any of the locals. Chances are, someone down there would pass her details back to Solomon.

Like every other tragedy in Sarah's life, she tried to tackle it with the same mindset; consider it a problem for another day.

She was snapped out of her dilemma by the sound of approaching footsteps as Kate and the librarian both descended the stairs together, Kate holding the librarian by the arm as though supporting her. The librarian looked as though she had gone a different shade of white.

"What did you do to her?" asked Sarah, half-joking.

"I told you," said Kate simply. "I have a way with people. And now, we have a new destination, thanks to this lovely creature here." She pressed her hand into the librarian's shoulder, who visibly recoiled from the touch, but tried to keep the discomfort off her face with questionable success.

***

They cleared out of the library quite quickly. Neither of them had bothered to take any of the doctored adoption papers, Kate having reasoned that there would be no use for any of them.

They piled back into the rented car and continued driving to their destination.

"She gave me an address for the person who likely has information on these adoption papers. With any luck, he should still be in the area and should be able to provide us with some answers."

Sarah looked at Kate, who was driving the car with a steely command. "You seem very sure of yourself, you know that?"

"Well, we need that kind of certainty if we're going to get anywhere."

Remind me again why we couldn't just bribe that librarian?" asked Sarah.

"Thought you were trying to avoid leaving a paper trail," said Kate. "Besides, judging by the look of her, I doubt she'd even know what a credit card looks like. The poor thing might as well have lived her life trapped in that attic. It was a calculated risk getting her to talk and point us in the right direction."

"And what do we do if the source isn't where she says he is?" asked Sarah, certain that there was a flaw in the plan she wasn't seeing.

"I've thought about that" said Kate briskly.

"And?"

"And we'll be back at square one. You, see? I've thought about it?" Kate took her eyes off the road just briefly to take in Sarah's perplexed face. "You worry too much, Sarah. You always act as though your life is one disaster away from imploding. You need to take things as they come, let them wash over you."

"When I'm in the mindset for poetry, I'll pencil it in" quipped Sarah.

***

When they arrived at the location, Sarah almost understood why the librarian had been reluctant to open up.

The buildings were in varying stages of decay, deplorables coming in and out. Sarah could see a group of people stood close together watching them. To them, the car must be some kind of rare jewel, thought Sarah. She tried to imagine that at night, the streets came alive with a vibrant carnage, people dancing in the moonlight basking in euphoria under cover of darkness. But in the daylight, that effect hadn't carried over, the buildings on either side of the road looking like oversized slabs as the car drove past, as though they were entering a gargantuan graveyard. Sarah would never be caught dead in a place like this.

The car pulled up outside what looked like a tavern, given the similar features of all the buildings, it was hard to tell. "You sure we shouldn't hide the car" asked Sarah, looking around at the people in the street who were eyeballing her. "I have a feeling that it won't be here when we come back."

"Why?" asked Kate. "You got any bushes for me to hide it behind?"

Kate watched a group of small children at least ten years old playing in the streets with a football. One of the boys kicked the boy, narrowly missing the car. "Sorry" he called out, expecting a reprieve.

But instead, Kate smiled. "Tell you what; how would you kids like to make a little extra pocket money?"

"What do you need?" asked the boy.

Kate pulled out a wad of notes, which prompted the attention of the other children to come running over. Neither of them had ever seen so much money in their life.

Kate took a note and passed one around to each of the children. "You can keep an eye on this car for at least an hour, there'll be another helping at the end of it, you got it?"

The boys all nodded, eagerly accepting the money.

"Really, Kate?" asked Sarah. "Anyone would have thought you were a charity."

"You were the one who was worked up about the car. Either we cough up a bit of dough to keep it safe, or we make it around Barcelona on foot. I'm guessing you have a preference?"

They walked into the tavern, looking around at the people inside. Sarah tried to keep her jewellery hidden in the event anyone tried to pounce on her. Kate rolled her eyes at the materialistic display. "For God's sake, woman, don't get so worked up over your jewellery."

"Easy for you to say" retorted Sarah. "Last time I checked; you weren't one lugging anything fashionable on your fingers." She surveyed the crowd once again, who seemed to be keeping to themselves, not that this did much to alleviate Sarah's anxiety. "I swear to you, one of these freaks is going to take my jewellery and then straight up kill me."

"That's impossible," said Kate. "Very unlikely to happen."

"Why?"

"Because this lot won't waste any time struggling with you; they'll just kill you, *then* take the jewellery."

Sarah looked pointedly at Kate. "Tell me, Kate, at any point in your past life were you a motivational speaker?"

"I had my moments" admitted Kate.

"I take it you lovely ladies are waiting for me?"

The voice came in between them, and Sarah almost jumped out of her skin. Kate seemed non-plussed, taking in the figure who was standing before them in the doorway. There was nothing to indicate he had walked in through the doorway, or that he had gotten up and walked towards them through the crowd.

It was as if he had just materialised behind them.

"You know how to make an entrance" said Kate, who seemed completely unsurprised by the intrusion.

"It helps for a man to be able to slip in and out of the world whenever he feels like it" said the man, stepping back. Now Sarah could see he was wearing a long black trench coat. "I am the Stream."

"Is that what your friends call you?" asked Sarah, unimpressed by the grandeur.

"Indeed, *petit ocell,*" said the Stream. "You might even get to call me that if you live long enough." He turned to Kate and made a slight bow. "My apologies for the goose chase, *bruixa*. Wouldn't have been my first choice, but when it comes to valuable information, there is very little stopping it from falling into the wrong hands."

"Well, thank God you're here to intervene," said Sarah.

The Stream was now studying Sarah, as though only just seeing her for the first time. "You know… I find myself struggling to comprehend what he sees in you. It's certainly not your intellectual prowess."

"Who?" asked Sarah, agitate.

"All right, cut it out, riddle-man" snapped Kate, impatiently. "Save that cryptic bullshit for the tourists."

The Stream looked at Kate, as though seeing her for the first time. "Very well" he said, speaking in a tone that was supposed to be natural, but instead came out stilted and he was clearly trying to contain himself.

"Why don't we take a seat?" suggested Kate, trying to prevent an altercation from breaking out.

The Stream led them over to a deserted table and ordered a drink. "Why do we have to meet here?" asked Sarah, glimpsing around at the patrons. "Among these… people?"

The Stream frowned. "These 'people' are lost souls. Whatever life they had beforehand has crumbled around them. What they have around here, it's not much, admittedly, but it's home. I apologize for failing to live up to your standards, *petit ocell,* but you see, not everyone has a castle to retreat to like you." He turned to Kate. "So" he said briskly, clearly wanting to hurry things along. "What has put you in my direction?" He downed his drink at that point.

"We're looking for information on an adoption."

The Stream smiled again, but this time, it didn't seem like a smile, more like a grimace. "I'd think long and hard before you go looking under that rock."

"It's important that we find this information as soon as possible." instructed Kate.

The Stream leaned into Kate and Sarah could see he was inhaling deeply. "You are not one to be trifled with" he said plainly. He leaned back, impressed and to Sarah's surprise, a little subdued. For a few minutes, they sat in silence, until the Stream finally said, "In Zaragoza, there is a nun. I believe she goes by the name Sister Veronica. To the best of my knowledge, she should still be alive. I suggest you pay her a visit. She will tell you all you need to know."

"Is she going to tell us about Nathaniel?" asked Sarah impatiently.

The Stream looked at Sarah with interest. "Ah, I'm guessing he's not been entirely honest with you."

"What are you talking about?" asked Sarah, trying not to freak out.

"He was worried that you'd run a mile if he told you the truth. Not that I blame him, I imagine that if I had that kind of background, I'd be keeping a tight lip." He then added in a sotto voice; "And that's not actually too far off from the truth.

"But I must insist, *petit ocell,* for your own sake, go home, forget about what you are looking for."

"What?" exclaimed both Sarah and Kate, Kate in particular looking at the Stream with fiery eyes.

"I don't think you fully comprehend what you are looking for" said the Stream, taking on a more serious expression and trying to visibly ward off Kate's angry gaze. "You must know that no good can come from any of this, don't you? It will wreck a lot of lives; probably Nathaniel's, certainly yours. It's not the kind of damage you can contain.

"Now, this man clearly loves you, loves you enough to try and keep you out of Hell, even if it means condemning himself in the process. That kind of love is incredibly hard to come by and in my experience, it always comes with many catches. Go back to your old life. This isn't your life; it isn't even your world. You should forget about all of this. Even now, it's not too late to turn back."

"I can't" said Sarah numbly. The words that came tumbling out, they hadn't been there a moment ago. But the feelings, the feelings had been there for a long time, and it was only now that she was able to put words to them. "I love Nathaniel, I've spent a good portion of my life pining after him. If there are going to be any challenges, I want to be able to face them with him. And…" She looked down at her belly. "…I think we're having a baby. Whatever happens to this child, I don't want it to go through the same hardships as its father."

The Stream appeared sincerely moved by this and for a moment, seemed lost for words.

"Well, I must say, I admire your commitment. If you're absolutely sure, then I will give you what you need, and I will be on my way."

"I'm sure" said Sarah, like a gambler who was placing a bet she was certain would pay off.

But Sarah would not have been quite so confident if she had known what she was gambling.

After the Stream had conveyed the information, Sarah got up and made her way to the entrance, determined to find this nun. But Kate hung back briefly to glare at the Stream. "What do you think you are playing at?"

"I had to give her the choice," said the Stream. "Now it's out of my hands and in yours. So do with it what you will."

***

The drive to Zaragoza was a difficult one for Sarah. Everything that she thought she had known about Nathaniel was now being called into question. At first, she had been angry that that heartfelt confession had been partially engineered. But when she thought about all that she had learned about his brother, the life that he had led – the life that he had been forced to lead – she felt a pang of sympathy. It would take a lot for a man living in darkness to force himself into the light with the constant risk of it weighing him down.

As they drove, Sarah looked over to Kate, who didn't seem fazed by anything she had learned that day. In some ways, Sarah admired that unbreakable demeanour. It was like looking at a woman who would willing swim with the sharks without fear or trepidation.

As they drove, Sarah noticed a road sign pointing them in the direction of the small town of Burjaraloz. As she glanced at the sign, something shifted in the back of Sarah's head, an idea that had been planted there by the Stream.

"Let's go down that route" said Sarah to Kate, who was sat behind the steering wheel as though petrified.

"You sure?" asked Kate.

"Trust me, this is the road we need to take" said Sarah, unable to explain the hunch she had. Then again, today was a day where explanations could not be attached to current events.

"As you wish" said Kate, and she turned off the road and turned into Burjaraloz.

By the time they had arrived in the village, the sun had begun to set, and a cool evening air began to seep into the atmosphere through the humidity. Sarah hadn't realized how much time had gone by. She hadn't expected her search to take her this long, and she knew that Solomon would likely to be asking after her for her whereabouts. Sarah knew that if Solomon didn't know her comings-and-goings right down to the minute, he would assume the worst. Although knowing Solomon as she did, Sarah knew that he would likely find something – or someone – to help him past the time. Sarah couldn't afford to think of Solomon right now. She had come too far to let doubt drag her back into his arms.

If the village had once been touched by countryside, then there was no sign of it, the plant life far and in between, the buildings standing tall like temples of worship. Everything in the area was aged. It felt to Sarah as though nothing new could grow here. If anything, this felt like a place where things go to die.

And yet, there was a silent beauty to the village as the evening sun shone over it, casting it in an illuminating light.

"I think that's our pitstop" said Kate, pointing a gated building which wouldn't have looked out of place in a gothic novel. Kate stopped the car and the two women got out.

The gates were not locked, and it took a mild shove from Kate to pry them open.

"So, where do we go from here?" asked Sarah.

"I don't know" said Kate sarcastically. "I didn't see the directory for back-alley adoptions."

They tried to look around the place for anything that might seem out of place.

Their answer came in the form of a faint cloud of cigarette smoke.

"Interesting" said Kate, deciding to follow the trail.

They followed it and came into a vineyard, rife with ripe fruit and indeed, the only part of the entire village that didn't look like it had been abandoned and left to die.

They followed the trail to its original owner, witnessing a sight that felt so paradoxical in nature, Sarah had to blink to make sure her mind wasn't playing tricks on her.

It was a Black nun taking long thick drags on the cigarette, twirling it between her fingers with the grace of a sculptor managing their tools, inhaling the thick, black fog into her lungs before blowing out again, letting loose an air of catharsis every time. In between drags, she was taking large, healthy swigs from a glass of red wine… although in this case, it was less of a glass and more of a goblet which had been filled to the brim. She set the glass down next to her on the bench, which contained at least two bottles, one of which had already finished and a fresh bottle about to be opened.

Kate coughed, half to get her attention, and half to clear her airways from the cloud of smoke. The nun turned to her with a bored look on her face. As she turned, Sarah almost gasped at the sight of three tribal scars on each of her cheeks. "Don't pity them" said the nun in a thick African accent. "They're a rite of passage, a mark of where I come from."

"I thought nuns were supposed to be all about abstinence" remarked Kate.

The nun smiled, an old smile that had once been used to charm many people that had come her way, but now held a faded energy. "My child, when you get to my age, when you have found yourself exposed to many ungodly things in the world, the most natural reaction is to distract yourself. After all, they say that alcohol is the world's great numbing instrument. I took my vows expecting to lead a life of piety… but then decided that I preferred a life of pleasure." She held up an unopened bottle of wine. "Would you like to join me for a glass or two? Perhaps even a bottle. I can assure you that this is nothing like the cheap cat piss you get in restaurants. This selection comes from a lovely little winery called Solar De Urbezo, found in Carinena. I believed that the winery was named after a famous painter, under the pretence that wine-making was like all art, painting a transcending picture that touches its drinkers in varying ways."

"And you drink for the artistry?" asked Kate sardonically.

"Oh, no, I drink purely for the pleasure. Any higher meaning continues to elude me. Normally, they would charge a fortune for even one bottle, but then again…" she smiled a lopsided smile. "…that's the beauty of letting God into your heart and home. You'll always find someone willing to provide an offering." The eloquence of her speech was ruined by a slight hiccup. "How rude of me, I haven't offered introductions; my name is Sister Veronica. Who are you charming creatures and what turn of events has placed you in my path?"

As she spoke, Sarah noticed something that was hanging around her neck. A chain of some kind. Upon closer inspection, Sarah could see that it was a pendant.

But it was like no pendant that Sarah had ever seen. It looked like a mandala sun, and inside it, there appeared to be crescent of some kind. There was a stab of recognition in the back of Sarah's mind. But she couldn't place it just yet. But she already knew the dread that such a symbol would likely bring.

Taking charge of the situation, Sarah reached into her bag and took out a recently taken photograph of Nathaniel. "We're looking for information on this man, more specifically the circumstances surrounding his adoption."

Sister Veronica took the photo in her hands and ran her finger over it, giving nothing away. "Where did you get this photo?"

Before she could decide the practicality of the question, Sarah blurted out, "He is my boyfriend."

Sister Veronica looked down at the photo and ran her finger over it once again, but after a few moments, a single tear fell onto the photo. "Astounding" she whispered. "So many of them come to us, full of promise, full of potential. But as is the way with our world, we seldom get to see that potential fully realized. He seems to have grown into a magnificent specimen."

"'Specimen'?" repeated Sarah incredulously. "He's a human being you're talking about, not a fucking piece of meat!"

"Ah, but you see, child" said Sister Veronica in a subdued tone, leaving Sarah to wonder just how inebriated the nun was. "When these wayward souls come our way, that's exactly what they are, meat. We raise them like livestock until they become a child worth having."

Sarah was thoroughly disgusted by what she was hearing, even more so by the cavalier attitude with which she was speaking. "Is this the part where you tell us you've got a slaughterhouse for kids hidden somewhere?"

Sister Veronica waved a hand dismissively. "Girl, you show the ignorance of all your generation. It is not our intention to kill these children. Far from it. These children have the capacity to be a part of something greater in life. They would waste away, never having anything to offer. They would lead their lives, coasting through life, taking from their environment, but never giving anything back to it."

"Is that what you told Nathaniel and his brother?" asked Sarah. "That they were going to be a part of something greater?"

Sister Veronica avoided her eyes. "Children seldom understand their purpose in life, especially at a young age. But I have found that children are often much more compliant when they are told that they are special. And I remember their mother; an opinionated creature not unlike yourself, unprepared for the trials of motherhood. I do believe she loved her two children. But would she have been prepared for them in the long run. I know the expression, 'love overcomes' has been thrown around quite freely, but in this case, I fear, it did not prevail. She had already begun resenting their presence, feeling as though she was at the end of her life because of them, that she had to put her hopes and dreams on standby for her two boys."

"But when I saw those two boys, I saw the promise that they would bring. And I knew that one day, they would prove themselves useful. I convinced her that the boys were gifted, and it was a God-given right that those gifts be nurtured. But rather than see them disappear into a biased care system…" she snorted derogatively. "I swear when they say 'care', it is used ironically, I persuaded her that I was the boy's best chance of a proper education."

"And you know everything that happened since then?" asked Sarah disbelievingly.

Sister Veronica shrugged. "I know enough."

"And you feel no remorse? For all the suffering that has been caused. Have you no conscience?"

Sister Veronica did not alter her manner in any way. "We all knew what was expected of us. We all knew the risks we were taking, just as the two boys did when they escaped. The younger brother…" she paused. "…that was unfortunate. But it was clear that he was not meant for the Moirae. Unfortunately, Ben shared a troubling mindset shared with children of his age; they always seemed to believe that they are the centre of their own little worlds. They have no idea the consequences that their actions have on others, how wide reaching they can be. And we certainly paid the price for his actions."

Catching Sarah's dirty look, she snarled, "And don't you presume to pass judgment on me, child. I made my choices willingly and I stand by them. I won't apologize for the actions I have taken. God will be my judge."

"Looks like you'll be meeting up with him a lot sooner at the rate you're going" said Kate, gesturing to the wine and the cigarette.

"Sometimes" said Sister Veronica. "To do what we do requires a certain numbness. I don't know why you feel the need to look at me with such disdainful eyes, child. I am not the instigator of this comedy of errors. I am but a simple chess piece, fulfilling my place on the board so that others may advance."

"What others?" asked Sarah.

"Well, this… operation could not have been carried out alone" explained Sister Veronica. "There was…" She looked up to Kate, and for a split second, it almost felt like a request for permission to carry on. "…a judge who signs over closed adoptions."

"And where can we find this judge?" asked Sarah impatiently.

Sister Veronica scoffed. "You presume that he is someone who can be easily tracked down by a simple postal code?"

"We found you easily enough," said Sarah.

"I have very little to hide from you. And besides, if I had truly wanted to hide from you, why not just climb under a rock and stay there until the day I die? Granted, I wouldn't be able to sample this magnificent wine, but it feels like a small price to pay for security. How do you even know that finding me was a thing of ingenious deduction on your part?"

She took another puff on the cigarette, truly enjoying it before saying,

"You are always so quick to follow the trail of breadcrumbs. But did you ever stop to think of who left them behind and why?"

The words sent a cold chill running down Sarah's spine. And all of a sudden, her world seemed so much smaller, and she felt the same feeling a wild animal must feel; caught in a trap with no immediate escape.

She turned to Kate, silently pleading for answers. But if Kate showed any sign of distress over the turn of events, she did not show it, as stoic as ever.

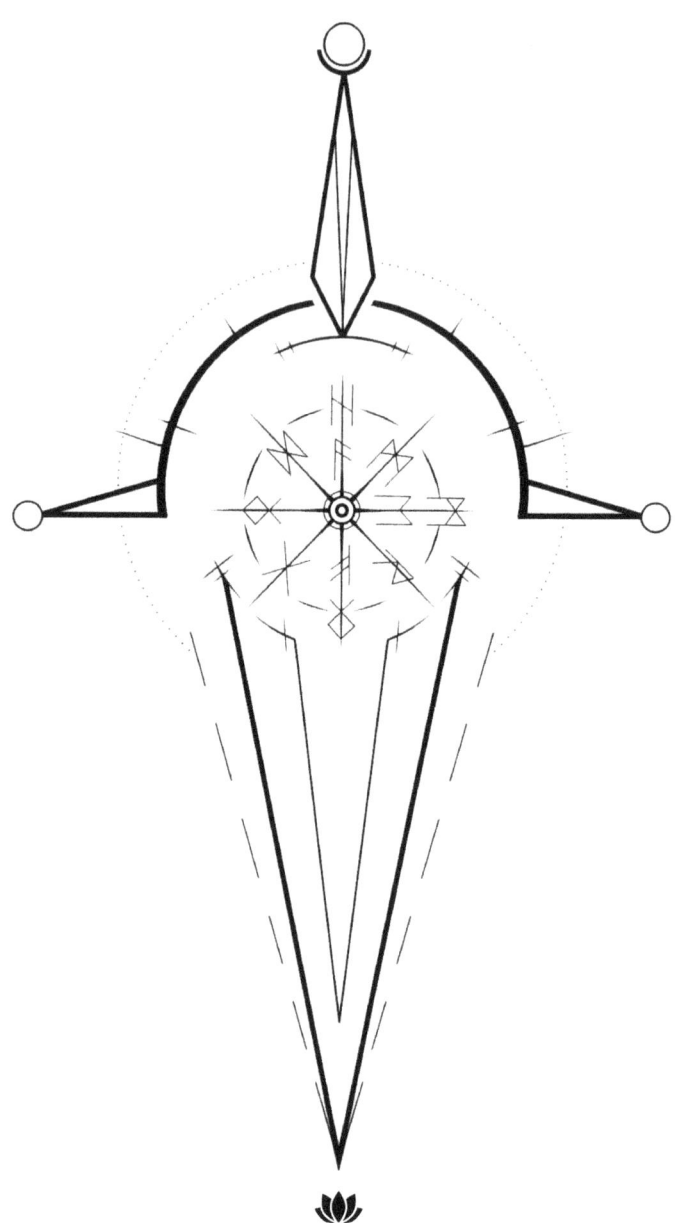

SETH
Chapter 19

The tension in the air was so sharp, it could be cut with a knife's edge. Hyienna did occasionally allow a scene in his mind to play out, to think of what would happen if he told Solomon that he wanted no part of this haphazard scheme... and every time he tried to imagine Solomon's reaction, it never ended well for him.

"Surely you've noticed it too, Hyienna."

Hyienna was snapped out of his daydream by Solomon's irate voice. "What?"

"Nathaniel's little habits. He's got to be the most pretentious bastard I've ever met. He thinks because he's a writer that he can look down on the rest of us. Flashing his money and fancy words around like a claim to Formentera. He likes to make out he's 'one of the people."

Hyienna cleared his throat. "At the risk of sounding pedantic, you're not exactly a local boy yourself."

"I never claimed to be" replied Solomon. "I've got no problem with telling people where I come from, and I certainly don't feel the need to parade it around the way Nathaniel does."

"I've got to ask, Solomon, in the interest of general sanity; what has Nathaniel ever done to you?"

Solomon didn't seem able to comprehend the question. So Hyienna continued. "OK, he may have been a bit full of himself and likes to throw his money around, but there is a difference between a guy who is just a pain in the ass and a guy who is out to screw you over."

"It's not about what he does to me," said Solomon. "It's about what he does to the people around him. You ever heard of a remora fish?"

Hyienna raised an eyebrow. "Do I strike you as a marine biologist?"

"Thought as much. Well, a remora fish is known as a parasitic fish. The only way it can survive is by latching to a bigger fish and feeding off of it."

"You mean like a parasite?"

"Exactly! That is how I feel about Nathaniel. He is feeding off other people in order to survive. No man, ever gets to where they are without climbing over the backs of everyone else."

"This is all about Sarah, isn't it?" asked Hyienna. "You just don't want to see her with anybody else other than you."

"Hyienna, she's your cousin. You and she are bound by family, as will you and me once the wedding is underway. If I came to you with irrefutable proof that Nathaniel would be the worst thing to ever happen to Sarah, would you honestly tell me to go screw myself? Or would you start trying to work out how to keep her safe? And of course, there's the fact that she's having my child. I never had a dad who taught me right from wrong, showed me how to make a trade or how to love. I had to learn the hard way. I had to make my own mistakes and pray they didn't cost me in the long run. If Sarah is going to keep this baby, then I want to make sure that I am there for my child."

Hyienna could not doubt the passion and sentiment in Solomon's voice, but he knew Solomon well enough to know that he was not about using honest feelings to do dishonest work. Everything he said was an excuse to justify his crusade against Nathaniel.

"All right" said Hyienna, trying to force back the uncertainty in his words, not truly believing them, but feel that Solomon could be better manipulated if he heard what he wanted to hear. "I'll help you. But I need you to give me a few details."

Solomon shook his head. "Sorry, Hyienna, I'm not sure how much I can tell you-"

"You've ambushed me, asked me to help you bring down a man who has done no harm to me as of yet. I think I'm entitled to a better explanation than no explanation."

Solomon sighed. "You drive a hard bargain, Hyienna. OK… we're going to see Seth."

Hyienna sat upright in his seat. "You're joking." He remembered the fleeting glimpses he had been lucky – or unlucky – to catch of the imposing man, a man who radiated brutality and had no issue with unleashing it on anybody who had wronged him. "Why the hell would Seth get involved in this mess?"

"Seth is a man in high places. He knows every single facet of Barcelona's underbelly, every dirty little secret floating in the air, nothing escapes his notice. Most people pass him off as a thug. And admittedly, I made the same mistake. But I'm telling you, Seth is a man who knows how to play his cards. He knows the value of information, and more importantly, how to weaponize it."

"Hyienna scoffed. "I knew you and Seth were close, but do you really think he is the one to get you out of this?"

"It helps to have friends in high places," said Solomon.

"And what are you giving him in return? Seth is a great many things, but a charity case? No, he'd never stick his neck out like this if he didn't think he was getting anything in return."

"At the moment, he's not asking for anything. He's doing this for me with the understanding that I'll get round to scratching his back one day."

"And you really want that kind of debt hanging over you, Solomon?" Hyienna briefly became aware of the irony of the statement, considering he had reached out to the Stream for information on Nathaniel without truly considering what he would need to give in return.

As if he had read his thoughts, Solomon said, "We're almost there, Hyienna, so I suggest you get your ass off that high fence and decide whose side you're on. If you're not handing me the nails to Nathaniel's coffin, you'll getting caught in the crossfire with him. I mean, being honest; what do you really know about this guy? He's not some secret brother, he's family. I wouldn't even go as far as to call you friends. So, what is it about him that makes you want to risk everything you have for him?"

Hyienna couldn't truly answer him. He barely knew Nathaniel and knew that the carefully cultivated peace he had carved for himself in Formentera was in danger of being disrupted. But he still felt that to betray Nathaniel was to sacrifice his own soul. "Depending on what Seth has for us" said Hyienna slowly. "Are you going to kill him?"

"Not if I can help it" said Solomon, the casual manner of which told Hyienna that he had at least considered it. "No, what we'll do is risky, but nowhere near as risky as leaving Nathaniel to sow his own seeds in Formentera. In an ideal world, Nathaniel would pack his bags and head for different pastures. No one else needs to get hurt."

But Hyienna knew that Nathaniel's feelings for Sarah ran too deeply for him to just give her up without a fight. "And if Nathaniel won't cut and run?"

Solomon met his eyes with fierce determination. "Then he'll wish he had never set foot in Formentera."

The car pulled up outside a small café. Hyienna recognized the venue as one of the first places he had visited when he had arrived in Formentera. But he didn't feel the same warm sense of warm welcome. If anything, the air seemed to take on an icy chill as he drew nearer.

And there was Seth, sitting in a seat, stirring a spoon in a cup of coffee.

"A word of advice" said Solomon just before they exited the car. "Let me do the talking. No offence, but when you shoot off your mouth, it tends to do more harm than good. This kind of conversation needs someone who won't fly off the handle at a moment's notice."

"And you think you fit the mould?" asked Hyienna.

But Solomon didn't hear the comment, too wrapped up in greeting Seth. As they walked over to the table, Hyienna caught sight of the knuckles of Seth's right hand.

They were bruised and bloodied.

For all they knew, Seth could have just beaten a man to death and was now sitting here casually drinking coffee as though nothing had happened. Hyienna did not want to get mixed up with a man for who casual violence was as natural as breathing. But he was already in far too deep to back out now.

"Seth" said Solomon. Hyienna watched as the two exchanged a soul brother handshake and giving the slightest of nods, as though they were conscious that their body language would give anything away to Hyienna.

"Thank you for coming," said Seth.

"So, what have you got for me?" asked Solomon.

But Seth held up a meaty hand. "First thing's first; I believe you have something for me."

Solomon nodded and reached into his jacket pocket, pulling out a wadded envelope. Seth took the envelope, scanned the contents with a bored expression, before tucking it away in his coat. Hyienna once again caught glimpse of the Hammer of God tattoo on his forearm.

"So… what have you got for me?" asked Solomon again.

"Well, I did a little bit of digging, and despite your man's claims about being a writer, he's not published anything of note. An aspiring Fitzgerald, he is not."

"So, how is he able to afford all that fancy shit?" asked Solomon. "Is he a bootlegger? A gun runner?"

"No" said Seth, smiling thinly. "Nathaniel doesn't seem to have his fingers in those particular pies. If he did, I imagine they wouldn't take too kindly to him flaunting his cash around like that. But I did find something else. I was tracking down some of his purchases and the cash he uses seems to be above board, but… he had to do a fair trading beforehand."

"Trading?" asked Solomon. "For what?"

Seth took something out of his pocket and slid it across the table to Solomon.

It was a raw-cut ruby, unlike anything Solomon or Hyienna had ever seen before. Solomon's eyes lit up at the unprecedented wealth represented by this ruby.

"I… I can't say I'm familiar with this kind of currency."

"Nor should you be," said Seth. "It is a currency used by an underground trade. How much would you say that ruby is worth? At a guess?"

"Ten?" asked Solomon. Seth shook his head, enjoying the suspension

of disbelief.

"Fifty?" asked Hyienna.

"That ruby on its own is worth one thousand euros. Apparently, the group that traffic in these rubies believe that possession of these rubies gives them a frontline to God or some religious bullshit."

"I'm guessing you're not a believer?" asked Hyienna.

"I'm a simple man" Seth said. "I only believe what is right before my eyes. And they have yet to deceive me. I am happy to swim within these waters, but I refrain from the deep dive altogether."

Solomon clasped his hand greedily around the ruby, as though he had just stumbled across a great fortune. "And how many of these does Nathaniel have?"

"It's hard to say for certain," said Seth. "He seems to have dipped into that fund and traded them in for euros over a number of years. And the kind of people that he traded with aren't exactly the kind that keep receipts, if you take my meaning. He's done very well to not leave a paper trail behind. You've got to admire how careful he has been."

"'Admire' is not the term I would use" said Solomon, his hatred for Nathaniel too settled in to be shifted at all.

"What can you tell us about this group?" asked Hyienna.

"Word on the grapevine is very hard to snag" said Seth grimly. "But they're very well-connected. They take kids from birth, kids who maybe haven't been dealt the best hand in life and they go about selling them on."

"Who to?" asked Solomon.

"Anyone who is willing pay top dollar. My guess is that Nathaniel is one of those kids who was sold to a load of traders."

"Well, that's surely not his fault" said Hyienna, hoping that Solomon would see Nathaniel in a more sympathetic light.

But Solomon was more focused on other matters. "What can you tell us about this group?"

Seth winced. "That information has been a little harder to come by. People seem to remain tight-lipped about them. They seem to be small in numbers, operating like a family unit. They never stay in the same place for very long, always moving on to find new prey. It's how they have been able to remain undetected for as long as they have."

"Well, there's got to be someone who knows something" insisted

Solomon, who was used to having an explanation for everything in life.

"Oh, yes, probably," said Seth. "If you want to set off on a fact-finding mission, why don't you check out the numerous unmarked graves scattered around Barcelona; see where that gets you. What I know for certain is that there are two kinds of people in the world. Those who have never heard of this group. And those who piss themselves in constant fear."

"You don't seem to have done too bad for yourself" said Solomon, not appreciating the potential danger.

But Hyienna could see the shift in Seth's mood to something resembling dread.

"I made sure I got the information from a distance and that my enquiries came at the end of a chain so far from the source that it couldn't be traced back to me, complete deniability."

"And if they take umbrage with you poking your nose into their business?" asked Hyienna.

Seth shifted uneasily in his seat, as though becoming increasingly aware how out of his depth he was. "Then I'm going to have to find myself some new couriers sharpish." He leaned in closer.

"Do you have anything like a name for this group?" asked Solomon.

"Apparently, they are called the Moirae."

Hyienna had to fight like hell to not show his discomfort. He thought about all the information he had accumulated from Nathaniel and the Stream. He had never been much of a clairvoyant, but he could instantly see the trouble Solomon and Seth were inviting their way. Bringing down an otherworldly curse on them.

Hyienna couldn't help, but chuckle to himself about how all of this had been brought about by a relationship squabble.

"I will be honest," said Seth. "When you first contacted me for this job, Solomon, I figured it was a waste of time. All this trouble for a woman. But I played ball. I figured the worst I would have to do is rough up the man and get him to stay away from Sarah. But hearing about this group… and if even half of the things that are said about them true… then this becomes a very different matter altogether."

"What's that supposed to mean?"

"It means that all of our lives may be in danger."

"Why me?" asked Solomon. "I don't even know these crazy bastards."

"You've been poking your nose into their business, therefore making it yours," said Seth. "And that's how they are going to see it."

"Well…" stammered Solomon. "Maybe I should talk to them. I can handle it-"

"For God's sake, Solomon" said Seth exasperatedly. "You're not negotiating a scuba-diving trip! You don't 'handle' the Moirae! You just keep out of their way and pray that you go a lifetime without having to go anywhere near them."

"I haven't done anything to them!" exclaimed Solomon. "Why should I pay the price because Nathaniel did a runner on them?"

"The Moirae are going to want their pound of flesh" explained Seth. "And if they can't get Nathaniel, they'll get the next best thing."

"Like Sarah" said Hyienna breathlessly.

"Exactly."

"Well, we've got to protect her" said Solomon desperately. "We've got to find a way to keep her safe. We'll run. We'll hide somewhere, somewhere they can't see us. I have a passport; we can just leave the country."

"You take that approach; you'll be living on borrowed time," said Seth. "They'll find you eventually. Sure, you may be able to buy a few more years of peace for yourself, but that will just make it all the worse when they finally find you."

"Then, we'll take the fight to them!" said Solomon. "We can kill them! You can take them all down."

Seth held up his hands. "Whoa" he said. "I think you're confusing me for a martyr. I am not going up against these people. I mean, I like you, Solomon, but I like my own skin even more."

"So, what are we supposed to do?" asked Solomon.

"The only thing we have any power to do; give them what they want."

Hyienna once again wished he could be anywhere, but here. "Please tell me this isn't going where I think it's going."

But Seth confirmed his worst fears. "We're going to have to give them Nathaniel."

"You can't be serious!"

"If you have a better idea, I'd love to hear it."

Unable to muster anything else to say, Hyienna tried to appeal to what little morality Seth might have. "If we do this, it's murder!"

"I think not," said Seth. "As far as I'm aware, they won't want Nathaniel dead. He's the jewel in their sordid crown. They wouldn't want to waste something like that. So, technically it's not murder. Just… a fate he'd rather not have any part of."

"Is there nothing else we can do?" asked Solomon, who at least had the decency to be taken aback by the plan.

"Not unless you want to offer up yourself or your woman as an offering," said Seth. "For what it's worth, it's not the course of action I would have taken, but it's the only one available to us."

"You're forgetting something" said Hyienna. "Nathaniel won't go to those people. He's already spent half his lifetime running from them."

"I never said that he would go willingly," said Seth. "We're going to need someone to get close to him, close enough to trap him. And sadly, I'm not exactly Mr Approachable."

"And he already hates my guts as much as I hate his," said Solomon. "So that's me out of the running."

Hyienna suddenly realized that both sets of eyes were on him. And even though they said nothing more, he knew exactly what was expected of him. "Goddamn it" he muttered. "You want me to be fucking bait?!"

"You don't put it in the best of lights," said Seth. "But more or less, yes."

Hyienna looked to Solomon accusingly. "Is that why you dragged me down here, Solomon? To be your goddamn point man?!"

Solomon held up his hands, affronted. "Hey, I had no idea what Seth would be putting on the table."

"But you'll willingly go along with this?"

"Nathaniel's fate was decided long before we came into his life,

Hyienna" said Solomon, who was now taking care to promote Hyienna's name correctly. Whether that was as a show of respect or simply because he wanted to get Hyienna on his side, it was hard to tell. "We don't have a choice. If I could see a way around this without anyone getting hurt, believe me, I would take it. But I can't."

"Bullshit" said Hyienna loudly, prompting a few of the café patrons to turn and look in his direction. "You've never liked Nathaniel; you've made that obvious enough and you'll happily throw him to the wolves if it means you'll have Sarah all to yourself."

"Keep your voice down" said Seth in a hushed voice. "It's bad enough we've been dragged into this mess. You really want to put all these other people at risk too?"

"I'm not doing it" said Hyienna, shaking his head. "You're asking me to betray a friend."

"And does Nathaniel think like you?" asked Seth pointedly. "He has lied to you, endangered yourself and your cousin. Hate to break it to you, but those are not signs of friendships. Those of the signs of a man who knows how to use people to get what he wants. If Sarah wasn't your cousin, if you were just some wandering soul, he bumped past in the street… do you really think he'd have gone to so much trouble to bring you into his circle?"

Hyienna didn't respond to that because he himself had always considered the possibility that he was just a means to an end for Nathaniel, a steppingstone towards the one who had captured his heart. They might never have crossed paths if not for Sarah.

Seth continued. "You're just a means to an end to him. Let's say, speaking hypothetically, the situations were reversed, and it was you that needed to settle a blood debt. Can you honestly tell me, hand on heart, that he would move heaven and earth to keep you safe? That he wouldn't just offer you up just to save his own skin?"

Hyienna wanted to say 'yes', that Nathaniel had a sense of honour that would prevent him from sacrificing anything else. But how well did he really know Nathaniel? He knew that Nathaniel had done many shady things to survive. Things that conflicted with his own principles. And when Nathaniel had made that heartfelt confession the other day,

Hyienna felt as though it was coming from a different man.

Was each persona that Nathaniel offered up one that was best suited to serving his purposes and getting what he wanted out of people? Did he even know the real Nathaniel? What if everything he had seen up to this point had been a performance?

But Hyienna would not abandon his morals just yet.

"You said you would help me" insisted Solomon. "This is me, asking for your help now. I don't expect you to do it for me. And I wouldn't blame you for wanting to turn me away. But I am begging you, for your cousin's sake, let us be free of this burden."

"OK" said Hyienna, trying to play out the scenario in his head. "Let's say, speaking hypothetically, I help you turn Nathaniel in, what happens then?"

"It's simple," said Seth. "I will go back to doing what I do best. You can continue building the life you wanted to build on Formentera. And Sarah and Solomon can enjoy a future that isn't weighed down by the past."

"And you can both live with yourselves?" asked Hyienna. "You can live with sending an innocent man to his demise?"

"Climb down off your high horse" said Seth derisively. "I have done far worser things than this in my lifetime and I haven't lost a single night's sleep over any of them. I doubt I'll lose any sleep over this. Believe it or not, this is not the worst thing I've ever done."

"And you, Solomon?"

Now Solomon was squirming in his seat, aware of how far out of his depth he was. "I won't be happy about having to do it. And I won't take any pleasure in doing it. But… yes, I think I can live with it."

"And what about Sarah?" asked Hyienna. "Are you willing to break her heart?"

"Sarah is an adventurous woman" said Solomon hesitantly, as though he was trying to commit himself as much as Hyienna. "Nathaniel is not the first infatuation she has ever had and probably won't be the last."

"God forbid you both take up monogamy" said Hyienna derisively.

"It takes all sorts to make a world" said Solomon defensively. "She will get over Nathaniel, in time."

"You really don't know my cousin, do you?" asked Hyienna. "She has held a torch for Nathaniel for years. He was the reason she had wanted to come down to Formentera in the first place!"

"Bullshit. She came down here because she wanted us to start a new life together."

"You're living in a dream, Solomon. You were never the destination. You were the pit-stop." And then, before he could consider the wisdom of the statement, Hyienna said, "You really think that's going to be possible when she's having Nathaniel's baby?"

Solomon's entire body went rigid. "What?"

The smart thing to do would be to back down, not let Solomon get himself hyped up. But Hyienna was psyched, too far provoked by the sheer immorality seated before him. "When Sarah gives birth, and she is looking at a constant reminder of Nathaniel, do you really think she'll have time for you?"

The words hit Solomon with more force than any other punch. "That… that's not possible. That's my child."

"Sarah and Nathaniel have been seeing each other for a while now? Did you honestly believe that their 'infatuation' would go no further than that?" Noticing Solomon's shock, Hyienna said, "My God, you actually did. You actually felt that even when Nathaniel was seducing her, you honestly expected her to maintain a flame for you?"

"No, Sarah's not pregnant with Nathaniel's child" said Solomon insistently. "She would have told me."

"Having a philanderer for a boyfriend doesn't do much for confidence" said Hyienna, not sure how much of what he was saying was retribution for Solomon's previously poor treatment of him. "She was expected to turn a blind eye whenever you went out to play 'hide the sausage', but if you had known the full extent of Sarah and Nathaniel's affections, you would have considered her defiled forever. And let's be honest, Solomon. You never wanted a kid. You just saw that child as something you held ownership over. And your interest now is just about Nathaniel taking away what you consider yours. When you wanted Sarah to get rid of that baby. You didn't want a child cramping your style."

Hyienna didn't care for the unmeasured cruelty in his words. Solomon had likely gone his entire adult life without having to face the consequences of his actions, never seen the destruction he had left in his wake. But now he was forcing him to look upon it.

He had expected Solomon to either hit him or deny it. But he hadn't. He had simply sat there and taken it in stunned silence.

Because deep down, he knew it to be the truth.

Hyienna continued his verbal assault. "And when you actually think about it, Solomon. Do you really think you could have been a father to that child? After the bang-up job you had done with Yasmina?"

Now Solomon looked up. "What?" he asked.

"Yeah, I know about Yasmina. How that little fling resulted in a baby. A baby that was since lost. And when she came to you and tried to tell you, you tried to brush it off, dismissed it has her trying to get you in her pants."

"That wasn't true" protested Solomon desperately.

Hyienna thought back to Yasmina, the night she had appeared at the Green Lizard seeking refuge after the incident with the rucksack.

She had been cleaning his room when she had happened upon the rucksack. Hyienna had chided himself with how carelessly he had placed it. Anyone could have come in and seen it.

But even if Yasmina hadn't, she would have still been drawn to the tinnitus sound emanating from the partially-open wardrobe door, where Hyienna had hastily stashed it, too preoccupied for what to wear for his date with Kate, an indecisiveness that seemed to stalk him all the time. The only thing that seemed to keep him grounded was the anchor in his pocket, the only thing in his life able to offer him a modicum of stability and calm.

By the time Hyienna had found Yasmina and happened upon her discovery, she was already quite high when he found her, thus her defences had been lowered. She wouldn't never have confessed those secrets to someone she had barely known, but in that moment, the pain had become too much for her and she needed to share it with somebody lest she go mad. So, she had told Hyienna all about the child. How she had hesitated to tell Solomon. Had decided against terminating and raise the baby as best she could. She had even found herself mapping out her child's life. "He's not going to settle in life" Yasmina had said. "He's going to be someone who matters, a doctor or a lawyer. Someone who helps people. I had opportunities to make something of myself. But I never did anything." And then she had lost the baby in tragic circumstances. And the pieces had clicked together for Hyienna.

Inside, his mind explored those memories. But outside, his verbal assault on Solomon continued. "Who else was Yasmina going to sleep with, huh? They weren't exactly lining up. You were the only person who fit the profile. Solomon. And Yasmina was actually foolish enough to believe that you would settle down with her. But you didn't. And I think that deep down, she knew that too. That's why she didn't tell you about her pregnancy. That was why she felt as though she needed to suffer in silence while you go gallivanting around Barcelona with no goddamn idea that you'd just lost her child. You ever wonder why she smokes so much weed? Because that's the only way she can cope with the loss. Who knows, maybe if you had been willing to step up, your baby might still be here-"

That had been the final straw. Solomon roared with anger and grabbed Hyienna by the throat, slamming him into the ground, much to the shock of the onlookers. He raised back his fist, clearly intending to bring it down on Hyienna's face…

…but he didn't. As Hyienna looked up, he could see Solomon's eyes brimming with tears, finally confronted with the horrific truth and unable to hide it. And Hyienna knew that he had found it; the open wound that would never be healed.

Seth rose from his seat and placed a hand on Solomon's shoulder. "Not here, Solomon. We have business to attend to, and I would prefer not to carry it out before the eyes of prying citizens."

Solomon hauled Hyienna to his feet and dragged him over to the car, shoving him into the backseat before clambering into the driver's side. Seth inserted himself into the passenger seat. Hyienna barely had time to gather his bearings before the car pulled out of its parking spot and drove away.

"Where are we going?" asked Hyienna worriedly. Solomon didn't answer, his eyes focused on the road ahead.

"We're going to find Nathaniel," said Seth. "We're going to scour the entire island if we have to. And when we do, you're going to help us bring him in whether you want to or not."

"You can't do this!" protested Hyienna. "You can't-"

Seth turned around in his seat revealing a bladed weapon. "I'm not used to people telling me what I can't do. You want to be a brave man and start trying?"

Hyienna kept his mouth closed.

"Goodman," said Seth. "I like you, Hyienna. You've got a fire in you that isn't easily quelled. I don't want to have to dump you in with Nathaniel. But I will, if I need to. Now, first thing's first. Is there anything you can tell us that might make finding Nathaniel a lot easier?"

Hyienna tried to think of something that would throw them off the trail. He didn't think he could escape from these two. Solomon was clearly a man on a mission, and he wouldn't stop until he found Nathaniel or die trying.

But even if he managed to find Nathaniel, packed him off to the Moirae, settled his debt with them, life would never be the same again. Hyienna had opened his eyes and made sure that they could never be closed. Solomon would never be able to enjoy a comfortable life with Sarah. He would always look at her and see Nathaniel. And he would be forever reminded of his sins regarding Yasmina. Hyienna wasn't sure whether this qualified as a victory. On reflection, he had wanted to get back at Solomon for some time, but he didn't relish the idea of breaking a man.

Hyienna's mind quickly flashed to the rucksack that he had failed to discard. He remembered the elderly woman who had given it to him, and whom he had been unable to return it to.

He wondered what would happen if they turned up at the lighthouse with the rucksack in tow? Would the woman be willing to hear out the demands of two men, one of which so driven by vengeance that reason had long since abandoned him?

It was a risky maneuverer but considering that the alternative was handing Hyienna over on a silver platter, he needed to divert their attention.

"I… I think I have something that can help us track down Nathaniel."

Seth glanced at Solomon. "Sounds like music to my ears. Start singing."

"I was given a rucksack, something that we can use to find Nathaniel. It holds… a message."

Seth looked to Solomon. "Is he pulling our leg? If we're going to be meeting up with these people, I hope to have more to offer than a rucksack."

"We can use it to our advantage, return it to its rightful source." But in his heart of hearts, Hyienna knew that this was contradicting every instinct he had built up over the rucksack. He felt as though he had been tasked to deliver a message by a higher power. Hyienna had never been a superstitious man, but he felt as though fate had put the rucksack in his path so he could carry out a specific task… and now he was about to contradict fate to save a friend.

"And where is this rucksack?" asked Seth.

"It's at Yasmina's inn" said Hyienna.

"You'd better not be lying to us, Hyienna" warned Seth before turning to Solomon. "Looks like we've got ourselves a little detour."

Solomon looked as though he was going to be sick. Given what he had just learned, the last thing he wanted to do was face Yaz.

But he felt as though his life was now on a collision course from which there was no return.

He drove towards the Green Lizard and Hyienna climbed out of the car, starting for the Green Lizard before Seth grabbed him roughly on the shoulder.

"Now, now" he said softly. "We don't want you doing a little disappearing act on us now, do we? I'm coming with you, just to make sure that this thing is the real deal."

Hyienna marched into the Green Lizard with Seth right behind him. Yaz looked up from a magazine as he walked past them. "Hyienna?"

she asked, moving forward, before immediately shrinking back at Seth's presence. "What's going on?"

"I've... just got to pick up a few things before I head out for the day" said Hyienna, hoping it was a convincing lie as his life depended on it. "You wouldn't happen to have that rucksack I found, would you?"

Surprised by the peculiar request, Yasmina nonetheless said, "Sure, I put it in your room."

"Thank you" said Hyienna. "Just going to go upstairs and get it."

"Why is he coming with you?" asked Yaz nervously.

"I'm giving him some money to drive us around" said Hyienna.

Yaz nodded. "OK."

As they disappeared up the stairs, Seth whispered, "So that's your cover? That I'm your chauffeur?"

Hyienna whispered back, "Well, somehow, it sounded a lot better than saying you're threatening me at knifepoint."

***

Once they were gone, Yasmina turned her attention to another person standing in the doorway.

It was Solomon.

"What do you want?" asked Yaz, immediately feeling the sting of rejection from that night when she had tried to tell hm the truth.

"The other night" he said, carefully choosing his words. "When we spoke... and you told me about your baby..."

"*Our* baby" insisted Yasmina.

"You were telling the truth, weren't you?" asked Solomon, knowing that the words he spoke would be the last time he ever felt any comfort in his life, the last time anything would ever be OK.

"Course I was telling the truth!" said Yasmina. "Last time I checked, weed doesn't make me hallucinate."

"What was he like?" asked Solomon, daring himself to move closer, while knowing he had no right to do so.

"What does it matter now?" asked Yasmina. She had never seen Solomon like this; a complete shell of himself, his once-unbreakable bravado shattered.

"Please" pleaded Solomon, and Yasmina could see his eyes were red from crying. "I need to know what he was like."

Yasmina sighed, reopening the wound that would never heal. "His name was Samuel" she said wistfully. "He was a beautiful little baby. I had never thought much about having kids, but I knew that the moment I lay eyes on him, I was meant to be a mother.

"Even from a young age, he was more aware than any infant I know. Most babies are normally scrawling messes. But Samuel? He seemed to be aware of the entire world around him."

"How so?" asked Solomon, feeling the need to lean against a desk.

"I can't explain it, but whenever I looked down at that little face, I could see all the love and care I'd given him staring back at me. And when I took him to places, he would always remember them, pointing to trees or people. He would take in everything around him."

She found herself thinking about those moments when she was pushing him around in his pram, little Samuel squawking happily at his surroundings, feeding him baby food in the form of an aeroplane…

…and not for the first time, she found herself thinking about the kind of life she would have wanted him to have, tried to imagine him growing older, getting to a point where she would be the one who had to chase him for attention. She thought about him leaving education to go into a job that made him happy, before one day finding a woman to complete his life, at which point they'd be starting a family. And Yasmina would be made a proud grandmother.

Solomon found himself trailing down the same flood of memories, inserting himself into Yasmina's daydream. He tried to imagine himself in the role of a father. He had thought of himself as a great many things, a ladies-man, a diver, but the idea of being a father felt like an ill-fit to his persona. But as he imagined himself giving a child the parenting he had never received, he realized that it was a side of him that he'd never known had been there.

"Why didn't you come to me?" asked Solomon breathlessly, bringing Yasmina crashing down to reality.

"You're joking, right? You would have seen Samuel as some kind of marriage trap."

Solomon's first instinct was to deny it, but deep down, he knew he was exactly the type of man who wouldn't welcome a child into his life.

"How did it happen?" he asked, daring. "What happened to him?"

Yasmina felt her stomach turn as she relived the moment her son vanished from the face of the earth. "Honestly, I have no idea. One minute he was there in his crib, the next… he was gone."

"How?"

"I don't know!" shouted Yasmina, exasperated. "I've spent ten years trying to work out how it happened! There was nobody around the apartment within a ten-mile radius that night. It was as if he had completely disappeared from the world altogether… and he had."

Solomon thought on what he had learned only hours ago from Seth, about this clandestine group who profited off the backs of children, who seemed… more than human. "Do you think… there's a chance that Samuel is still alive?"

"Don't" said Yasmina sharply, turning away from him. "I spent many years holding out the hope that one day, I would see my baby again. But he's dead."

"Surely, we can find him-"

"No. I'm not going to help you with your fantasy of playing the doting dad. Why do you even care now? What does it matter to you?"

Solomon wanted to tell her about the Moirae, how they operated, how they dealt in gifted children. But to tell Yasmina would be to put her in harm's way.

As Solomon's mind raced, he realized that he was on a one-way collision course with the people who had unknowingly robbed him of his child. Solomon gasped as he took in this newfound fate.

Steadying himself for Yasmina's sake, he asked himself, "If you could find the people who took Samuel…" The name pained him like a knife to the gut. "…If I could put you in a room with the people who took him, what would you say?"

"Solomon, I'm not indulging your hypothetical crap-"

"I need to know what you would say to them!" pleaded Solomon, laying his soul bare for her to see. "Please!"

Yasmina sighed. "If they were here. I'd ask them why… why they felt the need to separate a child from his mother. What a baby could have possibly done to deserve such cruelty. Why most of us were left to grieve so that a few could profit? But I don't think I'd ever get an answer. And even if they did, I'm sure they'd explain it away."

Solomon bowed his head. "I'm so sorry, Yasmina. I'm sorry about everything. I'm sorry I couldn't be the man you needed me to be." He wondered to himself; if he had been a better man, if he had been a man worthy of parenthood, if Yasmina had felt brave enough to come to him, would the tragedy have been averted? Would Samuel be alive today?

The weight of it all was too much for Solomon to bear. Suddenly, Hyienna and Seth came walking down the steps, bag in hand. "We're all set," said Seth. He turned to Yasmina respectfully, kissing her on the hand. "A pleasure to see you, my dear. As always."

Yasmina watched as Hyienna walked out of the door with her rucksack… holding the final link she had with her son.

And then Solomon turned and followed without another word.

Now that they had a rucksack, all that remained was to find Nathaniel and then they would be set to confront the Moirae.

The question was what would Solomon do when confronted with his child's abductors?

The Nephilem

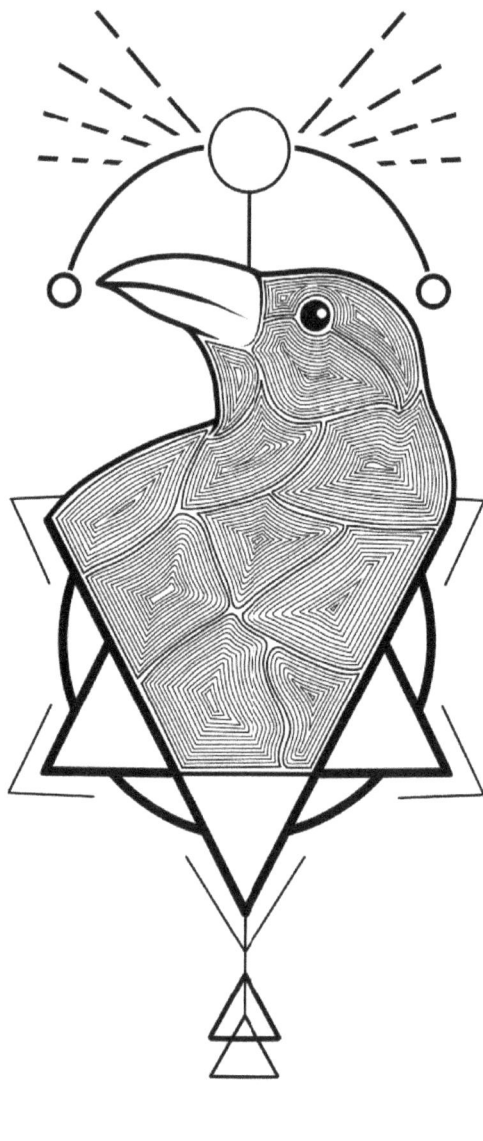

S'PALMADOR
Chapter 20

Even though he was supposed to be driving towards his salvation, Solomon felt as though he had wanted to drive to his destruction.

He hadn't wanted to leave the inn and thus, Yasmina. There were so many questions he had wanted to ask her. But he couldn't. He didn't want to dare thinking of tomorrow until today was sorted.

He tried to set his mind on the task ahead. He had always thought of Nathaniel as his enemy. The man who came into his world, lording it over with his wealth and a non-existent background that was supposed to make envious. Solomon had wanted him out of the way, certainly. And wasn't above letting Seth beat him black and blue to do so. But could he actually *kill* him?

He had never killed a man before, Solomon told himself. Never come close to killing one.

But that wasn't strictly true. He thought back to when he was first taking tourists out into the sea. He remembered one woman who seemed so delicate and fragile, almost like a bird that was on the verge of being wounded. He would have liked to have made a conquest out of her, but the man accompanying her – her boyfriend, presumably – had made a point of watching her watching everyone else. There was something about the boyfriend that Solomon hadn't liked. The way he moved and stood perhaps a little too close to his girlfriend. But not like a man about to take his lover in his arms, but like a coiled snake waiting to strike.

Solomon figured that he didn't want to bring any negative attention to his then-burgeoning business, so he backed off and tried to keep it professional.

But a few days later, he saw the woman walking through the town centre by herself, looking down on the ground. Solomon had gone over to ask her if she was OK. When she looked up at him, Solomon had assumed that the woman had overdone it on mascara, but as he looked closer, he could see the black eye starting to swell.

He hadn't asked her why it had happened, only where the boyfriend was now. She had directed him to the beach where he was staring out into the sea. No words were exchanged, only a flurry of fists as Solomon lay into the man until by the end, he looked as though a train had hit him.

Solomon had held the man under the seawater, as his opponent thrashed madly for air, clawing at Solomon's face in an attempt to get him to loosen his grip. Solomon could feel the life leaving him. But he returned to his senses, and pulled the boyfriend out of the water, throwing him onto the beach. No one dared make any eye contact with Solomon.

The man had gone to the local hospital, and despite only being a tourist, news travelled fast, and Solomon found himself waiting for the moment the police would come for him. But they never did.

It was around that time he had started socializing with Seth. And as he got to know Seth, and the kind of grip he held over Formentera, he found himself wondering whether the feared man had pulled some strings to keep Solomon out of trouble, taking it upon himself to act as a guardian angel. He had expected Seth to ask for a favor in return. But Seth made no such requests.

Even though it had never deterred him, Solomon had always known that his philandering would bring about a heavy price. And he wondered if now, by killing Nathaniel, he was about to pay it.

He tried to mentally gear himself up for the task, picture Nathaniel's body lying bloodied and broken beneath Solomon's triumphant form. He tried to imagine that all of his problems would die with Nathaniel, and he could renew life with Sarah, the way it was supposed to be. He imagined she wouldn't be too happy to find out what he had done. But he would help her get over it.

It did briefly occur to Solomon that it might not be too late to deviate from this course of action, call it off and walk away with his humanity intact.

But he looked at Seth, hands clasped tightly around the wheel, a man set on his current course with no interest in deviating. Even if he wanted to, there was no going back now. He had already come too far.

He looked to Hyienna, who was sat in the backseat, looking as though he'd rather be anywhere, but here. But he had a part he needed to play in this. "Hyienna… it's time for you to work your magic. I need you to get Nathaniel somewhere remote. Somewhere where we won't have… interference."

Seth looked over to him. "You'd do well enough to help us, Hyienna. I doubt you've ever taken a stupid step before. Don't start now." The tone was polite and calm, but there was a slither of ice present.

"Call him," said Seth. "He trusts you."

Seeing he had no other choice, Hyienna got out his phone. "Remember" warned Seth. "We'll be listening to every word. So, we'll know if you try and give him a heads up."

Even without the cramped space in the back of the car, Hyienna could feel the walls closing in. He dialled the number on his phone for Nathaniel and held the phone to his ear, praying that Nathaniel wouldn't pick up.

But to his dismay, there came a "Hello?"

"Hi, Nathaniel" said Hyienna, trying to put on his best 'calm and relaxed' tone, as Seth watched him with an eagle eye. "Just wondered how you're doing?"

"OK, all things considered" said Nathaniel on the other line. "I was wondering if you talked to Sarah… about what we discussed."

Now Solomon briefly took his eyes off the road to look at Hyienna, now quite aware of the lapse in information Hyienna had been providing him with. "I… haven't, really" said Hyienna. "I figured that was a conversation that was best left to the two of you."

"Thank you, Hyienna. I really appreciate your integrity throughout all this."

Hyienna gulped at the oblivious guilt-slinging Nathaniel was unknowing piling on him. "Not at all, Nathaniel. Not at all." Seth gave him a pointed look which was clearly a sign that he was losing patience, so Hyienna spoke quickly. "I was wondering if we might be able to have a catch-up to chew the fat, see where we stand with everyone else."

"Be happy to do so," said Nathaniel. "I've just got to finish up a bit of fishing-"

"Oh, where are you fishing?" asked Hyienna before quickly reminding himself to dial back the eagerness.

"On S'Palmador," said Nathaniel. "Lovely little patch of land. Thought I'd do some fishing down there. Sometimes it's nice to get out and enjoy the simple things."

"Yeah" said Hyienna wistfully. "I might see you later."

"Let's hope so" said Nathaniel, who had no idea what he was inviting his way.

Hyienna hung up before his emotions gave away how he was feeling. "For what it's worth," said Seth. "I think you're doing the right thing."

"Remind me again how killing Nathaniel is going to solve anything" asked Hyienna, hoping, even at the edge of the abyss, that he could pull Solomon away from the edge.

Solomon didn't quite answer straight away, so Seth answered for him. "Nathaniel is a Nephilem, Hyienna. Imagine a jewel perfectly crafted by the Gods. The type of jewel that would drive others mad with envy. Imagine if that jewel was thrown down to the world of the mortals. Let's say… a group of peasants, who have never experienced such riches in their lifetime. They all want this jewel, and they will gladly bury each other in blood. An entire land decimated. Now you could easily imagine the peasants being at fault. But if you really think about it, introducing this rich element into their lives changed their very nature. That is what Nathaniel is. He needs to be removed altogether-"

"-returned to the Gods?" finished Hyienna, suddenly feeling brave. "And you're OK with all of this, are you, Seth? I know for you, Seth, brutality is as natural as breathing, but are you really buying into this supernatural bullshit?"

"We all answer to a higher power," said Seth. "I do not control which direction the wind blows me in."

"Funny" retorted Hyienna. "I didn't think a hammer could be blown."

Seth's face darkened at the reminder of his lack of autonomy, but Solomon quickly interjected. "Let's just focus on the task at hand. I sort this out; you get to go off and live your life, Hyienna. And Sarah and me can recover from this. Everyone's a winner."

"Everyone except Nathaniel" said Hyienna.

***

Nathaniel gathered up the fish that he had caught and was hanging them up by the tree.

He loved visiting S'Palmador, it was a tranquil and beautiful place that had yet to be touched by the outside world. He felt that this stretch of the island had looked much like it did centuries ago, and today, felt like a stronghold from the likes of industry.

He had once heard that appearance was reflected by experience. Once you had been exposed to the elements that had altered your way of life, they were immediately set in stone, and you were given the face to go with that. That was what Nathaniel loved about S'Palmador more than anything, its untainted purity. Based on this expression, Nathaniel had found himself wondering how he might look if life had taken a more optimistic course with him.

He thought about his brother, about the type of man that he would have become had he lived.

He pushed these thoughts to the side, tired from his fixation with the past and daring to dream of a brighter future.

But even that seemed difficult given the current events taking place. He had been naïve enough to think that he could outrun the Moirae and hide from them, disappear from sight altogether. But that was the folly of youth; one always overestimated how safe they actually were.

He imagined that they would always be there in the shadows, waiting for the moment to strike. Nathaniel wondered if they would be the ones to kill him, granting him this borrowed time until they arrived to take it back.

But one thing that Nathaniel knew for certain about the Moirae was that they took every slight, no matter how small, personally. And when they came to collect the bill, they would ensure that their victim knew exactly what they had done to bring them to this point. However, he hypothesised, death would wear a familiar face…

"NATHANIEL!" shouted Solomon who was rushing over the island to get to him.

Nathaniel rolled his eyes at the interruption to his tranquillity as Solomon came rushing forward. He did not have time to deal with this-

And then he saw a glint of metal in Solomon's right hand, brightened by the sun.

It was a knife.

Nathaniel had barely enough time to knock Solomon's arm to the side before he was tackled to the ground, the knife lying a short distance away in the sand.

But Solomon was already on top of him, pummelling Nathaniel over and over, bloodying his fists in the process. "Not so pretty now, are you?" shouted Solomon. "Let's see if you're going to be picking up anyone with that face!"

Nathaniel didn't retaliate. At least not straight away. Instead, he gathered up a handful of sand in his outstretched hand and thrust it into Solomon's face, temporarily blinding him and giving Nathaniel the opening, he needed to shove Solomon away.

"Is this all about, Sarah?" demanded Nathaniel, getting to his feet, spitting out a broken tooth.

"Don't you fucking mention her" growled Solomon. "Sarah was fine before she met you. In fact, more than fine. She was perfect. And then you ruined her, you Nephelim bastard."

Nathaniel stopped dead in his tracks, alarmed at hearing the word that he had tried so hard to elude.

"Oh, yeah" said Solomon, soaking up Nathaniel's surprise. "I know everyone else in Formentera is too chickenshit to mention it, but not me. I know exactly what you are! And soon, everyone else will!"

The idea of the peaceful life he had envisioned with Sarah being snuffed out like a candle was enough to rouse Nathaniel to action and he kicked Solomon in the leg and began returning with blows of his own. He elbowed Solomon sharply in the ribs, recalling a lesson Kal had once given him.

"Always go for the weak spot" he had once said. "There's no such thing as a clean fight. If one of you is marked for death, you make sure it's the other guy."

The irony of relying on the advice of a man who had caused him nothing, but grief to get him through this was not lost on Nathaniel.

Solomon returned the favour with a sharp punch to the throat.

As the two men grappled with one another, ironically, they found focuses for each other's anger.

In Solomon, Nathaniel saw Kal, the Moirae and everyone else who had permanently marked him as damaged in the world.

In Nathaniel, Solomon saw the assailants who had stolen his and Yasmina's child and denied him the chance to be a father.

Yet unable to target these forces directly, the two men only found each other as a means of venting their hate.

Nathaniel was quicker on his feet, able to dodge various blows and kicks from Solomon.

But Solomon was the bigger man, and when his blows connected, it knocked the wind out of him.

The two men were evenly matched. It was just a question of whose determination would die out first.

***

Meanwhile, Seth was waiting with Hyienna in the car parked by the side of the road. Hyienna wanted to jump out of the car and warn Nathaniel, but he knew that Seth could be quick on his feet when he wanted to and if he tried anything, it would well be the last thing he ever did.

"How can you do this?" asked Hyienna, still uncomprehending despite all that he had seen. "How can you allow this to happen?"

"For what it's worth," said Seth. "Nathaniel's card was marked long before you came into his life. We just needed to find a suitable instrument."

"Too afraid to get your hands dirty?" asked Hyienna, daring himself to be brave.

Seth smiled thinly. "Let me be clear, while we're on the subject of getting our hands dirty. We all answer to higher powers. There are forces at work that you cannot possibly understand so it would be pointless to try and understand. The Moirae will have their blood oath restored no matter what. At the end of the day, Hyienna, we are all, but links in the chain. You should be grateful that the Moirae isn't coming after you simply by guilt of association."

"So, that's it, then?" asked Hyienna. "Solomon kills Nathaniel and that's the end of it all?"

"I would imagine so," said Seth.

"Except it never is, is it?" said Hyienna. "I don't know enough about the Moirae to be an expert, but I know that they won't stop destroying lives or finding people to do their dirty work for them."

Seth shook his head sadly. "I feel for you, Hyienna. You complain about the Moirae, about the work we do on their behalf, but the truth is, you have only scratched the surface. You have no idea the reach that they possess. Tell me; are you familiar with the legend of the Vampire of Barcelona?"

"You've got to realize my answer is no" said Hyienna sardonically.

"Around the early 20th century, the people of Barcelona believed that there was a vampire haunting the streets. Now, unlike the vampires you know from Stoker's fable, these vampires were said to roam during the day, looking for children to abduct before draining their blood to make potions.

"For many years, this vampire eluded the authorities, and their legend rang out for the world to hear.

"But in 1912, the authorities arrested a woman named Enriqueta Marti, a woman who had quite a colourful background, having worked as a nanny, a prostitute, and a witch doctor. It was discovered that she also ran a brothel that specialized in supplying child prostitutes to wealthy patrons."

"Jesus" whispered Hyienna, horrified.

"Jesus didn't have anything to say on the matter," said Seth. "The Moirae on the other hand...

"The police found the remains of several victims in her home. But despite the overwhelming evidence against her, she never faced trial. It's funny how despite the limitations she faced in that time because of her gender, she was still able to avoid a sentence that would have certainly seen her executed. Some believed that this was because of her clientele who were terrified of her own name being dragged through the mud. But, fifteen months later, she was beaten to death by her fellow inmates."

"Is there a point to this historical horror or am I supposed to guess?" asked Hyienna.

"She was supposed to be bringing those children to the Moirae," said Seth. "She went against the oath that she swore and used those children for her own benefit and profit. And she damn near shone a light on their workings. The Moirae would not let such a slight go unpunished. And justice was eventually served. As certain as is death, the Moirae will eventually collect all debts. It has been their way of existence long before you and I came into the world and will continue to operate as such long after we have returned to the soil. We're puppets that exist to be pulled on the strings. And the only thing we get to decide is whether we are the lapdogs of the higher power or their cattle."

***

The fight between Nathaniel and Solomon continued to rage on, and Solomon was quickly finding the advantage. He headbutted Nathaniel repeatedly, dazing the man, before dragging him by his shirt to the sea and thrust his head underwater.

Solomon had been here once before, when he had almost drowned the abusive boyfriend, and back then, he had wondered whether he had the nerve to kill. Now, time would tell if he had overcome this weakness.

Nathaniel thrashed underwater as Solomon kept his grip on Nathaniel's throat.

Solomon found himself swept away in the animalistic rage of drowning Nathaniel. Only a few more seconds and all his problems would be over.

But then Solomon caught a glimpse of himself reflected in the water. And to Solomon's horror, he did not recognize this monster staring back at him. It took him a moment to realize that this monster was him.

In that moment, Solomon knew that there were many things he had been in life. A partner, a diver, a father, a philanderer. Patterns of life that he had fallen into, some of which had been his own making.

But he could not bring himself to become a murderer.

He released his grip on Nathaniel and stood up.

Nathaniel came bursting out of the water and pummelled Solomon repeatedly, punching him over and over until the blood flying from his face meshed with the water.

But when Nathaniel saw that Solomon wasn't fighting back, he relented, suddenly gasping for breath, as though he had never tasted oxygen before. He was surprised by Solomon's lack of action, having been moments away from drowning him. Reason told him that he should kill Solomon while he had the chance. But Nathaniel's mind was working quickly. He was only alive because of this act of mercy. And he saw not a dangerous opponent lying before him, but a man who had been broken by unseen forces.

Possibly the same forces that had broken him.

"You don't like me. I get it. But I think I have a good idea as to why you're out here. And I'll be damned if I'm going to die for another man's sins" he gasped between breaths.

He stood up tall over Solomon who looked lost and confused, like a child.

Taking this in, Nathaniel said, "Let me guess; someone put you up to this, right?"

Solomon nodded.

"I think I have a pretty good idea who that is. Now, we can either keep going until one of us is dead, or you can tell me what you know and find the bastard who deserves to sleep with the fishes. What do you say?"

SWIM TO SHORE, SWIM TO ME

Chapter 21

Seth checked his watch. "Funny, Solomon should have been done by now."

Hyienna turned to Seth. "I'm sorry, I didn't realize there was an average time for carrying out a murder" he said sardonically. "So, what happens to me? How do I factor into your plans?"

Seth's face twitched in disgust. "You make this sound like we're moustache-twirling villains looking to hold the world to ransom. This is nature taking its course. Your petty issues with the Moirae are no different than if you were holding a grudge with a storm. And returning to your earlier question, you will be free to go. We have no use for you."

"Um, thanks, I guess" said Hyienna. "And what will you do?"

"Me? I shall go back to what I have always done. Life is one big wheel. You're either being crushed underneath, or you're the one turning it. I know which one I'd rather be-"

Seth stopped, for the first time in his life at a loss for words.

Solomon was walking back to the car, but he wasn't alone. Nathaniel was walking alongside him.

"Please tell me I'm hallucinating," said Seth. "You were supposed to kill him!"

"It's nice to see you too, Seth" remarked Nathaniel.

"Why is he still alive?"

"We need him," said Solomon. "And he's no good to us dead."

But Seth was starting to panic. "Do you realize what you've done? You were supposed to settle a debt! They will come for all of us, and-"

"I know," said Nathaniel. "And unless you want to stick around to see what we can do, I suggest you find a way to help us through this mess and get our lives back."

"Your lives were never your own to begin with!" shouted Seth. "You cannot outsmart the Moirae. Doesn't matter how many years they wait; they ALWAYS settle all debts-"

He was silenced by Hyienna elbowing him in the face, knocking him out. "You don't know how long I've wanted to do that."

As Seth slumped down in the car seat, Solomon and Hyienna climbed into the car and drove off.

***

Yasmina took a long drag on the spliff, letting its spacey air fill her lungs and easing the mental burden she was experiencing.

Everything she thought she knew had been called into question.

"How you doing, Yaz?" asked Ermina, who had come round to see Yasmina in her hour of need.

"I've been better" admitted Yasmina, taking a long drag.

"I don't know why you're bothering with that piss-poor shit. I can get you in touch with the holy trinity."

"Ermina, I'm not turning to bloody religion. If God exists, he's probably laughing at me."

Ermina looked quizzical. "No, I was thinking pills, powder and grass. The perfect push to send you flying out of reality."

"I've been thinking about Solomon."

Ermina raised an eyebrow. "OK, I think you've been smoking too much of that shit if you're still holding a candle for him."

"I'm not" protested Yasmina, knowing that she would be earning Ermina's eternal disproval. "But he seems different. Ever since I got that blanket, he seems remorseful. Like he wants to be better."

Ermina interrupted, having been brought up to speed on the blanket. "So, let me get this straight; you're saying Solomon's out-of-control libido was cured by a bone-lined blanket."

Yasmina shrugged, too zoned out to grasp the ludicrousness of the statement. "You could say that."

Ermina shook her head. "Actually, no. I never want to have to use that sentence ever again." Turning serious, she said, "Look, Yaz.

You've given him chance after chance after chance. And he'll make all these fancy promises, he'll say that you're the girl of his dreams. But how long will that last? How much time do you think you two will have until he starts wondering that there's always someone better on the island? How long until that little voice in his dick starts reminding him of all the bimbos he could be fucking?"

Yasmina couldn't bring herself to disagree with Ermina. She knew Solomon well enough to know his patterns.

But this time was different. He hadn't known about the possibility that he might be a father, that he had been shown the life he could have led. It was easy for her to say that she didn't have feelings for Solomon anymore. But she still held a candle for him. The intimacy that they had shared, and the life that they could have led with their child… one didn't experience that level of intimacy and not come away with lingering feelings.

Before she could protest even further, the door opened and in walked Solomon, Hyienna and Nathaniel. "Yaz, you all, right?" greeted Nathaniel.

Taking in Nathaniel's swollen lip and mildly torn clothes, Ermina commented, "You look like someone's knocked ten types of shit out of you." She turned to look at Solomon, her distaste palpable. "So, you were trying to kill him and chickened out?"

Solomon and Nathaniel shared a look as Ermina had no idea how accurate her statement was.

"Yaz, we've got something we need to discuss," said Nathaniel. "I think it would be better if Ermina left the room. The less people know, the better."

"Oh, no, I'm not going anywhere," said Ermina. "The second I'm out of sight…" She pointed to Solomon. "…he'll be forcing that silver tongue of his down your throat."

Ignoring the comment, Solomon said, "This is for your own protection."

Ermina scoffed. "You're joking, right? You're the one who needs protecting. From me!"

"I'm not here to cause any trouble," said Solomon.

"Bullshit. You've never laid eyes on a woman you didn't want to fuck!"

"Things are different now" insisted Solomon.

"How? You padlocked your crotch?"

Nathaniel did his best to stifle a laugh, at which point Solomon looked in his direction. "Sorry, couldn't help myself."

Seeing the desperation in Solomon's face, Yasmina turned to Ermina and said, "Look, I can handle this. I promise."

Seeing her sister's pleading expression, Ermina relented. "Very well" she sighed. "But I'll keep in hollering range if he tries playing hide the sausage." And with that, she left out the back.

"Yaz, do you know anything about where Sarah has gone?" asked Hyienna.

"Should I?" she asked. "I thought you never let her out of your sight" she said to Solomon.

"She went off with Kate" Solomon replied.

"We need to find her" said Hyienna, quickly making for the door, leaving Yasmina alone with Solomon and Nathaniel.

"How come you two are so chummy all of a sudden?" she asked.

"We're not" insisted Nathaniel. "But I think all of us might be in danger. Including Sarah."

"I knew it," said Yasmina. "This is all about protecting her. You just want me as your bit on the side before you go back to her!"

"It isn't!" protested Solomon. "Sarah is carrying my baby! I've already lost one child to those Moirae bitches! I don't want to lose another!"

Nathaniel bit his lip. He knew that there was a 50/50 chance that Sarah was carrying his child, and indeed, had this conversation taken place hours ago, he would have gleefully rubbed it in Solomon's face.

Instead, he said earnestly, "I'm so sorry, Solomon. I know how it feels."

"Do you?" said Solomon, turning on Nathaniel. "Do you know what it's like to lose your child?"

"Thankfully, no," said Nathaniel. "But… I do know what it's like to have your childhood taken from you. And… I know what it's like to lose someone you love to the Moirae. I lost my brother Ben because of them. There were so many things I wanted to do, so many things I wanted to be. But my fate was decided for me. And I thought that if I came here, I could reinvent myself, maybe start afresh. But I see now I was just kidding myself. They will always be coming after me."

"Why?" asked Solomon. "No offence, but what makes you so special? What is it that you've got that makes them want to chase you down?"

"I'm like human jewellery to them" said Nathaniel, shrugging. "So was my brother Ben. Only they didn't get him in the end. You know, the night we ran away, I often asked Ben what would happen if we got caught. But he refused to even consider that possibility. He said he'd rather die than go back to the traders."

"I'm sorry, mate" said Solomon heavily, feeling a kinship with the man he had once loathed. "Is there any way we can move forward through all of this?"

"Honestly, I don't know," said Nathaniel. "Our best option is Seth. He's the most visible player in this sorry game."

"Seth?" asked Solomon, then shook his head. "No, no, no. Me and Seth are like brothers. He'd never go against me."

"You really sure about that?" asked Nathaniel. But Solomon couldn't bring himself to answer, so Nathaniel continued. "His loyalty is to the Moirae only."

Hyienna came into the bar, dragging Seth's prone body. "Speak of the literal devil" remarked Nathaniel as Hyienna slumped his body on the floor.

"We're going to need to restrain him" said Hyienna.

Before anybody could answer Yasmina said, "Ermina has some handcuffs from when she had a guy round last week."

"Please, don't add anything else to that sentence" pleaded Nathaniel.

Within a short space of time, Yasmina had retrieved the handcuffs from Ermina, handcuffed Seth to one of the poles in the lobby of the inn. Nathaniel kicked at the body with his foot. "Get up, you bastard."

Seth stirred as he came to. His eyes opened, settling on the four faces looking down on him. "So" he said confidently. "It seems we're all about reopening old wounds."

"What do you know about the Moirae?" asked Nathaniel.

Seth scoffed. "Have you not been paying attention? You really need me to spell it out for you?"

"We're know you're connected to them. We know that you've been helping them" said Hyienna.

Seth did a mocking clap. "Bravo, Hyienna. For an interloper, you're surprisingly astute. The Moirae may see value in you yet."

"You son of a bitch" said Solomon, kneeling down in front of Seth. "Did you know that you were helping the bastards who took my child? All the times you were in my home, drinking my wine, you knew that you were making it possible for them to get away with this? DID YOU!?" he demanded, gripping Seth by the shirt.

But Seth's demeanour did not change. "For what it's worth, Solomon, I'm sorry you had to go through all that pain. I've always liked you. In another life, we might have been friends. But when the Moirae set their sights on what they want, it's not a question of if they'll get it, but how many bodies they'll leave in their wake to get it. Your son had more value among the traders than the life he would have led beforehand."

"How many children?" The question came so quietly, delivered in the form of a whisper, that it took everyone a few seconds before they realized Yasmina had spoken. "My baby was obviously not the first to be taken. And neither was Nathaniel. So, how many families have you demolished for the sake of the Moirae."

Seth shrugged. "I couldn't tell you. I don't keep a tally."

"You know," said Nathaniel. "For a guy that is being threatened, you seem alarmingly calm."

"Because I know that whatever you plan to do to me is incomparable to what the Moirae will do to me," said Seth.

"I think you're overstating yourself," said Solomon. "They can't be that powerful."

Now Seth roared with laughter. "You want to tell us what's so funny?"

"You really don't know anything about them!" said Seth between laughs. "You know, they're on the other side thinking that they need to be looking over their shoulders, taking extra measures, when the truth is, you really don't know anything about them!" He burst out laughing again.

"Well, we're quick learners," said Solomon.

"Oh, sure, sure, if you say so," said Seth. "Well, the first thing you should know about them is that they settle any and all debts. You can't cheat the Moirae."

"So, why are they after me?" asked Nathaniel. "Last time I checked, their business was kids, and I don't exactly fit that mould anymore."

"Yes" said Seth slowly, taking Nathaniel in as though really seeing him for the first time. "I had heard so much about you from the Moirae. You know, your little great escape had dire consequences for the Moirae."

"Oh, my heart bleeds" said Nathaniel dryly.

"It should" assured Seth. "One of the sisters was killed because of your folly."

"So why has it taken this long for the Moirae to kill me?" asked Nathaniel. "After they lost me all those years ago?"

"'Lost you?'" repeated Seth. "They never lost you, Nathaniel. What they did was tantamount to giving you the afternoon off. They always knew where you were. They just wanted to make sure all their targets were in the same area."

"Who else, then?" asked Hyienna.

"The collector Kal. He purchased Nathaniel and his brother when they were boys. And then the two ran away, Kal managed to kill the younger brother. But disobedience should not be possible for these children, so Kal assumed that there was some foul play on the part of the Moirae. He tracked them down and was able to kill one of them. He marked himself for death that day."

"So, how do we kill them?" asked Solomon.

"You can't" said Seth simply.

"Kal managed it" said Hyienna.

"The Moirae have taken precautions ever since Kal's run-in. You underestimate the power that these people have. You act like they operate in the shadows, but in fact, quite the opposite is true. We live in their shadows. We live and die by their beck and call."

"And who are you, in the grand scheme of things?" asked Hyienna.

"I'm a Hammer of God," said Seth. "Guided by the Moirae's hand."

"Oh, I get it," said Nathaniel. "You're the Moirae's pet."

Rather than blow up at Nathaniel, as everyone present had expected, Seth studied Nathaniel. "It's actually a miracle you're still alive, Nathaniel."

"What do you mean?"

"You defied the Moirae. And yet they still saw fit to let you live on borrowed time. You know, I never met your brother, but I know that he was braver than you. Ben was willing to face down Kal, own his defiance and die for it. You, you were just content to skulk around Barcelona like rats through a sewer, squandering the borrowed time you've been living on, living a life that was never your own. Even willing to abandon your own brother to his fate so you could-"

That was enough. Nathaniel screamed primally and started pummelling Seth over and over. But Solomon grabbed Nathaniel and pulled him back. "STOP!" he commanded. "I feel you, Nathaniel, I really do, but this man has information we need and we're not going to get it from him if he's fucking dead."

In between deep exhales, Nathaniel said, "Sure. Sorry."

Seth added spitefully. "Of course, if you had stayed with Kal, you would have learned about self-discipline."

"So, how do we kill the Moirae?" asked Nathaniel, trying to keep calm.

"You can't" repeated Seth.

"Kal managed it," said Solomon.

"Kal got lucky. He didn't overcome them by skill or intelligence. I can assure you; the man falls considerably short regarding both those faculties. He won by the same luck as a child handling his father's gun."

"Well, we'll just leave," said Solomon. "Pack up, take Sarah and go somewhere where they can't reach us."

"For God's sake, Solomon" said Seth, exasperated. "You're not trying to outrun a Starbucks. They have links wherever you go. The only option you have left is to go to them to fulfil your debt. You'll only make it harder for yourself, if you resist." He paused, before deciding on his next few words. "You know, Nathaniel, you are a lot like Kal."

"No, we are nothing alike" insisted Nathaniel.

"You both thought you could fight fate. Kal is determined to outrun his fate, doing whatever it takes to stay one step ahead of the Moirae... even if it means going after Sarah."

"What?" said Hyienna, Nathaniel and Solomon simultaneously.

"You heard me. He took her, thought he could use her to settle his debt."

"You're lying" said Hyienna. "Sarah is with Kate. She's on another part of the island."

"One thing I've learned about Kal is when he sets his mind on getting something, he normally gets it."

"We've got to stop him," said Solomon. "We've got to get Sarah back." And at once started for the door.

"Hang on" said Nathaniel, holding up a hand. "Somebody needs to stay here and keep an eye on him." He gestured to Seth.

"Well, I'm not leaving Yasmina alone with that animal" said Solomon, and Yasmina found herself touched by Solomon's concern.

"I'll stay" volunteered Hyienna. "You both need to try and get Sarah back. I'll stay here and make sure Seth doesn't go anywhere."

"Good man" said Solomon, grateful.

"Just one thing" asked Hyienna. "Can you guys get to Kal without tearing each other's heads off?"

Solomon and Nathaniel looked at each other before Solomon said, "We're good. We've both got a mutual fucker to take out."

Hyienna looked down at Seth. "Where can we find Kal?"

"As far as I'm aware, he should be hanging around La iglesia de San Miguel. It's funny, him spending a fair bit of time around dead people, while working so hard to avoid joining them."

"That's all we need to know," said Nathaniel.

"You can't keep me here," said Seth.

"Watch us" said Hyienna as Solomon and Nathaniel set off with Yasmina.

In the car, Yasmina once again handled the rucksack containing the blanket, tears dropping onto the garment. "My baby…" she whispered, reliving that same heartbreak.

Solomon turned round in the passenger seat and said, "I promise you, Yaz, we're going to get justice."

"Yeah" said Yaz, nodding her head. She felt a sudden urge to numb the pain she was feeling and downed some of the pills Ermina had given her. Within minutes, she was experiencing a mild high. She leaned over to Solomon and whispered in his ear, the winds have changed, the sky, the sea, all are the same once you are under it and your tide has come in, swim to shore, swim to me."

Solomon did not think he had ever heard a statement that had simultaneously reassured and terrified him.

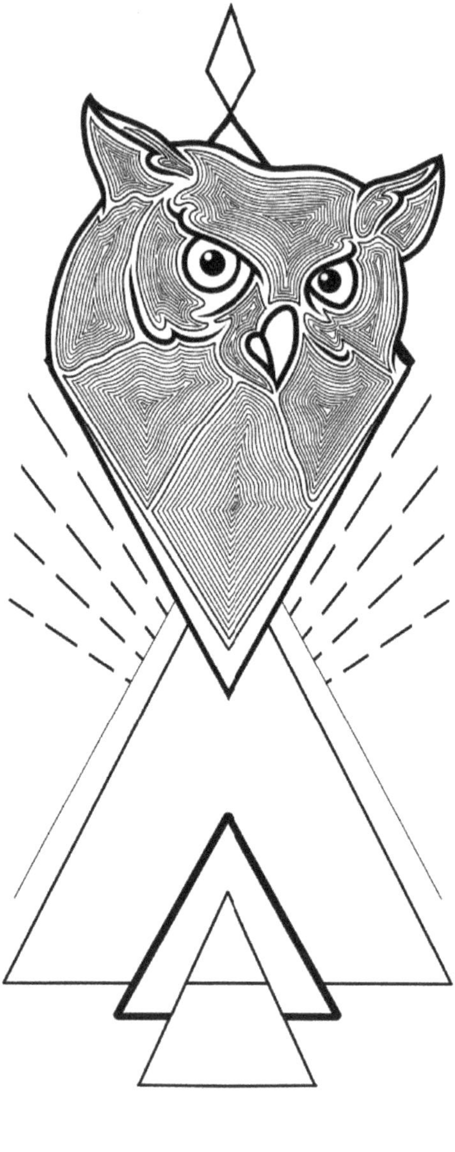

MOIRAE:
OF OWLS AND CROWS
Chapter 22

Sarah felt her entire world reeling. Everything she thought she knew about everything was being called into question.

After Sister Veronica had dropped that particular bombshell on the two women, Sarah had made their way back towards the car, with Kate in close pursuit.

"Sarah? What are you doing?"

"We've got to get back to Formentera. Got to warn Nathaniel." Sarah said the words so fast they could have easily been one word. She was driving behind the wheel of the car, picking up an alarming speed as though the road ahead had become a racetrack.

"You're crazy, Sarah, we're talking 7 ½ hours of driving. And that's without stopping and resting."

But Sarah was lost in a manic frenzy, reason having little effect on her. "We'll make time" she insisted, pressing down the pedal as the car picked up speed, the rest of the world rushing by in a flurry of incomprehensible colours.

"Maybe you should be letting me drive" suggested Kate cautiously.

"No, we have to get back!" shouted Sarah, almost manically.

When Kate spoke again, she did so in a calm, soothing voice that caught Sarah off-guard. "I'm afraid I can't let you do that, Sarah."

Sarah turned to look at Kate. "What?"

Out of the corner of her eye, a car came blaring into view, and Sarah had to swerve to avoid it… but she was unable to avoid the second car and the collision of grinding metal.

***

Kal felt as safe as he ever would as he wandered through La iglesia de San Miguel. The sun was still hanging in the air, which unnerved Kal as he felt that it left him exposed to all of his enemies.

It wasn't that the church was protected by any kind of barrier, far from it, it wouldn't take much for the ancient walls to come crumbling down. It wasn't that it was well-protected because today, as with every other day, Kal only had the dead to keep him company.

But he had heard that sometimes, the whispers of the dead would overwhelm the Moirae's hearing, thus giving him some protection among the restless souls.

Kal reflected on the events that had brought him to this point. He entered into the slave trade business with the interest of gaining plenty of wealth in his flesh for cash business. He didn't make any apologies for the events that had led him to this point. He had enjoyed the power that came with it. There was something about holding someone's life in one's hand, to bend them to your will, which elevated one to godhood.

He remembered as a boy his father had shown him entire cattle of livestock and had given young Kal a small device that would release a gas that would kill all the cattle. He told Kal to imagine the idea of all those animals lying dead. The decision he would take made little difference, but it was the capacity for that decision. To know that the difference between life and death was his and his alone. To know that all it would take is a small impulse to end so many lives. Kal had relished having that kind of power, and through the Moirae, he believed that he would be able to hold that power.

To this day, he couldn't understand why he had decided to target the Moirae. When Nathaniel and his brother had first escaped, he should have seen it as the act of a foolish boy rather than the machinations from an ancient conspiracy. But Kal felt as though his pride had been wounded by that event, and with Nathaniel out of his grasp seemingly forever, he had wanted to find someone to pay the price.

So, he had settled on the sisters.

He was still not entirely sure how he had pulled it off, killing one of them. He couldn't be sure whether it was down to luck, skill, or a tragic miscalculation on the part of the sisters.

Either way, he had had his revenge. But he quickly realised that the Moirae would come for him. They would not stop. And Kal knew that it would not just be a straight-up killing. He knew his history. He knew that the sisters would want to inflict some kind of poetic justice on him.

Even though he knew his days were numbered, that the Moirae would not allow him a peaceful death – he wondered if they would follow him into the afterlife – he couldn't bring himself to regret the actions he had taken. Killing the sister to the horror of her siblings, Kal had remembered all those years ago the lesson his father had imparted to him.

What it felt like to be a god.

***

"So, what's the plan?" asked Solomon, agitated. Yasmina had passed out in the back of the car. Neither Nathaniel nor Solomon could tell whether it was the drugs or whether the events of the day were finally taking their toll on her.

"We find Kal, get him to tell us where Sarah is, and we'll kill Kal and get her back." The way Nathaniel said he, he sounded so sure of himself. It sounded so simple, but in truth, there was little to no guarantee that he could actually pull it off.

"And what happens afterwards?" asked Solomon, knowing that he shouldn't be thinking about who would own Sarah's hand, that there were more pressing matters at hand here. But after everything he had been through for Sarah's sake, he still wanted to know if they had a future together.

Nathaniel understood what Solomon was saying and said, "Look, if you're asking me to just roll over and let you have Sarah all to yourself, I'm afraid I can't do that. And I'm pretty sure you would say the same."

"Everything I've done…" said Solomon, coming to terms with how far he had fallen in life and trying to desperately convince himself that he could be a better man. "I've done it for her. I thought she could make me a better man."

"I felt the same thing" said Nathaniel sympathetically. "I wanted to be better. To live a life free from the Moirae. I felt that Sarah would be my chance of a fresh start. And I still feel like that. I love her, Solomon. For me, the sun rises and sets with her. I haven't got anything else in my life worth having if she's not a part of it."

"Did you ever think about telling her about the kind of life she'd be entering into?" asked Solomon. He didn't ask the question with edge, just deep curiosity. "Did you honestly believe you could go your entire life without Sarah being none the wiser to where you come from? You've swam in those waters, my friend. So, to think that you can outrun or even outlive the Moirae, you must have been packing some serious naivety."

And Solomon could see that Nathaniel hadn't considered this. He had spent so long fixated on a particular future – his and Sarah's future – that it had left him blind to the fractured past catching upon him.

Instead, Nathaniel said, almost petulantly, "I don't think you're really in a position to condemn me for lying, Solomon."

"Well, comparing a few flings with a blood feud with a sisterhood, I'd say you're coming out pretty much ahead," said Solomon.

Nathaniel couldn't argue with that. Instead, he said, "Look, I can't walk away from Sarah, because she is my only hope for a normal life. And besides, I've come too far already to just walk away. And I'm not going to insult your pride by suggesting you walk away. We'll have plenty of time to fight over her when this is over. But for now, we both have a common goal, to get Kal out of the way; the enemy of my enemy is my friend."

Solomon sighed. He wouldn't call Nathaniel his friend, but the two men reached a silent understanding. Finally, Solomon spoke up, "I really envy Sarah right now."

"Why's that?"

"She's having a much easier day than the two of us."

***

Sarah slowly opened her eyes, waiting for the flash of pain to ripple through her body, waiting to see bone tearing through flesh, her baby killed in its womb, her body facing damage that matched the wreckage of the car…

…but when she opened her eyes, she could see she was completely fine.

The car had crashed into the side of the road and was torn to shreds, but she was completely intact.

So was Kate.

Kate manoeuvred herself out of the wreckage and offered Sarah her hand to help her out.

"How?" asked Sarah, who as soon as she was stood up started backing away from Kate, feeling as though her faithful companion was now truly alien to her.

"I have my methods," said Kate. As she spoke, Sarah noticed something different about her voice. It had lost much of its contemporary accent. It was as though an age long since gone was speaking through Kate.

"What… are you?" gasped Sarah, overwhelmed by the whole thing.

Instead of answering, Kate said, "Allow me to tell you a story. It's not like you have anywhere else to be.

"Let me tell you about a gipsy girl who found herself wondering by a riverbank late one evening. She noticed a silhouette of woman digging in the sand just yards away by the river. The gipsy woman hid in the bushes nearby and watched as the woman dug an egg from underneath a rock. The old woman clasps the egg in her hand tightly and whispers a few magic words, only faint enough for the gipsy woman to hear. The woman put the egg into the water and as it floated away it turned into a boat. The gipsy woman watched as it floated down the river mouth and away into the wide ocean.

"The gipsy woman, so intrigued and curious, slept in the hideout of bushes waiting for the old woman's return. Just before sunrise a loud clatter on the rocks woke the gipsy woman and the old woman appeared with many baskets of fresh and exotic fruits and flowers.

"The woman got out of the boat, and it promptly turned back into an egg. The woman put the egg back under the rock deep in the sand of the riverbed. The gipsy thought to herself, 'I want to do that, and followed the woman all day throughout the village and saw the woman sharing the prizes of her voyage with her neighbours. When evening fell, the gipsy went back to the riverbank and listened carefully for the footsteps of the woman approaching.

"The gipsy was still making up her mind whether to take the egg and sail for herself down the rivers stream or leave the egg where it rested. Just as the noise of the approaching woman got louder, the gipsy ran for the rock where the egg lay under. Digging as quick as she could, she unearthed the egg and remembered the *magik* words. When the egg was let into the water, sure enough it turned into a boat. Into the boat the gipsy climbed and away and far she went into distant lands gathering spices unheard of and exotic flowers and fruits.

"On her return, after hiding the egg in the sand at the rivers' bank, the gipsy woman went into town with her new treasures and bought a house. In her house she had the finest crafts and furniture in the village. But all was not well. One of the women in the village was jealous and suspicious of this newcomer with wealth. She tracked her movements closely. Time passed and again the gipsy woman seen fit to travel to the riverbank. On this occasion, the jealous woman followed in the shadows of nightfall.

"As the gipsy woman watched and listened out for the witch to come to the riverbank, she crept to the rock where the egg was hidden. The jealous woman watched as the Traveller began to whisper *magik* words. Just then a noise nearby disturbed the jealous woman as she turned to see where the noise came from. In another quick turn she found the gipsy woman in a boat floating away downstream. The jealous woman ran toward the riverbank and behind her stood the witch with the rock in hand.

"The witch asked where the egg was and when the jealous woman replied with a story of gypsy woman taking the egg, the witch cursed them both and their children and the entire village until the egg was rightfully returned. The next sunrise, at the gipsy woman's return as she made her way down stream noticed drowned elders in the water. The closer she got to her destination the lumpier the river got with bodies. Out of the boat the gipsy climbed with much gold and silk and exotic things in baskets. All along her path back to the village, the dead counted numerous. Even children and animals had not been spared. The gipsy was horrified and ran back to the riverbank but when she arrived the river had turned and rolled and washed away the rock and the egg along with it from its bank."

Kate sighed with deep contentment. "You know, it is so rare to hear that story in its true, unfiltered form. Contemporary retellings almost always find some way to neuter the imagery or the meaning. They always tried to paint me as some lunatic witch with an insane cackle. I know one iteration of the story even gave me a broomstick if you can believe it."

"Why are you telling me this?" asked Sarah. "What do you mean 'paint you' as…" Her voice trailed off as though invisible scales were slipping from Kate's face, and she could see the vindictive, ancient soul beneath. "Oh, God."

"'Catherine' will suffice," said Kate. "I am the Decider of Fates, spreading throughout this world like the air seeping into your lungs. I am everyone you turn to. And if you are foolish enough to seek solace in the subconscious, you will find me waiting for you."

"What the hell are you?" stammered Sarah, truly terrified, but also too paralysed to run or do anything about it, simply stand in horror of this woman.

"You should not be concerning yourself with what I am, but what I want," said Kate. "Because of events set in motion by your lover, I lost my beloved sister. We went into hiding after that for years. We wondered if our age was over, whether it was time for the Moirae to pass into legend. But we were patient.

"But Rosalita and I soon realised that as we have tested the faith of thousands before us, we ourselves were being tested. Losing our sister was meant to determine whether we deserved to lord over this world. And I promised Carmelita that I would make her proud and I would find the bastard responsible for taking her from us and I would make them pay with the full force of centuries behind me."

"Who?" dared Sarah to ask.

"Nathaniel" said Kate.

"What… what does he have to do with this?"

"He's a Nephilem, a great prize in high corners. If humans were a currency, he'd be the finest of them all. He was marked for glory. But he refused the path offered to him. He escaped into the night like a rat seeking scraps. But it wasn't enough for him to escape."

"He used his own brother as a decoy."

"What?" asked Sarah, Kate's words contradicting everything Nathaniel had told her about himself.

"Yes. We have always believed that it is a sibling's responsibility to stand by each other, to shield our skin from the world. And yet Nathaniel offered him up like a sacrificial lamb. And because of that, we lost our sister. I failed my blood bond to Carmelita because of him.

"And now he has to pay. That is the way of the Moirae."

***

They had finally reached the church. Solomon stopped the car a distance away at the edge of the church as Nathaniel climbed out of the car. Solomon was about to follow suit, but Nathaniel stopped him. "No, you need to wait here."

"Hell, no" protested Solomon. "If he's got Sarah, I've got to-"

"Kal is a ferocious fucking fighter. And no offence, Solomon, but I've seen how you scrap. Kal would wipe the floor with you. If we go in at the same time, Kal will kill both of us and there will be no chance of helping Sarah. And besides…" he looked into the church. "…I've got a score to settle. Wait here. If I'm not back in ten minutes, you know what to do. And keep an eye on Yasmina. From the looks of things, she's had her fair share of sufferings."

And with that he took off, moving into the church. He could have done without the location. It was hard enough warding off his own ghosts without being overwhelmed by other people's.

He saw Kal standing at the end of the long hallway, clearly fancying himself a king of his own little world. Even now, at the point of no return, Nathaniel's first instinct was to run, to seek shelter away from this man... but then he thought of Ben... Ben, who had been so brave, even in the face of death... and he knew he had to see this through.

He walked up to the altar as Kal locked eyes with him. "Well, well, well," said Kal. "This is most certainly a sight to behold. I always thought I'd have to drag you back to me kicking and screaming, I never thought that you'd actually come to me willingly."

"Where's Sarah?" demanded Nathaniel. "What have you done with her?"

Kal looked about, using mockery to cover his own confusion. "I think you're over-estimated my reach, dear boy. She's not here."

"Don't lie to me. I know she's here."

"Nathaniel" said Kal in an authoritive tone. "I have done many things to you in the past, but I have never lied to you. We both know that I'm not above getting my hands dirty, but I am not some wildfire destroying everything in my path. I target my fury specifically, and there was no point in targeting Sarah."

"I know you're lying" insisted Nathaniel. "Seth told me you had her."

"Seth?" asked Kal, looking confused for the first time, before breaking out into laughter. "Of course, he did. I must admit, it's an impressive move on the Hammer of God's part. The idea that I was responsible for holding your lady love gave you all the incentive you needed to come find me. There's a savviness there you've got to appreciate. In hindsight, I should not have held the Moirae responsible for your abdication. But, back then, I had a serious impulse control problem. Now, we have been set on a collision course, both of us played for fools, while the Moirae retreat into the background, satisfied that they had had their revenge. I wouldn't be surprised if they had her already."

A pit opened in Nathaniel's stomach. If anything, that Kal was saying was true, then Sarah was lost forever. He would never get her back from the Moirae...

...No. He would not believe it. Sarah was his salvation. She had dared to show him a better path untainted by sin and he would not give it up without a fight. "You don't tell me, I'll gut you where you stand" said Nathaniel, pulling out a jagged blade.

Kal gazed at it, fluctuating between admiration and disgust. "So, you kept the blade I gave you? After all these years? I'm surprised; when you did your little runner, I figured you would want to shed anything to do with me. I'm actually touched that you kept it."

"Oh, you're about to have it returned to you" said Nathaniel, pointing at Kal's chest.

"I hope that Sarah appreciates the lengths you're willing to go to get her back. It's far more effort than what you showed your brother."

The blade quivered in Nathaniel's hand as if in response to Kal's words. "What did you say?" he asked, his voice a dangerous whisper.

"You heard me," said Kal. "You were a capable young lad. You probably could have taken me. You might have lost, but you would have been able to get at least a few nicks in with that blade. But no. You ran like a coward."

"Shut up," said Nathaniel.

"And you didn't just leave your brother to die. You set him up in your place so that you could get away scot-free. Your brother, who you were supposed to protect. And you left him to the mercy of a man like me."

"Shut up!" Nathaniel snapped.

"Maybe that's why you held off confronting me for so many years," said Kal. "Because you didn't want to be confronted with the knowledge that you'd sacrificed your own brother-"

Kal wasn't able to finish his sentence. Nathaniel roared and charged at him, knocking him to the ground. He brought up the blade, preparing to bring it down on Kal's skull, but Kal ducked out of the way and the blade scratched against the stone floor. Kal pulled out his own blade and drove it into

Nathaniel's side.

Nathaniel screamed in pain as Kal pulled back his blade for a second blow, but Nathaniel delivered a kick that connected with Kal's arm, knocking the blade out of his hand. The two fought hard and bitterly, letting years of anger and resentment power their blows.

Despite his older age, Kal was nimble on his feet, moving with the agility of a man half his age. Nathaniel for his part, was weakened by the knife wound in his side which was now leaking blood.

But in that moment, Nathaniel saw the image of Ben's face, looking at him, pleading, trusting, and Nathaniel punched Kal repeatedly with renewed vigour.

But Kal retaliated by punching Nathaniel's wound, causing Nathaniel to double over. Kal got Nathaniel on the ground, pulled Nathaniel's blade out of his hand and positioned it just over Nathaniel's throat.

"You're just not meant for this world, Nathaniel" said Kal between heavy breaths. "Maybe you'll have better luck in the afterlife. Give my regards to Ben."

But before he could bring the blade down, Kal screamed in pain. Behind him, Solomon was standing tall, having used Nathaniel's fallen weapon to stab Kal in the back.

But Kal quickly whipped around and backhanded Solomon hard in the face. "Wrong move, boy," said Kal. "You should have stayed out of this. Now your fate will be yours."

But then Nathaniel charged at him, gripping the wrist holding the blade, unable to get Kal to relinquish it…

…so instead, Nathaniel drove the blade into Kal's stomach.

He repeated this motion as the two sank to the stone floor, their blood desecrating the holy place.

Solomon stumbled over to the two men. Kal was unresponsive. So, Solomon went over to Nathaniel, turning his prone body over…

…to be met with Nathaniel's half-open eyes. There was no sign of life.

Solomon shook him, imploring the man to get up, but he knew it would be no use.

Nathaniel was lost to the world. And yet, despite the last violent moments of his life, the expression on Nathaniel's face was one of peace. As though he had finally been able to leave behind the torment that had long since plagued his life.

SAY GOODNIGHT TO TOMORROW
Chapter 23

Solomon wanted to shake Nathaniel awake, but he knew that there was no point.

It was a bitter irony that only hours ago, Solomon had wanted to see this man dead if only to guarantee his salvation.

But it wasn't just Nathaniel that was dying. Any chance Solomon had of getting Sarah back had died with him. If anything, if what he had learned about the Moirae was true, Sarah was lost to him forever.

Solomon wanted to weep. Weep for the loss of Sarah, and for the child that had once again been stolen from him.

He didn't know what to do. He couldn't fight for there was no one else in the area. He couldn't plea Sarah's case, for there was no way he could bargain with the Moirae. In that moment, he felt no different than Nathaniel.

He just slumped on the ground, completely paralysed.

***

Sarah had only just noticed the cool breeze of the increasing wind blowing through the night air. It briefly occurred to her, that perhaps Kate – or Catherine as she seemed to refer to herself – was mustering some control over the elements. But then reason started to settle in, and Sarah dismissed the notion.

The sun had disappeared from view, shrouding Sarah and Catherine in darkness. Sarah wished the light hadn't deserted her so. There was something hidden about Catherine, something incomprehensible to the human eye. But Catherine's own eyes glistened like those of a predator finally cornering their conquest.

Catherine inhaled deeply, as though tasting the essence in the air. "Well, it looks as though the fates have spoken. Nathaniel has met his end."

"What?" asked Sarah. "Nathaniel can't be dead. He-"

"I'm sure there are many things in your life you're unsure of" said Sarah, almost sympathetically. "But be assured, your lover's fate has been set in stone."

"No" said Sarah, shaking her head, refusing to believe her. "Nathaniel wouldn't leave me, wouldn't leave us-"

"Oh, he didn't," said Catherine. "If it makes you feel any better, Nathaniel died fighting for you. Not that it would have made any difference."

Sarah collapsed to the ground, clutching her belly, the only reminder of Nathaniel left to her.

Catherine was moved to feel some pity for Sarah; a pawn in a game she could not possibly understand. She considered letting the woman go free. After all, Nathaniel was dead, Kal was dead. Honour had been satisfied…

…but then she thought of Carmelita, dying from wounds inflicted on her by Kal. How she and her sister had fought to keep her with them. But there was nothing they could have done. All those powers, the might of the Moirae had allowed them to transcend to become the apex predator… and they were powerless to save their own sister.

And then she thought of Nathaniel. All this because he had absconded, because he had rejected his birthright. Which meant that the Moirae had been short of a Nephilem.

Now Catherine was looking at Sarah's belly. She could feel the child inside her, radiating power. The sensation was delicious.

Vengeance now at the forefront of her mind, Catherine said, "Of course, I cannot let you go, Sarah."

"Why?" asked Sarah through tears.

"Your baby is a potential Nephilem. Nathaniel was a rarity, hard to come by. And you may be the key to restoring power."

"What are you talking about?" asked Sarah, the emotion having overwhelmed her and leaving her fast approaching a daze.

"Nathaniel was my property. He may have turned away from his birthright, but he was still my property. And that means that your child is my property as well."

"Go to hell" managed Sarah. "I'll be damned if I let you anywhere my child." She looked around the wreckage, trying to find anything that could be used as a weapon.

"What are you going to do?" asked Catherine. "Kill me? The last time the Moirae fell prey to mortal hands, we were foolish enough to let our guards down. We were so convinced of our invincibility that we left ourselves wide open. Well, I won't make that mistake twice."

Sarah laid eyes on a piece of broken glass from the windshield, brandishing against Catherine. When she saw that Catherine was unfazed, Sarah held the glass to her own throat. "What if I kill myself? Stop you from having me or my baby?"

Catherine smiled humourlessly. "Sarah, my dear, I just saved you from a car crash. Do you really think it's beyond the realm of possibility for me to save you from yourself? I know, the glass is at your throat, all it will take is one swipe. But do you honestly believe that you can do your little trick before I do mine?"

Sarah saw the conviction in her eyes and knew that Catherine wasn't bluffing. Determined not to let this be the end, she said, "I'll run and get help" she said. "Hyienna and Solomon-"

"Don't you think they've been dragged through this enough?" asked Catherine. "I have an associate in waiting who will gladly come for those two, and anybody else who tries to come between us. We will raze the entire island if we must. You won't have any tears left to shed before I settle your debt."

"People will come looking for me, you know" protested Sarah. "I have friends who will turn this whole island upside down to find me."

"For their sake, I hope they don't," said Catherine. "And even if they did, I could just as easily tell them that you were killed." She took on the appearance of a limping, wounded survivor, struggling to say, "Sarah... killed... by somebody... almost killed... me." She straightened up again, performance over.

"They won't believe you," Sarah insisted.

"'Won't believe me?'" repeated Catherine. "Sarah, I have been by your side for a long time now, and you were none the wiser as to the trap around you. Maybe because you spent so much time in the company of fraudulent men, you did not to notice the bird of prey."

Even though they were on an open road, when Sarah looked around for possible escape, she saw nothing, but barriers.

"You come with me now, Sarah, nobody else needs to die, nobody else needs to get hurt. I don't want to have to destroy your every single human connection in the world. But I will. You would not be the first mortal to defy the Moirae. And you won't be the last. Our plans are measured in centuries."

"What do you want to do with my child?" asked Sarah, daring to ask the question, terrified of the possible answer.

Catherine could see exactly what she was trying to say and switched her tone to a more reassuring one. "Oh, I don't intend to hurt your child. That baby is a rare commodity. We will ensure he gets the finest treatment."

"And what will happen to me?" asked Sarah, breathlessly, as though the oxygen had left the atmosphere.

"You will be settled into your new home… under the lighthouse."

Sarah gulped as her fate was spelt out for her.

"You will have everything you need down there. But you can never leave. You will be there until you die."

Sarah tried to picture the image of her living beneath a lighthouse, never able to leave, never feeling the sun on her skin, or the touch of a lover, the rest of her life, defined by isolation. The image made her fall to the ground, at which point Catherine shot forward to catch her. Sarah was surprised by how gentle the woman's touch was.

"I know it's a lot to take in" said Catherine soothingly.

Sarah looked up at Catherine with pleading eyes. "Is there anything I can say or do that will-"

Now Catherine's tone was harsh again. "Don't waste my time bargaining with alternatives because there are none. This is your best and only option. Think of it like this. If I didn't get what I want, I would have to torch this entire island. Every single soul wiped, like a bug underneath my foot. And since my potential killing of the population or by leaving them be, depends solely on whether you are willing to come with me, it's almost as if you're more responsible for their fates than me, wouldn't you agree?"

Sarah forced herself to nod her head.

"Good girl" said Catherine, seeing that she had worn the young woman down. "Deep down, you know in your heart that this is the right thing to do. Say goodnight to tomorrow."

She placed a hand on Sarah's trembling shoulders and said, "I am the wolf dire and transforming, God killing, Scythe, and all-knowing. I am the glory, sun-taking, beauty in blackness, all hope, and nothing in forgiveness. And you, you are more precious than rubies to me."

And Sarah felt an invisible force taking hold of her, and in her mind, she knew that no matter what she did, she could never leave, she would never know free will ever again. Every action she took from this point on would be under the direction of the Moirae.

She had become a puppet on strings.

***

Solomon stumbled back to the car in a slow daze, just as Yasmina was starting to come out of her drug-induced stupor.

"Everything OK?" she asked in a daze.

Solomon didn't say anything. He simply climbed into the car and started the engine. Part of him felt as though he shouldn't have left Nathaniel like that. That whatever he thought of the man, he at least deserved a proper burial. But he had to get out of there. He couldn't stay a moment longer.

Yasmina sensed the tension on him and had enough of her wits about her not to say anything.

It felt as though there had been a shift in the earth. Nothing seemed to have changed outwardly. But the wind brought with it a colder chill.

***

Meanwhile, back at the inn, Hyienna was pacing up and down, trying not to make eye contact with Seth who just sat there, handcuffed to the pole, locking eyes with him.

"There's nothing you can do," said Seth. "Events have been set in motion by forces greater than you or me."

"Shut up" muttered Hyienna.

Seth shifted where he sat into a more comfortable position. "Just out of curiosity; how did you think this whole scenario was going to pan out, hmm? You'd find the Moirae, take them out, get the girl, walk off into the Barcelona sun?"

Hyienna didn't say anything out of sheer embarrassment, but Seth was completely accurate.

"You know, I was a lot like you once," said Seth. "I used to have romantic ideals. But once you cross paths with the Moirae, you see the fairy tale for what it is."

"And you're OK with that?" asked Hyienna. "You're content to be a puppet on strings?"

Seth's face did not shift at all. "I made my peace with my place in life a long time ago. You should too."

"No, I refuse to accept that" said Hyienna, shaking his head.

"But you must" said Seth softly. "There are things going on that are beyond your comprehension. You have only dipped your toe into that other world, and despite your best efforts, you're lucky you haven't been dragged under. Hyienna, listen to me. This is the life I chose, the life I lead. The same for Nathaniel. I know Nathaniel fought like hell to avoid his fate. But he was a smart man, smarter than any of us gave him credit for. And he must have known he was going to his death. In all honesty, it's a shame he dragged you into it. I mean, when you think about it, what was he to you?"

"He was my friend" said Hyienna, suddenly unsure.

"I don't doubt you felt a kinship with him, but do you honestly think he would not drag you down with him?" When Hyienna didn't answer, Seth continued. "A drowning man will always drag down those closest to him, if only so that they can have a few more seconds of life, anything to avoid being swallowed up. Nathaniel's fate was decided long before you entered the game."

"This isn't a fucking game!" shouted Hyienna. "You're talking about people's lives-"

"That's exactly what it is!" said Seth, raising his voice. "It's a big elaborate game. This whole island is a chessboard, and we are the pieces that are   moved thusly."

"I am not a pawn in your fucking game" protested Hyienna.

"You're right. You're just a guy who happened to settle in the wrong location with the wrong people at the wrong time.

"But it doesn't have to be your life. You came here a year ago because you wanted a fresh start. You wanted to know that there were pleasures in life that weren't closed off to you. That can still happen for you, Hyienna. Just pack up your bags, get a boat off the island and leave, never looking back, never coming back. Your life is a blank slate, and it will be down to you to fill in those blanks. Or you can stay in this rudderless world and get sucked up into a cause you don't understand. And please believe me when I tell you this, you will *not* want to pay the price."

"So, what exactly are you asking?" asked Hyienna.

"Just undo these cuffs and let me go. Let yourself go blind, Hyienna. I give my word, I'll hold no grudges against you, and I'll make no plans to call on you. You and Solomon will be exempt from any retribution. You have my word. And my word counts."

"What about Sarah?" asked Hyienna. "Does she get to walk away from all this?"

Seth's face crumpled. "There is nothing I can do on that front."

"Fuck that, I want Sarah's guaranteed safety."

"Even if I was in a position to guarantee that, I couldn't. Sarah's fate has already been decided-"

"ENOUGH WITH YOUR FANCY HIJINCKS BULLSHIT!" shouted Hyienna. "If I don't see Sarah or Nathaniel anytime soon, I swear to God-"

"Sarah's gone."

Both Seth and Hyienna turned in the direction of the door. Solomon strode in, taking Yasmina with him, who focused her eyes on the floor.

"And so is Nathaniel and Kal. I watched them die. They both took out each other."

The shock of Nathaniel's death hadn't registered with Hyienna. Before it could set in, he asked, "Well, what about Sarah, can't we-"

"I overheard Kal talking to Nathaniel," said Solomon. "They took her."

"What about Kate?" asked Nathaniel.

Had either Hyienna or Solomon been looking at Seth at that time, they would have seen a noticeable twitch in his face, but by the time they looked back at him, it was gone. Seth said, "They have probably killed her too" he said. "They were interested in Sarah. And I imagine they wouldn't want any witnesses to the taking."

Hyienna felt himself retching with the knowledge that he had lost three people. Yasmina buried herself in Solomon's chest, who wanted to comfort her, but didn't know how to.

This was a sombre moment for Seth. For years, he had been aware of the damage inflicted on mortals by the Moirae, but this was one of the very few occasions when he actually saw it up close, could see what this belief did to people.

But he buried these conflicted feelings deep within himself and said earnestly, "I'm sorry."

"'Sorry'?" repeated Hyienna. "We were supposed to protect her. And you're sorry?" He knelt and grabbed Seth by the shirt. "You've taken Nathaniel, Sarah, Kate from me – from us" he quickly corrected.

"Nathaniel is responsible for Sarah's fate" explained Seth evenly. "The minute he started courting her. The minute he entered her life, she was doomed."

Unable to hear anymore, Hyienna said, "Solomon, I say we kill this bastard right now."

"Hyienna" said Seth, who was not panicking in the slightest over the prospect of his impending death. "You're not a killer. Sarah is already lost to you. So don't commit a crime of passion and condemn yourself for nothing. Even if you leave the Moirae out of the equation, I don't think it would look well to the police if you had the body of a murdered man in the lobby of the inn."

"So, what are you suggesting we do with you?" asked Yasmina. "You people took my baby from me, everything worth living for. What could you possibly give us that would make all of this worthwhile?"

"Absolutely nothing" said Seth bluntly. "There is nothing I can say or do that would ever rectify the wounds inflicted on you all. And for that, I'm truly sorry. But I can stop any more damage from coming your way."

"How so?" asked Solomon.

"You release me, and I give you my word that I will not disturb any of you ever again for the rest of your natural lives. Whatever dealings the Moirae will have in the future in these areas, I can ensure that you are kept clear from them all. My voice carries a fair bit of sway. But I can't do that unless I have been released."

"So, what?" asked Solomon. "We're supposed to just forget everything that's happened and carry on as normal."

"Of course, not," said Seth. "I would not dare insult any of you by pretending to just forget about what has transpired here." He looked directly at Solomon and Yasmina as he spoke. "But if you feel there is any salvation to be found amongst you, then do everything that you can to be there for one another."

It was the longest moment of Solomon's life. He could kill Seth right here. Maybe he would not be directly avenging Nathaniel, Sarah or Kate, but he would be doing some damage to the Moirae, but he wondered if that would even leave a dent in their dealings.

Feeling completely exhausted and just wanting to lose himself to a deep sleep, Solomon took the keys from Yasmina, walked over to Seth, and unlocked the cuffs.

Seth rose to his full height, flexing his wrists where the cuffs had dug in.

He walked past them, where they all shifted from his presence like a mountain among clouds.

When he got to the entrance, he said, "There are still pleasures to be found in the world. I hope you all manage to find them."

And then he was gone. And Hyienna, Solomon and Yasmina were

left alone with the knowledge of all they had lost, trying to come terms with this new, misshapen reality that would become their life.

Hyienna thought about Nathaniel lying dead in the cemetery, his place in the world decided before he had even entered it.

Yasmina was feeling the pain of losing her child all over again, and now with the knowledge of losing Sarah and Kate, this threatened to emotionally cripple her.

Solomon felt himself walking back from a precipice, at crossroads in his life, only hours ago resolving to be a proper husband to Sarah, and now, he had lost her forever. Once again, he had been swayed with the temptation of family life, only to have it cruelly dashed.

Once all three people found themselves wishing they could be anywhere on the planet other than Formentera, the maafa was complete.

THE MENDING OF CATHERINE

Chapter 24

Aeons passed… worlds span and whirled… time had become a motionless entity…

…when in reality, only hours had passed for Sarah, but taking the flux out of time seemed to be the only way to cope with the enormity of what was occurring.

Every step Sarah took seemed more difficult than the last.

It was now early morning, and Sarah wanted to have one last chance to take in the beauty of the Balearic sunrise before it was lost to her forever.

She tried telling herself that this was the right thing to do. That by condemning herself to a life of solitary confinement, she was sparing the lives of all the people on Formentera, that she was giving Hyienna and Solomon the chance for an ordinary life.

But she wondered how long that motivation and determination would stay with her.

The lighthouse loomed in front of her as Catherine guided her towards it. Even though Sarah knew she could make a run for it, but she knew it would be pointless. There was no escaping the Moirae.

Catherine had assured her that a living space had been prepared for her and that she would have everything she needed.

Except her freedom.

As they moved closer, Sarah saw an opening underneath the lighthouse that she knew would be invisible to anybody who crossed by.

Sarah tried to take in all the sensations surrounding her one last time, the feeling of the sun gently burning onto her skin, the feeling of sand crunching beneath her feet, and the gentle spray of the sea splashing onto her. She tried to memorise all of these sensations because she knew she would never feel them ever again. Memory would be all she ever had in place of the real thing.

She tried to leave behind all her personal ambitions at the foot of the entrance, all the things she had wanted to do with her life, all the things she wanted to be. She found herself wishing that she had never had those feelings, they were both comforting and soul-destroying, a remainder of the promises she could no longer keep.

Part of her still wanted to lash out at Catherine for robbing her of her life. But she couldn't bring herself to do so. Because in the end, Catherine was all she had.

This was the way of the Moirae.

They made their way down into the cave, Catherine shining the way with a torchlight.

Sarah tried to understand her new surroundings, trying to find the will to accept them and not silently implore someone to save her.

As they passed, she happened upon a painting on the wall, a shadow-like piece of street artwork.

As she walked, she noticed something lying on the ground. It was a card, titled 'Burden Bearer'; it showed an oracle on the front. Sarah clutched the card to her chest, knowing that she would have to become the card's namesake. For the sake of Solomon, Nathaniel and of course… Hyienna. She could not save Nathaniel. But there was a chance she could save Hyienna.

She held the thought at the front of her mind, letting it empower her and push her further into the darkness…

***

Solomon had put all his pictures of Sarah into a box. He had been tempted to burn the box, to do away with the memory of her, as though that would somehow spare his pain. But he thought of the joys they had shared together, how she had ultimately set him on the path to being a better man. Instead, he had placed the box in a small cupboard. Maybe he would revisit it sometime from now, to honour her memory.

He had taken a small sabbatical from work, cancelling all his assignments and tours for the next few months. He had tried returning to work after Seth had been released. He had thought that surrounding himself with people would make it easier for him to move on, return to normal life.

But everywhere he looked, he found himself seeking traces of the Moirae, or some higher power manipulating things from behind the scenes. And his clients had noticed the distance in his once-charming demeanour, one of which even asking if he had undergone a personality transplant.

In the end, he had decided that it was too much to be around ordinary people after everything that had happened, so he had stepped back.

This was an equally unfulfilling idea. He found himself going out of his mind with angst. Even when he tried to sleep during the day, the trauma of the past few days trickled into his subconsciousness, and he found himself haunted by images of Nathaniel's broken body.

When they had first met, he had loathed the man. In some ways, he still loathed Nathaniel, for it had been his infatuation with Sarah that had seen her taken away from him.

But such feelings exhausted Solomon. And he remembered how close he had come to killing Nathaniel. And the only reason he was still alive today was because Nathaniel showed him mercy. For that, he knew he had to be thankful to Nathaniel.

Solomon wished he had gotten the chance to know Nathaniel better. Whether, in another life, they might have even been friends.

One day, he headed for the cemetery where Nathaniel had had his life cut short

He had expected a visit from the police, someone who had seen him driving in the area and might want to ask him some questions about the two bodies lying there.

But there had been no such visit. And when Solomon headed to the cemetery, there was no sign that a fight had ever taken place. It was as though the bodies of Nathaniel and Kal had disappeared altogether.

He wondered if Seth had had anything to do with it. He had not seen his one-time friend since the day he had walked of the inn. He wondered what had become of the man, whether he had left Formentera altogether, or whether he was still there, simply retreating into the shadows.

Solomon felt sombre that Nathaniel had no such gravestone. Nothing to mark his passing or his life. And as far as he knew, there would be no one coming to mourn him. Whatever facets of his life there were to uncover, Nathaniel had taken to his non-existent grave.

He hadn't spoken much to Hyienna since that day. It was as though there was an unspoken agreement between them to never utter another word while they both lived. He had wanted to speak to Hyienna, to apologise for dragging him into the firing line, for putting him up against Seth. But he knew that there was no moving past what had happened. Maybe there was no closure to be found.

Not for the first time, Solomon considered whether he should leave Formentera, travel abroad, see the world.

But the more he thought about it, the more unfeasible it sounded. The world had no new sights to offer him. Like a child walking in on a primal scene, Solomon could only see life through a cracked lens.

And though he would never outright say it, Barcelona was in his blood. No time and distance would ever change that. And one day, Solomon would occupy a space in the cemetery here.

He remembered that today was Hyienna's last day on Formentera. He figured that if he hurried, he could catch him. At the very least, they could exchange goodbyes, both bidding goodbye to a turbulent period in their lives. But Solomon knew that such an attempt would be self-serving, more for Solomon's benefit rather than Hyienna's. Hyienna didn't want anything to do with Solomon and Solomon couldn't find it in his heart to blame him.

But he knew that there was somewhere else he needed to be.

***

Yasmina had not opened the inn for business, despite Ermina's insistence that she was bleeding money. In the end, Ermina had taken over responsibilities keeping the bookings herself. And to her credit, she seemed to be doing a good job of it. She had stopped counting down the days when potential visitors would catch a whiff of whatever chemical concoction Ermina had been inhaling.

Yasmina spent most of her time looking out to the sea ahead. The blanket had since disappeared from the inn. She was still in two minds as to how to feel about it. On the one hand, she had wanted to keep it, to maintain a part of Samuel. But then she remembered that a blanket was no substitute for a living baby.

She thought she had gotten over the pain of losing her child, that the wounds had slowly started healing. Now they had been pried wide open and Yasmina did not think she could ever close them again.

She had once heard the expression 'it is better to have loved and lost than never loved at all'. But Yasmina disagreed. She would have rather never fallen pregnant, never entertained the idea of becoming a mother if it was going to be ripped away from her.

She had hoped that the blanket would supply some kind of closure, that now she knew for certain what had happened to Samuel. But then she wondered if it had been better to keep on hoping rather than have the reality crashing down on her.

She looked out into the sea, beautiful and merciless, just like the Moirae.

Not for the first time, Yasmina thought about walking into the sea, wading into the waters, and letting them pull her under, taking her out of a world filled with pain and regret.

But that wasn't a decision made once. It was a decision made over and over, every time Yasmina thought about what she had lost, the life she could have had, how the only way she could numb her pain was to dope herself silly.

And every time she made the decision, the sea looked more and more inviting.

***

Ermina was busy looking through the register when someone walked into the inn. "What are you looking for?" she asked without looking up. Her new responsibilities meant she needed to keep a clear head, something she envied considerably. Although she wanted Yaz to get her act together for her own sake, part of her hoped that Yaz would step up again so that Ermina could go back to being stoned 24/7.

"I want to speak to Yaz."

Ermina looked up. Solomon was standing in front of her. Her first instinct was to tell him to 'fuck off' as she had done on numerous occasions.

But there was something different about him this time. He no longer looked smooth and imposing. He looked like a shell of himself, as though all the joy and the ability to feel joy had seeped out of him.

"She's not seeing anyone at the moment" said Ermina plainly.

"I just need-"

"It's not about what you need!" said Ermina. "She's lost her son. She needs to heal. She doesn't need you getting her hopes up again."

"I just want to help her" pleaded Solomon.

"What, are you a doctor all of a sudden? You offering a prescribed shag?"

"No! Nothing like that!" snapped Solomon. "Look, you don't like me. I get it, I don't blame you. Right now, I don't particularly like me very much. But Yaz is hurting badly. I know because I added to that. And I honestly don't think anything I say or do is ever going to make up for that. I'm not going to ask you to forgive me because I don't know if I can forgive myself. But I want the same thing as you; to make Yaz better."

Ermina studied him. She had expected some suave chat-up line from him to charm her. But the reply had been earnest and had clearly come from the heart.

She remembered that Solomon had lost a child too, and he had still been feeling that pain on his own. Maybe the two could help each other.

And it wasn't as though the two had a collection of people to unload to. Everyone would think them insane if they spoke of witches or supernatural curses.

"All right" she finally said. "She's out the back." As Solomon began to move past her, Ermina quickly added, "She's in a difficult place. There's a lot of things she's uncertain about. Things that I can't convince her of no matter how hard I try. But one of the very few things she was ever certain about was you. So, if you get that second chance – and that's one big if – try not to squander it."

And she stepped aside, letting Solomon pass.

Yasmina could sense Solomon's footsteps as he approached her. "You mind if I join you?" he asked hesitantly, estimating his right to be here.

Yasmina shrugged. "It's a free country last time I checked."

He took a seat next to her as they both looked out into the sea.

Solomon did not dare look into her eyes, feeling he had not yet earned that right. Instead, he looked out ahead into the unyielding, merciless sea stretching into the distance.

And as they both gazed, Solomon's hand gently rested on Yasmina's.

But she didn't pull away from him this time. Instead, she took his hand in hers, allowing herself that small solace and him the promise of a better tomorrow.

***

Catherine had always admired gorges.

So much land had been taken up by industries. She remembered a beautiful field that she had loved to run across when she was a girl. As far as she could remember, there was now a supermarket where it once stood.

She loved patches of land that had been untouched by the world.

It also meant that she was safe from civilisation and thus, potentially prying eyes.

She thought about her girlhood home in Trasmoz. It had been some years since she had been there and would like to revisit it again now that Kal had been dealt with and Carmelita had been avenged.

"Enjoying the view?"

She turned around to see Seth making his way towards her. "I take it's done?" he asked.

"Yes, it's done" she said simply, unwilling to dwell on it any more than she needed to. "No one's asking questions?"

"No, the cemetery was cleansed of all traces. Think of it like cutting out pages in a history book. No one will be reading Nathaniel or Kal's stories anytime soon," said Seth. "So, what's next for you?"

"Tamil Nadu, India. I've got to tidy up some loose ends regarding the blanket. I managed to swipe it from the inn with nobody any the wiser."

"Ah" said Catherine with a slight smile. "Give the Martial Arts Master my regards."

"What about you?" asked Seth. "What will you do?"

"I'm on my way to Africa" answered Catherine. "Oyala, to be exact. With Kal gone, there is an opening for a Collector. A void I am all too happy to fill."

"Congratulations" said Seth plainly.

There was a pregnant pause in the air, and she faced Seth again. "Got something you wish to share?" she asked.

"You played a very dangerous game in Formentera" said Seth without accusation.

Catherine nodded in acquiescence. "Restoring the balance in life is always a turbulent process."

"I'd prepare yourself if I were you" warned Seth. "Your power play may have gotten Kal knocked off the board, but it still cost the Circle of Judges a Nephilem. So, if you're expecting them to coat you in glory, I wouldn't hold your breath. At any rate, you won't be forgetting 2006 in a hurry."

"It was a price worth paying to avenge my sister. If I can't have her by my side, I shall settle for revenge."

Seth shook his head knowingly. "Catherine, everybody is happy to pay the price… until they're actually paying the price. Your card will be marked. So, if I were you, I'd think long and hard about what your next move is going to be."

Catherine turned and faced him. "That's the beauty of the Eternal Game. There are endless moves to make."

***

The ferry was going to take off within ten minutes and Hyienna could not get off the island fast enough.

His decision had been made for him the moment Seth left the inn. It was the formalities that hammered it home. Sarah had been a major reason why he had stayed for as long as he had, Nathaniel another. And with both gone…

He hadn't said goodbye to Yasmina or Solomon. There had been nothing more to say. They all knew that they were bound by the events that had transpired. But in the interest of everyone's lives – at least, those that remained – they needed to remain silent.

He thought about the loss of Sarah from his life. When it became clear that she was never coming back, that he had lost her forever, he had broken down screaming the scream of the damned. He had dared himself to envision a future with her in it, the only person who he felt could help him turn his life around, to find the good in life. Whenever he dared to look into the Sarah-less future, he recoiled as though stung. She had been his light in the darkness. And now the world had gone black. There were so many things he had wanted to say to her. And now he would never get the chance. It was almost enough to convince him to say, if only so he could say them one day. But that dream had been ripped from him. And he had to stumble, wide-awake, through this new, bitter reality of a world he struggled to recognise, a world he didn't want to recognise, a world that seemed determined to remind him of his loss.

It was hard to believe that there had ever been a time when Hyienna looked on Formentera with excitement, its buildings with its rich history, a beacon that called to him every time he stepped into the streets, only to lose its charm gradually as the rot underneath became increasingly clear.

He didn't know where he would go from here. There was no plan; he had no idea what he would do with himself, no idea what work would look like.

But most of all, he was uncertain as to whether he would ever be able to inhabit a part of the world untouched by the Moirae.

He thought about Sarah, the closeness they had shared. He wondered how he could think back on the times they had spent together when she occupied a space in his mind reserved for darkness and tragedy. He wondered if he could ever bring himself to reflect on her again, or whether it would be better to push her from his memory to spare himself the pain.

As these questions shrouded him like a black fog, Hyienna felt something bump into him, knocking him off balance and almost over his case.

"I'm so sorry" came a familiar voice.

Hyienna turned around and got a look.

He recognised the woman. She had been with him the day he had first arrived in Formentera. And standing next to her was her son, now older, aged by a year and slightly bigger. "I remember you!" said Hyienna cheerfully, pulling the same funny face he had pulled from what seemed like a lifetime ago.

The child chortled with laughter at the faint memory of the amusing man with the sunglasses.

"So, what's pulling you away from the island?" asked the mother, having no idea how loaded the question was.

Hyienna's mouth hung open as he considered the question. He could give any number of explanations, all of them false and impossible for her to understand. So, instead he settled for the simplest answer he could think of.

"I'm looking for a change of scenery."

"Me too," said the mother. "I'm taking this little one to see his daddy."

The need for small talk quickly passed as the ferry prepared to pull away and she said hurriedly, "Nice to see you again" and hurried onto the ferry with her son.

Hyienna envied the small child, displaying an innocence that Hyienna would have loved to recapture.

He thought once more about his friend Nathaniel. But this time, he didn't find himself thinking of Nathaniel's final end. Instead, he thought about the life Nathaniel had wanted with Sarah, basking in the sun, the spray of the sea on his face, knowing what it meant to love and be loved, finding an anchor in the form of a family of his own. The kind of life that would have always been denied to Nathaniel, right up to the end...

...but not to Hyienna. Those possibilities were still open to him and as he clutched the anchor buried in his pocket, he tried to imagine himself in Nathaniel's place, holding down a job, starting a family of his own. It had all the makings of a good life. He could do and have all the things that Nathaniel should have had. That was how he would honour his friend's sacrifice. That was how he would keep himself going for now.

As Hyienna moved onto the ferry, he still struggled to think of what his life may look like post-Formentera...

...but for the first time, it didn't scare him.

He was determined to find a peace for himself in the world, a peace untouched by the clutches of the Moirae. He did not know how long it would take him to find that peace. But he had the determination to last a lifetime. He hoped to lead a good life to enjoy all the pleasures that Nathaniel had spoken about.

And as the ferry pulled away and Formentera faded into the background, Hyienna looked to the sea and to the future with renewed hope.

THE END

AUTHOR'S NOTE

Pennsylvanian native, S.E Wilson, pen name Exquil, has been writing in one form or another since his middle school years. He was writing poetry, learning song writing in his teens to help craft his narrative technique. A Nottingham Trent University graduate in Multimedia Production BSc (Hons), Exquil enjoys building a world that a character and persona can brood away in. He gets satisfaction in offering heart breaking truths of one's human condition, with a poignant touch of mysticism.

Exquil is also a doting husband, a proud father of two, an evil stepfather of two, a discerning media studies teacher, a secondary school basketball coach (championship winning!), an enthusiastic dreamer, and a bit of a foody. When Exquil is not dreaming up schemes, plot lines for future books to fit into his Conspiracy of The Eternal Game masterplan, you can catch him spending time on his PlayStation, watching his favourite TV Shows, or supporting his beloved sports teams.

Now residing in Peterborough, England, catch Exquil in his full over-enthusiastic flow about the world The Nephilem is set in and anything Eternal Game related on his website's mini blog.

Brand hashtags: #whatistheeternalgame, #thenephilem, #exquilofficial
Exquil (pronounced ézé-quil)

 Exquil Official  Exquil Official

Exquil Official Exquil Books

www.exquil.com